My Sweet Broc
Bad Boys Book One

Christine Young

ISBN: 978-1-62420-532-3

Credits

Cover Artist: Designs by Ms G
Edited by Christie L. Kraemer

Chapter One

Scotland 1823

Broc Wallace leaned on the saddle horn, watching the intriguing lady fly recklessly across the open field on her horse. Her hair coming loose from the pins previously holding it and streaming out behind her, his heart caught in his throat. Afraid for her safety, he set his black stallion after the woman. Hooves pounding on the ground, he raced after her, praying he could reach her before she fell off.

Gaining ground and finally coming abreast with her horse, he reached out and holding on to the reins brought the mare to an abrupt stop. The horse reared and the lady slid from the back of her mare, a satchel of papers and pencils flying into the air then spreading along the ground in wild disarray.

"Bloody hell!" she cried out. "What do you think you are doing?" She sat on her arse, staring at him as if he was a fool. Her aqua eyes blazed, simmering with anger or perhaps passion.

He slid off his horse, reaching her in a quick stride, ready to examine her for broken bones, "Are you alright, Miss?"

"Yes, but no help from you." She pushed hair from her face, grimacing slightly as she tried to move. "I've lost my glasses." She started crawling on hands and knees, seeming to search with her hands. "And my papers, they're everywhere."

Feet braced apart, his hands on his hips, "I rescued you," he said indignantly yet somehow he couldn't stop looking at her shapely rear as she searched the ground.

"If that's a rescue then I wouldn't like to see what would happen when you wanted to completely incapacitate someone. I'm perfectly capable of riding a horse without incident." She continued to search the ground, mumbling words he couldn't make out, her rear sticking higher into the air as she bent closer to the earth.

"What did you say you were looking for?" He got down on his hands and knees, now eyelevel with her. He needed to help her find whatever it was she lost, owing her something but he wasn't quite sure what.

She glared at him, her cheek smudged with dirt, "My glasses. I lost my glasses and without them I don't see too well."

He chuckled despite his best efforts. She was incorrigible and at the same time possessed a sweetness about her he couldn't deny. He found himself drawn to her. "Is this what you're looking for?" He held up what appeared to be a pair of glasses. "Do you have a second pair? These don't look to useable."

She snatched them from him and sat back. "Thank you and yes I do." Her voice was curt. "Now tell me why you thought I needed rescuing. Do you just assume that a woman galloping on a horse is out of her element?" But she didn't seem to pay attention to him. She began to pick up the other debris and stuff the things into the satchel she'd been carrying. When everything was picked up and in their proper place, she grabbed the reins of her horse and walked toward the river.

Broc caught up with her, his hands stuffed in his pockets, wondering what she was going to do next and if he dared play a role. "You didn't need rescuing? It certainly appeared your horse was racing uncontrolled."

"You saw wrong. You should check your eyesight." She puffed a breath of air, moving a strand of hair that lay across her face.

I'm not the one wearing glasses," he told her, grinning.

"Perhaps you should be."

He stuffed his hands in his pockets. "I know what I saw."

"For your information I'm a very good horsewoman. I've never ever needed a man or anyone else to save me." At the river she found a grassy spot. After spreading a blanket on the ground, she pulled out the papers she had recently packed away.

"You could have been hurt racing that way." He continued, unwilling to accept the fact he might have been wrong about what he saw.

She hummed softly, ignoring him and sketching the scene in front of her, effectively overlooking him. The drawing developed as he watched, intently captivated by everything about her.

At a loss for anything to say, he continued to watch. Relaxing and stretching out on the blanket she spread for herself, he casually leaned on one elbow. The natural sounds of the river and the meadow encompassed the little scene.

"What's your name?" she asked, suddenly breaking the silence and setting her pencil on the paper. She gazed at him then with those aqua blue eyes that captivated him, reminding him of the Mediterranean Sea at its bluest. He wanted to see inside her soul.

"You tell me yours and I'll tell you mine." He wasn't sure why he challenged her, but he needed to see her reaction. She looked somehow familiar, but he couldn't place where he'd seen her before.

She shrugged her delicately slim shoulders. "Bliss." She shot him a quick smile before her attention focused on the sketch again. Pencil in hand she appeared not to have a care in the world. Yet somehow he knew that wasn't true about her.

"Bliss? Bliss what?" He pressed her for an answer, wanting to reach out and smooth the escaped strands of hair from her face. He needed to feel its texture and see if it was as silken as it looked.

"Just Bliss," she said, her voice soft and it seemed that was all she meant to say.

"I see." Two could play this game. "Broc. Just Broc," he told her, reaching for a piece of grass to stick between his teeth. Despite his best efforts to appear relaxed, his body tensed. His reaction to this lady was unusual and put him at unease.

"Nice name." Bliss continued to draw, seeming to pretend he wasn't sitting so close to her he could reach out and touch her.

"What are you going to do with the sketches?" He wanted to thumb through them, all of them but didn't think she'd go that far to give her approval of the invasion of her privacy.

"I turn them into paintings, oil or water color then I sell them in town." She set the pencil down. "I earn my living that way."

"Don't stop on my account, and why would a young lady such as yourself have to pay their own way in this world? Surely there is a man..." He started to reach out and touch her but caught himself, quickly withdrawing his hand.

"I'm done and you're making me nervous." She turned to stare at him. "Don't want anything to do with men. At least not the ones my..."

"Sorry." He couldn't believe he apologized for watching her. "The ones your..." he cocked an eyebrow, daring her to continue. "Care to enlighten me."

She laughed softly, "No, you're not sorry and no, I don't have any intention of telling you what I almost said. You've probably never been sorry for anything in your adult life."

He liked the way her voice sounded when she laughed and she was right. He couldn't think of a single time he apologized to someone and really meant the words. "In my defense, until now, I've never had anything to apologize for."

"So, you believe you're always right."

"I didn't say that." Unable to resist any longer he picked up a strand of her hair, rubbing it between his fingers. "So soft, is the rest of you this soft?"

"Didn't you?" she queried, pulling away from him. "You didn't say the words but you talked around it enough for any intelligent person to come to the conclusion."

It seemed she ignored his second question. "I was raised to be confident," he answered, grinning and thoroughly enjoying the conversation. "What about you? Do you apologize if you know you're wrong?"

She cleared her throat, continuing to draw. "Never wrong, just like you."

"Are you through sketching?" he asked her, picking up the pad that was sitting on her lap. "May I?"

She nodded a few times, "Nothing too unusual about the sketches. That's just what they are, simple drawings I mean to put on a canvas. That's where they come alive."

His breath caught when he ran across a sketch of him, riding on his horse. "You know who I am?"

Several times she was shaking her head as if she meant to say no. But, "Of you, I've seen you riding across this meadow before. And yes, I know who you are and who doesn't know who you are?"

"You did these from memory?" He was impressed with her ability but was even more curious about who she really was. And there were more. She'd watched him chopping wood, half naked. The thought sent a wave of hot and very potent desire through him. He wanted to investigate further with her this seeming infatuation with him. Too soon, though, it was way too soon for her to understand what he craved from her.

"I'm good," she told him, grinning as she said the words almost as if she meant to challenge him.

"You should never say things that aren't true." He closed the pad.

She started to protest his words he was sure, but he didn't mean to give her a chance. "Hush." He placed a finger on her lips, a bit presumptive, he knew, but once again he couldn't seem to help himself, his blood suddenly pumping double time.

"You, my sweet Bliss, are very good, amazing even, particularly if you can sketch these from memory."

"I've watched you cutting wood, too, over by the stables. Indeed, one day I..." she moistened her lips but stopped short of telling him what she was thinking.

"You watched me and I had no idea that was what you were doing, no comprehension you were even there." He wasn't sure where to go with this new knowledge. He would have to think about it for a while.

"Would you like to walk along the riverbank and discuss this a bit further? I need to stretch my legs." He stood, holding a hand out to help her up. Her hand in his was a simple and non-intrusive step to her seduction, because he did want her in his arms and craved her in his bed.

She accepted the help, letting him enclose her small hand in his larger one, "A walk would be nice. I'm a bit restless."

Broc didn't want to let go of her hand, at least not until she made it clear she didn't like this tiny advance. He was inexplicably drawn to her and hoped she wasn't some debutant who would seek a commitment. He liked his freedom and didn't mean to lose it anytime soon.

"Bliss," he paused, "where do you live?" he asked, trying for a bit more information from her. The thought of a debutante seeking him out sent a wave of precaution through his head. But what would some random debutante be doing riding hell bent across a meadow on MacTavish land? A debutant would not have to earn a living.

"Why?" Her answer was curt.

"Just curious. It seems you know more about me than I do you. It's only fair, don't you think?"

"No, fairness has nothing to do with any of this. I barely know you," she said. "I'm not going to give you my address. A lady needs an air of intrigue about her."

"You know me well enough to watch me half naked chopping wood," he told her, thinking he'd like to see her naked. Her dress hid her curves fairly well, but he could still tell quite a lot about her body. "I'm sure you know exactly where I live."

"And you weren't a wee bit bashful either. I also saw a beautiful woman ride to the stables. I saw you kiss her. When you were half naked. So," she paused gazing at him, her eyes simmering, "I'm sure you don't care if I saw your chest and rippling muscles." With that said she looked away as if she didn't want him to see her reaction. He was sure he saw more than she intended.

"Jealous?" Good lord but that was at least two months ago. His mistress paid him an unusual visit and he sent her away with the order to never come to his home again.

"Of course not," she protested to quickly.

"The blush rising on your cheeks tells me you're not speaking the truth. I think you should apologize or let me kiss you. Perhaps we should make a bet. Every time you lie you have to kiss me."

"No, I wouldn't like to make a bet like that with you. I've been told you're a very bad man where it comes to women."

"Who told you that?" He could only think of a few people who would say that about him, and it would be in jest or to warn a debutant away.

"Just heard it. Don't remember where. Probably one day when I was in town to sell my paintings." She smushed her lips together, squinting, her eyebrows drawn together as if she was thinking.

"Something doesn't ring true."

"Don't know why you say that?"

"Back to my question, are you jealous? Should we find out if you like my kisses?" He grinned at her hesitancy, but the way her tongue swept across her lips told him she was thinking about telling him yes, or at least about a kiss.

"Probably not a good idea." She backed away from him, but she didn't take her hand from his. "A kiss. No something like that could lead to other things a lady shouldn't do."

"Other things? What do you know about other things?"

"Nothing really."

He decided a bit more persuasion might be appropriate here. He traced gentle circles on her wrist with his thumb and he watched her eyes cross for a second. "Probably not, but what if kissing you is a very good idea? What then? You'd miss something you would enjoy."

"Again, I barely know you. It's not proper to kiss a man when you've only known him for a few minutes. One must wait..."

"Proper!" he roared then chuckling. "You are the least proper woman I've ever met. And we've known each other over an hour now, not a few minutes. So a kiss would certainly be proper."

She pulled her hand from his. "I..." She walked away from him hurriedly, not really paying attention to where she was going. She stumbled but righted herself quickly.

In any case, he wasn't sure how well she could see without her glasses and perhaps that was why she quit drawing with only one sketch completed.

"Bliss..."

She stopped and turned. "Perhaps I'm not proper, maybe I don't want to be. But it doesn't change the fact that you hurt my feelings when you made that statement."

"That had not been my intention. I'm glad you're being honest with me, at least about that. I like honesty in a woman. Don't like to be blindsided by falsehoods."

"So you say." She started walking again.

A few rapid strides and he was beside her once more, walking step for step with her, wondering how far she meant to go. The horses were still tethered a ways back and the sky was darkening. He didn't like the idea of a rainstorm catching them out in the open and unprotected.

"We should go back." He set his hand on her shoulder, turning her slightly.

She stared at him then followed the direction of his gaze. "I suppose you're right. It could rain."

They reached the horses before any showers started, but a brilliant crack of lightning brightened the sky. Quickly, he set her on her horse. "My drawings." She reached out seemingly intent on dismounting.

"I'll get them. Head for the stables at my place. We might make it that far before the storm hits. Would rather not get a drenching." Yet if they were soaked through to the skin, he could think of some delightful possibilities, all included being naked with her.

She had turned her horse, seeming to head in the opposite direction then she nodded to him. He swept the items into his arms before mounting. Following her they raced the storm.

The tempest raged behind them. The little mare she rode seemed to be a good sound horse. She kept the animal under control despite the noise and the lightening. He realized she was right. She was a damn good horsewoman, and this afternoon she had not needed saving.

He had no regrets.

Inside the stables, she slid from the horse, rubbing her down with a cloth she found. Seconds later hail pounded the top of the barn while wind howled around the eaves. Darkness seemed to enshroud the inside of the barn.

"It seems we just beat the tempest," she told him, rubbing her arms and looking a bit forlorn and cold. "I would have never made it home."

"You're chilled." He wrapped her in the blanket she'd spread on the grass earlier then he sifted through her sketchpad. "Everything seems to be in order."

"I'm glad we had some place dry to go, but I'm not sure about getting home if this rain keeps up. I don't like to ride in the dark by myself."

"Are you asking me to accompany you home," he asked, grinning, understanding he might just learn more about her than she'd been willing to tell him earlier this afternoon.

She bristled, her back stiffening. "I'll have to think about it. I didn't mean to say anything to you. I'm perfectly capable of doing things I don't like if the situation demands it."

"Makes sense to me. It's settled then. A woman shouldn't be out by herself in the dark. I would be remiss if I let you go by yourself."

"Would you?" she asked, "Be remiss? I think you just want to learn what I didn't want to tell you."

"I can't visit you and watch you paint when you're not looking if I don't know where your home is." He chuckled at her look of chagrin.

She found a bale of hay and sat down, keeping the blanket wrapped tightly around her and shivering uncontrollably. She didn't say anything but he heard a heavy sigh. For a few seconds she fiddled with the edge of the blanket.

"Why?" He sat down beside her, stilling her fingers by taking them into one hand and wrapping an arm around her.

"Why what?" She kept her face turned from him.

"Why indeed. What is it that you need to keep so secretive? The more you try to evade my questions it seems the more I want to know what you hide." She was mysterious yet it seemed to him, she liked him, seemed to feel at ease with him, perhaps even wanted to divulge more about herself.

"It's just that I like my privacy. You're a man and you don't have certain things to worry about. I don't want to seem overeager or jealous or whatever men think about women. I'm not chasing you and have no intention of doing anything of the sort."

He touched his lips to the back of her hand, wondering what it would be like to explore her mouth and if she would let him discover untold mysteries. But she thought of him as a bad man. He didn't believe her story about hearing it on the streets, so where did those words come from?

"What is it you have to worry about?" he asked, turning her hand over and kissing her palm, his tongue making gentle forays across the tender flesh.

She shivered from his caress. "Well, right now I have to worry about a man seducing me," she told him but she didn't take her hand from his.

"Is that what I'm doing?" he grinned shamelessly. "Seducing you?" He brushed his lips on her neck.

"Perhaps. Not really sure what a seduction entails."

"I believe it's to lead astray."

"Then you couldn't be seducing me," she said, her voice a thin whisper.

"Perhaps you're enticing me to engage in a relationship with you."

"Me enticing you?"

She let her head fall back, giving him better access to her neck. "I'm still not sure what it means."

"Some more of this." He brushed her hair from the back of her neck then kissed her gently, delighted by the tiny noise she made. "And more of this." He explored her ear with his teeth and tongue.

Her breath caught in the back of her throat. "Should my heart race?" she asked and her voice broke on the words.

"If I'm doing it right." He pulled the blanket from her shoulders before turning her and drawing her into his arms. What he craved and what he was going to do right now didn't match even though she seemed more than willing. If he took his time with her, she would be his.

"Does this make you a bad man or does it take more than this?" Her breaths seemed to come sporadically while she spoke.

He paused a moment, wondering at her words once more. "No, just a man who wants to learn more about a very special lady."

"I suppose seducing and enticing someone requires more than just a kiss on the back of the neck." She touched his lips with a finger before running the tip across his mouth. "How much more?"

He groaned, wondering at her innocence. "You presume right and as to how much, that's a discussion for another day." The relationship was one he needed to pursue longer than one night. The way her body responded to the slightest touch gave him reason to smile, but he wanted this connection with her to last longer than a few enjoyable hours.

"What are you going to do now?" Her eyes were wide pools of liquid passion.

"After I kiss you, I'm going to see you home." He wanted to undo all the buttons on her dress and... Bloody hell, but he needed to make love to her but tonight he wasn't going to be a bad man. He was going to be a very good one.

"You're going to kiss me?" she asked, her voice whispered across him.

"Nothing to be afraid of. I promise you'll like it and beg for more," he told her, running the back of his hand along her cheek. "Have you ever been kissed before?"

"Arrogant man."

"Confident," he told her, his hands on both sides of her face. "That's it, get ready for me, let me see your tongue run along your lips, just like that." He wanted to know if any man had ever kissed her but realized if she told him yes... Good god, but he felt jealousy rise to the forefront of his mind.

"My...me..." Her hands rested on his chest, her fingers winding into the fabric of his shirt.

"See, I am good. You can't even talk you want me so much." His lips molded on hers, his tongue searching for entrance. His body ached with a thrumming desire to be inside her. Soon he told himself but not too soon.

For a second he pulled away from her. Bliss' eyes were closed, her fingers digging into his shoulders. He kissed her again, encompassing her mouth within his, probing inside with his tongue and playing with her then pulling away.

"Did you like my kiss?"

"Am I seduced?"

~ * ~

"Not even close, little minx. When I seduce you, you won't have to ask. You'll know, ah soon, my mysterious woman."

His roar of laughter startled her, the kiss making her head spin and her heart beat crazily out of control. She punched him in the chest, "Why are you laughing at me?"

"Hopefully, with you. I'm laughing with you."

"I'm not laughing." She turned from him, her back stiff, feeling a wave of inadequacy and innocence sweep through her. She needed to get away from this wonderful crazy man and his potent charm then sift through all that happened this afternoon. "The rain has stopped. I need to get home."

"You don't want to stay and let me coax another kiss from your sweet lips?" he chuckled, refastening some buttons that had inadvertently come undone on her dress.

She couldn't recall when he unfastened her dress, or had she? "No."

She had to get home or her brother would be out searching for her, but she couldn't tell Broc about her brother or that she was a MacTavish. Broc and her brother were best friends and she knew personally neither one would ever marry, at least not until they found a need for an heir and that didn't appear to by any time soon, at least not for her brother.

"Since I'm seeing you home you could stay a bit longer. We could explore some other avenues of your seduction or you could seduce me. You seducing me, leading me astray, I find that thought fascinating."

"I have to get home, my..." She almost said her father. Her father was dead as was her mother. Flynt, her brother, was charged with taking care of her and her sisters and of finding them a husband.

"And where is home?" he asked, still seeming to probe for answers when she didn't want to give any.

She inhaled long and deep searching for the courage to continue this lie, this necessary lie. "The whereabouts of my home is none of your business, but if you must know, I rent a small cottage nearby." She didn't want to bring up the name MacTavish or lead him to the estate where she grew up. If she did, he'd never see her again.

"You do?" he questioned. "How?"

"Painting money. Both my parents have passed on." The tears at this memory filling her eyes were not a lie. They were very real. "I have to live somewhere and I have to earn an income. So..."

"I see." But the expression on his face told her he wasn't believing a word she said.

"You can take me to the cottage," she told him, placing her hand on his. When he left her there, she would ride the rest of the way home by herself. It wasn't far and she'd done so several times at night when time slipped by and she realized too late it was dark outside.

Truly, she didn't think Flynt would miss her tonight. He rarely checked in on her or her sisters. He was just too busy with his affairs. Before she left to sketch this afternoon, he'd told her he was heading into Glasgow for a night of carousing. He didn't say the word carousing but that was what she told herself he was doing. He was going there to be a bad man or bad boy as he and his friends called themselves. The only difference this time was that Broc wasn't with him. He was with her being bad. Well not really so bad, probably not what he anticipated when he kissed her.

"I would like to see where you live and to make sure you're safely inside before I leave for home." He brought her horse to her and helped her up then mounted his stallion.

The tempest that passed through the area left a trail of broken branches and debris on the ground. The ride was slow in the dark of the night. Despite her fear at Broc seeing where she lived, Bliss was happy to have him by her side and even more pleased to see the tiny cottage in front of them.

"Is this it?" he asked, pointing to the cottage she called her studio. "You even have a small barn." He turned his horse in that direction.

"You're not staying," she told him, eyeing him critically. "Told you, you could take me here not follow me into the house."

"No, of course not." He grinned at her, "But a gentleman would never leave a lady to groom her horse and he would never leave without checking inside to make sure no one was inside the home."

She caught the retort in the back of her throat. "Another something I'm quite capable of, grooming my horse." He caught her reins, stopping her mare.

"Then come with me and I'll watch before I accompany you inside the house and make sure everything is safe." It seemed he wasn't going to get caught up in the game she was trying hard to play just to keep her emotions from showing.

"I'm not going to change your mind, am I?" she sighed, resigned now to letting him do just about anything he wanted. He would have an argument for everything just to get his way.

"Nope." He dismounted, leading the horses inside the stable. He reached up to help her down.

Shaking her head several times, she allowed him his gentlemanly gesture, "Something else I can do by myself. Could get off a horse before I was five." She had to admit to herself she liked the feel of his hands on her waist and the unsolicited attention he lavished on her. She'd never been treated so well.

"I wouldn't be a gentleman if I left you to your own devices. Now you spoke of taking care of your horse." He stood back, his arms crossed. "I'm going to water and feed mine too."

He allowed her to do as she asked and when they finished with the horses, he held out an arm to escort her.

At the door he stopped, "It's not locked?"

She looked at him surprised, "I never lock the door."

"Something we need to discuss," he told her, a sudden darkness covering his face, his brows drawn tightly together.

"Whatever are you talking about now?" This time she was truly baffled with his comment.

"An unlocked door? You're far too trusting." He stepped aside so she could enter the room. "What if someone let themselves in while you were gone?"

"Perhaps," she agreed with him, but she didn't mean to tell him he was right. If she actually lived here, she would keep it locked. As it was there was nothing here to steal except her painting supplies. Besides the door didn't have a lock, so what could he expect?

Following her, he stepped inside. He paused for a moment, searching the room, seeming to absorb the absence of everything that would make it livable and come to some conclusion. Then, running a finger along a shelf, he looked at her, a wide grin on his face as if he found something amusing.

"Not much of a housekeeper, are you?"

She stiffened, wishing she had protested his entry into what she was pretending to be her home. "Never said I was. I've more important things to do than clean house." She set the satchel carrying her sketches on a table. Her discomfort grew with each second. He would see through her ruse, figure out who she was and leave.

She would never see him again.

"I see supplies but no paintings." He investigated the living room before making his way to kitchen.

"I was in town yesterday with all of them. Sold them all so I could pay my bills," she called after him, watching his departing back.

She stayed put, listening to the cupboard doors as one by one he opened and closed them. His footsteps on the kitchen floor thundered in her ears. Inhaling a long deep breath, she paused, hands clasped in front of her, waiting for his assessment.

Broc stepped out of the kitchen, a bottle of brandy and two crystal glasses in hand, "Not a bite to eat and nothing to cook with but you've got something to imbibe on a cold night, or hot one. Care to have a brandy with me."

"What does that matter?" Why she asked that question, she had no idea. She didn't want to hear his evaluation.

He shrugged broad masculine shoulders, "One has to eat. Would you like a drink?"

She didn't answer, instead she fidgeted with the satchel and the sketches within. Before she could say no, he had poured her a drink and was handing it to her. He sat down in an overstuffed chair, dust flying. He coughed then sneezed, brushing imaginary or perhaps real dust particles from his jacket.

"I'm going to send over a housecleaner tomorrow." He sipped the drink, staring at her. "Could clean and tidy up this room before the morning passes."

"No." She bristled, displeased with the fact he was beginning to assume rights he didn't have. "No, you're not."

He smiled and sipped, looking more relaxed than anyone should. She knew her *no* meant nothing to him. He would do as he pleased when he pleased. He was just like her brother. "I wouldn't have it any other way."

"I won't let a housecleaner inside." She protested adamantly; her hands fisted at her side. "You can't take over my life. We barely know each other."

"Won't be much trouble with an unlocked door. I just want to make your life easier, give you more time to paint." Nonchalantly, he rose from the chair, once again walking around the room, picking up things and tracing more dust lines on the furniture.

"A lock will be on tomorrow. I promise." Exhausted from the exchange, she sat down, the glass of brandy in her hand a tempting diversion from this complication she brought home with her and could not get rid of. Well, she didn't want him to come into the cottage for this very reason.

"Not by the morning."

She wanted to throw the glass at him even while she wanted him to kiss her again. The lies of omission seemed to grow too rapidly for her to explain anything away. Not that she should have to clarify what she did and didn't do to him. If he'd just act the way she expected of and wanted, everything would be fine right now and she'd be on her way home.

"Drink your brandy. At least it will be something in your stomach and it will help you relax. Your shoulders are rigid and that can't be comfortable." His voice sounded harsh for a moment. Then he grinned, showing perfect white teeth. "I could give you a massage."

She wished he would go home. She did sip the brandy though, and the potent liquid pooled in her stomach like a brick. "Don't you think you should leave?"

"Too many questions," he told her, stepping through another door into the smaller bedroom as if he owned the cottage.

Bliss didn't know why her heart raced and her hands shook. At this moment Broc was nothing to her. Just a kiss in the stables, just someone she'd like to spend time with and perhaps kiss again. Having heard enough of her brother's stories, she understood this man would never have a meaningful relationship with her. Would never ask her to become his wife. And yet...

"I'm not giving you any answers." She turned away as he walked into the second bedroom.

"Ah a bed, so you sleep." He set his brandy on a side table and plopped on the bed, crossing his long legs that were stretched out in front of him. He patted the space beside him, "Care to join me?"

Bloody eyes, but she'd like to know what he was thinking. "No."

"I could easily convince you otherwise."

"Let's move on to the discussion about your departure." She couldn't help herself. She walked into the bedroom, needing to see him and his expressions to help her understand what might be in his head.

"Not leaving until I have answers and I know you'll be safe at least until morning." He patted the bed beside him again, his grin still broad as if he thought she would do his bidding.

She inhaled several short rapid breaths of air, her body quivering and unable to think of anything to say. "I'll be safe." Stupid man. As soon as he left, she meant to ride to Deepwood, the MacTavish estate. It didn't seem he meant to depart anytime soon.

"Join me." He made circles with his hand on the spot next to him. "While the bed is clean, which does surprise me given the condition of the rest of your home, it's not comfortable. Too many lumps."

"It wasn't meant for your comfort." Yet she walked to the other side of the bed and sat down next to him with her back against the headboard.

"You shouldn't have a bed unless it's comfortable to everyone who is going to sleep in it." He placed her hand in his, bringing it to his lips for a quick kiss.

He was incorrigible. "Broc, no." She tugged it back, afraid of what might come later if she allowed him to many liberties, understanding his reputation.

He shrugged. "You liked your hand in mine only an hour ago. You also liked the kiss. Me thinks you protest too much, *mo mhilse,* my sweet."

She turned to face him, her legs curled around her. "What are you really doing here?"

"I've been more upfront with you than you've been with me. You're not telling me something and I'd like the truth. In fact, I don't believe anything you've told me today is true except perhaps your name."

She gritted her teeth together, frustrated and confused. "Those are truths I'm not comfortable in giving you. Can't you just forget about what I haven't told you? We'll probably never see each other again, and..."

"We will see each other," gazing at her, "again and again, until we tire of each other."

"You won't give up and neither will I." She liked the part of seeing him again and the promise the words held but not the part of until they tired of each other.

"All the evidence, except this bed, point to the fact you don't live here. I'm suspecting that as soon as I leave, you're going to hightail it home, wherever that is."

She felt the color drain from her face and after she looked away, he touched her chin with a finger, effectively turning her so she had no choice but to look at him.

"I'm not going to another home because I don't have one." She persisted in her story, intending to beat him at this game he was playing of truth and lies. Perhaps omission was a better term than lies. He was waiting for her to slip up which she wasn't going to do. The dratted man couldn't take no for an answer or an answer to a question either for that matter.

"You're very beautiful but there's a haunting look in your eyes. You don't lie easily. In fact, I think you have very little experience in subterfuge." He stopped for a moment, gazing into her eyes. "There is something so familiar about you, but I can't figure it out. I will though."

"I don't know what that could be." She tugged her hand away then walking from the room and to the front door, "It's time you left." Hands clasped in front of her, she stood beside the door.

"We are at an impasse then. I'll just make myself comfortable. It would be nice if you had some food in the cupboard. My stomach is rumbling." He shirked out of his waistcoat before loosening his cravat.

"What are you doing?" She was inside the bedroom again, watching as he pulled off his Hessians.

"Getting comfortable as I said I intended." He crossed his feet again as he settled back on the bed.

"You can't do that."

"Bliss, really, pacing will do you no good while the truth will exonerate you and I'll leave for my home. Although as the hour grows later, I believe I would prefer to remain here. I don't relish a cross-country ride in the darkness of the night. I believe you've waited too long."

Bliss walked back to the sitting room and poured herself more brandy. Talking to him would do no good. She pulled a pillow from another couch and found a blanket back in the main bedroom.

"What are you doing?" he asked her, his voice deep and gruff. "You can't sleep out there on a chair." The command in his voice was evident.

"I'm not going to bed with you," she told him, angry with him, angry with herself and the situation she got herself into. Thinking if she could turn back time, she would have made different decisions.

"But you're bedding down out here." He hovered above her. "I'd never keep a lady from her bed."

Sometime in the last few seconds he'd removed his shirt and his pants were unfastened. She inhaled a swift deep breath of air. "You're naked."

"You've seen me without a shirt."

"Not this close," she told him, her voice a squeak. Reaching out to touch him then realizing what she was doing she pulled her hand back as if she burned it. Despite the real and powerful draw to him, which she felt, that action was not well done of her if she wanted to dissuade him. She understood from listening to Flynt what bad boys were like.

He was grinning, clearly enjoying her impulsive actions. "You can touch me any time you like."

"No."

"Don't trust yourself with my body? Afraid I might find a way to get you on your very own bed and have my wicked way with you? I won't, you know. Not unless you tell me how much you want me."

She pulled the blanket over her then punching the pillow, she tried to get comfortable. Before she could close her eyes, she was in his arms and she found herself on the bed with him beside her, closer than she'd ever been with a man, a very nearly naked man.

"Bliss, truly I'm not trying to give you a bad time and I'm not going to ravish you unless you ask." He brushed hair from her face, his lips so close she could almost feel them against hers.

"Kiss me," she told him, her voice quivering but she meant to say don't, simply because she was afraid of her feelings. The palm of her hand rested against his chest, touching him. "Please Broc, I... You need to go home."

"Why, Bliss? You didn't mind my kiss before and you just asked me to kiss you." He persisted, his breath ruffling across her face.

"Meant to say don't. But no, you're right. I liked your kiss but now...

Not when you're on a bed with me and it doesn't seem you're going anywhere." She trembled, wishing for one thing but her mind telling her something else entirely.

"Tonight at least I'm staying with you, just for your safety."

"If you go home, nothing will happen to me. I promise." Her fingers dug into his shoulder and she pushed against him, but this time it wasn't to push him away. It seemed she was pulling him closer.

"I'm going to make sure nothing untoward occurs here tonight. I wouldn't be able to sleep at night if anything happened to you because I was careless." He kissed her cheek, the line of her jaw then.

"Broc, please. This is all happening to fast." *Even though I want that kiss and another one after that.* "I'm not your whore."

"Never." But he pulled away as if she slapped him. "I realize I've overstepped some bounds. But I've never in the few short hours I've known you have I thought of you as a whore. And there is something about you Bliss. I want you."

"I won't be your mistress either."

"No, I don't suppose you will. I have a mistress."

~ * ~

Flynt sat back in his chair. A barmaid brought him and his companion, Cam, a second pint.

"Where's Broc?" Cam asked.

"Must be with his mistress," Flynt said, having wondered that same question several times in the last two hours. It wasn't like his best friend to miss this one night out every week. The five of them had a pact. This night was sacred to their friendship and their dedication to stay single. No simpering, music playing and ball-dancing debutantes for them.

"Nope, not there," Donal said, pulling up a chair and sitting down. "Rode by the house on my way here, and his horse wasn't tied up at the hitching post."

"Where the blazes do you think he is?" Flynt asked. He was leaning back, watching the barmaids as they plied their wares. No one here bedded any of these women. Didn't want to take the risk of the pox.

"Told me he was going for a ride. Was looking for something he'd seen another day," Cam said.

"Sounds like a riddle to me," Flynt added with a frown. But something niggled in the back of his head. Something his sister Bliss had said, but for the life of him, he couldn't think of it.

"When are you going to present your oldest sister? Isn't it time for her to have a season?" Donal asked. "You've got to do your duty by your sisters or they're going to be living in your home until they're old and gray. Doubt if you want anything like that. Could get in the way of other endeavors."

"Stuck on the shelf, so to speak," Cam added with a hearty chuckle.

Flynt ran his fingers through his hair, knowing he left it in a disheveled mess. "She doesn't want a season. Says they are ridiculous."

"Then she's going to stay a spinster?" Leslie asked. "Don't know her well but I doubt if she's meant to be celibate for the rest of her life."

"Bliss doesn't care about any of that. I've presented several men to her. In fact, there's one coming to call on her in two days. She doesn't like any of them. Finds something wrong every time." Flynt knew exactly why she didn't like them, but bloody hell, she needed someone who would stay true to her. Not someone like him or his friends, acknowledged bad boys. Men who, in time, would break her heart.

"And who pray tell have you sent her?" Leslie asked, laughing hard. "Not one of those bookish men who sit and read all day. Those types are really too boring for any of your sisters, and they would never succeed in making them happy. You are going to have to go beyond what you want and think about what your sister and later on sisters will want."

Flynt rambled off a list of the eligible suitors he sent her way. "She says she could never go to bed with any of them."

"Why is that?"

"It seems there have been a few evenings we've not been discreet in our carousing. She's seen more than one of us without our shirts on and as my sister tells me, she's not going to settle for anything less in a man."

"You have power over her. Tell her who she has to wed and be done with at least one of your sisters," Cam said dryly.

"Then you'll have three left to find husbands for."

"I can't do that to her." He was shaking his head, feeling the need to see Bliss happy. He had to do that for her, didn't need to feel guilty for the rest of his life. It was just that someone like him, a known rake would not make her happy in the long run.

"Your heart is too soft."

"Perhaps, but put yourself in her place and you will soften too. She doesn't care about a title or money, she cares about the man, perhaps even what's beneath the surface. I've got to say, I respect that sentiment too much to gainsay her or force her into a marriage where she'll be miserable the rest of her life. Not really sure what I'm going to do." Flynt gulped down the last of his drink.

"You could always let her find a man on her own," Cam suggested, grinning. "That might prove interesting and amusing to watch."

"That could be a complete disaster. She's an innocent in the ways of men. What if she fell in love with a complete cad, someone like us who would break her heart and leave her pregnant?" Donal asked.

"Men like us are who Bliss is attracted to along with her sisters," Flynt said, sipping the brew he just ordered and refusing to let his emotions get the better of him. "Never bargained on having to find husbands for three sisters."

"Who's left?"

"All of them after Bliss and I've accomplished nothing with her. Chelsea, Daryl and little Lacie are all in need of husbands."

"You've got some time with Lacie and Daryl, though," Leslie pointed out, his eyes alight with humor.

"A respite, just what I need but I doubt if they'll be any easier. Mother and Father raised them to have a mind and think for themselves. They know what they want, and I'm sure they won't settle either."

"Focus back on Bliss. What does she enjoy?"

"Music," Flynt began, "and painting."

"Problem solved. Find some who appreciates the arts."

"The men she would find suitable appreciate the art of seduction above all else," Flynt said, tossing back the Guinness and motioning for another one before making a mental note to stop at his mistress' home tonight for some much needed relief.

Chapter Two

Broc left the tiny cottage with the rising of the sun and a smile in his heart. Taking a moment to gaze at the sleeping and still fully clothed Bliss, he knew what he needed to do. This was going to be a very good day, a very good day indeed.

Whistling as he rode, he headed into Glasgow with several destinations in mind. The first was the locksmith and the second was to his mistress' home. No, he needed to visit his bank first and place a substantial amount of coin in Edina's account, enough so she would have enough money until she found a new man to keep her.

Perhaps a housecleaner should be approached after he addressed the locksmith. If what he saw last night was typical, Bliss was in sore need of one and he hoped she wouldn't object overmuch.

Yesterday, he knew the moment he kissed Bliss, she would be his next mistress. He understood how difficult handling that situation would be. She would not accept the status easily, so he would have to dance around the title making sure she never suspected his intentions.

It was the middle of July and the day would soar into the upper eighties, hotter than normal. At least the cottage surrounded by oak trees would remain cool through the heat of the day. His thoughts traveled back to Bliss and how peaceful she looked sleeping, so different from the feisty lady of the day before. She matched him intellectually and she would never give in to his dictates unless that was what she wanted also. He respected that even though there were some who would not.

He reached the locksmith and gave him directions to the cottage then secured a key for himself before leaving for his second and third destinations. The third one a task that would not be as enjoyable as knowing

Bliss would be safe and he could come and go in her home whenever he wished.

So far all had gone according to plan. The account was set up in Edina's name and should last her for several months. Now he stood in front of her door, the townhouse she lived in was near the center of town in one of the wealthier districts. He'd made sure she lived in a reputable neighborhood when he purchased the home. When she found another man, he would sell the townhouse.

Making a mental note about Bliss, he meant to purchase the cottage she lived in now for her so she wouldn't have to pay rent. It was on MacTavish land and if Flynt wouldn't sell, then he would make arrangements to pay the rent each month. He could imagine Bliss' expression when she discovered what he'd done. A smile spread across his face, thinking of the passion the deed would provoke. And he realized he enjoyed provoking her at least a little. He knew making up would be sweeter.

The door opened, "Edina," he acknowledged with a nod but no welcoming smile.

"Broc? I expected you last night. What happened to you?" A frown etching her pretty face, she stepped away to let him inside.

"Busy." He was curt, never liking to explain himself or his actions. The last thing he would do is mention Bliss to Edina. He respected Edina too much, but he'd grown tired of her just as he had every other woman in his life.

"Can I get you anything?" she asked, following him as he strode into the parlor. Tapping his riding gloves against his leg.

"A whiskey would be nice," he told her as he walked to the sideboard and finding two glasses he poured them both a drink. "You should sit down."

"I'd rather stand," she told him but she did sit, holding her glass with both hands, rolling it between her palms.

"You've probably guessed why I'm here." He sat crossing his legs and leaning back. She would do well as she was still attractive and her figure enticing. Her disposition was also pleasant. Any man would be happy to have her.

"No," she said, sipping the whiskey then coughing slightly. "I've no idea why you're visiting in the middle of the afternoon."

"Really." He didn't believe her for a second. While Edina had never been guileless, she only lied on occasion and when it suited her. This must be one of those times.

"To what do I owe your afternoon visit? I take it you're not here for sex. And since you usually send a note when you intend to see me, I am rather surprised."

His attraction to her now seemed baffling. Compared to Bliss she was a hollow shell with little to make her standout. Perhaps at the time he wanted a woman who would do his bidding and never gainsay him, or maybe he just needed a pretty face and nice curves.

"I've come to tell you it's time for the two of us to move on. I no longer want to see you or pay for your frivolous whims."

She inhaled swiftly, her hand rising to her throat. "Frivolous? No, you can't mean it. Who is it? Are you wedding?" She cleared her throat then, "We both know that wouldn't make a difference."

He realized suddenly it was something he'd never really thought about before but if he did fall in love, give his heart to a bonny lass, he would never keep a mistress on the side.

"None of your questions have anything to do with you or your business. Why we are done is not yours to know. Just be aware of the fact I've left a suitable amount of coin in the bank under your name. It is sufficient to carry you over until you find another protector."

He watched as a tear slipped from an eye. Somehow he felt it was contrived and he wasn't about to acknowledge the fact. She never loved him; perhaps cared for him a little. They were compatible and served each other well while it lasted, but it was over now and nothing would change that fact. He'd made it clear to Edina from the first day of their relationship; she would not be with him forever.

"I see." She folded her hands in her lap and sat up straighter. "Then I won't see you again."

He was shaking his head, "Not unless it's on the street. You may keep everything I've given you and as you well know I've been generous. When you find another protector, I'll sell the house. You can live here until then."

"Thank you." She tried to speak softly but the underlying current of anger could easily be heard in her voice.

He had crossed her and she might become a formidable enemy. Watching his back and Bliss' might not be a bad idea to keep in mind. He rose then, setting his glass on the end table.

"Take care, Edina. I wish you the best. I'll see myself out." He felt as if he couldn't get out of the oppressive home fast enough. The lightheartedness he'd begun the day with vanished. After he closed the door behind him, he heard the crash of one of the expensive crystal glasses he poured the whiskey in shatter against the brick fireplace.

A part of his life was over, and he was about to embark on a new scenario, one he hoped would prove satisfying and quite enjoyable. He had thought to return to the cottage after he ended the relationship with Edina but now he had a different idea.

Bliss wouldn't like it, but he intended to buy a few things for her home, one he planned to spend a lot of time in. The first item was going to be a comfortable bed then he would meander over to the dressmakers and purchase a few things including some lingerie then he intended to buy food and a few pots and pans so she could cook. He wondered if she did know how to cook.

With all the errands, the morning and afternoon had flown by. Now he was driving a cart filled with items for Bliss' home, and his stallion was tied to the back. Anticipating her reaction, he thought for a moment that perhaps he should have purchased a shield for himself when she started throwing things.

Yesterday she didn't seem like a violent person. Indeed some of the outrageous things he said and did to provoke her, she simply did not respond to them. Yet he'd felt the underlying passion between them, the desire for something she'd never encountered before simmering raw and deep inside her. He wanted to unleash that hunger simmering in her sweet curves and reap the rewards.

When he started down the lane to Bliss' home, the sun was still fairly high on the horizon. Light shimmered through the leaves on the trees, creating dancing shadows on the ground. Squirrels scurried up the trees to get out of the way as he passed by. The air was redolent with the scent of summer flowers.

He reined in the horse pulling the cart, "Ah, it doesn't seem Bliss is home. Wonder where she could be?" In any case, it gave him some time to set the scene. Humming he strode to the front door and successfully unlocked it with his new key and saw Bliss' key had been left on the table by the door just as he instructed.

The house was clean, dusted and swept from one room to the other. He smiled, pleased with himself and the tasks he'd set in motion. Well, he had a lot to accomplish in what could be a short amount of time.

If he guessed right, this wasn't her real home, but it could be their sanctuary. She might not even show up here today, yet again she could arrive at any minute. Setting about unloading the cart, he didn't have a moment to waste.

By the time the sun was just starting to set, the new and much larger bed was inside and made with quilts and lavish pillows. He'd purchased a longer bed and mattress to fit his frame. The new dishes and kitchen equipment was put away and food was stored. On the way here, he stopped at a small restaurant he frequented and ordered a meal, which he set on the counter.

A nice kitchen table should be my next purchase to replace this tiny one, he decided. He stood back, hands on his hips and surveyed the small home, pleased with what he accomplished this day and hoped tonight would be well worth his efforts.

Now with everything finished, he was on lose footing. Pacing, he tried to think of all he should do. He didn't like waiting, especially when he didn't know if she was coming here today or even next week.

During the ride to the cottage, he thought of several scenarios if he had time to carry them out and decided to grab a bite to eat before pouring himself a drink. Then he would present himself as he was last night, on the bed and with his chest barred. Would there be fireworks or silence?

He didn't hold out any illusions he could sit and do nothing for very long, but he would try just for the chance to see her reaction.

In the bedroom he disrobed from the waist up then after loosening his pants for comfort, he set his glass of brandy beside the bed. He poured another for her and placed it on the other side. His hessians were the next articles of clothing to come off.

Now he was ready for her to appear and all he had to do was respond to Bliss' reactions to all of this. He turned in a three hundred sixty degree circle inspecting his handiwork.

"Very nicely done, Broc Wallace if I do say so myself."

At the window, he peered outside, hoping to see some sign of her appearance. But he only saw the darkening sky and decided if she wasn't here by the time night fell, she wasn't coming.

Relaxing on the bed, Broc closed his eyes, listening to the soft sounds of a small creek running behind the home. He must have dozed because the next thing he realized was the sound of horses' hooves and a lumbering cart coming to a stop in front of the cottage.

He grinned, knowing he was about to have his second encounter with Miss Bliss. Good lord, but he wanted to learn her last name. Perhaps she'd let it slip or perhaps not. She was too cagey for a mistake unless he caught her off guard.

Crossing his hands behind his head and stretching out on the bed, he watched for the door to open. He'd left it unlocked and slightly ajar.

The creak of the hinges caused him to hold his breath in anticipation. She pushed open the door, stumbled on her skirt before dropping an armload of packages on the floor.

He grinned at her when she looked up and knew the second she saw him and realized he was here for a visit. What kind of visit he was in for, hinged on her feelings for him. She would dictate what happened this evening between them, but he certainly meant to challenge her and he wouldn't leave without another kiss or more if she allowed it.

"Broc." Her voice died away in a whisper of air and the last remaining package in her arms fell to the ground with a definitive plop. It seemed she didn't move for several seconds.

His mind raced with different scenarios as how to proceed. First, he craved a kiss, anything else would be an extra bonus, no maybe two kisses. Then he needed to make sure she understood how he felt about her and what he was willing to do to help her out. Using the word mistress was out of the question, denying it a necessity.

"At your service. As you can see, there has been a substantial upgrade to your home." He smiled at her, patting the bed beside him.

Without answering or commenting, she spun on a heel, showing a shapely amount of ankle, and left. Bloody hell, he couldn't let her leave. It was growing dark, would be dark in minutes since the sun had already dipped below the horizon. If she left, where would she go? Good lord, he hadn't thought that far ahead.

He started to move from the bed, a position he didn't want to abandon but stopped when he heard the creak of the door and watched her bring another armful of packages into the house.

After dropping the parcels on the floor again, she stepped back, "You could help you know." Pausing to inhale a breath of air. "A gentleman would give assistance."

"Never really claimed to be a gentleman unless it suited my motives," he told her, once again patting the spot beside the bed. "In this case it doesn't. Besides, you've implied numerous times that you're more than capable of doing anything a man can do."

"Couldn't possibly sit down beside you. Who knows who will show up at my door and unload the contents of my cart before I can."

He grinned again, acknowledging he really should help and wondering how he could turn the act of chivalry to his advantage after abandoning his strategic position on the bed. "How much do you have left?"

He heard her huff of indignation, he assumed, as she turned again. Reluctantly he rose, following her from the house. Evidently she wasn't going to answer his question.

"I'll get what's left." He stepped in front of her, picking up the remaining packages.

Still she didn't say anything but marched into the bedroom and grabbed the brandy he poured for her before returning to the sitting room. She downed the contents then set it down.

"What the bloody hell have you done?" She looked over the room before marching into the kitchen and discovering additional purchases.

He shrugged, still unable to stop grinning. "Do you like it?" Lord but that was a baited question.

"I can fend for myself. All of this," she swept her arms around the room, "is going back first thing tomorrow morning. I refuse to use any of it. You can't buy me."

"Nope." He stepped up to her, touching the underside of her chin and lifting so he could look into her eyes. "It's all staying right where I put it. Now that that discussion is finished, are you hungry? I purchased a few things at a restaurant since I didn't know if you could cook, and I certainly can only boil water."

"It's going back." She wrenched away from him. "Especially the bed."

He supposed he should give her something else to think about because the discussion was pointless and a complete waste of time. Returning anything was out of the question. "You could say thank you instead of being so negative." Somehow he couldn't resist and knew she would either stay silent or put him in his place.

It seemed she chose to remain silent for the time being and marched into the bedroom to discover the small packages he set on one of the chairs near the bed. Opening one, she uncovered the lingerie, the thin filmy lingerie he'd die to see her in tonight even though he knew that wasn't going to happen.

Then, "I won't ever wear this." Quickly, she placed it in the paper and wrapped it back up.

"I think you will." He rocked on his feet, hands behind his back, enjoying the way her hurried breathing was assisting in the swift rise and fall of her breasts, a very attractive view he appreciated.

The other packages were unwrapped and placed back into their containers. She was looking at him and shaking her head as if in disbelief. A moment later she rushed at him and slammed her fist on his chest. "You don't understand anything about me. Gifts won't buy me. They won't buy you sex. I can't be bought."

"What do you expect? You've told me very little about yourself so all I know is what I've observed."

"Then you think I would stoop so low as to be your mistress? Is that what one kiss yesterday told you?" She slammed her hands against his chest again. "If that's the case, I take it back."

"You can't take back a kiss already given."

"Then there will be no more."

For the moment he had the losing hand. "I don't want you for a mistress. You couldn't even pass the interview."

"Interview." She walked the length of the room and back. "Interview!" Bliss plopped down on a chair, her eyes closed and seemed to be trying to slow her breathing as well as the speedy beating of her pulse, which he could clearly see.

"Yes, an interview. I always interview the women I choose to be my mistresses and they tell me their names and whatever they can about their families, their backgrounds. I need to know everything about a woman I mean to invest a large sum of wealth and time into. I want to know what things they like and what they enjoy doing. What you see here is just a man being nice to a woman he likes."

She bolted upright, eyes wide open before she waved her hands in the air again. "This is a substantial amount of money. You've got to take it back."

"Hardly any money at all, not for a man of my means anyway." He smiled at her again. "We really should get something to eat." He stood over her, but far enough away so he wouldn't appear intimidating.

She sighed heavily, seeming to realize some of what he was about was acceptable. "You do have a way making a point. I'm starving. What did you bring from town? A meal I can accept as long as you don't expect anything from me in return."

"Come see." He held out his hand and relished the feel when she placed hers into his.

Before she could object, he wrapped his arm around her, drawing her close. She let her head settle against his shoulder almost as if she was telling him that at least for the moment she was giving up the argument.

Then she turned in his arms, gazing at him before moistening her lips as if she anticipated or longed for a kiss. "You really have to stop doing this," she paused, "assuming things about me, buying things for me."

Slowly he lowered his head to her, and with his mouth less than an inch from hers. "Never, I'll never stop kissing you or giving you things I think you'd like, at least not until I stick my spoon in the wall."

31

He longed to touch her gently and tenderly in so many ways, explore and discover all that made Bliss the beautiful feisty woman he was coming to know and enjoy more than any woman of his acquaintance. He never knew how Bliss would react to his outrageous challenges.

His lips touched upon her, traced the seam of her mouth. Good god, but her taste was an aphrodisiac calling to his soul. She was his for the rest of time. He would move heaven and earth to make it happen. Heat rushed through him, pooling in parts he'd rather not think about right now. It would be a long night if this kept up.

Together their tongues danced with each other. She responded so sweetly and so passionately he almost forgot that he meant to feed her not take her to bed. Although the bed certainly called to him.

"Broc," she whispered, seeming to come up for a minute to gather air into her lungs. "Didn't you want food?"

"Too hungry for you." His mouth found hers once more. Yet he knew asking her for more was too soon in the scope of things. "Yes." He breathed in deeply steadying himself. "I'm going to feed you so you'll have the strength for more playtime."

She punched him on the arm, smiling this time. "There will be no more playtime for you. You've presumed way more than you should, and your haughtiness won't allow you to confess your sins."

"Yes, I've plenty of sins," he agreed, taking her hand and leading her into the kitchen. "And we're going to commit more together." Just not tonight, he reminded himself.

"Dreams, Broc, you've only dreams to keep you going. I don't plan on bending to your whims. I won't be party to whatever you planned. Tonight you're going home."

"We'll see about that." He raised her into his arms then inside the kitchen he set her on a chair.

This table was tiny but still sufficient for their needs. Using the newly purchased dinner and silverware, he scooped food onto the plates. He opened the bottle of wine and poured the liquid into cups.

"Venison stew and biscuits." He smiled at her. "Eat up. We've a long night ahead of us."

With knife and fork in hand, she leaned forward, "You are not staying and there is not going to be a long night. Just because you bought gifts, doesn't mean that's a payment for something more. How many times do I have to say the same thing for you to understand?"

"Alright then, if you tell me your last name, I'll go home, but I promise you I'll be back in the morning." He said the words but realized he couldn't see her tomorrow or for at least a week. It might be the end of July before he could get free. He had important and time-consuming business in Glasgow and would have to stay in his apartments there.

She sighed deeply, seeming to realize she lost this battle between them. "You've won this round but you can sleep on the bed in the other room." She leaned forward as if she anticipated his reaction.

She couldn't know because the door was shut and she must have assumed he kept the old bedraggled bed. But he tossed it out. "There is no bed in the other room, and I'm not sleeping on the floor."

Her bewildered, look sent a brief moment of compassion for her distress pummeling through his veins, but he had to look out for both of them. If she had another bed she could escape to, he might not ever consummate this relationship. While he was a patient man, he didn't intend to wait forever.

"What happened to it?" Her face drained of color at the realization of what he anticipated. For a second, he felt the cad but he wasn't going to force her to make love with him. After last night's chaste hours she must know that fact.

"Needless to say it's gone."

"Gone? You had no right."

"No, I suppose I did."

~ * ~

Bliss woke up to an empty bed but a feeling of lightheartedness she hadn't felt since her parents died. Broc was gone or at least not in the house. She enjoyed sleeping beside him but understood it was just a matter of time before he would claim more from her.

She had been half in love with him since the first time she set eyes on him nine years earlier. She'd been all of ten years old, but she'd thought he was the most handsome boy she'd ever seen. Well, at the time he was more of a man than a boy.

Her grandmother was the only person she ever told about him and the way she felt, not even her sisters were privy to her thoughts and she told them almost everything. She washed then dressed before she locked the house and headed toward Glasgow to see her best friend and absolutely best confidant in the whole wide world. Grandmother would help her figure out her feelings for Broc Wallace, a self-proclaimed bad boy.

As far as she was concerned the only kind of man or husband, if that was possible, she wanted was a bad boy. She didn't want someone who didn't challenge her and surprise her. Whether the surprise was outrageous or sweet it made no difference to her. She didn't want a man who was not debonair and handsome as sin.

Before she returned from her visit, she would purchase a few more things for the kitchen as well as bring a few dresses from home and hopefully would have a little time to set up her new canvases. If the place looked more lived in, then he might believe what she told him and not keep pressuring her for her last name and a real address.

He didn't say as much the evening before, because she didn't think he wanted to argue with her. She touched her lips. No, he had other things on his mind as did she.

Her grandmother's home was slightly northwest of Glasgow about ten miles from the MacTavish estate. She could easily ride there and back in one day. She would take one of the stable horses not her own so she could leave that one and ride a fresh horse back to the cottage after her visit.

A couple hours later she pulled up in front of the house. Her grandmother had been sitting on the porch. When she saw her, she walked down the steps arms open wide for a huge hug.

"What brings you all the way out here?" Arm in arm they walked up the steps.

"Have things to talk about with you," Bliss said, thinking that was an understatement. "Important things and they couldn't wait another moment."

"That sounds ominous," Catherine laughed softly. "About a man? Has that brother of yours set you up with someone completely unsuitable?

I'm going to have to have a talk with your big brother and change his mind about possible suitors for you as well as your sisters."

"Flynt isn't involved at all. I found someone on my own, but he's just like Flynt. Doesn't want anything to do with marriage. He does everything by his own rules, only wants a mistress." Bliss let out a heavy sigh wondering what she could possibly say or do to change Broc's mind.

"Remember, you cannot change a man. So if you can't live with him the way he is, best you say goodbye before you lose your heart to him."

With a long indrawn breath of air to fill her lungs and give courage, "My heart was lost to him when I was ten."

"Don't exaggerate. Best you explore more of your feelings now. A school girl crush is not something that will necessarily last a lifetime."

"It seems so real though."

"Come inside and I'll fix us a pot of tea. Maybe cook left some ginger cookies. Have you had breakfast?"

"No, not yet anyway. Seems I forgot about getting anything to eat." Bliss sat down in the kitchen while she watched her grandmother bustle around the room humming to herself.

When the tea was ready, she poured them both a steaming cup and sat down across from her. Reaching out she took both of Bliss' hands in hers and smiled at her. "Now tell me everything about this young man of yours and don't leave a thing out."

"Do you remember Broc Wallace?" Bliss began, watching her grandmother carefully.

Her eyes brightened and she smiled. "He was the young beau you were smitten with about ten years ago as you just said. I remember everything you told me about him. It seems as a teenager he was incorrigible. He and Flynt are best friends."

"More like nine. I remember I saw him out chopping wood by the old stable. He's rebuilt it now and it's nice inside not all dusty and crumbling wood." At her grandmother's tilt of her head, she realized she might have said too much.

"I see you've been inside. Was Broc with you?" Catherine's stern voice reverberated.

"It's not like it sounds. I was out riding, going to sketch if I need to be precise. He saw me and tried rescuing me." Bliss waved her hands in the air, "None of that matters. We were almost caught in a thunderstorm. The closest shelter was the stable."

"Makes perfect sense. Did he try to take advantage of you?" Catherine smiled as if she was remembering another time, one she would probably never share.

"Yes and no. We beat the storm and didn't get wet, but he did kiss me and grandmother, I really liked it." Bliss broke off a piece of the ginger cookie but held it between her fingers for a few seconds.

"That's good. Was that all he tried? He didn't do anything bad did he?" Catherine asked.

Bliss shrugged her shoulders, wondering just how this would sound. "It was dark so he insisted on riding back with me. Then he stayed the night with me at the cottage. Didn't dare take him home. He would have figured out who I was."

"No." Grams hands fell to the table.

"We didn't do anything. Just slept." She pulled in a deep breath of air. "I do think he cares about me, but the way he talks and provokes me, sometimes I don't have any idea what to say in response so I stay quiet."

"You're on delicate ground, my darling girl. I see by the light in your eyes when you speak of him, you like him more than you should. Keep in mind that right now if he cares about you it's just to get you into his bed. Now that doesn't mean his feelings can't change, but you mustn't let him seduce you."

"I've liked him forever and now, for the first time, he seems interested in me. But he's just like Flynt who vows he'll never marry until he's over thirty and wants an heir anyway."

"That brings up another important point. Does Flynt know about Broc?" Catherine asked. "And this budding relationship between the two of you."

"No, and I don't plan on telling him until there's no other choice. Flynt would find a way to keep us apart if I did."

"He would and perhaps that would be for the best. Your difficulty stems from the fact you don't know if Broc likes you and considers you someone he might court or if he just wants you in his bed."

"He's led me to believe he wants me in his bed but nothing more. Just like Flynt he's never going to court a woman." She sipped her tea waiting for advice she was beginning to realize wasn't forthcoming.

"Next question, does Broc know you're Flynt's little sister?"

The question hung over her head for a few seconds as she watched tealeaves settle in the bottom of her cup. With a feeling of dread, "No, he doesn't and I don't mean to tell him."

"That could hurt you in the long run." Catherine reminded her. "Honesty is always best."

"If we have a long run. Right now it's been one afternoon and two nights. I've no idea if I'm ever going to see him again."

"Oh darling, I'm sure you will encounter your new love again. You kissed him. He spent the night with you. If he didn't like you or intend to continue the relationship, he would never have stayed all night. He would have left as soon as he saw you in your door."

"I hope so. I can't stop thinking of him and while I understand Flynt is going to be furious with me when he finds out, I still want to see what happens between us. I don't want to give up on Broc before anything has had a chance to start."

"My grandmotherly advice to you would be to stay strong. Don't give in to his seduction of you. He will try, you know. It's a man's nature. If you sleep with him, then he'll have what he wants. If you want marriage, you need to make sure he doesn't get what he wants."

Bliss grimaced feeling as if she didn't have a chance to stay strong. With just one kiss, she almost gave into his gentle persuasion. He understood how and where to touch her, caress her. He was the one who didn't pursue more.

"I'll try," Bliss said.

"That's all a girl can do is try. I wish you luck with both men, your brother and Broc. They both will find out the truth, you know," Catherine said, patting her hand. "As I said a few moments ago, sometimes honesty is the best tactic."

"I understand it will all come out in the end. I'm just praying I will see Broc again and that the truth will be discovered later not sooner. I couldn't bear to lose him before I have a chance to form a relationship and see where it might lead."

"My darling, you already have a relationship with him. You need to form one that is long lasting now."

"I don't know how to do that." Bliss looked down, thinking about how much he provoked her and so many times she was at a loss for words.

"Just be your beautiful self." Catherine said. "Come now, put a smile on your face and wipe away that dreary expression. That's no way to catch a man."

"Could we go for a walk? I'm a little stiff from the ride and need to loosen up my muscles before I ride back. Besides the bright sunshine and the sound of the river might clear my mind."

"Looking for more things to sketch?"

Bliss nodded, relieved for the respite of talking about Broc. "I've sold more paintings and I've a tidy little sum in the bank. I could move out if I wanted, and Flynt wouldn't have a thing to say about it."

"Flynt doesn't know about that either, does he?" She looked to Bliss for an answer.

"Why should he? If he learns I've funds, he'll think he should control them." As far as she was concerned men had too much power over women. She wasn't about to tell him about her personal life.

"As will the man you wed. Hopefully, it will be someone who is strong enough to allow his wife to be self-sufficient."

"It's not fair." Bliss mumbled, thinking about all the things men could do that women could not.

"Life's not fair and well you should know it. Your mother and father should have never died either. Keep in mind we never know what is around the corner, so live each day at its fullest."

"That sounds as if you're giving me two different pieces of advice. One, not to sleep with him; the other life could be short so do what makes you happy." Bliss challenged her grandmother, needing to understand. Yet she knew she would sleep with Broc sooner than later whether he asked her to wed him or not. Where he was concerned, he could play her body with hands that seemed magical.

"Think about both then act with your heart. Don't give away your soul until he can return the gift with his own. Remember there are other consequences to having sex with a man than just losing your heart." Catherine went on to say, "Do you see any places you'd like to sketch?"

Pregnancy was a very real consequence. She knew that. "The river Clyde is beautiful, as you well know. I'm sure that on another day I'll come visit and spend the evening too. I am running out of inspiration at home."

"Except with your young man. Have you painted him yet?" Catherine asked.

Bliss felt the heat rise to her cheeks. "He saw the sketches of him and seemed pleased. It was hard to tell."

"What makes you blush?"

"He was shirtless. I was out riding one day and I saw him chopping wood. One thing led to another then a sketch."

"I see and you didn't present yourself to him." Catherine laughed. "Come, the day is getting late. Best you get home and see if your young man has plans to see you today. Think long and hard about allowing him to spend another night in your home as well as your bed."

"Bye, grandmother," Bliss kissed her on the cheek, "Thank you for listening. You gave me a lot to think about."

Bliss stopped at the MacTavish estate and picked up some of the items she thought might be necessary to make the cottage appear more lived in before heading to her new home.

Loading her arms with packages, she walked to the door and pushed it open with one foot. She stumbled, most of her parcels falling to the floor at her feet. When she regained her balance and looked up, once again Broc sat on the bed, his hands behind his head as if he belonged there.

Her mind seemed to go blank and the ensuing conversation made no impact on her brain. If asked to recount it, she wouldn't be able to remember anything except the fact he bought her things and they ate something, she didn't know what.

"You threw out the bed and bought a new one. You've purchased things for me that you say you're not taking back. Then I'm going to pay you for them and not with my body." Her voice and words echoed in her brain. She meant to stand her ground.

"Never asked for your body as payment nor do I want coin." He spoke softly, the underlying current sending heat within. "You're well-being and happiness is all that matters to me. These are gifts, nothing else."

"That's what men do," she told him, her voice a quivering sound that didn't sound anything like her, overlooking his last words. "Buy women things so they can have sex with them."

"Buy women's bodies?" One eyebrow rose. "Novel idea."

"For their use," she finished, swallowing hard at the way the words sounded to her now. "I..."

"What you said is demeaning although I understand the point you're trying to make. As we discussed earlier, we should end this discussion because it's simply not going anywhere. I'm not asking you to be my mistress. Does that bother you? You think I don't want your body?"

She turned from him, attempting to mull over the arguments he just made, her mind a congealed mess of words that made no sense. "You're confusing me."

He swept her into his arms and striding to the couch, he sat down with her. "I'm not going to stay the night even though I would like to." He placed gentle kisses on her face then whispered kisses down her neck and across her collarbone. "But I am going to introduce you to a few more things that happen between a man and a woman when they care for each other."

"Broc..."

"What, little minx *mo mhilse*?" His fingers danced along the fastenings of her dress until she felt the fabric fall away.

"Should you be doing that?" She could barely breathe. Because she'd been riding she hadn't worn a corset, just a thin chemise. She felt his fingers against her flesh.

"Do you like this?" He didn't answer her question, instead he used his lips to caress her and explore her more intimately.

Then his lips seared hers and his body burned against hers. She imagined how perfectly they would fit together. His kiss deepened as she ran her fingers through his hair, pulling his head closer, clinging to him with an intensity she truly didn't understand. She felt his hands below her breasts as they slowly rose higher to encompass them in his hands.

She closed her eyes, giving in to the magical and enchanting sensations coursing through her, enjoying the moment and how he was making her feel. Her grandmother's advice entered her mind for a fraction of time then it vanished to be replaced by the myriad of sensation streaming inside her body, the heat and the pleasure.

His fingers touched and explored then his lips closed over a nipple, sucking it deep into his mouth. She couldn't help the tiny sounds of pleasure rippling through her.

Breathing was impossible as was thinking. Making a conscious decision to end this unreasonable. All she could do at the moment was feel and react by discovering more of him. She smoothed her hands along his chest, touched and explored his muscles, enjoying his groan with the knowledge she could give him pleasure as well.

He returned to her lips, caught by his. His kiss now all but consumed her. His tongue swept, hard and passionately, deep into her mouth, her throat. Molten fire rushed throughout her limbs, radiating from between her thighs. Good lord, but he made her feel things she'd never before dreamed of.

She heard or felt the pulse of his heart or hers, and it was as if drums pounded in her head. She could not think, only feel and the intimate sensations were both heady and oddly delicious, mesmerizing, so engulfing that his hands were moving again before she realized it.

Searing sensation remained; the pleasure faded. His lips parted from hers, touched them again. His hand gently stroked her cheek, her breast. A whisper of tantalizing flame licked over her, inside her, a hint of something mercurial and as excruciatingly sweet as the sensations had been intense. His lips encompassed her once more, his hands discovered the flesh of her inside thigh and higher.

She could not dissuade him; she could only cling to him, ride out the wildness of the storm he created and feel strange whispers of promised pleasure within. She became increasingly aware of him, the corded muscles of his body straining, the fluid movement of him as he touched her and her body cried out to his for something more.

Life is short, she reminded herself of her grandmother's words even as he drew away from her, holding her at arm's length and gazing at her with a tender smile. Don't let him make love to you until he commits to you were her other words of advice.

Lord, but he wouldn't have even needed to ask for her to let him do whatever he wanted with her body and he seemed to understand that fact. He played her, hands and lips dancing over her body with knowledge she could only guess at.

Once again with the back of his hand he stroked her cheek and her breast then with a heavy sigh, he fastened her dress. "Are you alright, little minx?" he asked her smiling at her.

"I don't think so. Don't think I'll ever be right again," she whispered softly. "What are you doing?"

"I'm putting you to bed."

"To bed? With you?" she asked, her eyes closing as she tried to digest the words he spoke.

"Without me." he told her as he strode with her to the bed and set her down. "I'll let you undress yourself."

"You don't like me?" she asked, still barely breathing and after all his teasing he was leaving. She sounded like a ninny.

He chuckled softly, "You are amazing but I don't want to take what you're not ready to give me."

"I thought I was ready." She suddenly felt self-conscious and lacking.

"Hush, don't doubt yourself. I can barely walk I want you so bad. There will be another night, another time when you know what I'm asking of you. Your innocence amazes me, touches my heart in a way no other has. But I'm not going to steal your virtue."

"So, you're leaving. Just like that?"

"I'm leaving and I won't see you tomorrow. I've business in Glasgow. I'm going to stay in my apartments there. I'll be gone about a week. If all goes well, less time than that. I want you to remember this night and how you felt. Don't forget me. Promise?"

~ * ~

Catherine sat in the parlor, Nial, her husband, at her side. "I'm worried about Bliss. She's found someone who could rip her heart out if he's truly a cad and womanizer as Flynt and his friends like to believe."

"I think they call themselves bad boys not womanizers or rakes, but they aren't really. They just haven't found the right woman," Nial replied with a soft chuckle, picking up Catherine's hand and kissing the back. "I do remember my younger days, and all I would change about them is that I would have met you sooner."

"Thank you," Catherine felt the blush rise to her cheeks. "Back to Bliss, she's been ill prepared to go up against someone of such vast experience," Catherine said, recalling her first time with Nial as well as her first husband. Both times they had prepared her, had helped her overcome her shyness.

"She will do just fine. Bliss has your backbone as well as the wisdom of your advice. What else does she need except a man who cares for her more than his own desires?"

"That's my worry. Does he care for her or will he use her and toss her away like he has all the other women in his life?" Catherine asked as she relied on Nial for support. "Bliss is such an innocent and so sweet she would give her heart away without thinking."

"Men like Broc have a way of figuring out when a woman is innocent and truly loves him. If she is the right woman for that man, you will have nothing to worry about. If she is not, he'll ken it and not take advantage. They are both just trying to figure it all out."

"I hope you're right, but what you say isn't going to stop me from paying more attention to my granddaughters. They are all vulnerable and they've no one to guide them now that their parents are gone. Flynt is no substitute for a mother or even a father. He has no idea, no idea what the girls might need and want."

"You're planning a visit then?" he asked. "I do think you should stay in the background a bit more."

"Flynt has no experience as to how to raise a daughter or daughters. He's now in charge of four young ladies, and he's more concerned with his own love life than he is of his charges."

"You don't know that."

"Of course I do. He's a bad boy and he's trying to steer his sisters away from men like him. What he doesn't know is that a reformed rake makes the best husband. I've married two." She finished with the emphasis on married and two.

Nial grinned shamelessly and Catherine felt a tiny shiver of anticipation sweep through her. "Are you calling me a bad boy?" He brought her hand to his lips then pulled her close.

"Should we explore this more upstairs?" One eyebrow rose expectantly.

Breathlessly and anticipating the night of lovemaking, she said, "I do believe we should."

"Then you need to make a promise or two to me." His lips met hers in a heart-stopping kiss, one that left her gasping for breath and her heart beat doubling.

"What is that?" She could barely breathe but knew he meant to give her directions where her granddaughters were concerned. Deep inside she understood what he might be telling her. It was much the same as her advice to Bliss.

"The promise, my darling, is that you continue to give your advice but do nothing to keep her from her heart's desire. I understand how hard that will be, particularly if there are mistakes made along the way."

"As long as I don't have to remain silent, I'll be fine with that. I've already imparted a few tid bits of advice which I hope might help her sort out her feelings." Sighing softly, she leaned into his embrace, absorbing his strength into her.

"Promise me?" He ran a fingertip across her cheek then her breast, lingering in enticing places.

"I will keep my distance as long as it seems Broc has her best interest and not his own in his mind."

"If she gives herself to him before a commitment?" he queried. "What will you do then?"

"As long as it was her decision, I will support her," she told him, hesitating but acknowledging that Bliss wanted to be an independent woman and that she would understand the possible repercussion of sex. Yet she had been deprived of a mother for the last few years. What did she know of the repercussions of sex?

"Promise me," Nial insisted.

"As long as I can talk to her mother to daughter about what can happen when she lets a man take advantage of her sweet generous nature," Catherine insisted.

"I think you're forgetting women have sexual needs too." Nial said.

"I would never forget that but Bliss has no idea...and absolutely no experience with the opposite sex."

Chapter Three

The day dawned sunny and promised to be warmer that the last one. Broc mounted his horse, setting off for the MacTavish estate and a conversation with Flynt before leaving for Glasgow. Once his plans were completely set in motion, he'd find a way to win over the stubborn yet very beautiful Bliss. In time, she would come around to his way of thinking and become his mistress.

He admitted to himself he was infatuated with the lovely and precocious woman. Last night when she told him she was confused, he couldn't agree with her more. Around her, he didn't even act himself. He would have stayed the night, if Bliss had been any other woman. He would have made love to her. But Bliss was more important to him than he ever imagined a woman could be, and he sensed she wasn't ready to have an intimate relationship with him.

Somehow she had found a way inside his jaded heart, and all he wanted was to make her happy and watch a smile form on her face. Today, he would set the wheels in motion to purchase the little cottage for her. Hopefully Flynt wouldn't mind selling the home where no one really lived. Although, he was still trying to decide if the cottage was truly Bliss' address.

A short time later Broc stood in front of the heavy wooden door of the estate, knocking. The MacTavish butler opened it. "Why, Master Wallace, what a nice surprise. I'm assuming you're here to see Flynt's older sister?" He bowed then stepping back allowed him room to walk inside.

The man's words stunned and shocked Broc. Why would the man think such a thing? He and his friend's never courted debutants never came anywhere near them. "No, I'm here to see Flynt." His voice was curt and to the point. "Have important business to attend to."

"That's good because you'd be the third man waiting for the lady to arrive. She's not here and Flynt has the men cooling their heels while he sent the stable boy to look for her." The butler chuckled as if he knew something Flynt didn't. Broc thanked his lucky stars that he didn't have sisters he had to find husband for, a horror filled task in this day and age.

"Do you want to wait in the parlor or his office?"

Out of curiosity he wanted to see the men who were here to court Flynt's oldest sister and size them up. Who was Flynt recruiting? Certainly, no one like them would be suitable.

"I'll wait in the parlor." He stepped passed the butler, purposefully striding into the room where the two men waited.

Both men rose when he walked through the door, momentarily thinking he was Flynt.

"Good day," one said.

"You're here to see Flynt's sister?" he asked, realizing both men were unsuitable for a beautiful young lady. Why he assumed Flynt's sister was beautiful he had no idea.

One of the men was short and sported a sizable belly, the buttons on his shirt unable to keep the fabric from separating to show his lily-white skin. He wore a wig, which undoubtedly meant he suffered from hair loss. Broc hoped the diminishing hairline was not from the pox and if it was, Flynt would realize and claim that suitor as unacceptable.

The second man was tall and rail thin. His ginger hair was thick as was his beard as well as his eyebrows. He wore tiny little spectacles and his stovepipe pants left little to one's imagination. Although he didn't have as much to show off in that department as any of the bad boys.

"Poor woman who is expected to marry one of these men," Broc chuckled. "They would never be pleasured."

The butler seemed to hover nearby. Broc turned, "Believe I'll wait in the office. I know the way." What the devil had Flynt been thinking? Neither of those men was suitable for any of his sisters. Granted, he'd only seen Lacie in the last year, but if the others were as stunning as the youngest, they didn't deserve to be courted by men who were years older and were lacking in physical charm. Come to think of it, too many years had passed and Flynt rarely if ever spoke of his sisters. Except for Lacie, he didn't even know their names. In any case it wouldn't matter. He had no need to learn Flynt's sister's names.

Inside, Broc poured himself a glass of whiskey then sat down in a luxurious chair, intent on making himself comfortable until Flynt was notified of his visit. Once this transaction was complete, he'd have to wait several weeks or more before he could show Bliss the deed and inform her she didn't have to spend more of her hard-earned money on rent.

He grinned thinking of the myriad of ways Bliss could thank him when he pointed out what awaited Flynt's sisters. Perhaps that wasn't such a good idea. He'd have to think on that.

"Broc?" Flynt stepped inside. "Missed you the other night at Lucky Black's Tavern. You find something or someone better to fill your time with than your friends?"

"I'm sure you had just as good a time as you would have had with me. The wine and the women must have flowed all night long." He handed Flynt the second glass he'd poured.

"What can I do for you?" Flynt sat behind his desk, resting his forearms on the top. Flynt was a handsome well-muscled man with dark black hair and steel blue eyes, ones that could light up in humor and simmer with anger when provoked.

"I'd like to purchase the little cottage you own. It sits on the edge of your land and is close to Wallace property."

"Close to yours, you say. I'm trying to recall. Been a long time since I've ridden in those parts."

"Very close," Broc grinned, thinking of the woman who occupied it now.

"May I ask why? It will need a lot of cleaning up and it's small. Is it up to your standards?"

"It's for a special friend. She's a bit of a recluse, likes to paint and sketch. It's perfect for her and I'll be close by to make sure no harm comes her way," Broc said realizing the last thing one could call Bliss was a recluse, so why did she rent the tiny cottage that wasn't close to anything or anyone?

"A new mistress, so soon. Just heard you split ways with Edina.

Can't say I blame you. That lady can be a real bitch."

"The lady in question is not my mistress," Broc said, although if she gave any indication she would like the title she could have it. Still he meant to give her everything she wanted or he thought she needed. So by definition she would be his mistress.

"You protest too much and too quickly," Flynt laughed, eyeing him critically. "Not that I care who you take for a mistress as long as it isn't Muria."

"Go against the bad boys code, never." Broc sipped the whiskey enjoying its smooth glide down his throat. "Now about the cottage. I understand someone is renting it."

"You understand wrong then. No one has lived there for years. Not since before mother and father died."

"Oh." He rolled that answer around in his head, wondering if he should confront Bliss with the information or ignore it. For the time being he meant to ignore what Flynt told him. Perhaps Flynt just forgot. If Bliss made her payments on time, Flynt would never be reminded that someone indeed rented the cottage. The transaction was most likely done through his solicitor.

"I'll sell it to you with the stipulation that when you move on to another lady friend, you sell it back. It is on MacTavish land, and I don't want to lose a part of my heritage."

"Agreed. When can you get the papers drawn up? I'm going to be in Glasgow for about a week on business." Hopefully less. He couldn't wait to get back here and see Bliss.

"If there aren't any complications, should be done in several weeks' time. I'll drop them off when all the legal stuff is completed."

The two men shook hands, Flynt walking him out. "You really should look for men more suitable for your sisters. Those men..." He was shaking his head and laughing. "Your sisters will never agree to a marriage with anyone like those two."

"Are nothing like us, which makes them infinitely more suitable. I don't want my sisters to be cuckold."

"Not if you wish them a life of happiness," Broc said as he was walking down the steps whistling a bawdy tune. "Haven't you heard, reformed rakes make the best husbands?" He laughed as he left.

He was pleased with the transaction and could now get on with his business in town. If his business transactions went as expected, he'd be back before the end of the week. The ride to the city was pleasant, but he sighed when he strode up the steps leading to his apartment. Flopping on the bed he closed his eyes, conjuring visions of his sweet Bliss, imagining the way she felt when she was between his arms. He should have seen if she would have liked to come to town with him.

If the selling of this ship wasn't so blasted important, he wouldn't have come personally. But this client required wining and dining. He needed to outdo his competitors and sell that ship. If he did, he most likely would gain a contract for more boats.

This could be a very prosperous week for him. Tomorrow he'd give his client a tour of his shipyard then take him to one of the most prestigious restaurants in town or perhaps the Glasgow Golf Club.

The knock on the door surprised him. He rose, unloosening his cravat and sauntering to the door. When he opened it, he was surprised to see huge redheaded bear of a man standing in the doorway with a very tiny dark-haired woman on his arm.

"Wanted to see you sooner than tomorrow." James MacMurra stood outside his door with his wife. "Do you think that would be possible? I understand this might be a bit of an inconvenience, but if we can take care of everything tonight, it will free up the rest of the week for my wife, Tavia and me. We'd like to return home as soon as possible."

"I just arrived a few minutes ago and am hardly set up here to do business." Broc stepped back, gesturing for them to come into the room. "Can get you a something to drink, a brandy perhaps and we can talk."

"I'm impatient to return to London. As you can see my wife is expecting and we want to return home as soon as possible before the baby is born. Don't want to be on the high seas during childbirth."

"So, you've made up your mind about my ships?" He wanted to find his way home as soon as possible too. Fatigue didn't matter right now, only the sale of the ship and getting back to Bliss.

"I've interviewed a few ship owners and they all stand by the fact your ships are the best made. They say you're an honest man who I can deal fairly with. These are all men I feel I can trust."

"Do you want to go to my office?" he asked, as his stomach rumbled. He'd eaten little today and was looking forward to a nice dinner.

Tavia stepped in, "Sometimes my husband is a bit obtuse and single minded. It's clearly dinner time and I'm sure we're all hungry." Then she turned to her husband, her hand on his arm, "Could we eat something first. Mr. Wallace probably knows a good restaurant that is close by. The two of you can talk business while we make ourselves more comfortable."

"We can go to Mrs. Pullock's Prince Street Hostelry," Broc suggested hoping he would take him up on dinner before business.

"Of course." James was clearly confused and distracted from his single-minded pursuit of the ship he was about to purchase. Then he smiled at his wife. "Whatever Tavia wants."

Broc wanted to laugh at the way James was so clearly smitten with his wife. He would probably jump off the tallest bridge if Tavia asked him to. He wanted to feel that way about a woman someday.

Broc grabbed a jacket then led the way to the restaurant he'd been thinking about earlier. It was pleasant and the best tables looked out at the river. The food was satisfying and the conversation interesting.

James told him of how Tavia had pretended to be a lad, finding a job as a cabin boy on his ship. The ship that was lost in a hurricane on its last voyage. Tavia didn't seem to enjoy the little tale as much as her husband, blushing prettily while he spoke of her sleeping in the hammock.

"You married?" James asked pleasantly.

"No, don't plan on it any time soon." Yet at the word marriage Broc's mind travelled in the direction of Bliss. He shook his head as if the gesture would rid himself of the notion. "I'm not the marrying kind."

"Thought so myself," James said, laughing as he stared at Tavia. "Until a pretty lass posing as a boy stole my heart when she fell from the hammock right into my waiting arms."

Tavia appeared to want to throw the glass of water she was holding in James' face. "You don't have to tell him anymore of our private relationship. What happened on board that ship needs to stay between us?"

"I like to watch you blush though," James said, bending close to her and quickly brushing a quick kiss on her lips.

"If you keep doing that...making me blush," she paused, lowering her eyelashes, "you might find yourself on the couch tonight."

James let his head fall back and roared with laughter. "You could never keep me there. All I have to do is kiss you and you beg for more. Your threats are empty and we both know it."

Uncharacteristically Broc thought once more he'd like a relationship like theirs, lighthearted and filled with humor. They clearly cared deeply for each other and enjoyed each other's company so much that James brought his pregnant wife with him.

Confused by his wayward thoughts and finished with the meal, Broc pushed back his chair. "Shall we go to my office now?"

"You should find a good woman," James said. "It's obvious no one has sparked your interest yet. Just keep an open mind when the right lady is staring you in the face. When that happens, you will know. Don't let her get away."

Tavia held James' arm as they all walked down the street to Broc's office. His solicitor should have the papers drawn up and ready for signing. If he sold the ships tonight, he would almost be done here and after completing a few other business dealings, could return home before the end of the week and surprise Bliss.

Tomorrow he decided he should shop for some baubles for Bliss. He liked the sound of that but was sure Bliss would have a different opinion. The thought of the expression on her face gave him reason to smile. She would refuse them of course and he would make sure she wore them at least once, perhaps when they made love the first time. The thought of her naked and wearing a necklace that held aqua marina stones the color of her eyes, he groaned.

In his office the papers sat on the desk, two sets, one for the sale of the first ship and the second set of papers a contract for three ships to be picked up as soon as they could be finished.

With his business concluded, Broc walked the short distance to his apartments. Candles were lit when he stepped inside. "Bloody eyes," he whispered, his hand reaching for the small knife he always kept close at hand.

"What took you so long? I've been waiting for what seemed an eternity." Edina purred as she rose from the couch in the sitting room dressed in nearly nothing. It was a piece of lingerie he purchased for her but he had no wish to see her wearing it any longer. When he said goodbye to her, he meant never to see her again unless it was passing on the street.

Broc searched for something to cover her with but was unsuccessful. "You don't belong here. Go home, Edina." He had no idea how to extract her from his apartment, but she wasn't staying the night and she would not find her way into his bed.

"Of course I do. Who knows better how to make you feel good?" she queried, batting her lashes at him and moistening her lips in a calculated gesture.

"How did you get inside?" he asked but he knew. He'd forgotten to retrieve the key to this apartment when he called on her the other day.

"The key you gave me." She held it up in front of her then slipped it between her breasts. "You can come and get it if you like."

"You can give it to me." He growled.

"More fun if you retrieve it. You don't mean to take it away?" she asked as she watched him slip his fingers down her cleavage. Once he was successful, he slipped it in a pocket and backed away from her.

"You cannot come and go as you please. I never allowed you to do that anyway. The key was to be used just for an emergency."

"Well, this is an emergency. I heard you were in town and thought you might be lonely and want me." Slowly, she walked toward him, her hand resting on the small fastener that would undo the gown. "You won't make me leave will you? At least not before," she moistened her lips.

"You thought wrong," he growled low in his throat, displeased with the situation and his inability to convey his desire. "Get dressed." He would dress her himself if that would get her away from him sooner. He had no idea what he'd ever seen in this woman.

"Thought you'd like to play a little bit," she said, her sultry voice irritating to Broc now that he'd let her go, now that he'd found someone else to fill his thoughts and soon his bed.

Hell, Edina had never filled his thoughts, never really been a part of his life. She relieved sexual tension and for the most part she was the perfect mistress because she understood the boundaries, until now. She'd been a convenient diversion for over a year. He meant to get rid of her, sleep a few hours then tend to the rest of his business so he could return to the cottage.

Broc strode past the woman and into the bedroom, picking up her discarded clothing as he went. When he returned to the sitting room he handed them to her. "Get dressed," he repeated, barely able to keep his anger under control. "You're not staying for another second let alone the night."

She pouted, a feminine ploy she'd used before to get her way but Broc was immune to it. "Do I have to?" she asked in a soft whisper of a voice meant to entice. She looked to him then in a single fluid move she unfastened the lingerie and let it slip to the floor.

"I'll call you a cab. You can either go home like you are now or you can put your clothes on, Edina. I ended it almost a week ago and thought I was very generous, but obviously you didn't understand. We are through." There was nothing about this woman that intrigued him. He wondered if there ever was.

As he turned, he heard the huff of indignation and wondered why he'd spent so much money on her. At the door he paused, thinking he should say something else but was at a total loss for words.

"I don't have any say in this?" she asked, still naked.

"Five minutes."

For a few seconds he thought of leaving and just not going back to his apartment. He wanted to get to his horse and ride to the little cottage. He needed to make sure Bliss was fine. Instead he was in town, with his ex-mistress naked in his sitting room.

"Blessed hell," he swore as he raced down the steps, jumping the last five to the first floor.

Outside, he summoned a cab, paying the fare and for the time the man would have to wait for Edina to put her clothes on. She had better be dressed and ready to leave.

Once again taking the stairs two at a time, he reached the apartment. She was dressed and sitting on the couch, her face scrunched into lines of anger.

"This was your last chance, Broc," she said. "You'll regret what happened here tonight."

"After you." He didn't know how to reply to what she said. Her words made no sense to him. She had no power to make him regret anything.

With her nose stuck in the air, she walked past him. From the top of the stairs he watched her leave through the front door. He hoped she took the cab and he prayed fervently she would leave him alone.

~ * ~

Bliss raced her horse to the stables and dismounting quickly she handed the reins to the stable boy. "Take care of her for me, please. I should be back in an hour." Not wasting any more time she ran through the backdoor, headed for the upstairs and her room.

"Hold on there," Flynt grabbed her by the arm stopping her and hauling her against his chest. "Where have you been? You were supposed to be at home," he said, his voice harsher than Bliss could remember hearing before. She didn't know why he was angry and she really didn't care.

"Around," she told him, trying to shake off his hand to no avail. "It's none of your business. Let me go I've things to do and not a lot of time." Truly she had more time than she wanted. Broc told her it would probably be a week before he returned. She would ride to Glasgow and surprise him, but she had no idea where he lived. Asking Flynt was of course out of the question.

"You have suitors waiting for you in the parlor. I expect you to change your clothing to something more suitable then fix your hair. It's a mess. After that you will politely meet these men who've already used up too much valuable time waiting for you."

"Who brought you up to be so rude? Mother and father would have washed your mouth out with soap," she told him, wondering how and when Flynt had changed from the doting older brother to this bear of a guardian.

"Do it now." His words were a command and she didn't mean to obey.

"No," she told him breathing hard and still trying to shake off her brother's hand. "I don't want to meet anyone now or tomorrow or the day after that." No, she already met the man she wanted to be with for the rest of her life. Convincing him was going to be harder though.

"If you don't go to your room, and do as I say..."

"I'm not going to..."

"You will. I've a duty to you and your sisters and I mean to fulfill that obligation. If you don't pick someone to wed, I will do it for you. Now go, or do I have to dress you myself?" His eyes blazed with anger and perhaps a bit of frustration.

"Am I keeping you from your mistress?" she asked defiantly not believing for a single moment Flynt would haul her upstairs and change her clothing. He hadn't seen her naked since she was a toddler, she was sure.

His voice softened a bit and his smile seemed genuine, "Go upstairs then spend a little time with these men. Don't judge them so harshly before you meet them. God knows I've looked all over Glasgow for suitable men to court you, and I can't seem to find any."

"I'll go see them as I am. I'm not going to change for any man and if they don't like what they see, then too bad for them." She would give them five minutes of her time to appease her brother then she was off to see if any of her sisters were at home.

"You need to look presentable," he growled, his anger seeming to simmer just beneath the surface.

She twirled in a circle letting her skirt flare out. "I'm not presentable?" She laughed, loving the look of chagrin on Flynt's face. "Then they would never love the real me. You know as well as I do, half the time the real me has oil paint on her face and clothes."

"No." He was running his hands through his hair, clearly frustrated. "Your hair is a muddle and your blouse is smudged with what I can only assume is paint. In short, Bliss, you're a deplorable mess."

"Then my benevolent suitors will see me as I will be if they decided they want me, a mere woman, is good enough to become their wife." She approached her brother and poking him in the chest several times to send her point home, "I promise you this is a waste of time, I'm not marrying either of those two horrid men even if they like me the way I appear right now." And she thought of another man who didn't mind her when she was a deplorable mess. Indeed, he seemed to like her that way.

"You don't know if they're horrid. You haven't met them yet," he shot back too quickly.

"What aren't you telling me, Flynt? Are they short and fat or perhaps thin as a rail with no manly muscles," she challenged him. "I will never say I do to either of those two men and you know you can't make me."

"I've confiscated all your funds, my dear. You don't have a penny to your name, so you can blather all you want and pretend to be independent but you're not. You're under my thumb so to speak."

Bliss inhaled a sharp deep breath, wanting to lash out and slap her brother. But she willed her mind and her body to calm. "It makes no difference if you took all my money. I can sell more paintings, and this time I'll do a better job of hiding my earnings from you. Grams will help me."

"I had every right as the man of this family and you know it. British law gives me that right. Now go upstairs." His anger having built to a crescendo his hand shook when he pointed in the direction of the stairs.

"You may pretend you have every right to confiscate all my worldly belongings including my money, but only a scoundrel would take something like that away from his sister. You feel guilty as hell." She fisted her hands and ignoring her brother she stomped toward the stairs, hoping to take so much time doing Flynt's bidding her would be suitors would leave.

Once more he stopped her, his hand on her shoulder. She brushed it off. "I've your well-being and future in mind. Both these men have substantial means to give you anything you want, and I'm sure children too."

"They can't give me what I want and while I haven't seen either of them yet, I'm sure climbing into bed with either man would be repulsive. I would never let them kiss me let alone touch me intimately." She couldn't stop the shudder of revulsion sweeping through her at the thought of any man except Broc touching her.

He stepped back, seeming to study her. "You're an innocent and you won't know the difference between an experienced lover and one who is not. At least I think you are. What haven't you told me, Bliss?" He looked as if he wanted to shake her.

"You know my life's story." If she had her way, she wouldn't be innocent for long. "Would you get into bed with either of those men," she pointed in the direction of the parlor.

"Bliss, that's hardly..."

"Well, if they were women and I was trying to find you a wife? Would you climb into bed with them?" She challenged him again, the attempt to calm herself wasn't working very well. She had things to do and this was cutting into her planned schedule. And now with the confiscation of her money, it meant she had to go to work again sooner than she had intended. Time was fleeting.

He looked in the direction of the parlor then back to Bliss, "Of course I wouldn't," he admitted reluctantly. "But..."

She waved her hands in the air, unable to inhale a breath to respond she was so furious. "But what? You wish something on your sister that isn't good enough for you?"

"It's not your place to question me." He tried that tact again.

"Marrying either of those men is out of the question. Threatening me will do you no good. Grandmother will take me in as long as I need a place to live and in time I'll pay her back. If you stole my money, you know I had a sizable amount in the bank. Are you going to also put signs on my paintings telling people not to buy them?" Bliss was beside herself now, yelling at him as she paced the kitchen.

"You're misunderstanding everything."

"Am I?" she questioned, her hands on her hips. "I'm going to go introduce myself to those men right now and if you want me to look more presentable, you're going to have to make the changes in my appearance." She turned on a heel and marched into the parlor.

"Good morning, gentleman. I'm Bliss MacTavish. So sorry you wasted the morning. I'm not going to let either of you court me let alone wed me. My brother was mistaken if he told you I might be interested. I am not. No one can make me say I do against my wishes and that is also British law." Bloody hell, but she could not fathom what Flynt could have possibly been thinking when he brought these so called men to court her.

The chubby man stood, sputtering, "You are very lovely, Miss

Bliss. Perhaps you would like to go for a carriage ride. The weather is nice and I do think you would find my company entertaining. It's been said I've a wicked sense of humor."

"I would be happy to take you to the Tontine Coffee House and Reading Room." The other man not to be out done, smiled and she could almost see his lips behind the bushy red beard.

"That wouldn't be fun. They don't allow alcohol or tobacco. I do so like to have fun and enjoy my wine."

He cleared his throat, coughing slightly. "I don't drink or smoke," he told her.

"What kind of man are you then? My brother and all his friends drink and smoke. They would never go to the Reading Room. Instead they would go somewhere that allowed alcohol. What do you do there?"

"Read."

"How tedious," she spoke softly.

"We could take a leisurely ride." The other man spoke up.

"I won't ride in a carriage and on a horse it's always astride. Now that I've convinced both of you I'm not suitable for your mate, you can leave." She whirled and in leaving the room, she ran into her brother.

"Not so fast," he whispered close to her ear, both hands on her shoulders. "You need to apologize."

"No."

"I will tan your backside if you don't," he growled and it seemed she'd pushed her brother to what appeared to be his breaking point, yet she didn't believe for a moment he would hit her. If he wanted to tan her backside, he would have to lift her skirts and get rid of all her underwear. He would never do that either.

"Something else you won't do," she told him, feeling a tiny bit cocky. She would not let her brother or any other man dictate to her and control her life. At that moment, she believed being a spinster had countless possibilities since she had a means to support herself or would have in a few days. Perhaps in time she could convince Flynt to give her back her money.

"If you push me too far..." he began but stopped himself when one of the suitors cleared his throat.

"Miss Bliss doesn't seem to want anything to do with us." The two men looked at each other and in unison rose and left.

"I will bring more men. You can't avoid this forever."

"Just watch me." She turned from him and raced up the steps only to stop at Chelsea's door. There was only one man Flynt could bring to court her. She would be very agreeable if he brought Broc.

Bliss knocked. "Are you in there?"

"Bliss, you're home. Wherever have you been? If Flynt knew you weren't home at night, he'd be..." Chelsea pulled her inside. "I don't know what he'd be, I can't even imagine how furious he could get. This last year he's changed so much. One minute he's laughing with his friends and the next he's pacing and muttering about how unfair his life is."

"He was just angry with me now. I told him no to the suitors," Bliss said, pushing back the strands of hair Flynt complained about earlier. "Once he realizes he can't push me around, things will get back to some normalcy.

"You said no?" Chelsea asked, a look of awe crossing her face. "You give me hope for my future."

"I did and he threatened to change my clothes for me and tan my backside. He didn't do either as I gambled he wouldn't. If he had, I would have never forgiven him and most likely never come home again even to see you. You understand grandmother will always take us in even though she encourages us to forgive Flynt as well as make excuses for him."

"It's good to know you've set the standard for the rest of us. Those men were horrible," Chelsea said. "I watched them come to the house."

"I asked him if he'd go to bed with them and I thought he'd choke," Bliss laughed. "Anyway, you asked me where I've been and thank god Flynt is so busy with his own life he really doesn't notice any of us."

Chelsea fell back on her bed, giggling. "You didn't." She sat up quickly, "Where have you been?"

"You have to promise on your life you won't tell Flynt." Bliss held her breath as she watched her sister mull over the words. "Promise me."

"You're not doing anything dangerous, are you?" Chelsea asked, seeming to hesitate on that pending promise.

"Dangerous, no, not really but I've talked to grandmother and she gave me some advice which I've taken to heart. I won't do anything rash, and I understand all the consequences of my decisions. I want to steal my own bit of happiness while I can."

"You have me so curious I'm near to bursting at the seams," Chelsea said. "I promise. When Flynt brings us men like those two who were in the parlor just now, I'll keep any secret from him."

"Well, you only have a few months before you turn eighteen and Flynt starts in with you and possible suitors."

"I'm dreading that. I want to find my own husband, and I do have someone in mind," Chelsea said.

Bliss inhaled a long breath before blurting out, "I'm in love," she paused, "or lust. I've really no idea which one it is but I don't care. I'm seeing a man. One who Flynt would heartily disapprove of."

"No, are you sure?" Chelsea took Bliss' hands in hers. "I'd like to be in love someday."

"You have time," Bliss said, smiling and feeling the relief of finally telling someone how she felt. "You're the only one I can tell, you know."

"Who is it?" Chelsea's curiosity seemed to grow along with the size of her smile.

"That I won't tell you. Don't want to take any chances with my secret, simply because accidents happen. What you don't know you can't say out loud." Bliss didn't feel she could risk an unintentional slip of the tongue by her sister. If that happened, so much could turn back on her. Flynt would be angry but Broc would leave her.

"How did you know you were in love?" Chelsea's grin now seemed to run from one ear to the other.

"When he kissed me," Bliss whispered. "I knew the moment he kissed me." She smooched her lips together, remembering other things too. The way his hands caressed her and his fingers played with so many sensitive spots on her body. The magic and the mystery of his loving was so captivating, all she could think of was actually making love with him even though she wasn't entirely sure what that entailed.

"He kissed you." Chelsea clapped her hands together then leaning forward, "I've been kissed by a boy, but I didn't like the way it felt. His touch made my skin crawl."

"What did you do?"

"I slapped him."

"I'm not going to ask who kissed you, but if it's the right person the touch won't make your skin crawl. No, it will do so many other delicious things."

"I wonder just who my love will be?" Chelsea sighed deeply, her mind seemingly in the clouds above. "I'm happy for you."

"You've less than one year, really only a few months before Flynt will start bringing strange men here. Stay strong or you'll find yourself in bed with a man who makes you unhappy and you don't want that for the rest of your life." Bliss felt a sense of peace at finally making a decision about Broc. She wanted to pass grandmother's knowledge on to her sister.

"A few months," she paused, "I already have a crush on someone, and Flynt will never let me see that man. He's one of the..."

"Bad boys," Bliss finished for her, "Oh no, well, you're going to have to figure out a way to meet him on your own. I'm sure a woman of your intelligence can find a way."

"He's been at the house playing cards and I'm not sure Flynt is going to bring his friends around here much longer now that we're all getting older. He's afraid one of them will take advantage."

"True, if he wants to keep us from falling in love with his friends, because they do have this fatal attraction about them." Bliss looked out the window for a moment, thinking about Broc and wondering exactly what he was doing right now. "He's going to have to lock us up."

"You've fallen in love with a bad boy" Chelsea inhaled a deep breath then holding it said, "Please say it's not Cam."

"No, not Cam although I remember him. Cam is just like our brother. He's not one to fall in love with. He's one to take a mistress. Keep that thought in mind. There are some good reasons why Flynt is keeping us away from the bad boys."

"What if he never gets a chance to meet me and falls in love with someone else?" Chelsea questioned with a sigh.

"You are going to have to make sure that doesn't happen. I don't have any advice on how to go about that, but you need to find your own happiness in this life. If Cam makes your heart race, then he's probably the man for you. Grandmother says the best husbands are reformed rakes or bad boys. She should know, she's married two of them."

"Well, I don't even know where Cam lives or anything about him except that he makes me swoon when I see him. They were outside one day kicking a ball around and he had his shirt off." Chelsea's hand was pressed on her chest. "He's, well… 1 don't really have words."

"He was amazing?" Bliss asked. "I know the feeling, heart and breath racing. You could barely think let alone speak when you saw him."

"I wanted to touch him, run my hand along his chest and find out what his muscles felt like."

"I understand those sensations and more."

Chelsea nodded, the discussion seeming to come to a halt, both seeming to think about the conversation and the men they were falling in love with. "Are you staying here tonight?"

Bliss was shaking her head, "Something else you're not to tell Flynt, although I think I heard his horse's hooves pounding on the ground a few minutes ago. I'm staying at the cottage near the Wallace land. That's where I'm painting. Something else our brother did was to steal the money from my sales. He had absolutely no right to do that, yet the law gives him the ability. It's not fair. I just don't understand why men have all the power."

"What…?" Chelsea asked. "Flynt stole your money. How dare he? What are you going to do?"

"Sell more. Grandmother will help me. I won't make the mistake again of giving Flynt the opportunity to pinch what is not his, especially not my future." She would have to come up with some way, and at the moment she wasn't completely sure what that was.

"Come see me more often. I need these talks. I don't know what I would do without you."

"Me too, I've got to go now. The sun isn't anywhere near to setting, but I don't want to ride in the dark. Time seems to get away from us, doesn't it? Whatever you do, don't go to the cottage."

The sisters hugged and Bliss made her way down the servant's staircase in order to avoid Flynt if he was still in the house, which she didn't think he was. When she pulled up in front of the cottage, it was still light.

A few hours at least remained and after she took care of her horse and stepped inside, she discovered that once again the rooms had been thoroughly cleaned.

She wasn't sure if she cared any more. It was one less thing she needed to do now that she was living here. She hated housekeeping, but it was something else she intended to negotiate with Broc, knowing she was slowly and not so subtly becoming his mistress. Yes, a talk with the man would be wonderful. He told her he'd be gone for a week. Four days had passed since he left. She could only hope the last three days would not seem such an eternity.

That was a long time as far as she was concerned. Four days was longer than she wanted to go without seeing him or feeling his kisses against her lips and the rest of her. Once inside the silence seemed overwhelming. Rubbing her hands up her arms, she tried to ward off the Goosebumps. Everything in the house reminded her of Broc. She inhaled a long deep breath, stifling a tiny cry of despair or wistfulness she wasn't positive which.

So much had happened, including the very real threat of Flynt asserting his will in an attempt to give her to any man who would have her whether she agreed or not. She pressed her lips together trying to keep those thoughts from her head. Fighting her brother for her rights as well as her sisters was imperative. Flynt needed to learn his sisters wouldn't allow him to shove them around.

She pushed her loneliness to the back of her mind then set about the most important task she had right now. Bliss sat down and rifled through all the sketches she'd made over the last week, searching for the ones that would make good paintings.

Her fingers hovered over the ones of Broc, giving her good reason to smile. She was so lost in her dreams she didn't hear the soft knock on the door.

"You've got to remember to lock the door." Broc stepped into the room, grinning. He set a few packages on the table while he opened his arms.

Unable to help herself, Bliss ran to him, throwing her arms around him, reveling in the feel of his hard body against hers. "I just got home myself," she said as she gazed at him. "I think I missed you."

"Just think?" he asked, laughing.

"No, I missed you." She almost told him about Flynt and what he tried to do today and what he did do with her money, but she caught herself before it was too late to take anything back.

"Would you like to take a ride with me to the stables? I've something to show you?"

"I don't know." She thought about the stolen money and the work she needed to do to replace it.

"In the stables," he told her, "Yes, something to show you and you can have one if you like."

She touched his cheek. "Can it wait for another day? I have to work. It seems I don't have as much money as I thought." Bliss didn't want to admit her mistake, a mistake she was determined not to make again.

"Of course tomorrow or the next day would be fine. Can I stay the night?"

"You're asking?"

"This time, maybe every time."

"I'd like that but what would you do with yourself?" She knew if he stayed she wouldn't get anything done, and she didn't want to tell him he needed to leave.

"I'd probably keep you from getting anything accomplished," he spoke as he pulled her into his arms, his lips finding hers in a long drugging kiss, one she didn't want to end.

"And I'd let you, but Broc I can't afford food or rent or anything unless I sell some more work." She knew he would probably ask why or tell her she didn't need to make any money, but he'd be wrong on that count.

His eyebrows drew together. "You shouldn't have to work. If you'd let me, I could take care of you."

"Painting isn't work. It's a calling and even if I didn't need the money, I would want to create paintings." His hands on her waist tightened, and she understood he was thinking and trying for the best response.

He was shaking his head, a dark look on his face as if he wanted to argue. Instead he kissed her again, long and deep, their tongues playing and dancing together. Heat swept within as she felt the pounding of his heart and understood the need he generated within her. His hands cupped her breast, teased and tantalized even through her clothing.

"Bloody hell, but I've missed you and I want to talk to you, kiss you, lie down with you, hold you so close there would be nothing between us."

"You have to understand," she whispered, wishing he would stay, despite the fact she asked him to leave.

"I can't but..." His lips met hers this time in a quick kiss, "But we'll finish this tomorrow. Be ready by noon, or sooner."

~ * ~

Frustrated, irritated and a host of other feeling rushed through Broc as he rode hard and fast to the stables. Jumping off his stallion before he was barely inside the barn, Broc took care of his horse before picking up the axe and striding around the structure to the woodpile.

Minutes later sweat dripped down his forehead and body. He picked up one piece after the other as he split the wood in half with a single swing, the pile of split wood growing.

"You like cutting wood?" Lacie MacTavish asked. "Don't know why. It looks like hard work."

Broc set the axe on the woodpile then slipped on his shirt before walking to the rail fence where Lacie sat. Her coal black hair caught the sunlight and in places highlighted with blue shimmers. She sported the largest and most gorgeous brown eyes he'd ever seen. At the moment she'd put her hair in a braid hanging nearly to her waist.

"I do enjoy cutting wood. It's a great way to rid myself of frustration and annoyance." He wanted to laugh at the way she scrunched up her face.

"Well, I get frustrated and annoyed with my brother. Sometimes he just doesn't consider anyone's feelings but his own. He's acting horrible to my sister and ignores me."

"Frustrated, huh." He leaned against the fence, thoroughly enjoying the short reprieve. "You should not be frustrated ever. You're much too beautiful. How old are you?" He enjoyed the slow rush of color to her cheeks when he spoke of her beauty.

"Sixteen. How old are you?" she shot back.

He laughed chucking her under the chin before returning to his work. "Too old for you. I'm twenty-four."

"You won't be too old when you're thirty because I'll be twenty-two." She jumped from the fence, striding to him. Her boyish figure had yet to turn into the beautiful curves that would appear in a few years. "Can I try?"

Broc stared at her, open mouthed for a moment. Then shaking his head, "You mean cut wood? No, don't want to be responsible if you get hurt."

"I won't hurt myself. I promise." She stood in front of him, her chin jutting out in a determined stance.

"That's why it's called an accident. No one intends to get hurt but it happens."

She walked back to her perch on the fence. "Alright then. You're just like my brother."

"Am I? How?"

"Thinks he's always right."

"And can I assume most the time he is?" Broc was laughing inside. He supposed if he had sisters and was responsible for their well-being, present and future, he'd be demanding and autocratic too. Her complaints reminded him of himself and the way he dealt with women. He coughed, clearing his throat and trying unsuccessfully to vanquish his thoughts.

"Well, he's not right about the suitors he's bringing to the house for my oldest sister. They're absolutely repulsive. There is no way she will ever say yes to any of them. In the last few days there have been six total. Of course, she hasn't been home to meet any but two which also makes Flynt angry."

"Saw two of them a few days ago when I stopped by to see Flynt. I agree with you. No woman as pretty as you and probably your sisters could be expected to get into bed with those gentlemen. Not that appearance is everything, mind you."

"Since he can't keep track of my sister, he's been harder on everyone else. I probably should get going before he sends someone after me or comes by himself." Yet she didn't make a move to get down.

"Probably should get home," he agreed with her.

"You know what else he did?" She didn't wait for him to answer. "Told my sister if she didn't go change her clothes to meet the suitors he'd change them for her and then he told her he'd tan her backside if she didn't do what he commanded. Of all the nerve."

He had to agree. While the woman was a sister, Flynt shouldn't be seeing her naked. "Flynt is in over his head in this situation and just wants to do what's best. His heart is in the right place even though his actions are more than misguided," he said, musing over what the youngest MacTavish lass told him.

Chapter Four

Two days later, Broc spent the morning pacing the room and glancing at the big grandfather clock in the parlor of his home. One day had turned into two and he was impatient to see Bliss. He checked with his cook three times to make sure the basket of food was packed to his liking. Slowly he inhaled a long deep breath of air when the clock finally chimed twelve times.

When the door to Bliss' home swung open with a gentle nudge, Broc wasn't surprised. He understood she didn't believe she needed to take the judicious precaution of securing her door. "Bliss, hope you locked the door two nights ago after I left."

Ignoring his statement, in any case refusing to answer, "You're here." She held a paintbrush in hand and puffed a strand of hair from her face. "I'm so glad you came."

Holding the picnic basket high, "I brought lunch."

"Thank goodness, I'm starving. Sorry I couldn't come see you, but I did need to finish these so I can take them into town to sell. Can you set the basket in the kitchen? I'll be ready in a few minutes." She set about cleaning the brushes she'd used. "Do you mind if I change into something a bit cleaner." She wiped her hands on the apron, smearing wet paint as she did so.

"Not if you hurry." He found he didn't care what she wore. She was beautiful to him no matter what clothes she had on or he hoped she didn't have on. He'd always prefer her naked. The thought of eating at the table with no clothes on had possibilities, but he didn't believe she was ready for anything like that.

He set the basket on the table as asked then taking out the bottle of wine, popped the cork before procuring glasses from the kitchen then poured them each a glass from the Bordeaux he brought. Stepping outside to wait for her, he sat down at a small table beneath hanging wisteria. Bees buzzed around the flowers and a gentle breeze cooled the veranda.

The small area was beautiful and secluded from the road leading to the cottage. A very perfect private place to get to know Bliss better and he meant to use the setting to his advantage. So many unanswered questions swirled around Bliss and if he could uncover just one today, he'd be pleased.

For some reason he felt more at home here than he did at his estate. The cottage was comfortable as well as homey and with the pleasant day ahead, he looked forward to spending the entire afternoon and if he got lucky, the evening with Bliss as well.

He heard the whisper of fabric behind him before she spoke. "What's for lunch?" She sat down beside him. "Is this for me?" She tilted her head toward the glass of wine.

"It is. I should have set the lunch on the table. Stay there and I'll get everything. Just relax. I'll be more than pleased to wait on you. Have you been working all morning?" He bent toward her and kissed her on the forehead before leaving for the few minutes it took to assemble plates and silverware and bring them outside.

"I'm glad you're here," she told him, her gaze fixed on him. "I have been working and it's proved very productive. I've two paintings ready to take to the gallery in Glasgow."

Broc sifted through the basket even though he knew exactly what was in it. "Looks like we have ham sandwiches and potato salad and I think my cook put blackberry tarts and oatmeal cookies in for dessert." He pulled the items from the basket, placing something of everything on her plate.

They ate in silence for a few minutes. Broc wasn't sure why his nerves were rattling and ready to split. Getting to know Bliss seemed to grow in importance with each day he knew her. What he comprehended about her right now was just a handful of things and even though he was going to try to discover her last name, he didn't hold onto much hope for that. She was adamant about keeping that secret.

He poured them each a second glass of wine, stretching his legs out and settling back on the chair. "What are you willing to tell me about yourself? Am I worthy of knowing your last name?"

She stiffened before looking away. When she stood and walked to the edge of the terrace, he followed, understanding he could push her only so far. Placing his hands on her shoulders, he gently massaged her tight muscles, wishing he could do more for her. He could only do what she allowed.

"What would you tell me that you don't want me to know," she queried, turning in his arms, her eyes focused on him. "Would you reveal your deepest and darkest secrets?"

He chuckled softly, "I'm an open book."

"Do you still have a mistress?" She pushed away from him, her hand now rested on his chest.

He cleared his throat, feeling a twinge of discomfort at the probing question. Perhaps he wasn't completely honest with her. "No, no I don't, not since the day after I met you. I ended it that day. Does it matter to you so much then?"

She smiled then looked away again. Strolling along the path leading to a small creek, it seemed she didn't want to answer, perhaps craved time to think. He needed to figure out someway to make her feel more comfortable with the truth and expressing her feelings. What she decided not to tell him could affect both of their lives.

"I suppose it does. Thinking of you going to another woman after you've been with me doesn't sit well in my mind. Guess I want you all to myself but I understand I don't have the right to dictate anything." She stopped at the edge of the creek. "Is that's even possible? To have you to myself?"

If it had been any other woman but Bliss, he would have made it perfectly clear the women he saw or didn't see were none of her business. He needed to change this up now, before the evening dissolved and he left frustrated again.

"Come sit down with me." He tugged on her hand bringing her to a large boulder. "Let's play a game."

"I don't understand." Her quizzical look made him beam with pleasure.

Rubbing gentle circles on her wrist, he liked the way she smiled at him. "I ask you a question and if you don't tell the truth or you don't want to answer, then I remove an article of clothing."

She inhaled quickly, her voice wavering, "I've never heard of a game like that. It can only have one purpose."

"Indeed, one purpose," he repeated. "I'm certainly glad about that." He touched her cheek, and setting a lose strand of hair behind her ear, he craved pursuing that commitment.

"Then the same goes for you? If you don't answer true or refuse I remove something you're wearing?"

"I wouldn't have it any other way." Good lord, of course that was what he wanted, to be naked with her.

"How do I know if you're telling the truth?" she asked. "I'd have no idea one way or the other."

He shrugged, watching her closely. "Guess we just have to trust each other. Can you do that, Bliss? Can you trust me to tell the truth? Would you willingly tell me all your secrets?"

"I wouldn't be here if I didn't trust you, if you weren't important to me." She paused then, smiling at him, "If your object is to undress me then, the game will not be a success. You can only ask the same question once."

He kissed her forehead then the tip of her nose, "I guess its success will depend on what we don't want to answer. You asked me the first question so..." He wasn't going to ask her about her name again. That would be unfair. "I'll officially start."

She rested her hand on his leg. "You are worthy of my trust." It seemed she was thinking of an earlier question. "Its just there are things I know in time I'll tell you but not today."

"Like your last name."

"Yes."

"Where did you live before you moved into this cottage? In the city or a nearby village?" He watched the expression on her face, and he knew she would ignore that question also.

She was looking down and plucking at her skirt with her free hand. "I lived..." She began. "I don't want to lie to you. An omission of the truth is not a lie, is it?" Then she was silent, waiting it seemed for him to decide what piece of clothing he wanted to take off her.

"You're shaking." He felt a bit of compassion and perhaps the tiniest bit of guilt, but she did agree to the game. "First, I'm going to take the pins out of your hair. While I'm not sure they can be considered an article of clothing, I want to see you with your hair down."

Broc ran his fingers through her hair, pins flying in all directions. For a few seconds, he continued, finger combing her hair. It was brown and kissed by the son and the strands were so silken and soft. He wanted to wrap it around him, feel the fire against his skin when they made love.

"Is it my turn now?" She was moistening her lips, clearly moved by his attentions.

He watched her tiny pink tongue and its slow movements across her mouth. He groaned in the back of his throat, wondering just how he was going to prolong something he wanted this instant.

"Your turn," he agreed.

"How many mistresses have you had?" By the time she finished with the question her breathing had increased.

He didn't know if it was because of the question or because he was still running his fingers through her hair. "Are you jealous, little minx? I thought, and correct me if I'm wrong, you don't have any intention of being my mistress."

"You're not wrong. I think I am a tiny bit jealous of anyone who's been with you. So can you answer me?"

"I don't think I will just to equalize this game you see. It won't be much fun for you if you end up stark naked and I've all my clothes on." He wanted to laugh at her look of annoyance. "I thought you weren't jealous."

"I'm not." She said sounding defensive. "I...well my rational mind says there's no reason to be jealous of something that happened in a past I wasn't a part of, but my feelings don't always agree with my mind."

"It's your decision, what do you want to take off me?" He felt the beginnings of a huge grin now realizing he had a very good method to keep this game even.

She moved back, her hand on her chest as her eyes began to narrow. "I have to remove it from you? I don't know if I can. Can't you just take if off yourself?"

"That's not the rules of the game."

"I've a feeling you are making them up as you go."

He grinned, thoroughly pleased with himself and his idea for the afternoon. "Of course you remove my clothing. After all, I don't have any intention of doing that for you. Don't you want to see me naked? Well, we have to take it one piece at a time." Inwardly, he was applauding her. She looked ready to run, but she slowly brought her hands up to loosen his cravat, her fingers trembling against his skin as she undid the fabric.

When it was off and she was holding the fabric in her delicate hands, "What should I do with this?"

"Wait a moment." He swept her into his arms and strode back to the veranda then inside the home. "Let's continue this somewhere a lot more private. I know you don't have neighbors, but a chance passer by is always possible." He set her on the sofa in the main room before sitting down across from her. "Now it's my turn." He searched for something she could answer yet needed a question that would tell him something about her. "Are you ready?"

She wound the cravat around her hands then let it slowly slide through them. "I hope so."

"You told me you trusted me so, who else do you trust to tell intimate things to?" Perhaps this question would put him one step closer to knowing who she really was.

It seemed she breathed easier. "My grandmother. I tell her everything and she keeps my confessions to herself."

"I see the truth in your eyes. No one else?" He smiled, not giving her a chance to reply and said, "And I so wanted to remove your shoes."

"My shoes," she laughed.

"I'd have to remove them before I take your stockings off. I wonder what color your garters are. Are the tops of your stockings embroidered with delicate flowers? No, that's not a question. Besides, it's your turn."

"My question to you is the same as the one you just asked me." She tilted her head a bit sideways.

"Would you like me to tell you the truth or do you want to take something else off my person?"

"I want you to tell me the truth." She protested yet there was something in her eyes that told him differently.

"Liar," he told her. "Now what... Hmmm..." he slowly began to unbutton her blouse. Familiar territory, he'd seen her the other night, her breasts beneath her filmy chemise, touched them, sucked a nipple deep into his mouth.

Her eyes grew wide, "It was my turn. You can't..."

He stopped with the blouse still resting on her shoulders, "Alright then but after I answer then I'll finish removing this and you can ask a second question."

"I was going to ask the same question. Who do you trust to tell intimate things to?"

"Two people, you and Flynt MacTavish, my best friend. We've known each other for years, and it seems we both confide in each other."

"Would you tell him about me?"

"No." He would never tell Flynt about her.

She flinched when he uttered the name Flynt MacTavish. Perhaps forgetting to refuse to answer would tell him more than another question. He reached to her and gently slipped the fabric over her delicate shoulders, smiling when he saw her easy response and growing passion in the hardening of her nipples. Bloody eyes, but this was pure torture. He would have to refuse to reply to the next question.

She didn't pause. It seemed she needed to take his focus from her breasts, but it would be damn hard. "What's your greatest weakness?"

The question took him by surprise. He'd never really thought about a weakness, at least never really put words to it. He supposed he liked women too much and enjoyed giving them whatever they wanted. "That's a good question."

"You have an answer, but you're not going to tell me," she surmised, reaching for his shirt and slipping it over his head. Her fingers brushed against his chest and he really didn't think he could wait for both of them to be naked before he pulled her into his arms and laid her on the bed.

"Whose turn is it?"

"Mine, I believe. What to ask? If you had one wish, what would it be?" He smiled at her, wondering...

"If I had one wish, I'd want to be able to tell you everything you ask of me without it changing our relationship, without you becoming angry with me then leaving me forever." Her face turned red and she covered her mouth with her hands.

Her comment shocked him as well as her reaction. "What is it you want to tell me?" She wasn't going to answer that and he knew it. Out of turn, he really didn't care.

He reached for her feet and removed both shoes, sure she was going to argue with him. It didn't matter, though, they would both be naked soon and she would be in his arms in his bed and he'd make love to her.

His hands lingered on her feet, massaging then sliding upward as high as her garters then back down before he sat back and waited, his hands folded over his stomach.

"What would you wish for?" she asked.

He wanted to say for this game to be over. He didn't reply. Instead, he pulled his boots from his feet and socks along with them. "You wouldn't have been able to take them off yourself." Now he was left with very little to remove. Deciding this would be his last question, he needed to make it something she wouldn't answer.

"Who are you hiding from, Bliss. What can I do to help?" He was sincere and didn't care if he once more asked two questions.

She was shaking her head, her lips pinched together. "No, I can't answer and you knew it. That's not fair."

"Do you want to make love with me, Bliss?" he asked, removing her skirt then sweeping her into his arms and striding to the bedroom.

"I do. I want to live my life now. One never knows what might happen tomorrow, and I want my first lover to be you," she whispered softly against his neck. Then, "I do trust you, Broc."

"Not enough to just tell me what bothers you, but I don't care. In time I'll know all your secrets. And Bliss, I'm going to be your only lover."

"Promise?" she asked, running her hand along his chest. "I'd like for that too." Her lips touched him.

"I've waited what seems an eternity for this. Do you want me, all of me?" He needed to hear the answers from her before he took the greatest gift she could give to a man.

"Please..." she sighed as his lips molded against her. Bloody eyes, but this much of Bliss was not enough. He pulled her to a sitting position. "Raise your arms. I don't want to rip anything." Then she was naked except for her stockings and garters. The sight of her long sleek legs still in the delicate stockings leading to her woman's mound stopped his breath. She was exquisite.

"I want to see you naked too." She ran her fingers through his hair as she whispered.

"Soon." He kissed her again, teasing her lips to open for him. When she did, he touched her inside. Gently, he sucked her bottom lip into his mouth, biting gently. Her tiny moan thrilled him.

"Broc." She moved closer seeming to need more of him.

"What, my little minx. Tell me what you like? I want to please you." He'd had lovers and mistresses but no one as exquisite as Bliss and no one he'd ever wanted so much to introduce to sex as this woman.

"Everything. I don't know..."

His fingers danced over her body, played with the sensitive spots that would bring her the greatest pleasure. She was his now and no one would take her away from him. The truths or lack of didn't matter. Whatever it was she couldn't say to him would come out in the future and they would deal with it, the consequences be damned.

"Do you like me to touch you here." His mouth closed over one rosy nipple and he rolled the other between his fingers.

She didn't speak but nodded to him. Her fingers dug into his shoulders then moved higher, sifting through his hair.

"Perhaps you'd like this even more." He kissed and bit gently tender flesh, silken flesh as he moved down her belly then to her legs, touching every sensitive place he could find. With his teeth he tugged on her garters until they were freed and her stocking slowly slipped down her legs. He needed to explore all of her.

She cried out softly when his fingers settled in her most intimate folds, soft swollen petals, hot and wet from his attentions. Then he touched upon the bud, massaging until her hips bucked and her tiny cries were absorbed into his mouth with his kiss.

His fingers were on the tiny nubbin, his lips, and fingers dancing attendance on her breast, her body beginning to spasm in the sweetest agony and pleasure. Quickly, he pushed his remaining clothes to the floor then slowly entered her. His body quivered with the need to go slow and knowing she would feel pain this first time.

He was deep enough inside her. Felt the thin barrier that still proclaimed her innocence. She was running her hands up then down his back as if she meant to reassure him, her nails raking his flesh.

"It's alright. I understand what's happening, what's going to happen. Grandmother..." she sighed as he sucked a nipple into his mouth.

"Your grandmother told you everything about making love?" he smiled, realizing he was slowly learning tiny little things about her.

"Yes. Maybe not everything." Her hips moved as if trying to draw him deeper inside. "Mother died."

Her body wanted him, needed him to bring this to its conclusion. She was slick with her cream, more than ready.

"Are you stopping?" she asked, her nails sliding along his back. "This can't be all there is?"

"No, little minx, this isn't all there is." He thrust forward all the way to touch her womb, and she cried out as he ripped through her innocence, honored she wanted to give this gift to him.

Now instead of pulling him closer, she was pushing him away then pounding on his back. He saw tears running down her cheeks and he would take that away if it were humanly possible.

"It will be fine soon." He tried to encourage her.

She nodded, "Kiss me," she said, "Take the pain and away and replace it with pleasure."

And his lips fell upon hers, molded closely with hers, and it was the sweetest fire sweeping through him. He'd never felt anything so magical in all his life. When she started to move against him, he fell in rhythm then created his own with her.

Once more he found the most intimate spots and erotic places to caress until he felt the beginning of her release once more. He increased the tempo of his attentions until he felt the violent seizures of her body sweep through her another time. He cried out and it was primal as well as possessive as he poured his seed into her.

"Broc, I don't think I can move. Is this what it's supposed to be like?"

~ * ~

"Did Bliss really tell you she found the perfect man?" Daryl, the third youngest sibling asked Chelsea. "This man certainly wasn't one of the suitors our brother brought home to meet her."

Lacie giggled, "I've found a man but he's way too old for me right now. Saw him with his shirt off and I can bet none of those men our brother found for Bliss to court looked as braw and as handsome as Broc."

"You saw Broc Wallace without a shirt?" Chelsea asked, her heart thumping. Everyone knew he was a rake and far from eligible in the eyes of most mamas as well as Flynt.

Lacie was grinning and nodding her head. "He was chopping wood. It's not the first time I've seen him either. I always ride that way because he's at the woodpile a lot. Told me it was frustration that made him like to chop wood. Whatever that means."

"Back to my question," Daryl said. "Did Bliss find the man of her dreams and is that why she doesn't live at home any longer?"

"She's not this man's mistress is she?" Lacie asked, her eyes wide. "That wouldn't be very smart of her, to ruin herself. The man she gives herself to has be pretty special."

Chelsea didn't know what she could say or not say. She promised Bliss so much. "I think she's happy and she's taking grandmother's advice. We should all mind our own business and quit speculating about our oldest sister."

"And what was that?" Daryl asked. "Grandmother's advice."

"Something like don't live in the future. We never know what tomorrow will bring." Chelsea sat against the backboard of her bed, watching her siblings and wondering just how long any of them had to be together. Her sisters were gathered around her chatting about everything imaginable. She hoped that would never change even as they grew older and married.

"I do believe that is sound advice," Daryl said. "Pretend today could be the last day of my life."

"Me too," Lacie piped up. "I like that idea, seize the day, *carpe diem*. That way I won't have any regrets whatsoever."

"Did Flynt say his friends were coming to the house tonight and we were to make ourselves scarce?" Daryl asked with a wry chuckle. "Seems like I heard something to that affect, but I for one want to check the bad boys out again. Maybe they will have their shirts off."

"You sweet on one of Flynt's friends?" Chelsea asked, watching her sister's cheeks turn a vivid shade of red.

"What if I am?" Daryl shot back. "You like Cam. I watched you staring at him when he wasn't looking and even sometimes when he was. You know that he stares right back."

"Probably not wise for any of us to get our hopes up about the bad boys. There is no way Flynt will allow any of us near his friends or his friends near us," Chelsea advised while she wasn't ready to admit the fact to anyone but herself she was already smitten with Cam, and she was determined to find a way to be with him.

"Bad boys," Daryl said with a starry look in her eyes. "Such a suitable nickname, but if they were to find the right woman..."

"Bad boys," Lacie repeated. "But I'm not going to let any of that stand in my way. While Broc looks amazing without his shirt, I like Leslie too. I think he might be a bit younger."

"He's closer to your age." Chelsea grinned at her little sister who was growing up way too fast. They all were and Flynt was beside himself trying to be their guardian a task that the self-proclaimed rake wasn't up to although he believed his credentials proved him more than suitable.

"Who do like, Chelsea?" Lacie asked, probing into her sister's mind. "Bet it's one of the bad boys. Is it really Cam?"

With a heavy sigh and the realization her path to happiness with this man was practically impossible, "Cam. He stole my breath the first time I saw him, and when he looks at me my heart races in anticipation of something. Not too sure what that is though."

Thank goodness it's not Donal. I nearly swoon every time he walks through our door. One day, when Flynt was busy I sat down beside him." Daryl told her sisters.

"What did he say?" Lacie asked, her hand on her chest.

"Hello."

"Is that all?" Lacie's disappointment in the question gave the sisters a chuckle.

"What has Leslie said to you?" Daryl shot back. Not one of her sisters seemed amused.

"Now girls, let's not fight among ourselves. Let's try to figure out a way to sneak upstairs where we can watch them play cards and drink. We can see how long it takes for them to realize we're listening in on their bad boy or manly conversation."

"As far as we know they never lock the door. I've been up there before," Lacie said, but they never guessed. "I was quiet as a mouse and listened until I grew bored then I snuck down the back stairs."

"You tend to be far more adventurous than the rest of us. I'm not sure that's going to prove to be such a good thing," Chelsea said.

"That's because she's the youngest and doesn't know any better," Daryl said, seeming to still feel a bit of anger at her youngest sister. "We were all more impulsive when we were younger."

"With the least to lose," Chelsea said in agreement. "No one will judge her if she gets caught doing something foolish. We, on the other hand, could be ostracized. Lacie will have to change her ways as she comes of age."

"I'm not changing anything about me," Lacie said with a dramatic sigh to lend emphasis to her statement.

"Well," Daryl paused, "I want to risk going up to the attic. Seeing the men gambling and playing cards shouldn't be taboo for women. We should be able to do the same thing without all the gossip."

"I'd like to see what it's like to smoke a cigar," Lacie said.

"Whatever for?" Daryl asked, "they're smelly and make a person cough."

"Alright then," Chelsea said, inhaling a deep breath she hoped would give her courage. "I'll lead the way. We have to be very silent or they'll know we're in the room before we get a chance to listen in on a word they're saying. I want to know if they talk about women."

"They probably just talk about their mistresses," Daryl said.

"You want to eaves drop?" Lacie asked, clapping her hands together. "I'd give anything to hear what men talk about when there are no women around. Do you think it's sex?"

"Thought you've been up there."

"I was too young to appreciate anything they might have said," Lace told them with a dramatic sigh.

"Of course they talk about sex," Daryl looked down her nose at her younger sister as if she should learn a thing or two.

"Me too, I'd love to know what's on their minds. It might help me figure out how I can get Cam to pay more attention to me," Chelsea said dryly, wishing she were as confident as the youngest sibling.

"Then," Daryl waved her hand toward the bedroom door, "the servant staircase?"

"Seems the best avenue right now and perhaps the best path for escape when we're caught." Chelsea knew that running from them was inevitable, because she also realized she wanted Cam to catch her. She might even make sure that was what would happen. If he did catch her, it might give her a chance to be alone with him.

"Everyone stay clear of our big brother. He won't be happy at all when he realizes what we're about," Daryl said as if she was almost having second thoughts.

Chelsea looked in the mirror, pinching her cheeks and patting her hair to make sure every strand was in the right place then started out the door and to the room on the third floor where the bad boys always played cards, her sisters following.

The third floor room was lit with a few gaslights and the men were seated at a round table at the far end. Cigar smoke cast a hazy fog and Chelsea nearly coughed from the scent. Covering her mouth and holding her breath, she willed herself to silence.

They separated with the intent that everyone would flee in a different direction when they were noticed. There were three ways from this room; the way they entered, the main staircase and a hallway leading to various rooms on the third floor.

Chelsea settled in a dark corner nearest the tables watching as the men sipped their whiskey and made bets while they chatted. The other siblings took up places around the room.

"Whatever do you think has happened to Broc? This is the second time he hasn't come," Cam asked, setting his cards on the table and spreading them wide before leaning back in his chair and waiting for the other players to make their move.

"Don't know. Must have found a new mistress. Heard he dismissed Edina," Flynt said, seemingly unconcerned. "He'll be back with us as soon as the first infatuation wears off."

"Can't say as I blame him for looking for someone new. Edina was a real bitch. Saw Broc the other day and he told me she had the audacity to let herself into his apartment," Cam said. "I'll never give a key to my private residence to my mistress."

Chelsea covered her mouth with her hands, the ensuing gasp catching Cam's attention as she watched him look up from the table before turning towards her and showing his white teeth.

"I say is there someone here?" His hand traveled to the back of his waistband.

From knowing Flynt, Chelsea knew he reached for a gun. She pushed herself farther into a corner, but when she looked up, Cam's steel hard gaze met hers and he grinned knowingly at her.

"Don't think we need the guns lads, but we do have company," Cam paused, "in the form of your sisters, Flynt."

"There's more than one of them," Donal spoke, amusement tingeing his voice. "Can't say I'm too disappointed. The game was starting to bore me. Nothing like a little feminine diversion to spice up the evening."

"Suppose they must want to know what men do at night when they aren't playing cards," Leslie seemed just as amused as Donal.

"My sisters up here? I'll teach them a lesson they won't forget," Flynt said. "Tan their backsides. They won't come up here again."

"No, what is wrong with you? They are just curious." Cam set his hand on Flynt's arm to warn him off. "Let us do that, frighten them just a little. I think our involvement will have more of an impact than angry words from you or a thrashing, which is not appropriate in any case. They won't be as inclined to ignore your orders if they discover a few truths about men for themselves."

With Cam's words, Chelsea thought she might have found more than she bargained for. She didn't know if she should run now or not at all, but her legs didn't seem to want to move. Suddenly, Cam stood above her, gazing down on her, his hands resting confidently on his hips, a smirk on his handsome face. He appeared a man who ruled the world, at least his part of it. She bolted to the side while he lunged his hands grazing her arm but missing.

Breathing hard and wondering what the bloody hell she was doing, she darted through the door leading to the hallway. She should have headed down stairs to her room where she could bolt the door. His boot steps thundered behind her, closing the distance between them.

Without a thought, she slipped through an open door. Closing it quickly, she leaned against it, her heart in her throat and her breath racing. She thought she'd never been so terrified in her entire life yet so intrigued and curious about what he would do when he caught up to her.

"Open the door, Chelsea. I'm coming in one way or the other and I don't want to hurt you."

Unmoving, she closed her eyes. "I…" she licked her parched lips, "can't move," she whispered, hoping he heard the terror in her voice.

"Of course you can. Just step sideways."

She slid against the wall and away from the door. When he stepped inside the servant's quarters, his shadow, from the full moon shining through the window, seemed to fill the tiny space. Once inside, he closed and bolted the door.

"What are you going to do?" she asked, unsure of anything at the moment and questioning her judgment more so now than a few minutes earlier.

"I should turn you over my knee but no, not tonight. Tonight I'm going to do what you wanted all along, Chelsea. Do you recall what that was or do you want me to show you?" His large hand cupped her cheek, the other wrapped around her waist pulling her close against the hard length of his body.

"I wanted something?" she squeaked, unwilling to admit anything. His closeness and the feel of his hands pressing her against him seemed to render her unable to think.

"I believe so. You wanted this kiss. You want to know what it's like to be with a man, to make love, but I'm not going to teach you everything tonight." His mouth hovered so close to hers she felt his breath and the moist glide of his tongue across her lips.

Oh, he was right she did want this kiss and so many more, but she couldn't possibly tell him that. What would he think of her?

"Answer me," Cam persisted, his voice low and seeming to draw her into the delicious enchantment that surrounded him. "You want this kiss. All you need to do is say yes."

She nodded, hearing the deep masculine groan emanating from him. His lips molded against hers, encompassing them, absorbing them, the heated dampness of his caress searing her, reaching every nerve she possessed. He caught her bottom lip between his teeth and bit gently then sucked it into his mouth. She felt his tongue sweep across her lip as if soothing it then he bit gently again, repeating the gesture again and again. She could barely stand, hardly breathe but her heart thundered inside her.

Raising his head a fraction, "Give me your tongue, sweet imp. I want to taste more of you."

"Tongue..."

"Yes. Open for me and..."

She opened and was shocked when his tongue swept inside her mouth seeming to explore and delve so very intimately. She had never thought kissing a man could be like this.

"Do you understand now?" he asked, smiling at her as his other hand cupped her breast and teased a nipple. "No corset. Isn't that a little wicked? You wanted for me to touch you here, and here." He discovered more and more of her.

Cam didn't give her a chance to answer, his mouth closed over hers again, pushing hers open, sliding his tongue inside then backing out. She understood what he wanted now. Hesitantly, she touched his lips with her tongue ventured further inside his mouth while his nimble fingers tugged and played with her nipples.

When he pulled a way for a second as if to breathe, she said. "My legs...I don't think I can stand..."

He pressed his thigh between her legs, lending his support. Moving back a tiny bit he smiled at her, ran his fingers through her hair. She felt the pressure against her and wondered at the feeling in a part of her she'd never even thought about before. She ached with need for him and while she didn't quite understand, she knew if he touched her there she wouldn't say no.

"Your first lesson," he told her. "Did you like it?"

"When do I get the second one?"

"Meet me tomorrow at three on the southeastern edge of your property." He swept her into his arms. Leaving the room he descended the servant's staircase to the second floor. "Which one is your room? For future reference of course."

Chapter Five

"Wake up, sleepy head," Broc kissed Bliss on the cheek before running his hand lightly along her arm. He had too many plans for the day to count or he'd crawl back into bed with her and they would resume where they left off last night or perhaps it was early morning.

"You didn't let me sleep much last night," she yawned, stretching as the covers slipped from her shoulder. Reaching for them, she held the quilt to her chest.

"Tonight then you can sleep all you want after we finish our business, important transactions. I've a hot bath waiting for you and breakfast as soon as you're dressed."

"Really?" she asked, clinging to the constantly retreating covers.

He smiled at the small gesture hoping that soon she'd be comfortable with her nakedness when she was around him. "Has no one made breakfast for you before?"

"Mother and father, when I was a little girl," she told him, "but that seems infinitely different to me. You say there's hot water?"

He nodded in the direction of the small bathing area, deciding he'd pursue the topic of her mother and father at a later date and why they would stop making breakfast for her when she wasn't a little girl. He had to wonder just how young she was when she lost her parents. "Enjoy yourself and if you don't mind, would you wear the dress I set out?"

Bliss stiffened when he asked and he understood what she must be thinking but he just wanted to see her in the dress he bought with her in mind.

She moistened her lips as if mulling over his request. "I don't see where that would be a problem as long as you promise not to buy me anything else. I don't want your charity or to think you're paying me for sex."

"I would make that promise, but there are several packages waiting for you to open in the sitting room. Would you deprive me of my enjoyment?" he challenged her.

"I told you..."

"I couldn't help myself." He shrugged knowing that wasn't a good enough reason for her. "I'll try to do better," he told her knowing he would always do exactly what he wished and would buy her anything that caught his fancy.

He watched the soft rise and fall of her breasts and the slight agitation as she must be thinking over his words.

"I'll put the dress on, but if I need a corset, I might change my mind since I can't lace it myself." She graced him with a smile he didn't quite understand.

"You know very well, I'll help you with anything you ask, even a corset." He almost turned back to the bed, instead, "Call me when you're ready to get dressed. I've been known to lace a corset or two. My fingers are nimble."

"I don't like to think about you and other women, although I've no legitimate right to question what you have and haven't done before you met me. However, I'd rather think about you lacing than unlacing."

"My life is an open book and I did have one, a life, before I met you," he said grinning.

"I understand, just as you don't have a right to know my past either despite the fact you want to."

He remained in the doorway watching her and waiting for her to rise from the bed. She grimaced at him, causing him to chuckle softly. Truly, he didn't want to give her a bad time. "When you're ready, but you have to get up first," he conceded, eager to get the day started and looking forward to the evening in Glasgow he planned.

"When you leave the room."

Despite the fact he didn't want to leave until she rose naked from the bed, they could banter this back and forth and neither would accomplish anything. Resigned, he turned on a heel, heading for the kitchen where he finished with the breakfast he started earlier.

"Are you enjoying the bath?" he called out with a chuckle, "Do you need more hot water?"

"I'm fine."

He heard the rippling of the water and soft sounds and had real thoughts of joining her in the tub. "For another time," he murmured for his ears only.

While she was bathing, he set out plates and napkins. Then he placed the fried items on a platter. He indulged himself with coffee, but he made hot chocolate for Bliss thinking she might like the sweet beverage better than the bitter one. Hot water boiled on the stove in case she wished for tea.

"I'm ready."

In the bathing room she wore her underclothing, her corset against her breasts, hiding them from him. In time, she wouldn't be so shy about her body. In time, they would share so very much more.

"Thank you," he told her, "for wearing the dress. I've been waiting to see you in it for too many days to count." Quickly, he laced the corset, obeying her wishes when she told him not so tight then helped her with the back fastenings.

He turned her then, his hands lightly caressing her arms. "This is perfect for today. It will not be too hot, but you will need a parasol for the trip into the city. I don't want you to get burned."

She watched as he traced the low cut bodice with a fingertip. The neckline revealed yet covered and the tiny cap sleeves were barely sleeves at all. The scarlet fabric was trimmed in gold lace and piping and embroidered with the same colored flowers.

"I don't have a parasol, but I do have an old bonnet I wear when I'm painting," she said, seeming to stare at her cleavage. "I can put it on for the drive into town."

He wanted to laugh when she tried to pull the fabric higher. "I assure you the bodice is not too low. You're in the height of fashion and you're beautiful."

"I've never worn anything like this before." She looked at him, eyes wide seeming to question him, asking him if he was sure.

"Then enjoy the dress. Have you never cared about fashion? Seems unlikely for a woman of this day and age. Come, let's eat then we'll be on our way. I'd tell you I'd buy a parasol for you when we reach town but I know you'd refuse. So perhaps I can lend you the money and when you get paid and set up the new bank account, you can pay me back. Would that be alright?"

She smiled at him as if relieved. "That would be fine but until we reach the gallery, I won't know if I have money waiting for me or nothing to put in my brand new account."

"But you will." He tried to encourage as he pulled the kitchen chair out for her. "Now, coffee, tea or hot chocolate?"

"Coffee, please," she said, smiling at him. "You thought I'd want chocolate. Never chocolate in the morning, just on cold winter days. It's too sweet to start the morning with."

"I did, now I know one more thing about you." He poured the coffee before sitting down.

Later, with breakfast over and dishes in the sink, Broc held out his arm for her to take.

"The paintings? Are they ready to go?" She asked as they strode toward the old cart that would take them into town.

"I packed everything in the back while you were sleeping." He helped her onto the seat even though he expected a voice of protest.

"Thank you," she told him. "Don't you need sleep too? You didn't get any more than I did."

"Not as much as you. Too excited about the day to sleep."

"Oh..."

"What are you thinking, Bliss?" he asked as the cart started down the lane toward the main road into town.

"If I've sold anything, to begin with, and how you plan on setting up a bank account in my name." She rearranged her skirts then repeated the action. "The law doesn't allow for a woman's independence."

"It's not going to be in your name." He turned to smile at her.

"Not in yours then?" She breathed softly, the words seeming to linger in question.

"No, not in mine or yours but both of our names." He turned his focus to the road wondering how on earth he was going to justify this new action to her.

"How..."

Well, he knew she'd ask and he'd thought long and hard about just how to do it. Indeed he could think of no other way when he wanted to have some control of the funds, and he needed to make sure whoever it was who stole her previous earnings would never get their hands on this money.

"The account will have both our names on it, Bliss Wallace." He waited for another bout of protest. When all he heard was silence, he turned to look at her. What he saw was the most astonished expression.

"Bliss Wallace." It seemed to him she tried to swallow but was having difficulty with the task.

"What better way?" he asked, shrugging his shoulders to make his point. "With my last name on the account, no one can take it from you."

"But you will have all of the control." This time Bliss did protest. "You can take it from me."

"You told me you trusted me. Have you changed your mind so soon?" he said, watching her closely. He needed to know he had her confidence.

"I do. It's just that," she paused, sucking her lower lip between her teeth before gazing at him with huge wide eyes.

"Just that what?" He didn't want to sound harsh but bloody hell, he thought he'd made progress with her. At this moment he wasn't too sure.

She lifted her delicate shoulders, frown lines on her face. "I guess I'm just afraid to trust unconditionally. After what happened with my funds a few days ago, I do have reservations as well as questions. I can't keep my independence without that money."

"That's fair enough." He needed her to trust him unequivocally, but why would she? She'd obviously been hurt by a man and she would be stupid to give all she was over to him. And he had to admit she'd already given him more than any woman before and he appreciated it.

"If you could have any wish, what would you wish for?" she asked suddenly, surprising him.

"Ah, I asked you that last night, but it seems our attention was diverted from questions to making love."

"It was and I answered poorly creating more questions. Don't know why I felt the urge to remind you of everything I haven't told you about myself just now, but I do want to know what you would wish for." She placed her hand on his leg, gazing at him with sincerity.

"So what would I wish for? I have everything I want. I'm happy and..." he paused. He realized he would wish for a woman who would be loyal and true to him, who could trust him unconditionally. He was tired of being known as a bad boy. Instead, he thought it would be nice to be known as a family man, a man of character. Not that bad boys didn't have character, but somehow it wasn't the same and it was a title he no longer coveted.

"Nothing?" she asked, taking her hand away. "There has to be something. Perhaps you trust me about the same as I trust you and you're unwilling to tell me your deepest feelings."

"Perhaps." He wasn't sure he could tell her his latest thought. It might create optimism in her mind where he didn't know if there was hope. "I suppose if we were playing the game you'd have to take some item of clothing off me."

"Just thinking about that is very provocative," she said, her hands now clasped tightly together.

"Provocative, you say? I'd like to pursue that thought a bit farther when we finish with your business. Do you have anywhere you'd like to eat dinner?" He changed the subject unwilling to delve into such intimate issues while they were in the public eye.

"No, never spent much time in the city. Mother and father didn't like it, preferring the country. They chose to stay at home and since their death..." she paused, looking straight ahead. "I've only been in town long enough to sell my paintings. The city has no draw for me."

"There is a market not far from my apartment that sells food. We can purchase whatever we like there and take it home. If you'd like."

"One thing at a time. I didn't know we were going to stay the night. I didn't bring a change of clothes."

Looking at her he waggled his eyebrows grinning and feeling smug knowing she would protest, but once again she would enjoy what he had planned. "I've things at my apartment I purchased for you my last trip into the city, if you want to accept them. Of course you don't have to wear anything I purchased. I love looking at you when you're naked." Why he needed to challenge her, he wasn't sure but he did love the sweep of color reaching her cheekbones.

"You would say that." It seemed she almost laughed.

He held his hands as if they were scales. "Naked or clothed, your pick."

"So." She changed the subject. "You don't have a wish you want to voice my way then what do you want out of life. You must have some goals."

"Isn't that about the same thing?" he asked. "Are you trying to get me naked. Should I ride into town like Lady Godiva?"

"No, the questions are different." She swatted at his hand that seemed to be in the wrong place. "I'd like to become a renowned painter, but I know that's impossible because I'm not that good and I'm a woman. Things like that aren't possible for females, and I understand I'll have to enjoy making a living at my craft and settle for that, earning a living."

"You could sign a man's name to your paintings and pretend," he said, "but of course that doesn't address the first reason. Isn't the judgment of how good you are belong to the viewer not the painter?"

"Most likely, so what do you want out of life or even in the near future?" she persisted.

His answer would be the same one as the wish. He was tired of his life the way he'd spent it the last six years. He was ready to move on to the next phase of the journey, he just wasn't sure what that was and if Bliss would play a role.

He breathed in deeply. "I'm not really sure. You've given me reason to think about my life. I suppose I've lived the same way for several years. I don't know what I want in my future." *Liar, you just don't want to tell Bliss.*

"I think I know what you want tonight." She laughed, and with caution, she proceeded, "I want the same thing. Being with a man is too new for me to know how much time I want to spend with him. Never thought..."

"I'm glad being with a man is new to you and I'm even more

pleased that man is me." He pulled the cart to a stop, wishing he dared kiss her in front of the bank and all of Glasgow. He didn't have bad luck normally, but today of all days someone he knew would see and the rumors would fly through the city. He didn't want his newly formed relationship to be fraught with gossip.

"Are we here?" She sounded eager to get on with her life.

He couldn't help himself. He caressed her cheek with the back of his hand, excepting the fact that with each passing second she was becoming dearer to him than life itself.

"We have arrived. Do you want me to do the talking or do you want to take charge?" He loved the play of emotions across her face.

"I've set up an account before. The problem was my...never mind. I had to have a man to sign for it. I guess you are the man who will control all my funds." She breathed in deeply, looking to the bank's door.

He placed her hands in his, wanting to ask her, my what? "Truly, I won't steal from you."

"I was promised that once before too."

His heart went out to her and he wanted to right all the injustices that had been perpetrated against her. Strangling the man who absconded with her hard earn money becoming more and more a driving force in his thoughts.

"I can't think of anything else I can tell you that will clear your mind of any doubts. I want you to have blind faith in my integrity as well as my intentions, but I understand that won't happen today. If you can think of any other way to do this, I will stand beside you."

Her heavy sigh ripped his heart in two. "I want to have complete faith in you. At the moment I've no other recourse so let's do it."

He was too late to help her from the cart. When he reached her side, she was rummaging through the inside.

"Do you think these will be safe here?" he asked, suddenly concerned for the work she put into this endeavor they were about today.

"They always have before. No one has ever accompanied me on my trips to the gallery. No one is really concerned with what's inside the cart. I've never had any problems."

"Hope you're right about that."

Broc held out his arm for her and she closed her hand around him. Together they strode inside and a while later they left with an account set up for Bliss Wallace.

"How did you do that?"

"What?" he asked, comprehending her question.

"Get the manager to agree that your signature isn't necessary for me to withdraw money?"

"You like that, do you?"

"Yes and the fact you can't withdraw money unless you have my signature. I just don't know how you even thought about that."

"Do you trust me now?" He placed his hand over hers, focusing on her eyes and hoping to read the truth in them.

Her eyes, shining brightly, unshed moisture pooling in them. "I trust you completely and with my life. I've never known a man who would do something like that for a woman. That simple gesture means the world to me."

"And I believe you. Now we need to take these amazing paintings to the gallery and have any money you've earned from previous work transferred to your account."

A few hours later their mission was accomplished. He parked the empty cart in front of his apartment.

"I'm hungry, are you?" Bliss asked.

"Do you want to go upstairs before we find something to eat?"

"No, let's get everything we need then we can relax for the rest of the evening. I feel tired, hungry and ready to do absolutely nothing. I want to sip red wine and watch the sun set over the city."

"Maybe a nice hot bath? We could share." He lifted one eyebrow, waiting for an answer he was sure would not come.

"Do you ever think of anything but sex?" she asked laughing. The sound was music to his ears. He wanted to hear her laughter every day for the rest of his life.

"Not when you're around me. Well, no, that's not completely right. There were quite a few times I was thinking of your best interest and that did not include sex," he defended himself.

She pointed, "There's the market. What kind of food do you want?"

She skipped away from him then turned, backing up and watching him, her grin wide and infectious.

He caught up to her and they bought wine and sandwiches. He purchased a loaf of bread that should work for dinner as well as breakfast. She found oranges at another cart and a box of blackberries then purchasing several bottles of wine, they headed back to the apartment.

"I think I'm full just looking at all of this," she said, reaching into the box of berries. She picked up one, feeding it to him then popped another in her mouth. "Look, there's a pastry cart. I've a craving for sweets right now and pastries sound perfect."

"Should we get some for breakfast?"

"If I eat all this, I won't be able to fit into this corset or the dress. You'll have to shop for me before we leave tomorrow..." She covered her mouth with her hands for a second. "I'll pay for it."

"Bitch," Edina stepped in front of her, slapping her hard, Bliss' head reeling backwards at the impact. "You've no right to have Broc!" Spittle flew from the woman's mouth, her hands fisted at her sides.

Stepping between the two women, Broc wrenched Edina's arm behind her back, turning her away from Bliss. "Don't ever do that again." His anger simmering and ready to explode, he motioned for a nearby constable.

"You wouldn't dare." She looked to him then the suited man bearing down on them. "You wouldn't put me in prison."

"I would dare anything where you are concerned. I've told you twice that we are through, and you had the audacity to hurt the woman I care about." *More than life, more than my life.*

"Saw the altercation, sir. I'd take her to the station, but no one will hold her over slapping another woman. If she'd hit you..."

"That's alright." He understood the policies and the problems here. Then turning to Edina, "If you come near me or Bliss again, you'll stop breathing."

~ * ~

Bliss couldn't stop the quick inhalation of air that left her gasping.

Her cheek stung where the other woman had slapped her. She nearly cried out at the contact, now tears threatened to fall while she held her hand against her face. She couldn't recall another time anyone had hit her.

Gently, Broc removed her hand from her cheek, touching the bruised area with a fingertip. "Forget what has happened here, Bliss. I'll explain when we have some privacy, and I promise you it won't ever happen again. We need to get home." He wrapped his arm around her waist, guiding her though the throngs of people cluttering the streets.

She stumbled along beside him, her heart racing while she wiped moisture from her eyes. In all her life she'd never imagined anything like this happening. The woman must be a bit crazy. "I don't think I can do that, forget what just happened. That was hateful."

"I know it will be hard." He stopped then holding her by her shoulders, searched her eyes. "Please don't let this incident get in the way of everything good that has happened for you today. I want to celebrate with you as well as relax. Together we need to enjoy the evening."

"I'll try." Despite the fact she told herself to stop feeling sorry for herself, she couldn't erase the look in the woman's eyes when she first stood in front of her.

Broc's hands held either side of her head. His thumbs brushed tears away. "I don't ever want you to feel pain again. I will see Edina has another protector as soon as possible. That will be sure to take her focus away from you, away from us."

She was trying to smile and do as he said, put the incident behind her, having to assume this woman must have known Broc intimately at one time and must believe she'd taken her place.

The walk to Broc's apartment seemed to take an eternity, her cheek beginning to swell and throb painfully. She held back the sob threatening to escape and continued, holding tightly onto Broc's arm.

At the door to his lodgings, he ordered a block of ice then swept her into his arms after unlocking the door. Carrying her over the threshold, he set her on the sofa in the main living room. "Stay put."

She watched him disappear into the kitchen before reemerging with a cold damp cloth a tiny piece of ice inside. When he returned, his expression was so tender and concerned. She'd never seen this side of him.

"I think you you're going to have a black eye. Keep this pressed against your cheek and it might help reduce the swelling."

"You have ice?" She felt the cold against her cheek, flinching away yet she pressed her hand against the cloth to hold it in place.

"Yes, it was left over from last time I was at home. Keep this right here. I'll be back in a second." Before she could think to ask, he was out the front door. Baffled by his sudden departure, her thoughts random and confused, this day had so many ups and downs.

When he stepped back inside the door in just a few minutes, she asked, "Where did you go?" She took the frigid cloth from her face, but it seemed he wouldn't allow her to do so.

He placed it back on her face. "Just for a little while longer. As to where I went, I realized the lady who hit you, my previous mistress, might have more than one key. I sent a message for a locksmith to come here immediately. He should arrive in a few minutes."

"A second key?" More confusion swept through her. Why would anyone have a key, let alone one to his private residence?

Broc gently held her shoulders while he spoke. "Bliss, Edina was my mistress until the day after I met you. Remember when I rode into town?"

"I do, you said it was to do business." She recalled that day and while she was thankful for the time his absence gave her to think about him and the new feelings she was experiencing, she missed him inexplicably. "Did you lie to me?"

"And it was about business first. Business was the only reason I rode into town when I wanted to be with you. I sold a ship that first evening and signed a contract for a couple more ships. The day was profitable for me even while I missed you and wished you were with me."

"Ships? You never told me you sell ships?" She realized she had no idea what he did to make money, also realizing she never asked nor did she care.

"You never asked how I made my money. Money I like to spend on you." He laughed, gently stroking her other cheek then down her neck, his gaze riveted on her mouth. "If you'd asked, I would have told you."

She shivered at the caress. "Just thought you inherited your money and didn't have to earn an honest living. Guess I never thought much past that. My..." Good lord, but she almost just told Broc her brother's name.

"That's not a flattering assessment. I build as well as sell ships, but I won't say I do a hard day's work. The business is thriving and my employees do most of the labor, giving me time to pursue other pleasures such as you."

"And your mistresses."

A knock on the door ended their conversation. "Ah that must be the locksmith now or the new block of ice. Rescued from your last comment, although I do intend to answer you."

Broc opened the door. "You need a change of locks here?" The man stepped inside the room, the ice behind him.

"I do and I'd like two keys. How long will it take?" Broc looked to her then back to the locksmith before leading the other man into the kitchen.

"An hour perhaps?" The man eyed the previous lock, examining the work to see how to fix it.

"I'll double the money if you can finish it in thirty minutes," Broc said.

"Yes, sir."

Bliss almost laughed at the change in the man's demeanor. "What should we do while he's working on your front door?" Her stomach rumbled, suddenly feeling hungry after the day of controversy. She wanted to forget all the bad that happened and focus on the sales as well as her new bank account.

"Nothing I had in mind. Should we eat? An hour ago you told me you were hungry," He took the cloth from her hand to examine her face. "The swelling has gone down a little, but I still think you might have a bit of shiner tomorrow morning. How does it feel?"

She flinched at the gentle touch. "Eat, and yes, it hurts but it's nothing I can't ignore." Gently she touched her hand to the bruised flesh, wondering when he would tell her he no longer wanted to see her.

"This evening was supposed to be a celebration." He busied himself with the food then popping the cork he poured wine, seemingly unable to remove his gaze from her. "I understand you're nervous about the account, but I hope I've done everything possible to put your mind at ease."

"You have," she whispered, energy having drained from her body. "I never expected your generosity."

They ate in silence, seemingly unable to retrieve the easy conversation from before the incident. The locksmith finished then handed Broc two keys as he instructed. The payment was made and the man left.

Broc stood over her, his hand extended to her. She slipped her hand into his, wondering what he intended. "Let's take our wine outside on the deck and watch the sun dip beneath the earth."

"I think I'd like that," She smiled at his phrasing and let him help her to her feet. He wrapped an arm around her, guiding her to the couch overlooking the city and the western horizon.

A warm breeze blew off the river, ruffling the tree leaves nearby. Golden glints of lights were reflected from the buildings, casting warm shadows on the streets below. If she could let go of her fears from the earlier incident as well as the dark questions hanging over her head, the setting would be romantic.

When they sat down, he kept his arm around her, letting her relax into his body. She felt the slow steady rise and fall of his chest as he inhaled each breath of air and heard the beat of his heart so close to hers.

"How are you feeling?" he asked. "Your body still shakes. I would do anything for you to ease what's troubling you."

"I can't stop the trembling, and I can't keep the look in her eyes out of mind when she slapped me. She hates me." If he would kiss her and make love to her, perhaps then she could forget, yet she was loathe to ask when he seemed to be removed from her physically as well as mentally.

"I'm sorry about Edina. If I could rectify that, take it all away and replace it with a different memory, I would."

"What did you see in that woman to make her your mistress?" She didn't want to believe there were any similarities between the two of them, but there had to be some characteristic they shared.

He ran a soothing hand up her arm then down, resting his chin lightly on the top of her head. "For the love of God, I can't think of a thing. Perhaps when I first encountered her she wasn't like the woman you just met on the street. She was beautiful as well as willing, and that was all I cared about."

"Am I like her?" The question had been at the forefront of her mind for so long now, and she couldn't ask it with people all around them.

"Don't ever think anything like that. Well, except for the beautiful and willing part, not at all."

"But at first, before you ended things?" She didn't know how to stop thinking about that woman even though she wanted to.

"She is very pretty, and I thought she was nice. It must have been all a pretense. When I told her I was done, there was no more reason for her to lie about herself." He pushed her hair away and touched light kisses along her neck, stopping briefly at her earlobe.

"A pretense." Bliss sighed softly, needing to agree with him, even while she knew his intent at the moment. If he kept it up, his kisses would keep her mind from his past mistress. "Is anyone else going to show up and blindside me?"

"I don't think so?" His fingertip seductively followed the line of her bodice, dipping lower to investigate the exposed cleavage.

"Broc."

"Hmmm..."

It seemed he had no trouble forgetting the incident. "How many mistresses have you kept?" The answer to the inquiry was really none of her business, but truly she couldn't help posing the same question she'd asked once before.

"Why?" His lips resumed their conquest of her neck then turned their attention to her earlobes, biting then sucking. His hands toyed with the sleeves of her gown before investigating other parts of her.

She shivered with the pleasure coursing through her as he fanned the flames of desire, creating the passion he knew she would soon succumb to. He understood her body better than she did, comprehended exactly what would inflame her soul.

"I need to know how many irate women are going to come after me." Her words were barely a whisper in the night.

"No more questions." He pointed toward the horizon.

Between the few low lying clouds and the tops of the buildings vibrant colors painted the sky. Oranges, pinks combined with the summer blue as the sun spread its rays in the final descent. The day was ending and a new one would begin soon. Bliss wondered what the next one would have in store for her.

She snuggled into him, slowly learning to appreciate his strength and the feelings he invoked within. "It's beautiful. I would wish that picture to never disappear from my thoughts."

"You should paint it. I would buy a painting like that, one you painted. Hell, if I could, if you would let me, I'd buy all your paintings." Lazily, he trailed a finger up her arm, once more sending a mercuric heat coursing with her.

"Perhaps," she told him.

"Perhaps what?" he queried, picking up her wine glass and handing it to her. "Drink, you need to relax. You're still tense from this afternoon."

"Perhaps I'll let you do whatever you want." For a moment she turned in his arms. "Tonight at least." She needed to come to terms with the fact she was slowly becoming his mistress and she was allowing it to happen. Despite the number of times he denied the fact, she understood his ploy, comprehended each tiny thing he did that brought her closer to that position she meant to deny him or anyone else.

"Only tonight?" He kissed her. "What about tomorrow evening and the next then perhaps an afternoon of delight and unrequited passion?

The taste, the scent of him, evoked pleasure beyond anything she'd ever known. He didn't even have to seduce her to bring her cravings for him to a point of no turning back. "Maybe tomorrow morning too," she paused, "If you're nice to me of course."

An easy silence seemed to flow between them. "How many siblings do you have?"

The question seemed random and startled her. She gasped, inhaling a sharp bite of air, sending her into a quick bout of coughing. "Since my parents passed on, I've never felt safe. Now in your arms, I feel protected and nothing in the world can hurt me."

"Even though you're going to have a very pretty black eye in the morning. You didn't answer my questions and it seems to have made an impact. I wonder why?" he asked, gently stroking the bruise.

"Even though," she agreed, "Besides, you did protect me. Who knows what she was capable of if you hadn't been there? Do you think she would have known who I was if you weren't standing beside me?"

"Probably not, I want to make you feel safe, Bliss, but with Edina still in Glasgow, I'm afraid for you. I can't make her leave."

"Broc, you make me feel safe. I'm safe with you, and I've been so alone for the last five years. Since I met you, I don't quite understand how I survived those years after they passed."

"That's strange, I've a good friend whose parents died five years ago." He continued idly stroking her arm. "Strange that you would have the same circumstances."

"A coincidence," she murmured, wishing she hadn't let the wine and setting sun make her forget she needed to guard her tongue.

"Don't believe in coincidence," he told her, returning his attention to the bodice of her gown. The fabric seemed to be inching ever downward.

She didn't mind the easy slow seduction. Indeed, she enjoyed it more than she probably should. "Drink your wine," she told him, hoping to change the tone and the direction of their conversation.

"You too." He let a tiny drop fall on the top of her breast.

The moisture slid down her chest to pool in the valley between her breasts. With his lips he followed the drop, licking the moisture from her skin. A tiny little noise emanated from her.

She wanted to ask him if he should do that but knew she not only wanted to change the discussion to something that wouldn't give herself away, she needed the diversion he was creating.

"We can't make love out here where anyone can see us." Tenderly, she placed her hand on his cheek. "And I want to stay outside a little longer. So you must curb your baser needs." She wanted to laugh at the look he slanted her.

"Whatever you want. The bed will still be there in an hour or two, or do you want to play last night's game again? A bit of questions between the two of us?"

"No games," she murmured, nestling into him. "Just keep me safe and I'll reply to any subjects I can."

"Always," he told her, murmuring close to her ear, letting his lips and teeth explore the sensitive flesh.

But she didn't know if he would uphold his word when he found out who she was. No one liked to be lied to and forgiveness might be impossible. The hole she dug for herself was growing deeper and wider with each moment she was falling more in love with this man.

"You keep this apartment because you spend time in the city?" She really didn't know much about his everyday life or him but she was learning.

"Yes and no. I've a townhouse, too, but right now Edina lives in it." He spilled another drop of wine on her, continuing the seduction.

"Why would you do that? I don't know much now. I don't know anything about the goings on between a man and the woman he's keeping, but why would you allow her to stay there when you no longer want her for your mistress?" She would learn as much as she could.

"You pose a very good question," he told her, chuckling as he touched his tongue to another drop of wine. "You deflect very well. It's an unwritten courtesy. She can live there until she finds another protector."

"What if she never does? What then?" Bliss didn't like the idea of that woman still living in Broc's home.

"Are you jealous?" It seemed he enjoyed asking her that question.

"Not jealous, not after today even if I ever was. No, I'm angry and confused. What if she never leaves?"

"She won't stay forever. All women like her have certain cravings; some sexual, some stem from greed. I'm no longer buying her things or giving her an allowance. I believe she will want to eat sometime. All she has from me now is a shelter over her head."

"That's when you believe she'll look for someone else? When she's poverty ridden?" She didn't understand any of this. "That's why I'm glad I don't need a place to live. Independence from a man is important. I never intend to be beholden to a man."

She felt him stiffen at her words. "What if I don't want you to be independent?" he asked her, his fingers tugging on the tiny sleeves of her gown, lowering the bodice at least another fraction.

"Then you should never have helped me set up my bank account. But that wouldn't have mattered anyway." She turned then, staring into his eyes feeling as if his gaze drew her deeper under his control and power. "I would find some other way to feed and shelter myself, and I don't need or want a man to take care of me and dictate his wishes to me."

"I won't do that," he told her, his voice soft, compelling as he continued the slow caress of his fingers over her skin.

She turned back, looking at the myriad of stars that now brightened the sky. "If you see a falling star, you can make a wish," she told him. "What would you wish for?"

"For you to forget all this talk about mistresses, especially my past relationships and concentrate on us. I want you to think only about me, a bit selfish I admit but nonetheless..."

"I'll try." She would attempt to do what he was asking. That was a promise she wanted to keep. Perhaps tomorrow the effort would be easier. "What about us? Where do we go from here?"

He would make no commitments. To a man like Broc this was about sex and perhaps a little romance. He enjoyed her company and it seemed her body, but wanted or needed nothing more.

"And we both know what you would wish for. You answered last night." He stroked the top of her breast, pushing the fabric of her gown lower still.

"My answer was all wrong. That wasn't my wish." She shivered as he freed her breasts, her nipples hardening from his tender caress or the cool breeze flowing across them.

"What is your wish then?"

"That you carry me into the bedroom and make love to me."

~ * ~

Cam paced the eastern corner of the MacTavish property where he asked to meet Chelsea. Bloody hell, but the kiss last night nearly undid him and it took all his control not to toss her on the floor and take her in the tiny servants quarter on the third floor. He was not pleased with himself.

He'd never been affected as quickly or as intensely by a woman. One kiss from an inexperienced innocent sent his heart racing and all his blood pooling in his groin. She could do that to him now when he closed his eyes and remembered her sensual body pressed softly next to his, his hands bracketing her face, his lips molded against hers.

Hoping she wouldn't forget or decide not to come, he arrived early, spreading a blanket on the ground and surveying the area just to make sure there were no unwanted intruders, animals or human. He needed time alone with her, time to find out just how old she was and how she really felt about him.

He brought a picnic basket with wine and some food in case they needed something to do. That wasn't the only reason for the food. He didn't think she was eighteen yet, and he wasn't about to make love to anyone younger than that. He had little patience, but he could wait.

Cam heard the horse's hooves before he saw her through the trees. She was riding at a quick pace and when she reached the spot, she pulled on the reigns, dismounting in an easy fluid motion. He admired her even more, watching her competence and skill.

She was an accomplished horsewoman and he wasn't at all surprised. It was a well-known fact in this part of the country that the MacTavish children rode before they could walk. From the wild ride he assumed she partook of, strands of her golden blond hair had wrestled lose from the pins.

Confidently, he strode toward her, taking the reins and tying them near to his horse. "Wasn't sure if you would come. Glad to see you decided on this outcome to my proposition."

"Neither was I, sure that I would come. Seemed I couldn't resist." She appeared to look at him from beneath her dark sooty lashes. "No, my brother would have apoplexy over what I decided but you intrigue me and make me curious." One of his fingers rested against her mouth.

The gesture sent a wave of sexual need within as he watched her delicate yet innocent flirting.

She'd put makeup on for him, and the gesture was appreciated simply because it told him she cared. "Well, now that you're here, what would you like to do? Eat? Talk? Make love?" he paused, watching the rapid rise of color to her cheeks. "Or swim naked. I'm willing to bet you and your sisters have been naked in the loch over there more than once." Her bright red color darkened to an interesting shade.

She pressed her hands against her cheeks. "I..."

"So, I'm right about swimming naked." He let his hands fall back and he roared with laughter. "Someday, I promise you, we will do that together."

"I'm not going to lie to you. You're right."

"I would have liked to have seen that, no, I'd like to swim naked with you now, but that's going to have to wait for another time. I see you rode astride and you wore britches." He relished a woman who was not ruled by the dictates of society, one who made her own rules.

She shrugged small shoulders that seemed to want to hold the weight of the world. "Britches are who I am. Truth be told, I put on several riding habits before I left but decided you should see who I really am."

"But you've put powder on your face and shadow on your eyes." He touched her, couldn't help himself, "Some lip color too." He brushed a thumb across her mouth.

Her expression shuttered, she backed away a startled look on her face. "You don't like it."

"I do. Very much so." Truly, he didn't want her to think he criticized. "I appreciate all your efforts to look nice for me." Although she was beautiful without anything added.

For a moment, she looked at the ground before meeting his gaze. "Are you going to kiss me again?"

He chuckled, having planned to kiss her more than once. Indeed as many times as she would allow. "Ah, lass, do you want me to?" He brushed his knuckles against her cheek, craving her and feeling the need to do so much more than kiss.

Her cheeks colored and he noticed how her tiny pink tongue swept across her lips. "It's a very pretty day. Should we go for a walk?"

"You deflect well." He held out his arm and she placed her hand there. "Where would you like to go?"

"I've no idea. Is there a path of some sort?" She pushed hair from her eyes as she seemed to look over the area.

The laughter he felt settled in his belly. "Just ones the sheep and the goats take. Shall we follow one and see where it goes?" He set his hand on top hers, relishing the way they seemed to fit so perfectly together.

"If you want," she whispered. "Is the basket safe over there?"

He felt the slight trembling of her body as he pulled her closer to him. She was nervous and truly he didn't know how to set about remedying that. "Perhaps we should just sit and talk. I've questions for you as I'm sure you have some for me."

She nodded then, looking to the blanket spread on the ground then back to him. "Ah, lass, I'm not going to ravage you. At least not today." And he felt sure the longer he put off kissing her the longer she's be a tight bundle of nerves.

"I didn't think..." She licked her lips again then indignantly, "I didn't think you would," she paused, "ravage me."

He needed to put an end to the discussion before it got out of hand, needing to know if she was serious about courting him. Turning her and placing his hands on her shoulders, he studied her. She looked apprehensive and nervous, but her eyes flashed with what he hoped was passion and desire. He wanted to fan those flames and find out if she would burn beneath his touch.

"Kiss me, sweet one," he told her, his hands now bracketing her face. He bent so close he felt the whisper of her breath against him. The scent of mint hovered in the air.

She moistened her lips again, "I thought..." Her eyes closed for a moment and when she opened them, he knew desire flashed in their depths.

"That I would do everything? Have you forgotten your first lesson so soon?" His inquiry seemed to create a memory.

"No." She was shaking her head and he lowered his head close enough to her so her lips brushed across his.

"You need to place your lips on mine, touch them with your tongue. Do you remember or was last night so long ago all memory of our kisses have been lost to you?"

It seemed she didn't have an answer, instead she brought his face closer to hers. Their lips met, she did as he told her, swept her tongue across his mouth. The touch so innocent and hesitant, he nearly lost control. He opened his mouth, drawing her tongue deep inside his. Touching, exploring, he deepened the kiss, understanding she would give him whatever he asked. The tiny sounds rippling from the back of her throat told him, she was invested. He pulled away.

She touched his face, "Cam..." she whispered. "I... Did I?"

"You were perfect." He didn't think she should say anything more, at least not right now, not until he got his unruly body into some semblance of control. "Let's sit." With her hand in his, he led her to the blanket.

"Wine?" he asked as he pulled the bottle from the basket. Watching her, wishing he could see inside her head, he poured them both a glass.

"I've never had spirits of any kind." She accepted the drink from him. "Flynt won't let us drink at least not until we turn eighteen."

That answered one of his questions. What he had to ask now had him impatient and praying it would not be too much longer. "Try it. Your brother isn't here."

She laughed softly, sipping, "Thank goodness."

Thank goodness indeed, thank his lucky stars or he'd most likely be a dead man if her brother knew what was going on beneath his nose. "Do you like the wine?"

She nodded several times, downing the rest of it as it were water. Holding her glass out for more, "Please?"

He obliged and filled the glass again, "Chelsea, when is your birthday?"

She plucked at her dress, "Why?"

"Because you need to be eighteen before your brother will allow anyone to court you, let alone me."

"October eighth. You want to court me?"

"Two months," he murmured, groaning. He was hoping it would be a matter of days not months.

Chapter Six

Broc dropped Bliss at her house before heading home. She told him she wanted to paint the sunset they witnessed the previous night before the scene vanished from her memory. The painting would be his, at least that's what she told him before they kissed goodbye.

His main goal this afternoon while she was occupied with her art was to get Edina completely out of his life once and for all. While they were still in the city, Broc sent word to his solicitor to meet him at his home in the country. The sooner he sold the house the sooner Edina would be forced to find someone else to pay her way. Thoughts of the altercation at the market place left him shaking with fury.

Then later this evening he agreed to meet the bad boys for some fun and relaxation. It seemed they missed his company. If truth be told in the past weeks he'd been with Bliss, he outgrew their camaraderie, needing something more substantial and lasting.

Another warm August day loomed in front of him. By the time he reached his home, dark clouds materialized on the horizon, a brisk wind filling the trees and sending the long grass in the meadow swaying. So much for the heat, it seemed the afternoon and evening would cool off quickly.

He picked up his pace, meaning to get home before the sky opened up and let loose the barrage of water that seemed to be threatening in the distance. A smile crossed his face as he remembered the first day he met Bliss and the sky did that very thing. Luckily they were able to reach his stables before either of them was soaked to the skin.

They shared their first kiss that day, and he knew even before that moment he craved more of Bliss than he could claim at that moment. One kiss with his sweet Bliss was not enough to last a few hours let alone a lifetime. Now he didn't understand his feeling, confusion seemed to swirl in his head where it concerned Bliss and his future relationship with her. Everything he understood and accepted about his life had been turned upside down.

What did he want?

What he did know was that he should figure it out soon, recalling also he never took precautions with Bliss. When he made love to her all rational thought flew from his head. Even now as his muddled brain tried to decide what he wanted, she could be carrying his child.

Strangely the thought thrilled him and he wasn't sure he understood why, never having sired a child with any of the women he'd been with. He rode into the stables closer to his home, the main stables for the Wallace estate. Dismounting, he handed the reins to the stable boy.

"Take care of him," he told the boy as he sauntered purposely toward the house, hoping Conroy, his solicitor, had already arrived.

"Yes, sir."

Slapping his riding gloves against his thigh, he strode to the house just as rain sluiced from the heavens. He broke into a run, taking the porch steps two at a time until he stood beneath the roof, laughing. The run left him exhilarated and pleased.

Stopping to shake the rain off his jacket before he entered, he was satisfied to see his solicitor sitting in the parlor, looking bored and slightly annoyed. Well, it wasn't his fault he had to have a couple of kisses from Bliss before he left her for the day. Somehow over this short time, he'd become used to sleeping with her and he was sure he'd have a devil of a time falling asleep tonight without her wrapped up in his arms.

"Conroy," Broc held his hand out in greeting. "See you got my message. Glad to see you could make it."

"Good day," he said, "Came as soon as I could. Thought you'd be here waiting for me though."

"You been here long?" Broc asked. Hanging his coat and hat on the stand by the door, he strode to the sideboard. Nothing was going to change his mood, not today. "Brandy?"

Conroy chuckled, "Only about fifteen minutes and I'd love a brandy then you can tell me about the urgency of this meeting. It seems it might have waited until your next trip into town."

Broc poured the drinks, mulling over everything he meant to say to Conroy. He understood how imperative this meeting was. Edina needed to be out of his life and Bliss' and it had to be done now.

"How are you doing? Probably should plan on waiting until the storm passes before you head back to town. This won't take very long. I know exactly what needs to be done and what you need to set in motion." Broc sat down on a sofa, placing an arm along the back and motioning for Conroy to drink up.

"Better when we get down to business." Conroy leaned forward, asking, "I take it this has something to do with your new mistress. What's her name? Bliss? You need to set up a new home for her."

"What do you know about Bliss?" Anger simmered inside at the mention of Bliss equated to his mistress. He didn't like the fact people were talking about her even though he understood it was natural.

"Not much, just that I heard you were seen with the lady in the bank yesterday and some type of account was set up then later you visited a gallery. So, what is it you need from me and does it involve the lady?"

If he didn't know his solicitor as well as he did, he was sure the man was searching for answers that weren't his business. "Yes and no. I want to sell the home Edina is living in, and I want you to make sure she vacates it immediately. I was willing to give her time to find another man, but she broke my trust as well as my patience and now I've no intention of giving her any more time."

Conroy sat back, his hands resting on the arms of the chair, his expression intent. "After the sale..."

"You will need to see to her eviction. I'll send a legal note through you that she must relinquish the home immediately. Hopefully, the sale won't take more than a day or two."

"But you don't believe she'll do that, vacate the property." Conroy sipped the brandy, seeming to study him. "What's the urgency if you plan on purchasing another home?"

"I know she won't leave willingly. She's given me a couple of reasons this will not be easy. Don't know why I kept her as long as I did, but I just didn't see a reason to let her go."

"And now you've a reason." Conroy thrummed his fingers on the arm of the chair. "It's only my business because in order to evict the woman, I need to know a motive, your motive. Most times you just wait until there is someone else to take care of your ex and let it go."

"She's proven to be dangerous to the new woman in my life. Yesterday at the market she threatened her. I'm not going to take any chances with Bliss' life." Vividly, Broc recalled the stunned look of pain when Edina attacked Bliss. That wasn't going to happen again.

"Did anyone witness this assault?" Conroy asked.

"A lot of people but I couldn't tell you who. There was a constable, but he told me she wouldn't be prosecuted for slapping another woman." Once again the anger and frustration ate at Broc. He wasn't used to the idea of being a victim.

Conroy set the glass on the table. "I will do what you've asked and send a message when she has removed herself from the home. Will you purchase another house for your new mistress?" he asked, "If so, where?"

"She's not my mistress. I've already bought a nearby cottage for her." He realized the inconsistencies in the words he spoke. Under the circumstances everyone would believe Bliss his mistress. She wouldn't accept that title though and would deny it forever.

"I'm not sure I understand but that's not my place. What would you like me to do with the funds when it's sold?"

"In my account." He made a mental note to switch the funds to Bliss' account once the house was purchased. Hopefully, she wouldn't realize what he'd done, what with the sale of her paintings. She would have to be the type of person who kept an exact and accurate account or her purchases as well as deposits. He smiled to himself, thoroughly enjoying giving to this woman.

"I'll send a message as soon as everything is accomplished. Good day." Conroy stood, accepting his hat and coat then peering out the window. "Do believe the storm has passed through."

Broc poured himself another brandy, settling back in his chair and slowly sipping the potent drink. His mind rambled to the beautiful lady who stole her way into his heart. She changed him and how long had he known her? Less than a month now or was it more? How would he convince her to accept everything he wanted to give her?

He closed his eyes, thinking of the way she felt between his arms when he held her, slept with her, beginning to believe he was a maudlin romantic. Somehow in this one tiny slip of a girl, he'd found heaven and he wouldn't give her up no matter who she turned out to be.

He'd almost asked Conroy to find out who Bliss was, her name, where she came from. Conroy had connections that would most assuredly turn up pertinent information about his questions. Almost asked him, but he so needed for her to tell him. What would he do with the information if he gained it? Did he dare confront Bliss with the fact he went behind her back?

Probably not and he certainly didn't want to know something she didn't feel comfortable telling him. *You might not feel comfortable with asking Conroy for help, but you need to know.* He set the drink down, letting out a long deep breath of air, trying to persevere. "Patience, old man, patience. In time you'll find out all you need to know. Until then, let Bliss feel relaxed and happy with her secret lie of omission. You can deal with any fallout later. She says she trusts you so give her time."

He closed his eyes again, tempted to ride to the cottage and spend the night with her, but he'd promised to stay away so she could finish the painting. This evening with the bad boys was not something he was looking forward to enduring even though it used to be one of the highlights of his nights.

He had nothing to talk about and less in common with any of them now that he gave up his mistress, now that he'd been with a woman that meant something to him. At this point in time all he needed to do was figure out what that something was. Last thing he needed tonight was to talk about his exploits with his long time friends.

The time had come and gone for his turn to host their weekly card games. He didn't even know when the last one was, only that he had not been there. At the window he watched the rain as it hit the ground, drumming the puddles while he made plans for tomorrow evening. He hoped Conroy beat the storm, but he doubted it.

Tomorrow afternoon, Bliss was going to meet him at the stables, not the ones that were close to the house but at his private getaway, a retreat of sorts. He had a gift for her. He could hardly wait to give it to her. A shadow down the road caught his attention. At least one of his guests was about to arrive. Still he had another place he wished he could be.

Before cook left for the evening, she made sure food and beverages were sent upstairs. He didn't exactly know why but they always played on the third floor. Perhaps it had something to do with Flynt's sisters. If he had four sisters he wouldn't want them privy to men's conversations about sex and their mistresses. A lady had to be protected and kept innocent for her future husband. He'd want to keep his female siblings as unknowing as possible until they were at least thirty.

He chuckled to himself, trying to recall if Bliss ever told him her age. She couldn't be more than twenty. Hell, she could be even younger than that. Perhaps he should have asked but he was so caught up in learning her last name and or her address he didn't think of age. Truth be told he was so enamored of her those questions always took a second seat to her seduction and the physical side of their relationship.

"Cam," he greeted his friend after the man appeared on his porch steps.

"Good to see you. Haven't been around for a while. Do I need to ask why or should I just presume you've met another woman and she's more important than your longtime friends?" Cam laughed. "Believe I might have found a woman who falls into that category too."

Broc cleared his throat and for the first time in his adult life, he didn't want to bring the woman he was seeing into the conversation with the bad boys. They would want to know why he'd been absent for the last weeks. Plausible lies swept through his head, none that he would sully his relationship with these men with false tales. For him it was the truth or as little of it as possible.

"It's not what you must think," Broc said, his voice gruff and he hoped Cam would get the hint that this topic of conversation was off limits as far as he was concerned.

"Think I do understand. As I said, I met someone too." He cleared his throat, a strange smile forming on his lips. "Actually, I've known this someone for a long time. Just never approached her before. She was way too young, and now she's only a couple months too young."

"Not mistress material?" Broc asked, thinking the same about Bliss. So why was he treating her as if she was about to become his new mistress. Truth be told he didn't know how to treat a woman in any other way. With Bliss all he wanted was to give her things as well as make her happy. Well, he craved sex with her too, but with Bliss his feelings went deeper.

"No, but she's not old enough for me to court her properly. I've got to wait two months until she's eighteen. A month and a few days now," he amended, a wistful expression in his voice.

That sparked Broc's curiosity. "You mean to court her properly?" Broc wondered what courting properly meant. It certainly wasn't seducing the woman into his arms and his bed, and it wasn't wondering if she carried his child after a month or a bit more of sleeping with her. "Don't know if I could figure out how to do that? Court someone properly."

Cam laughed, "That's why we're bad boys, but I've got less than two months now to figure it out. Unfortunately, her guardian is going to be harder to convince I'm a gentleman than the girl."

"Who is it?"

Cam ran his fingers through his hair. "Can't say, at least not until I'm actually courting her. Don't want to risk losing her before I even get a chance to woo her with my kisses and gentle caresses."

"Can a man kiss the girl he's courting?" Broc mulled over everything Cam had told him. Probably kiss but nothing more.

"Hope so, since I've already kissed her twice." Cam's devilish grin told Broc he'd probably done a little more than kiss.

"You two going to open the door?" Donal asked with Leslie standing beside him. "Getting down right cold out here."

"Flynt here yet?" Leslie asked, looking around the room as he stepped inside. "Or are we the last?"

"No," Broc said, "Should we wait for him or head on upstairs?"

"There he is." Cam pointed down the road. "He's always the last one to arrive."

With Flynt trailing behind, the men strode up the steps to the third floor. Cook had not only set out all types of delicacies and drinks, she had lit candles as well as lamps so the men could see.

"Help yourselves," Broc said as he settled onto a chair, a glass of whiskey in hand, studying the bad boys while contemplating Bliss and thinking about what they'd be doing right now if he was with her. His mind was not on cards, and before a half hour passed, he lost a sizeable amount of money. Disgusted, he tossed in his cards.

"What you thinking about?" Flynt asked, "Your new mistress. The city's all-abuzz about the beautiful lady you escorted to the bank and the gallery the other day. Seems your past mistress slapped her in the market. Good thing you could escape to the country."

"Don't have a new mistress, an old one either," he mumbled, standing and striding to the sidebar to pour another drink, looking for the time to figure out how he was going to explain the last statement. "Don't want one anymore either." For days now he'd been realizing that fact and the feelings were increasing. He just didn't know how or what to think any longer.

"Where has Broc gone and who's in his body?" Flynt joked as he drew another card.

The men around the table all laughed save Cam. Cam seemed to seriously study him, his eyes focused on him as if he could read his mind. Broc felt a bit unnerved by the scrutiny but chose to avoid a confrontation.

"It's just that I'm feeling as if there is something more in life than debauchery, womanizing and keeping mistresses on the side. I'm tired of being associated as a bad boy with all of you. Not that I didn't enjoy and sometimes bask in the title for several years." He inhaled a long deep breath of air then downed the drink he just poured before filling his glass again. All he wanted at this moment was Bliss. He craved her arms around him the feel of her beneath him when they made love.

"Come back and play," Flynt said laughing. "I want some more of your money. Don't understand why this gal's got you all tied up in knots. You're going to have to rid yourself of those feelings, you know. Can't go on the way you are."

"Think I'll pass on the cards tonight. Don't relish the thought of losing everything." He brought a plate of delicacies to the table, passing them around then he sat, leaning back and folding his hand on his belly. He'd always admired these men, enjoyed their company above everyone else. Not any longer. Now it was Bliss who was on his mind, who he craved to be with.

"So, how is the business of being a guardian to four young women going?" Donal asked, a strange glint in his eye. "I certainly wouldn't want to have that obligation, and your sisters are all so beautiful."

"Horrid, my sisters hate me and swear they'll do whatever they want, when they want. They told me they are going to please themselves not me. They are not docile as I half expected them to be," Flynt said. "The oldest can never be found and the others don't want to tell me where she is. If I didn't know better, I'd swear she's found herself a beau and won't tell me about him. But Chelsea swears she's just off doing her thing, whatever that is. Truly, I don't understand women. They are such a puzzle."

"Can't live with them and can't live without them," Cam said morosely, tossing his cards on the pile. "Seems I'm done for the night too. Just want to drink and drown my thoughts in whiskey."

"Right now I just want to bed them," Donal said, grinning yet a moment later the smile faded as if he thought better of his words. "Need to get it out of my system until I'm ready to find a woman who will give me good sons. I do believe I'll ease my frustrations in the arms of experienced and willing women until that time comes."

"Believe I've already reached that point. I've just about had any woman I've wanted since I was fourteen. Tired of the parade of ladies in my life. I'd like to find one woman who will bear my children and be there for me night and day, one who can trust me with their life as well as the other way around." Broc thought more seriously about that. Bliss didn't trust him yet, not completely and he so needed that.

"Bite your tongue, old man. What are you saying? You want to get married? You have someone in mind?" Flynt asked, reaching for the pot in the middle of the table. It seemed Donal and Leslie folded also. "You're far too young for marriage."

"Is everyone love struck except me?" Flynt asked, sitting back and sipping his brandy. "What's happened to all of you? Where have the bad boys gone?"

"Yes, I think I've met a special lady," Broc said pensively. "The main problem is that she won't tell me who she is. I don't know where she came from or her real name. She's keeping something else from me, and that doesn't sit well with me. I've never liked lies or lies of omission. What she does tell me is all true, yet it's just there are certain things she's keeping from me."

"But you're willing to continue seeing her, even wed her," Flynt said, seeming to study Broc.

"I'm trying for patience. Don't know if it's marriage I want." Broc closed his emotions to these men. He'd already said too much. What existed between Bliss and himself was just that, between the two of them. Private. He didn't know where their relationship was headed yet. What he did know was that she needed to trust him unconditionally.

"Me too," Cam muttered. "I'm feeling the same as you, friend, but I have to wait. Something tells me you've already tasted her sweet charms but..." Cam stopped short.

"We need a change of subject. I sold a ship to James Macmurra a few days back, and we settled on a contract for more ships. This year has proven to be my most prosperous yet," Broc said as he attempted to switch the attention from his relationship with Bliss to anything else.

"What about you, Flynt? Do you have your sights set on anyone special save your mistress?" Cam asked as if he hoped for some change of Flynt's mind.

"Nope, don't intend to change my life anytime soon. I'd have to meet someone very special to make any transformations in my life."

"What about your charges?" Cam asked, "Don't you think you should take a different tack where they are concerned? Try not to be the autocrat."

"I will make sure they each find someone who is the direct opposite to each of us. I will not have them courted by a bad boy or anyone like us." He gritted out, his hands fisted tightly.

"What if the bad boy is no longer one, no longer a cad or a man who wants to keep mistress? What if the man has found the woman he wants to spend the rest of his life with?" Cam asked, his expression so serious it startled Broc and started him thinking. "Would you let one of us court any of your sisters?"

"What are you saying? Of course not, none of you are good

enough..." Flynt stopped short as if he realized the tenor of his words. "Of course you all are good enough, it's just that..."

"Who is good enough?" Broc had the distinct feeling Cam fancied himself in love with one of Flynt's sisters. "Those simpering men who wait in your parlor day in and day out expecting a glimpse of one of your sisters? Waiting for a chance to steal a peck on their cheek. Do you want one of those men who will make love with most their clothes on for your sisters?"

"They aren't real men," Donal spoke up. "If I had sisters I'd never saddle them with a man who couldn't or didn't know how to give his wife a woman's pleasure. That would be like a death sentence in my book."

"You would saddle them with a man who kept mistresses on the side then?

"Don't you think a real man would give up his mistresses when they wed?" Cam asked.

"Would any of you give up your mistress?" Flynt pointed out sternly. "And giving and receiving pleasure is not all there is to a marriage."

"What else is there?" Leslie asked as he swirled the liquid in his glass, grinning lecherously. "Sex and passion is pretty damn important in a relationship, in a marriage as well as raw desire and passionate lust. I have an appetite for all of the above. A man needs to know what he's getting into before he ties the knot."

Flynt seemed to bristle at the words and Broc was tempted to laugh. What Leslie suggested went against everything Flynt was trying to do with his sisters. Rumor had it, that all the men courting her had wealth and position, a few had titles but they all lacked what Broc and his friends would describe as experience with the opposite sex.

Where sexual experience or expertise was concerned, the men courting Flynt's sister were all lacking in that capacity. Broc actually was beginning to feel sorry for Flynt's oldest sibling who was destined to a life most likely of pain when it came to the marriage bed. Perhaps as the other girls got older, Flynt would improve as a guardian.

"He's going to tell us money and title are just as important," Cam said, shrugging his broad shoulders. "We've all money but not all of us have a title. None of us would cause any woman pain. Can you say that about the men who come courting your oldest?"

"If we weren't bad boys, we'd be perfect for your sister," Donal said, a broad grin painting his handsome face. Donal was probably the best looking of all of them. His features were perfect, his body well-tuned from the boxing ring. "We are good looking," he added, posturing to make an impression.

"Courting one of us would be just like eating butter on bacon." Leslie added his thoughts to the conversation. "Wouldn't you want something like that, someone like us?"

Flynt rose from the card table, his hands resting on it. "And I would never let any of you court my sister. I would add happiness to that list of money and titles. Not one of you could make a woman happy for a lifetime."

Broc thought Flynt wrong on that score. If they were willing to change their ways and devote their lives to the women they courted and would eventually wed, the woman should be happy, contented in this lifetime. He'd truly like to see Bliss contented.

"I'll take that as an insult," Broc said with a sigh that left him wondering about his life and direction, and the right angle shift it had taken in the last month.

"Are you looking to wed anytime soon?" Flynt shot back quickly. "If I were you, I'd take what I just said as a compliment. Who among us want to be tied down and committed to a wife?"

Broc ran his hands through his hair, thinking over what Flynt just pointed out. "Not anytime soon. I believe the original plan was when I turned thirty-five. I've got a while to go until then."

"That young?" Cam asked laughing. "I'm having thoughts of marriage and commitment as we speak."

"You've a special lady in mind?" Flynt asked, seeming to grow more irritated with each passing second, waving his hands in the air as if to make a valid point and the gesture would help. "Have all of you gone daft? The bad boys are vanishing right in front of me."

"I'm not ready to settle down," Donal said, quickly downing his whiskey then pouring another. "I'm enjoying my life just the way it is, thank you."

"Neither am I," Leslie said, looking from one man to the other.

"Want to keep my freedom for a while longer, but when the right time comes or perhaps the right woman, I'm sure I could be persuaded to change my mind. I understand that I will need an heir. So, I will be looking for the perfect specimen."

"Yes, you'll feel different when the right woman steps in front of you and blindsides you. She'll change all your well-thought out plans to ones of her own and you won't even know it." Cam sat down at the card table, shuffling the cards. "Thought I had my life planned out too, just like the rest of you but now..."

"Now what?" Flynt asked.

"Now I'm not so sure. A lady caught my eye, a beautiful lady and now all I can do is think about her," Cam said, still thinking about the idea she'd willingly and purposely made him reevaluate his thoughts about marriage.

A bit of relief swept through Broc. It was nice to know another of his friends was feeling the same. Yet he still wasn't ready for a commitment even though those thoughts had filtered through his head multiple times. Yes, Bliss blindsided and confused him, baffled him in most every way imaginable. Had Bliss really done that to him, changed his plans to ones of her own. Deeper and darker thoughts settled for the first time in the back of his brain.

"Then what are you waiting for?" Broc asked. "Haven't heard you were courting anyone yet."

"That's the problem," Cam mumbled, "She's not eighteen yet."

"More cards?" Flynt asked, seeming to understand the night was not turning out the way anyone expected.

"Think I'll go home," Cam said, starting for the exit. "This conversation is a bit too private for me."

"Suddenly there's a damper on the evening," Donal said, seeming confused. "This never happened before."

"Me too, got a big day tomorrow," Leslie said.

Flynt leaned forward. "Guess it's just you and me, Broc. Care to tell me what has you so morose?"

"It's personal." Broc ran over in his mind the fledgling relationship with Bliss, unwilling to speak of it when he had no idea exactly where it was going or how he felt.

"Here's to next time," Flynt downed his glass. "See you all next week."

~ * ~

When Broc dropped Bliss off at the cottage midafternoon a couple weeks later, Bliss knew she had to tell him who she was. Actually, she had two things she needed to tell him, settling her hands on her belly. Yet just thinking about it caused her body to shake, knowing full well the news would change her life and his also.

Well, that would be tomorrow, today she would try to finish her painting of the sunset over Glasgow for him. If he set her aside, the gift would be the only and last one she ever gave him. She felt resigned but also ready for whatever fate planned for her. Humming, she wandered into her bedroom and changed her clothing into something more appropriate for painting.

There were several canvasses all ready set up. Bliss chose the largest one, thinking it would look very nice in his apartment or possibly somewhere in his home. She recalled being in his house, Deepwood, once a long time ago but she couldn't remember what it looked like. It was big though and a painting like the one she had planned always looked nice over a fireplace.

The sun began to dip behind the horizon, a small breeze beginning to cool the room. She opened up the doors and the windows, enjoying the colors roaming across the sky.

"Bliss?"

She turned, startled by the voice at her front door, her hand on her chest. "Chelsea? What are you doing...? Daryl and Lacie. I didn't expect to see any of you."

"We came to visit. Thought you could use some company and we wanted someone besides ourselves to talk to." Daryl said. "Lately, we don't see much of you."

"Where have you been," Lacie asked, stepping inside and examining the room then sounding nonchalant as well as all-knowing, said,

"With the braw Scotsman who's stolen your heart."

"Lacie, no man has stolen my heart, at least not yet. I'm not going to let that happen. It's too dangerous." She lied too easily here and decided perhaps if she swore them to silence she could tell her sisters about Broc. After all, she meant for all the truths to be out in the open a short twenty-four hours from now.

"Well, I've a braw Scotsman who is stealing my heart and I've kissed him," Chelsea said, strolling into the kitchen then searching the room as if looking for something to eat. "I'm going to make a pot of tea." Stopping, she looked over her shoulder with a huge grin for all her sisters to see. "He gave me wine too. Wouldn't Flynt just have a bout of apoplexy if he found out?"

He would indeed. When he discovered her relationship with Broc, it might be even worse. She'd kissed Broc and more, something she didn't want right away for Chelsea, but she didn't know how to broach the subject without giving her condition away. Chelsea was too young to understand love.

Perhaps she wasn't.

Bliss set the brushes in the cleaning fluid and wiping her hands on her apron she joined Chelsea in the kitchen for a cup of tea, the others following her. Painting would have to begin in a few hours if at all. She might have time in the morning, if all went well.

"You mustn't give in to whatever your man wants, Chelsea. Unless it's a kiss, you need to say no. And keep in mind that kisses can lead to other things you might not be ready for." Bliss wondered how her and Broc's relationship would have progressed if she'd said no to that first kiss. She didn't regret anything.

"Kisses are fine, that's what grandmother says," Lacie piped in as if she knew everything about courting and love making as well as the opposite sex. "I wonder what else she's talking about." Lacie searched the cupboards. "Do you have any food in here?"

"If you're lucky there might be some day old bread in the far cupboard," Bliss said indifferently. She didn't want to tell anyone she'd been away for two days and for the second time she had spent the night with Broc in his apartment.

"You do know you need to eat," Lacie said as she found a few things to bring to the table. "This is incredibly ridiculous, and you haven't even been home to steal food from the main house.

"Been busy painting and I don't look on it as stealing. If I lived there, I'd be eating more than I take with me when I visit," Bliss said. "Want to give that one away when it's finished."

"You're not going to sell it? Why ever not? You'd make a small fortune on that one," Daryl said as she stepped back examining it.

"No." Bliss was shaking her head, smiling at her sisters. "This one's for a certain man I've come to care a lot about." She guessed she just gave away some of her secrets about the man she'd been seeing then she waited for their reaction.

"I think I know who you're seeing. It's all starting to make sense now," Lacie said a smug expression on her face. "When I talk to him, he's always looking wistfully in the direction of the cottage.

"If you've a guess, I won't confirm or deny anything, and I'd just as soon you keep your guesses to yourself."

"You haven't told him who you are." Her words sounded more like an accusation than anything else. "When I was ten I fancied myself in love with him. He's always so patient with me even when I ask him too many questions I know he doesn't want to answer. But last time I talked to him he told me he was frustrated and confused."

Bliss inhaled a long deep breath, wondering where all this was going and why she felt as if her life as she knew it was about to end. Well it might not end tonight, but tomorrow when she told Broc her last name...she didn't have any idea what would happen. "I'm telling him tomorrow and I might come to regret the words. Heaven knows it's about time he found out, and the truth has to come from me or the repercussions are going to be much worse."

"You think he's going to leave you?" Daryl asked. "Then he doesn't love you very much."

"It's what Flynt would do if he found out the woman he was seeing was also the sister of one of his best friends." Chelsea said. "Cam says when he comes to court me Flynt can't run him off and that he'll sit in the parlor everyday until Flynt gives in."

"Cam can do that but do you honestly think he'll be satisfied sitting in our parlor and just talking to you?" Bliss asked, holding her cup of tea while contemplating her younger sister over the rim. "You know his reputation as well as the rest of us, and that's just so not like the bad boys. They are men of action not given to sitting around doing nothing but wait."

"What I believe is that we'll find a way to be together without Flynt as our chaperone. I saw him a few days ago at the eastern edge of our property, and while he wasn't a perfect gentleman, he didn't take advantage of me." Chelsea smoothed her skirts, a whimsical smile on her face.

"Is that when he kissed you?" Lacie asked, looking upward, "I'd like to be kissed again, but I don't seem to have any prospects."

"You're not telling us everything," Bliss said. "Who has kissed you?"

Lacie looked away for a moment then with a soft sigh, "If you all must know, Leslie." Then she looked to Chelsea, "I suppose that's when Cam kissed you the first time.

"Yes, it was when we snuck up to the third floor," Chelsea agreed. "He found me in one of the bedrooms."

"Leslie found me in the stables. Said he was going to teach me a lesson about spying on men," Lacie said, laughing then touching her lips as if she remembered the kiss.

"You're too young to be kissing men," Daryl accused as if she had just become Lacie's guardian.

"I'm only one year younger than you," Lacie shot back. "And you're not too young?"

"Of course I am but like you there are no prospects lined up waiting for my attentions. Seems we've got some waiting and wishing to do," she laughed, "hoping our brother isn't so rigid as time progresses."

"Then Donal didn't kiss you the other night?" Chelsea asked.

"He did," Daryl admitted reluctantly. "And I liked it and I told him as much. He laughed then and told me I'd have to wait until I was older for more."

"Why did Cam want to meet you?" Bliss asked, thinking there was more to her sister's story than she was sharing. "He must have had a good reason."

Chelsea looked away for a few seconds before returning her attention to the group. "The other night we," she motioned at her sisters, "we snuck up the back stairs to the third floor and their card game. I wanted to see Cam but didn't have any idea what I was getting into. Before then he never really paid me any attention, at least not that I noticed."

"It was just a prank on our brother," Lacie interrupted, "I didn't think it was anything more until Leslie ran after me. I ducked outside and ran for the stables. Of course he caught up to me. When I peeked around a stall to see if he was gone, he was still there, leaning against the opposite stall arms crossed in front of him a smug expression on his devilishly handsome face. My heart nearly stopped."

"And Cam ran after me, followed me down the hall. Told the others exactly what he was about," Chelsea said.

"He didn't? He wasn't?" Bliss tried to hide her smile. "Is that what you wanted, Chelsea? For Cam to catch you?"

Chelsea's face turned a beautiful shade of red as she looked away in an attempt to avoid eye contact and more scrutiny. "I didn't know they would see us but I suspected. My heart beat so hard I thought it would jump out of my chest. And when he saw me I felt as if he could see into my soul. I knew then I wanted him to catch me, but I had no idea what would happen next or how fast I should run. I needed to look like I didn't want him to find me."

"What did happen? Did you allow him liberties when he finally caught up to you?" Bliss asked, understanding that if Chelsea was as attracted to Cam as she was to Broc then she allowed him to do anything he chose and he wouldn't stop with just a kiss.

It seemed Chelsea needed to think over what she was going to say then, "He touched my breast. Bliss, I felt things I never thought possible. How could that be?"

"It's just the way of things," Bliss said with a shrug and a grin. "They, the bad boys, know how to make you want them, how to seduce you to their way of thinking. Everything they do feels so deliciously heavenly. Chelsea, you have to be very careful not to give in to everything he does."

"Like you did," Lacie tilted her head sideways seeming to study her older sister.

"Like I did," Bliss agreed, understanding the real truth would come out all too soon, "I don't want any of you to find yourselves with child and unwed. You have to learn how to say no to your men no matter what they do or how much you believe you want them to do it." She paused, "Oh dear, I'm not sure any of that made sense."

"So, you are pregnant," Chelsea said, frown lines forming on her beautiful features. "I guess you know first hand what you're talking about."

"I haven't told him yet. It's going to be a big day tomorrow. I might need you all for solace after it's all said and done. I wouldn't be surprised if I never see him again, but I can't go on like we are. He means too much to me. We've made vows to be honest with each other, and I've lied by omission too many times to count. Of course, he knows I've omitted certain truths and he has been patient, but I can't do it, just can't go on like this any longer."

Chelsea reached toward her, placing her hands over hers. "We will stand by you no matter what happens. If he sends you away and doesn't want to see you again, he's a damn fool and not worthy of your love."

"You don't know what Flynt will do to you or your man for that matter."

"I almost fear Flynt's reaction more if he leaves me. It will only serve to prove Flynt right. He's only had mistresses, and he's started treating me as one. I've told him no, that I will never be bought for sex, but he continues to do just what pleases him as if I have no say in the matter."

"Men are so obtuse," Lacie said with a huge sigh that sounded much older than her real age.

Bliss and Chelsea both laughed then, "Of course, you're right. They do tend to be insensitive as well as overbearing. Even when I knew I wanted Cam to kiss me, it seemed he had to control everything. The first time I kissed him, while he asked me if I wanted the kiss, he was still in command of the moment. He took charge of every little detail."

"That's the way he is. Even though he knows I've a mind of my own because I've spoken up numerous times, he has to have everything done his way. In some respects it's endearing but... if I'm going to be happy and if he doesn't leave me tomorrow, I'm going to have to convince him to listen more to me. My needs and wishes are important also."

"You really are going to tell him," Chelsea said as if she too were resigned to the inevitable fall out if that actually happened. "Are you sure that's what you want?"

"I plan on it. Just hope I've the courage and strength. I almost told him yesterday on our ride home from Glasgow, but I couldn't seem to get the words out of my mouth. Kept making up excuses in my head not to tell him." She let out a long sigh that seemed to go nowhere, "There is the chance I won't be brave enough tomorrow, but I know in my heart if I don't speak up, I'm just putting off the inevitable. I guess I need to know one way or the other if he will forgive me. My lies are huge."

"I don't envy you. This could be so hard," Chelsea said, reaching out to comfort Bliss, covering her hand with hers. "At least Cam knows who I am and he is dealing with the fallout the best he knows how. Flynt will make our courtship a challenge but I think we can overcome anything he tosses our way. I believe Cam is a man who will fight back too if Flynt gets obnoxious."

"Anybody home," a small voice asked.

Bliss rose, striding into the main room to see a woman she didn't know standing just inside the doorway. "Who are you?" All kinds of thoughts filled her head including ones of Edina, but this wasn't the woman who slapped her. This was not Broc's mistress, unless of course he had another one.

A tall and very slim redheaded woman stood framed in the doorway, her hands clasped tightly together. She was exquisite and Bliss didn't believe she'd ever seen anyone quite so lovely, perfect. Her clothes were well made and fit her as if they had been made for her except the fact they were dirty and one sleeve was torn.

She moistened her lips before saying anything then looking at the floor, she spoke so quietly Bliss barely heard, "I don't know." She cleared her throat then a bit louder. "I don't know who I am."

"You don't know who you are?" Bliss wrapped an arm around the woman, leading her into the room, yet wondering if this were some con meant to get at her family or if she'd been sent by Edina. "Chelsea, will you get her a cup of tea? Are you hungry? Why don't you sit down and tell us everything you do know. There has to be something."

"No." The woman was shaking her head, her hands clasped tightly in front of her then inhaling a huge gulp of air, "Don't think I am," she paused, "hungry. But I should be. I've not eaten for a while."

"Where did you come from?" Bliss realized suddenly how Broc must have felt when she didn't answer those few simple questions he asked of her. She'd refused to tell him who she was or where she came from, denying him so many choices. He should have been able to make decisions about her from the first moment she'd met him. Selfish, she'd been very selfish where he was concerned, thinking only of herself. Bliss was suddenly ashamed of what she'd done.

"A carriage, there was an accident a ways down the road and no one but me survived," she told them, her voice barely a whisper in the night. "I was tossed around inside and when the vehicle finally came to a stop, I was able to climb out the door. That's all I remember, nothing more. I don't understand why I remember the accident and nothing before that."

"Our brains work in strange ways when there is trauma of any sort. I've heard of people forgetting their past lives and having to start fresh with just what they knew from that moment forward," Chelsea said.

"How far down the road did it happen? I can send someone to locate the carriage and find out if anyone survived," Bliss said, realizing the woman's hands were trembling. Her entire body was shaking.

"I don't know," she answered again, moving her head back and forth her voice thin a reedy sound emanating. "I've been walking a long time. My feet..."

Needing to discover more details, Bliss asked, wishing she didn't have to prod the woman. "How long is a long time?"

Chelsea handed the lady the tea, "I started walking yesterday morning, and I've been on the road ever since. Of course I've stopped a few times when my feet hurt so bad I didn't think I could take another step or when I was so exhausted I couldn't move any farther. Last night I slept under some bushes until the sun came up."

Bliss nodded to Lacie, "Go home and have Flynt send someone to locate the carriage. Quickly now, we need answers." Then she turned her attention to the lady, "What direction?"

"West, I think. I was walking away from the setting sun." She grabbed Bliss' hands. "I need to know who I am."

"Truly, you have no idea?" Chelsea asked, seemingly in disbelief. "Did you hit your head on something?"

"I don't think so," the woman said. "I'm so tired all I want is to lie down and go to sleep. It's almost as if I don't want to wake up and face the reality of the next day or even the next second."

"Well, there had to be some trauma." Chelsea said indignantly, seeming to ignore the woman's distress, "One doesn't just lose their memory unless something awful happens to them."

The woman was shrugging her slim shoulders, tears slipping suddenly from her eyes. "I need to find out who I am." Then she looked up, realization in her features, "You think I'm lying. I'm not."

"What if she's in some kind of trouble?" Daryl asked. "What if someone wants to hurt her and what if we don't keep her safe? What then? How do you think you'll feel if she dies?"

"Then we need to protect her," Lacie said, seeming to be the only real voice of reason in the group. "Flynt will make sure nothing happens to her. He's good at things like that."

"He better not take advantage of her," Daryl said, appearing to appreciate how beautiful this lady was.

"Of course Flynt would do nothing of the sort." But Bliss wasn't all that sure. Flynt was a man who was accustomed to getting what he wanted and he loved beautiful women. This lady was breathtaking even with the scratches and smudges of dirt on her face.

"She needs a name," Lacie said, hands on her hips as if she meant to punctuate her statement. "At least until she can remember her real name."

"What if I never remember?" the lady said, wiping tears from her eyes with the backs of her hand.

"Let's call her Fern," Lacie said, "I like that name. If I ever have a little girl, I'm going to name her Fern."

"Is Fern alright with you?" Bliss asked then, "Lacie, did you girls ride here or take the wagon?"

"We rode," she said. "I'll get going. I know you want me to get Flynt, but I don't think there's any hurry. He won't be home."

"Will you go to the stables then and get the cart ready? We're going to take her to the house and see what Flynt has to say about her staying here with us. She's going to need a roof over her head, and if she is in some kind of trouble, we can't risk putting her in even more danger by sending her away."

"And if Flynt is away, we'll just wait until tomorrow morning. It will be better that way. We can have her completely ensconced in our home by the time he returns. He will have a devil of a time turning her away."

"I remember the ocean," she whispered softly. "I think I was on a ship, but I don't know... I keep hearing the sound of seagulls and the lapping of waves."

"You don't know where you came from?" Bliss asked. "Well, you've a Scottish accent, so you must come from right here. Makes perfect sense even when it doesn't. The question is why were you travelling on a ship and from where if you are from Scotland?"

Once again she brushed the tears away with the back of her hand, sniffing at the same time. "It's horrible not knowing anything about yourself." Her hands trembled when she picked up the teacup to take a sip.

"It must be terribly frightening. I can only try to imagine how you must feel." Bliss was very nearly in tears listening to Fern's story or lack of a story. "I promise we'll discover who you are. You will remember."

"The wagon's ready, we'll follow behind on our horses," Lacie said, poking her head through the door. "Won't Flynt be surprised?"

"It will give him something else to think about when he finds out who I've been seeing," Bliss murmured softly, wishing what she just said wasn't real.

"And sleeping with," Chelsea added.

"Come, we'll take you somewhere where you'll be safe. Flynt, our brother will protect you and we'll do everything in our power to find out who you are," Daryl said.

The sky had darkened when they reached the house and few lights lit the front rooms. To Bliss the house had an eerie appearance, and she shivered slightly as she ushered Fern up the front steps into the home.

"Flynt isn't here just as we suspected." Chelsea said, searching the room for him as if she hoped he'd come striding from his office or the library when he heard the noise.

"It's his weekly night out with the bad boys," Daryl said matter of factly, hands on her hips as if she wondered why no one else thought of it.

"Bad boys?" Fern asked, her voice wavering with what seemed like another bout of fear. "Your brother is bad?"

Bliss waved her hand in the air grinning. "It's just what they call themselves, nothing to worry about at all. They are not really bad. We need to put her in a room upstairs. For now she's a guest so why don't you get her settled in my room since I'm not going to be sleeping there anytime soon."

"If things go badly for you tomorrow, you might be home sooner than you think," Chelsea said, concern touched her words.

Bliss was moved by that apprehension from her sister but, "No, even if he doesn't want to see me any longer, I won't come home. Don't want to. I've had a touch of independence, and the last place I want is to be under our brother's thumb, so to speak, and in easy reach of the suitors he brings here to court me."

"Is this Flynt such an autocrat then? He sounds absolutely horrible," Fern said, seemingly concerned that she just sidestepped one problem to land into another one that might be worse.

"Only when it comes to his sisters and their nonexistent beaus," Lacie said, grinning cheekily "I can talk about it since I don't have one yet, a beau. Even though I know who I want to court me when I turn eighteen. How old are you?"

"A beau," Fern looked puzzled. "I think I had a fiancé or a man who would claim me as his, but I don't recall how old I am."

"A fiancé...a man who would claim you," Bliss murmured. "Then he'll undoubtedly be looking for you, and what does claim you mean?"

Fern was shaking her head then backing further into the room. "He can't find me. Whatever happens I don't want him to discover where I am. Don't want to marry him. He doesn't love me and I don't love him." Her breaths came in uneven spurts and she'd turned pale.

"Why ever do you think that?" Daryl asked, tilting her head as if trying to figure out the puzzle in front of them.

"I don't know why or what," her voice a high wail, "but what I do know is that whoever he is, I don't want him to discover my whereabouts. He can't. He just can't. Something bad will happen to me if he does learn where I am."

"Alright then," Bliss said, wrapping an arm around her and leading the way up the stairs to her room. "For the time being we won't let anyone except Flynt know where you are."

With Fern finally settled in the bedroom and hopefully asleep, the girls gathered in the parlor.

"We should stay up until Flynt gets home," Lacie pointed out. "He needs to understand what we did and why. He will have to be assured she isn't a deceptive woman searching for an easy way into his life."

"That may be all well and good, but it's dark and if my, er, my friend still wants me tomorrow if he ever finds out I rode home in the middle of the night, he'll be furious. So, I have to leave now and I'm going to let the rest of you figure this all out without me."

Bliss left the girls behind, hoping for the best and wondering how her brother would handle the situation. She was sure Flynt would be skeptical and doubtful, but spending any time with Fern could be very convincing.

It seemed she jumped at every little sound that ruffled through the bushes and trees. She expected some unwanted fiancé to jump out from behind shadows created by the moonlight and trees and haul her away.

When she finally pulled up in front of the cottage, her nerves twinged at every little sound, her heart thundering in her chest. Putting the horse in the stable then taking care of it seemed too exhausting to describe.

The walk from the stable to the house seemed to take an eternity and her nerves skipped at every noise. Inside the cottage, she closed and locked the door, finally sitting on the couch and pouring herself some of the whiskey Broc left behind.

Slowly, she sipped the drink, thinking she should finish the painting. but she was unable to stand up. Suddenly, all the possible repercussions of her plans for tomorrow crashed down on her. She inhaled a swift breath, a cry of pain emanating from her a sense of impending doom swamping her.

Her thoughts were darker than ever before, and the premonition wafting through her sent her off the chair and to her knees. She had to see him tomorrow even though she knew it would be end of their fledgling relationship. He had told her he would always trust her and stand by her despite her secret.

But...

He wouldn't.

~ * ~

Flynt strode into his home and after slipping out of his raingear and hat, he poured himself a brandy. He sat down, stretching his legs in front of him and thinking. His friends, particularly Cam and Broc, said a lot of things to make him reconsider the direction of his life as well as his future. His plans for the future were changing right in front of his eyes, wanting things he understood all too well. He knew someday he'd be in the same place in his life, but he didn't expect that for several more years.

He had to meet someone first.

Closing his eyes, he groaned softly, thinking of Maura, his mistress. She was sweet and saw to his every need whenever he called, but she wasn't someone he'd ever wed. Maura didn't reach into his soul or call to his heart. He didn't need her any way, but he used her sexually and she seemed to enjoy his company. He gave her everything she asked for and treated her well.

"Flynt?"

"What?" Despite his reluctance, he opened his eyes to see Chelsea sitting down next to him a glass of whiskey in her hand.

"I need to talk to you."

"You shouldn't be drinking. You're not eighteen." He didn't have the strength or the will to argue with his sister, and he was sure this would end up in some type of disagreement. "Why are you still up?"

"Guess I drew the lucky straw. We need to talk and I don't want you to be surprised in the morning." She grimaced when she downed the potent drink. "How do you drink this stuff? Bliss too?"

"What kind of surprise can't wait until morning?" he asked sitting up a little straighter, curiosity drawing him toward the possible enlightenment that couldn't wait a few more hours. This wasn't at all like his sister.

"We have a house guest, a lady." Chelsea's voice was hesitant, but as she continued it grew stronger. "Flynt, she doesn't know who she is or where she came from. She couldn't remember anything about herself, nothing, nothing at all, not even her name."

"Nothing, you say." he paused to pour another drink then always the skeptic, "I've a hard time believing the girl doesn't remember a thing."

"Well, she seems honest and clearly in distress over her situation. I don't think we have anything to worry about." Chelsea looked toward the stairs.

"She's in the house? This house? She could rob us blind."

Chelsea nodded her head a few times while moistening her lips before shaking her head. "She won't rob us blind. I promise. We couldn't throw her out, just leave her to wander around in the dark and the rain with nowhere to go. Could we?" Chelsea seemed unsure of herself. "We needed to be charitable."

"It's not raining."

"Well the weather can change."

"Where is she?" Suddenly, Flynt was wide-awake, nerves on edge, stripped raw. He didn't want to tell Chelsea that was a foolish thing to do. Hell, he might have done the same thing and woke up in the morning to find the household in a shambles, everything gone.

"Up stairs in Bliss' room."

Flynt stood and after taking one step, turned, confused, "Then where the hell is Bliss?"

"In the cottage house. She wanted to paint tonight so she stayed there."

Bliss would have to change her ways and stay home. He was handing over the deed to the cottage. He meant to give it to Broc tomorrow. All the necessary papers had been drawn up. Now all that was needed was his signature. The cottage was no longer hers to come and go as she pleased. He should have sold it a long time ago and he would have had fewer problems with Bliss.

"Where are you going?" Chelsea trailed behind Flynt, who was striding up the steps two at a time. "Don't hurt her. I really think she's probably telling the truth. She is so genuine." Then she added, "Fern's the most beautiful woman I've ever seen."

"I won't hurt her, but if she isn't convincing then she will be set out in the dark. She can always stay in the stables if she doesn't like the dark. It's dry there and warm." He stopped at her door before looking to Chelsea. "Go to bed. What did you say her name was?"

"She doesn't know her real name. Lacie wanted to call her Fern. So for now Fern is her name."

"Bloody hell, what kind of name is Fern?" He chuckled inwardly. It was just like Lacie to come up with such an outlandish name. "Go to bed, Chelsea. Don't come out no matter what you hear."

It seemed she started to object then turned away.

Before Flynt confronted Fern, he watched Chelsea walk to her room and go inside. Then he turned his attention to the problem in Bliss' bedroom. He pushed open the door and let it hit the wall with a loud bang.

The woman bolted to a sitting position, covers drawn to her chin. Flynt didn't say anything, because he didn't have words. He was gazing at the most beautiful woman he'd ever encountered. All his condemning words caught and stalled in the back of his throat.

At the moment her ginger hair was in a tangled disarray across her shoulders and her blue eyes, highlighted by the moonlight slanting across her face, were wide with what Flynt could only describe as terror. She's a good little actress, better than he expected. He'd give her a lot of credit for that.

He strode to her bedside and sat down, reaching out to hold a strand of hair between his fingers. The tiny lock felt like silken fire in his hand, and he suddenly wondered what it would feel like wrapped around his naked body. Hell, that would be one way to make sure she stayed put in this bed, sleep with her.

"Who are you and what do you want with my family?" He rested a hand on her shoulder, feeling the trembling of her body beneath his touch as she pushed against the backboard, trying to get away from him. His first thought was that her fear was very tangible and real.

"Nothing." She inhaled a swift distressed breath of air. "I don't know who I am. Fern, they wanted to call me Fern. That's all I know."

"You're a good actress." He smiled softly, hoping to ease her into his fold enough so she would tell him more about herself. "What aren't you telling me? Out with it before I toss you out on your sweet little arse."

"I would tell you everything if I knew anything else. I was in an accident and I walked here. Who are you?" She sounded demanding as if she was used to giving orders.

"The man who's going to put you out on your backside if you don't tell me who you are. The truth now." Lightly he trailed a finger along her neck. "Do you like this? Is this what you wanted all along, someone to take care of you, protect you and give you pretty baubles?"

At his words she slapped his hand away, her eyes blazing with passion or fear. Flynt couldn't be sure. Then her demeanor changed.

"Don't touch me," she whispered, her voice desperate and weak. "Please don't touch me."

Her last words stopped him, as he drew away from her. "You're truly afraid. Why?"

She was shaking her head over and over, her eyes seeming to glaze over then she held herself still, too still and her breathing slowed so it was barely perceptible. Concern for her leapt to the forefront of his brain.

He didn't want to back away from her, thinking this was just another ploy to convince him she told the truth when indeed she was lying. Stubbornly, he held his ground, waiting for her to look at him and actually see him through the fog that seemed to be clouding her vision.

When her expression didn't change he rose, striding away from her, "I'm not going to hurt you, Fern. Just stop looking as if you're in some fantasy land far away."

He sat in a chair near the bed but not so close he would keep her in that trance-like state. Realizing that either way, if she was lying or if she really didn't know who she was, she would not recover from this daze unless he left the room or kept his distance.

After some time she slowly opened her eyes, "I'm sorry. It's just that... I don't know."

"If I truly terrified you, there is nothing to be sorry for. I apologize but I'd also like to know what happened here. Why did you draw into a shell so deep you couldn't see or respond?"

She grimaced, her hands plucking at the covers as if they would save her from something intangible. "I'll go. I don't want to put you and your sisters out or complicate anything for you. I don't know why but I understand that men don't like women who tell them no or deny them."

Flynt experienced a sudden an inexplicable change of heart despite his unwillingness to do so. He didn't want to believe this woman was capable of anything nefarious. Yet what just happened seemed so real and convincing.

He backed from the room, "I'm going to lock you in, Fern. Just a precaution. I will see you tomorrow morning and we can talk about this and what will happen to you."

Chapter Seven

When Broc woke the next morning, the sky was clear and a brilliant shade of blue, a shade matching Bliss' eyes. He anticipated this afternoon was going to be difficult but hopefully worth the delay. The surprise for Bliss waited for her in the loft in the stables and he meant to enjoy Bliss' sweet charms and perhaps speak of their future.

Making her his mistress was the last thing she'd wanted, but it seemed impossible to keep going in this way unless they both made a few concessions. He'd vowed years ago he'd never wed, at least not until an heir was necessary. Admittedly Bliss would have to make the biggest decisions and changes. Her concessions were appropriate and mandatory for their relationship to continue.

Hours until he could meet her ticked by slowly, too slowly for his frame of mind. The scene was set, however, and champagne along with little delicacies made by his cook were in the loft waiting for them. He stepped back after spreading the quilts on the straw. Having always wanted to make love here, he was thrilled now that the woman in his arms would be Bliss. Somehow this moment together with her seemed like the first time with her, and he needed to make this time magical.

On the trip from Glasgow a few days before, he thought there was something she wanted to tell him, but she didn't say anything and thoughts in his head piqued his curiosity. Perhaps today she would trust him, truly trust him with all her secrets.

Sounds of hoof beats echoed up the ladder to the loft. His heart in his throat, he peered over the edge. She was here. He inhaled a long deep breath, knowing this moment might change their lives indefinitely.

"Bliss," he said, taking the ladder rungs two at a time before jumping half the distance to the floor, eager to reach her. "I'm so glad to see you."

Broc pulled her into his arms, twirling in a circle and kissing her at the same time. She responded sweetly and passionately to his advances, his desire escalating with the feel of her lips on his and her body melded against his. When he finally set her on the ground, they were both breathing heavily.

"I missed you." She placed her hand on his chest, staring into his eyes. "I've so much I want to tell you today. It seems as if a lifetime has passed since we first met. We have to talk before..."

"You're right. We have to talk but not until later. For now I've plans for us. I'll take care of your horse. Go on up and take a look around." Unable to help himself, he kissed her again, this time just a fleeting brush across the lips, but he grinned knowing they would share so much more in a few short minutes.

"I'll wait." She stood back, her hands clasped beneath her chin, her eyes bright with hunger. She was staring at him and he realized how much he enjoyed her intense scrutiny, knowing she liked what she saw.

He didn't reply, understood he needed to be with her intimately; craved her, all of her so much he could barely contain himself. She was his for now and he prayed for always. He would have to make sure he gave her everything she wanted, needed, desired and more if possible.

Minutes later, he held her hand, rubbing gentle circles on her wrists before motioning for her to start up the ladder. She looked to him then the ladder, inhaling a deep breath tentative it seemed to make the ascent. He didn't think she was afraid of the climb, but something seemed to hold her back.

"What is it?" he asked, trying to give encouragement. This evening meant too much to him to have anything stand in his way. If necessary, he'd carry her to the loft.

"Nothing that can't wait, as you said we can talk about it later but it has to be today. Just don't know if I have the necessary courage." She touched his lips. Her fingertips soft, compelled him to act now and climb the ladder afterwards. But she turned away, proceeding as he'd bade up the ladder.

He followed behind her, entranced by the few glimpses of her ankle and leg he was provided. It wasn't anything he hadn't seen before and nothing he wasn't going to view many more times, but everything about Bliss stole his breath and made him feel as if he was an untried schoolboy, finding she completed him in a manner he didn't understand and was having a difficult time accepting.

At the top, he helped her scale the remaining distance then over the edge. "I've something to show you. A present if you like." He was eager and accountably excited to show her.

To Broc it seemed she bristled a tiny bit, "I don't need gifts from you. Don't want them either. I've told you I won't be your mistress, not today, not ever. Perhaps we should talk now."

But he was sure in time, soon in fact, she would succumb to his desire or perhaps it was more of a fantasy. "The gift is from the heart, nothing that I bought for you. Come." He held out his hand for her, "I think you'll like it. Trust me in this. I promise you will like this gift. Still, you can refuse it if that is what you want."

For a moment she held back, her body and mind seeming to resist his plea. "If you insist." She placed her hand in his and he felt the fine trembling beneath his hand.

"Don't be nervous. Truly you'll love this present." He led the way to the back of the loft where a mother cat and four tiny kittens were nursing.

Her expression changed from wary to one that was soft and compelling, "You could have told me."

"And ruin the surprise? Never." He crouched beside the cats and patted a spot beside him. "I want to give you one of these kitties if you like. You can choose any one."

"Really?" She sat beside him, picking up a tiny black and white animal. "Can I have this one?"

"As soon as they're old enough to leave their mother." He settled a hand on her shoulder, massaging gently the tight muscles and once more wondered at the way her body shook. "You need to relax. What has you so tense and nervous? You've never been quite like this before."

"I'm trying." She touched his hand with hers. "I don't understand. Like you said in a way this feels like the first time and there are so many things we need to talk about."

"Are you suddenly afraid of me or what we are going to do in a few minutes?" he asked, hoping the answer would be no.

"Not afraid." She set the kitten back with the others.

Her grimace didn't give him the reassurance he needed or craved. "A glass of champagne perhaps and a tiny delicacy cook prepared might ease your anxieties."

"Perhaps," she agreed, "I am nervous but it's not about making love with you. It's more about the things..."

He cut her words off with a kiss, her lips gently responding. When he drew away from her, she was breathing heavily, "Then don't worry about anything, just enjoy and feel. We've hours ahead of us. We can share our thoughts then, and for now we'll share our feelings. First things first; eat, drink, make love then talk."

Inhaling a long unsteady breath of air, Bliss nodded in seeming agreement. "Perhaps that is a good idea. I can do that but then I've really have some things that need saying today before I lose my courage."

"As do I," he told her, sweeping her into his arms and carrying her to where he laid out the blankets and set up the mini table of drinks and edibles. "Remember, I want only the best for you, for both of us."

Pouring her a glass of the bubbling liquid, he watched as she sipped, seeming to enjoy it. "I didn't get the sunset finished but I will. It's yours you know. Well, if you want it." She gazed at him over the rim of the crystal, her eyes seeming to shimmer, catching the sunrays cascading around them in the loft.

Sitting down next to her and pulling her against him, the sweet scent of vanilla and orange assailed him. "Of course I would like the painting if you're willing to give up the commission. I could also pay you for it."

"A gift should not be paid for."

He ran his fingers through her hair, divesting it of all its pins. As the strands slowly unwound from the coif she created earlier that day, the silken strands fell across her shoulders and breasts. Picking up a lock, he wondered at the way it felt against his flesh. He'd never felt anything so tantalizing and provocative.

She tried to turn in his arms, but he needed to savor this moment, cherish each second he enjoyed with her in his embrace. Bliss meant everything to him. In short, she'd become such an integral part of his life he thought he might die if he couldn't have her, keeping her to himself.

"More champagne?" she asked, holding her glass high. "Are we celebrating something?"

"I will explain everything," he paused, "later after we're both sated and I'm holding you—your nakedness against me."

He moved her hair to one side, kissing and exploring the length of her neck, up then down, felt the shiver of her longing as it poured through her and into him, felt the flames of desire lick at him. Heat coursed within, a molten inferno that only her body beneath his could quench.

He was consumed by her.

Her hands gripped his thighs, tightening then loosening in a pulsing cadence. She seemed to move to an ancient rhythm, primal and compelling. He sucked air, understanding he needed to prolong this as long as possible. She ran her hands the length of his thighs then back.

"Are you trying to torture me," she asked, her words a whispered caresses in the silent air, sunlight dancing across the light, spreading its warmth.

"Just give you more sweetly painful pleasure, promised agony and bliss at the same time. I want you to know how it feels to be thoroughly and completely loved by me. I crave for you to need me so much you'll never let me go." He knew he needed to wake up next to her more days than not, understood he didn't want to live his life without her close to him. But first, he had to convince her of something she denied with all her heart.

"I do believe you already accomplished that feat. Do you crave me so much you'll never let me go?"

Her query caught him by surprise. Earlier, he'd thought as much, and now he was sure there was nothing that would ever tear them apart, nothing that could separate them.

"I do," he said, suddenly realizing his admission was something he'd never believed he could say truthfully.

When his hands travelled to the fastenings of her riding habit, she let her head fall back, giving him better access, seeming to enjoy the slowness of the seduction. "Thank you," she told him.

144

"For what," he asked as he freed each tiny button.

"I wasn't going to wear anything you gave me, but after I finally gave in to my worst fears and wore the dress, I figured it wouldn't matter. So, thank you for your kindness."

One tiny step at a time, and soon she'd accept the title of mistress. He was making headway. "You're welcome," he told her as the bodice was open and all that separated her skin from his exploration was the thin chemise she wore. "No corset?"

"Not today. Today I wanted to have as little between us as possible." Tiny sounds fluttered from the back of her throat as he touched her breasts and brought her nipples to sudden hard peaks.

She was so responsive, seemed to explode with such delectable passion with the smallest touch. "Raise your arms. I want nothing between us, nothing at all."

"You should let me remove your shirt. It's hardly fair you get to look at me while you remain clothed. I want to discover every inch of you." She turned slightly, one breast pushing against the fabric of his shirt, teasing him.

Throwing his head back, he laughed then quickly he removed the shirt, "Now it's your turn. Raise your arms."

Bliss obeyed then there was nothing between them, so little to protect her from his gaze or his touch. Her breasts pushed against him and his groan of desire caught him by surprise. He'd meant to seduce her slowly and with finesse not the other way around.

Her nimble fingers found the fastenings of his doeskins. He pulled off his boots and rising, he disrobed, standing before her wearing nothing at all. "I want to see all of you now. Take your skirt off." He smiled as he watched her shimmy from the remaining garments.

"You're amazing," she told him, reaching out as if she needed to touch him, but as much as he craved that gentle caress, he wanted to prolong the inevitable sensual release that would come too soon.

"And you're the most beautiful, enchanting, bewitching woman I've ever had the pleasure of knowing intimately or otherwise." He came down between her legs, spreading them as he stretched out on the quilt, the length of his body caressing hers.

"What are you going to do?" she asked, her voice trembling once more but this time he didn't believe it was nerves causing the shaking but raw and so delectable passion and desire for him.

"I need to see you all of you, then I want to taste you, every part that makes you so special to love." He kissed and nibbled his way up one leg until he reached her core, the private folds that he was the only man to know and taste. She bequeathed her virginity to him and that meant the world to him.

With his tongue, he caressed the tiny bud and reveled in the cry of pleasure she blessed him with. This was what loving a woman should be like every day, and he knew he wanted to share this with her every possible moment they could be together.

"Broc." His name whispered from her lips, and his mouth discovered more places, intimate and private spaces, hidden parts of her only he knew. Her fingers wound tightly into his hair as her hips began to move, asking him to drive inside her, become a part of her and release himself into her.

He would oblige soon, but not too soon. One climax was not enough. This much of Bliss would never quench his thirst for her. Tonight he meant for it to never end even though he understood it would.

He lifted his head to see her, to gaze into her eyes where the truth of everything she was feeling could be read. Her eyes were closed to him and he wouldn't abide that. "Open your eyes, my sweet Bliss *mo mhilse*. I want to watch you when you reach that sweetly painful pleasure that will be yours time and again tonight and forever afterwards until we grow old."

She did and he watched as shudders of pure sensations, sweet sensations encompassed her body while he continued to stroke that tiny nubin that could bring her this overwhelming and intense pleasure. Sounds came from her throat, tiny sounds encompassing his heart and rewarding him for his patience.

He'd never been in love before and if this was the way if felt, he wanted to die in its sweet bliss.

When she settled and her body eased into a more tranquil state, one he didn't mean to last too long, he stroked her arm, ran his hands across her breasts, delighting once more in the sudden and swift hardening of her nipples as well as another sigh of blissful pleasure.

"Broc, I can barely breathe, hardly move and still you didn't..." Her words trailed away as he brought her hand to his shaft, her fingers hesitantly closing around him. She looked at him, wide eyed and questioning.

"Touch me, kiss me, do whatever you like?" he paused then, "As soon as you can move again." But he sat up, her hand falling away, and poured each another drink. "Fortification for the rest of the evening. Drink up."

She gazed into his eyes then directed her focus on his aroused heavy flesh then she smiled. "And you need to lie down again."

Seeming to remember another time, she poured small drops of champagne on his shaft before licking the tiny drops off. He groaned low and rough. Yes, this was surely deeply painful pleasure as he leapt at her every touch and each soft caress of her lips against him. Bloody hell, but what demon had he just released? One he wanted to encounter for the rest of his life. She would never bore him, always fascinate.

"*Mo mhilse* Bliss, you unman me." He felt the pressure of his release grow. "Put your hand on me." And it seemed she understood what he wanted as she tightened her fingers and moved with him. His cry reverberated throughout the stable as he reached his climax, his seed spilling and his body finally shuddering to a slow stop.

She touched his seed, seemingly fascinated by it. "This is what makes a baby." Her words were half statement and half question and filled with what sounded like fascination to him.

"It is." And once again he was reminded he'd never taken precautions with her and never would. What he knew was that he didn't want a bastard for a son or daughter. So where did that leave them? He had no answer to the question and supposed he would have to take this moment-by-moment.

Then she looked away, a dark cloud seeming to possess her features for a brief moment. "A miracle."

Indeed, but he no longer wanted to dwell on babies or miracles. He craved to be inside her, to feel her walls clench and unclench around him as they moved with the rhythm he set. He wanted to join with her and become a part of her.

"Two can play at your game." He dribbled champagne across her breasts, licking and sucking, using his tongue to play with the droplets and tease her to an aroused state of no return.

"You can't mean to do this again?" Her voice rasped and he was delighted by the impact he had upon her.

"I've not been inside you yet," he told her. "I've not truly made love to you until we are a part of each other."

The discovery between them, lips, teeth tongue played out until both were addicted with the need they created in each other. Tiny sounds, mewling noises, all told him she needed him. Her hips rose to meet his.

He thrust inside her before holding still enjoying the feelings sweeping through her and into him. She was molten lava, a heat so intense he could not endure it forever. He had to have her, finish this at least for the moment before they could begin again.

"My sweet Bliss," he cried out her name as they reached that deliciously raw tempest where their passion exploded in a magical dance.

Then she lay beneath him, so still he almost wondered if she lived. A soft sheen covered her body as he idly trailed his fingers across her collarbone as well as other places. "Broc, you've unraveled me and unnerved me one tiny strand at a time. If there were a fire, I would not be able to move."

"Never worry. If there was a fire, I would carry you out."

Time seemed to tick by as they lay together in each other's arms content for the moment with the silence. Thoughts raced through his head, dark thoughts of fears as well as denials, lies and unspoken truths. He tried to shake off the shadows in his heart and soul, tried to remove the terror that was suddenly growing inside of impending doom.

"Champagne?" she asked, sitting up and for the first time, failing to bring the quilt up to cover her. "I'm parched, my throat so very dry I can barely swallow. Perhaps we can talk now."

He poured them both drinks. They drank. They ate. Then, settling into an easy camaraderie, a friendship he hoped they would enjoy for a lifetime, she lay against him, her head placed on his chest, his arm wrapped around her. The moment seemed natural and right.

"Do you want to make love again, or talk?" he asked, chuckling softly as he ran a fingertip across her collarbone and enjoyed it as her body responded. As far as he was concerned they could talk later. He wanted to enjoy her now. "You're such a delight."

She looked down, not embarrassed then smiled at him. "I do believe I could do the same to you. Make you rise to the occasion." She nearly laughed but it seemed she held back a bit, unsure of herself.

"I like it when you talk dirty. Are you a naughty girl?" He stroked her cheek before leaning against the crate he'd set up for their food and drink.

"Was I talking dirty?" she asked, pretending innocence. "If I was, I learned it from you."

"I've created a monster, one I never want to leave me." He closed his eyes, still thinking of ways to approach the topic of mistress. Changing the mood and the tranquility of this priceless time was not on his agenda this moment.

While he was sure she'd come to terms with the gifts, the title would be another matter all together. While he had purchased the cottage for her, he'd yet to tell her, so she couldn't accept his generosity. Yet he knew she needed to understand what drove him.

He could well imagine her slowly explaining to him she had the funds to buy any home she wanted. And it was true; he checked the account in their name just the other day and it was growing. She didn't need to feel beholden to him, but he didn't think of the purchase in that manner. All he wanted was to make her happy, and he enjoyed giving.

None of that made a difference, he still desired to take care of her and protect her. Perhaps this conversation would be better left to another day. Ruining this day and these enchanting moments with an argument was not something he craved.

"I would never leave you," she said, gently stroking his lips with her tongue, her breast tantalizing him as they delicately touched his chest.

"Brazen hussy, you mean you've regained your strength and want to play again?" he asked, laughing while at the same time realizing he could put off the mistress discussion for a little bit longer, at least until they made love again, even another day.

"Oh, look," it seemed she sought a diversion also.

"At what?" he strained to see what she was speaking of, wishing she'd redirect her tongue to its last location.

"The kitty? It's come to see what we've been up to." She laughed as she snuggled into his arms, the kitten she'd picked out settling on his chest and making himself right at home.

"Do you feel as good as I do?" he questioned, hoping the answer would appease him as he stroked the kitten. "I think I could stay here forever, at least all night."

"Most likely better." Her voice was nearly a purr and he wondered if she understood how seductive she was. "But I think we'd run out of food so forever is probably not a good idea."

"Once again your innocence and sweetness unmans me. I've never met a woman as precious as you or one I can hold so close to my heart."

With that statement, she looked away but not before he noticed a whimsical expression a fleeting moment of disbelief, confusion and quite possible regret. "I'm not so sweet."

"It's all in the way a person sees another and what or who they have to compare with. In my case, the other women I've known have all been far from innocent. While they might have been sweet, they only cared about one person and that person was themselves."

"You really can't blame them. I'm astute enough to realize men will take advantage of a situation. I don't need anything monetary from you and that in itself makes me different."

"But not me. I'd never take advantage of you." He laughed, idly running a fingertip along her arm then back down.

"Not you...but if you want to be honest, I can agree with what you just said all you like, but I don't know how you've treated others. I can only say how you've treated me."

"Have I done well by you? Do you have any complaints?" he asked, simply pushing for more compliments yet needing an affirmative from her.

"Have I treated you well?" It seemed she turned the topic back on him and he wanted to think he'd done his best with her and she was happy.

"I asked first." He wasn't sure what to say. She treated him so well he was totally and completely enamored with her, never wanting to give her up for any secrets she might be holding.

"So far. As to date you've not pushed me to be or do anything that I don't want. As to the future, I can't say." She sounded as if she wanted to run away from here as if she was remembering their mistress discussions.

He held her possessively then, once again wishing for the day and night to never end. Outside the sun was beginning to set. Soft golden rays filtered in through the window of the barn. Soon it would be too dark for her to ride home and he couldn't let her go, not right now, not this evening. She would have to stay the night with him, in his home.

That changed things somehow.

This moment, the intimacy felt right and good, and he needed to hang onto it forever. Besides she told him there were things she needed to talk about with him as he had things to say to her. It seemed they both put the moment off as long as they could.

Holding her after their lovemaking was magical. She lightly trailed her fingertip along his chest. The sensations gentle, almost erotic but...

Broc laughed, stopping her hand. Then he chuckled again when she continued. "Bliss, that tickles."

With her head still on his chest, she continued then she looked at him, grinning. "A braw Scotsman, ticklish. Whoever heard of such a thing?" She laughed and the sound touched him intimately.

"You need to stop, Bliss."

But she continued, giggling at him as he suddenly returned the favor, tickling her as they both laughed and he rolled on top of her, holding her hands on either side of her head.

"What if I don't want to?" She moistened her lips, watching him, her eyes simmering with passion.

"Then I will have to find a new diversion for your attentions." His lips closed over hers, his tongue tracing the seam of her lips imploring her to open for him.

"You're going to make love to me again?" she asked when he pulled slightly away.

"Only if you want me to." He kissed gently as he kept the weight of his body from pressing into her. "Do you want me, Bliss? Tell me how much you want me."

"Aye, I want you. I want you so much I don't have the words."

"Bliss! Bloody hell where are you?"

~ * ~

"Flynt?" She breathed against Broc's lips, terrified and confused. This couldn't be happening.

"Bloody eyes." Broc rose from her, standing naked in the waning light. "How do you know Flynt?" It seemed he pulled his doeskins on and tossed her the second quilt before she could blink. His voice harsh, he turned to her, his words commanding obedience, "Cover up now."

He started for the ladder, but Flynt stood on the loft before Broc could waylay her brother. Then Flynt hit him. The sound of the punch resonated in the dark silence. Foreboding deep and resolute filled her soul. She had waited too long. Broc reeled backwards, staggering a few feet before rubbing his jaw, confusion etched in his face.

Her hands flew to her mouth, shocked by Flynt's actions. Her future with Broc vanished in that second when their gazes met and the realization of who she was settled into his head. *I was going to tell you. Her heart reached out to him, imploring him not to jump to conclusions. You seduced me from my intentions.*

Broc looked to her, his smile grim yet determined before turning back to confront her brother. "I'll give you that one. Don't try it again."

"Bliss, come with me now or you will regret it." The anger in Flynt's voice sent a wave of tremors down her spine.

"I already do." Her voice wavered on a desperate thin note.

She couldn't possibly get up this instant and go with him. She was shaking her head, praying for some divine miracle to swoop down and remove her from the scene. "No." It seemed no miracles were forthcoming nor was there any divine intervention on the horizon.

Broc stepped between her and her brother, his hands fisted at his sides, seeming determined at least at this moment to defend her. "Bliss is not going anywhere with you." Flynt still hovered at the edge of the loft, Broc blocking her brother's view of her.

"The hell she isn't," Flynt tried to step around Broc. "Try and stop me."

Flynt still hovered at the edge of the loft, Broc continued blocking her brother's entrance into their one time sanctuary. "Bliss is naked," he said, his voice shaking with the fury rippling across his muscles. "Is that what you want? To haul your sister out of here unclothed and embarrassed?"

Flynt stepped back a moment, seeming to let that statement hit home. "I'll wait for her below. And you're coming with me, Bliss."

Truly she didn't know what to say or how to interact with these two men who seemed to have gone crazy. They were both so angry, she couldn't breathe thinking about them and knowing she in part caused this.

"No, you won't," Broc's voice rose again. "I will see Bliss home and if we need to talk then we will. Bliss and I will sort this out and let you know what we plan. Other than waiting for our decision, you have no part in this. It is out of your hands."

"I'm her guardian, so I have the ultimate decision," Flynt grit out even while he seemed to concede and backed down the ladder.

With shaking hands Bliss held the cover up to her chin, wishing both men would vanish, at least until she could control her shattered nerves. All her plans to tell Broc the truth today evaporated with the setting sun and the untimely arrival of her brother. She had lost the opportunity. Good intentions be damned. Now she would never get the chance to prove herself to the man she loved. He would never know she had been willing to give him all her trust.

They were achingly alone now, the time bittersweet and empty. The sound of Flynt leaving ricocheted up the ladder. Tears she would give anything to hold back slipped from her eyes, turning into gigantic sobs of despair and longing for something that just slipped through her hands. Angrily, she pushed them away, determined to tell him... Tell him what? He knew everything.

Everything except for the baby.

He turned then the fury emanating from him that had been directed at Flynt was now focused on her. "Why didn't you tell me?" He wasn't looking at her but fastening his britches and slipping on his shirt before he sat down to pull on his flawlessly shined boots.

She made a slight noncommittal gesture with her head, still wishing she could disappear into the night or he would, either one would be preferable to this, this stilted compressed atmosphere. "I enjoyed your company too much at first. You made me feel like a woman, as if I counted somehow as if I was important to someone. You played my body as well as mind as if..." She moistened her lips trying to think of something to say. "As if I was your personal instrument. And you gave me an excuse to leave the house when Flynt asked men to come calling. I couldn't bear seeing those men or thinking about their hands touching me."

"You lied to me about something too important to overlook." It seemed he was focused on one thing and he didn't listen, at least not to what she told him only to what wasn't said.

"And at the time, you didn't seem to care, if I recall correctly. I never told you an untruth, explained to you there were things about me I didn't want you to know. You wanted me, I guess more than the omissions."

"No, you just neglected the most important piece of information I needed," he grit out, his fury seeming to grow with each second as it ticked by. "You lied about something more important to me than I could ever explain, and I don't think I can ever forgive you that transgression."

"And you've never lied to me?" she asked, unsure at the moment about her question but needing to put it forward.

"Only about things you shouldn't know, that could hurt you."

"Then we are not so different." Even though she pointed out that fact she understood, he still wasn't listening to her.

His hands were fisted at his sides, pacing the loft floor, seeming to refuse to look at her.

"I was going to tell you today. At least that was my plan when I arrived here. My name was what I wanted to talk to you about, my family, things you deserved to know." She inhaled a long shaky breath, forcing an unfelt courage to the forefront of her mind. "If you knew the truth about me, I was sure you'd leave me. Once you touched me, made love to me, I didn't have the courage to let you go."

"Bloody hell, I made love to my best friend's sister out of wedlock. Men don't do that. They don't take advantage of innocent girls of friendships." Seemingly frustrated he ran his fingers through his hair until it seemed to stand on end.

She bristled when he said those words. "You didn't seem to care when you broke through..."

"I thought you were nobody." He waved his hand in the air, pacing once more, seemingly beside himself with anger. "When I looked at you, I lost all sense of control. How the bloody hell was I supposed to stop myself when you were...are so seductive? I lost the ability to think every time I looked at you."

She cringed at his words, which confirmed her worst suspicions. If he had known about her, they would have never been together and she wouldn't have the memories or the child growing inside her. The baby was a part of him that would stay with her forever even when he wouldn't.

She didn't regret that.

She cringed against the backrest he constructed for this afternoon, her stomach rolling, waves of nausea keeping her immobile. "And now that I'm somebody you don't want anything to do with me? Is that it? I was perfectly fine to seduce when I was nobody." She shouldn't have said those words, but she couldn't help herself from tossing his words back to him.

He stopped, turning to her, his face strained with fury and other emotions she couldn't define, would never understand. She'd never seen him look like this, so angry, so furious he could barely speak.

"Get dressed, Bliss. I can't deal with this or the repercussions concerning you right now, but I will see you home. You cannot ride to the cottage alone in the dark." He left her then, with her clothes spread out around her, and disappeared to the floor below.

She pushed hair from her eyes, her body seeming to freeze for a moment. She couldn't move, could only feel the sickness invading her. Closing her eyes, she prayed the sensations would pass and she'd be able to think again. Minutes seemed to tick by until her stomach calmed and it appeared she could breathe once more.

Frantic Broc would come after her, she started searching for all the smaller pieces of clothing. Then slowly, meticulously as if the world had ended for her, she dressed but her hands and legs shook so hard, she didn't think she could climb down the ladder. She sat down, her head in her hands, silent sobs wrenching from her.

"Don't let him see you this way." She breathed slowly in then out then in again, repeating the process. "You have to be strong. He can never learn how he just devastated you, even though you knew it would happen when the truth emerged."

Gaining some control of her emotions, she inhaled several ragged deep breaths of air before she started for the ladder. She had trouble, her skirt catching on her boots and tripping her up. Finally, she touched solid ground.

On the stable floor Broc held the reins of her horse as well as his own. He remained silent and stoic while she mounted.

"I don't want you to ride with me," she said bitterly, knowing even as she said the words he once again wouldn't listen, no matter what he would follow. "I'm sorry I'm such a disappointment to you since I'm no longer a nobody. Truth be told, I don't ever want to see you again Broc Wallace. So you can just turn your horse around and ride to your home." Pain and anger swept through her. What she'd seen in him she didn't know yet those very thoughts were a lie.

She loved him more than life itself.

When she mounted and he handed her the reins, she didn't wait for him. She spurred her horse forward, galloping from the stables and the remnants of her broken life, never intending to look back. He would have to get down on his knees and beg her forgiveness if he ever wanted it. She didn't see him changing his mind though.

She prayed he wouldn't follow, but he did, it seemed keeping his distance. She heard the steady beat of his stallion's hooves. Turning her horse in the direction of the cottage, she meant to seek solace in the small home she'd begun to call her own.

Memories would have to be enough because she was sure this would be the last she would see of Broc, unless he found out about the child growing in her womb. Back at the cottage, she led her horse into the stable, groomed the little mare then left. Striding to the front door, she noticed him, sitting his horse, apathetic and mute, watching, still guarding her from some unknown evil.

He waited for her outside her door. "Make sure you lock it."

Before she closed the door, "Will I see you tomorrow?" she asked, knowing the answer would be no and unsure she wanted to see the odious man who gave her the most pleasure she'd ever known and now abandoned her because of her name.

"I have to think about what happened. This is not easy for me, knowing I betrayed a friend with his sister and knowing, too, the circumstance could have been avoided with a simple truth," he told her then turned his stallion and she watched him disappear into the darkness.

Didn't he betray her too?

For the longest time she watched the road, hoping he would think better of his sudden departure and turn his horse around, wishing he would beg her forgiveness and they could go on as before.

Only silence greeted her, nothing more. Inside the house, she locked all the doors before sitting down in front of the unfinished painting of the sunset. Thinking she could never put paint to the canvas again, she stared at it for the longest time. He could rot in hell before she completed this one.

The clock ticked then chimed nine times. Bliss rested her hands on her belly, recognizing Broc would never know he was a father because she didn't want him back out of sympathy or because she carried his child. The only way she would accept Broc Wallace into her life again was if he wanted her.

And he didn't.

She poured and drank brandy until she couldn't think and the world seemed to be a fuzzy haze. Her stomach threatened to erupt before nausea and dizziness enveloped her. She raced to the basin and emptied her belly's contents, groaning as she retched a second time then a third.

Kneeling, she rested her head on a forearm, waiting for the next bout. She wasn't disappointed though or perhaps she was. It seemed the retching continued until there was nothing left inside her. At the sink she dipped a rag in cool water, placing the cloth on her head.

"I hope I don't have this to look forward to for the next seven months," she murmured. Bliss curled up on the bed, clothes on then pulled a cover over her. The scent of Broc on the sheets lingered, reminding her of all she lost. She'd followed one avenue of her grandmother's advice and lived in the moment. Perhaps in hindsight she should have been more prudent.

Did she regret any of it? No, the moments with this man would stay in her heart for the rest of her life as would their child.

She must have dozed. When she opened her eyes, Flynt stood over the bed. "You look horrible."

She pulled the quilt over her head, reveling in the way the cover blocked both the sun and Flynt from her view. "Go away."

"You're coming home with me." His tone of voice was the one that told her she better not argue with him.

Beneath the covers, "Go to the devil," she mumbled and wondered if he heard her. The cursing and the pacing answered that question. "I'm not going anywhere with the likes of you. You've ruined my life."

"Bloody hell, Bliss, you can't stay here by yourself. The place has Broc's hands written all over it, even the size of this bed." His words thundered in her pounding head. Unable to help herself, she moaned.

Suddenly, she bolted from the bed to the basin, filling it again. Flynt stood over her then, offering no solace, not that her big brother knew how to do anything like that. The girls always had each other for that sort of thing.

"Drank too much I see. You can't drown your sorrows in brandy. Come home with me, Bliss. You'll be happier there."

At this time she wouldn't be happy anywhere. "How did you get in? I locked the doors."

"One was open. Now, you can change your clothes when we get home, come along." He turned to leave as if she would follow along mindlessly at his command.

The moment was here and she had no alternative but to confront him. "I'm staying here, at this cottage, and if you physically take me to the house, I will return when you're not looking. You can't keep me somewhere I don't want to be unless you tie me up."

"Broc owns this cottage now."

She closed her eyes, another gift he wasn't going to tell her about. "I'll pay him rent and you know I have the money."

"You're too damn stubborn for your own good but you can try. I doubt if he'll rent this to you." Seemingly resigned to her ultimatum, Flynt left with no more coercion or argument.

"Thank God and the only person I want to see is Broc, and at the same time he's the last person I want to see." Then she looked at herself in a mirror and changed her mind. If Broc saw her now, he would turn tail and run. Well, he'd already done just that so what did it matter even though he created this problem they now shared. Somehow, she would have to find a way to tell him about the child, their child.

At the moment, nothing mattered.

Her head pounding, she slowly heated water for a bath. When the tub was filled, she stripped and lowered herself into the warm water. Closing her eyes, she tried to recall everything that had been said between the two of them yesterday. Only pain and frustration rose in her mind.

He was gone from her life and there was nothing she could do, no argument she could present to bring him back to her. In his mind, he was a cad of the worst sort for deceiving Flynt. After all, he slept with the sister of his best friend because he thought she was a nobody. Well, she wasn't a nobody. *Go to hell Broc Wallace.* She deserved happiness with someone besides one of those loathsome men her brother thought would suit her. She'd rather be celibate the rest of her life.

She closed her eyes, dreaming of the wonderful moments with Broc, moments that would now be only memories.

Ach, stop feeling sorry for yourself, lass. You've a wee baron to bring into this world and dwelling in misery would not be wise. Take charge like you know you can do.

She finished bathing and dressing, finally wrapping her damp hair into a tight bun on top of her head. In the kitchen she rummaged through the nearly empty cupboards for something to eat. Stale bread and a chunk of cheese would have to do. She heated water to a boil before making a cup of tea.

In the sitting room she settled into a chair in front of Broc's sunset and decided she would finish the painting. Then one more aspect of her relationship with him would end when she sold it and it was out of her past for good. She could put that part of her life in the background and get on with her future since there was nothing left in the present.

A few hours later she was still painting, stopping to put her hands on the small of her back and stretch when she heard horse hooves. At first her heart and mind jumped to the notion Broc was coming to see her, but it was Chelsea who called out at the door.

"Will you let me in?" She was knocking incessantly and Bliss wished Flynt had not locked the door behind him when he left this morning. "I need to talk to you and find out what happened. Flynt is acting as if all hell broke loose yesterday, and you're in the middle of it."

"I'm not fine, Chelsea, anything but fine. I don't know what you know but..." She set the brush down before starting for the door. "I'm not sure I'm up to talking about any of this."

"All I know is that Flynt arrived home angrier than I've ever seen him, swearing and pacing. Then I heard Broc's name intertwined with yours. What the devil happened? I understand you don't want to talk about anything but this is me, Chelsea. You might feel better if you have someone to tell the story too, and you know I'm a good listener."

"The whole world I suppose will know by this time tomorrow or before by the way gossips spread the word." Bliss didn't want to think about yesterday or today. She wanted to forget anything happened. She needed to live in the here and now.

"Is Broc your lover?" Chelsea's eyes were wide with wonder or confusion. "He's Flynt's..."

"Best friend?" Bliss shrugged as nonchalantly as she could manage. "Guess the bad boys club continues. When he found out my last name, Broc left me just as I believed he would all along. Angry. Frustrated. I think he felt used by me. Perhaps that was the truth, but he used me too."

"What are you going to do?"

"Truly, Chelsea, I don't know. Keep going. Finish this painting and sell it. When I'm done, I never want to see this sunset or think about it again. I want to find some peace and quiet in my life. Broc is out of my future for good and forever, and I don't want to think about him again."

Yet she knew she'd think of Broc every time she looked at his son or daughter or when she grew big with his child and she felt the babe kick. She should tell him about the baby. If he ever came to see her she would, maybe. If she could find the words to get past the fact he liked her better as a nobody.

"So, you're not going to..."

"He made it clear that we are done. Broc and his feelings come before mine or ours. I thought we... I believed he cared for, me at least a little bit. I actually thought for a few seconds he cared for me enough he would try to work through the problems. But I was so wrong." She pushed the threatening tears to the back of her mind again. Intending to never, ever shed another drop for Broc Wallace.

"Alright then, are you going to stay in this home? I think Broc bought it from Flynt. I heard him with the solicitor the other day when they were finalizing the papers," Chelsea said.

"Would he toss me out now that he owns the cottage? Was that his intention from the beginning?" In her despair she was questioning everything about her relationship with the self-proclaimed bad boy. No, it was just one more ploy in his attempt to make her his mistress even if she didn't accept the title.

"I think he bought it for you. He said it was for his soon to be mistress. Could that be true? I know I shouldn't listen in on other people's conversations, but I couldn't help myself."

That information put everything in a new light. Was he going to ask her or tell her she was his mistress last night? He said he had something he needed to talk to her about. Or was the purchase for someone else? He couldn't be that cruel to take her home away. At this point in time, she had no idea who he was or what part she actually played in his life.

"I told him numerous times I'd never be his or any man's mistress." From the first day and the first conversations she voiced her opinion, and still he never listened.

"Men..."

Chelsea said with knowledge that went beyond her years and with a very feminine shrug, "Men only hear what they want. Anything else we say they think of as being trivial or a waste of their time then they continue on the path they deem to be the right one."

"And how are you and Cam?" Bliss so needed to change the subject, needed to dwell on someone besides herself.

Another shrug and a purse of her lips, "I haven't seen him in the longest of time. I guess he means it when he says he won't see me until I turn eighteen. That's only a couple of weeks away now."

"So, eighteen is the magic number?" Bliss nearly laughed as the darkness momentarily left her crushed heart. She turned nineteen in August and there was no celebration because of Broc in her life. She never thought twice about the lack of acknowledgment.

"You have nearly a month to wait. Any temptations to ride to his home and spy on him?" Bliss asked, deciding if the inclination was there, she would go with her sister. A diversion was so necessary.

"Too many inclinations to count, but I'm going to trust him. Besides we've no commitments as yet." Chelsea laughed outright then suddenly sobered. "I miss him and truly I barely know Cam. And now I wonder about his intentions. Was he sincere or did he just want a few kisses?"

"Cam seems up front and honest. Whatever you do, don't keep any secrets from him," Bliss said, plucking at her skirts, thinking about Broc even though she wanted nothing to do with him at the moment.

"So, did Broc seem sincere and honest? I suppose he must have or you wouldn't have spent a couple months with him." Chelsea reminded her. "He betrayed your trust too."

"He did seem to be that way, and I suppose he thought the same of me. I guess now that we know each other better we understand things differently." So much for changing the discussion to Chelsea.

"When you take the painting into the city, if you want company, I'll go with you," Chelsea volunteered. "You shouldn't go alone."

"I need to find out if Broc will do the same with my account as Flynt did. He stole my money, you know."

"No." Chelsea covered her mouth with her hands, clearly in shock. "He stole your money?"

"He did. Flynt took every penny and told me it was for my own good."

"Why?"

"Because he's a man and he couldn't stand the fact I could ever be independent from him or any other member of the male species." Bliss didn't understand but now she meant to tell Flynt her circumstances and no matter what he did or say, she wasn't going to be courted by anyone.

"Broc set up an account for me at the bank. I'm Bliss Wallace on it. How ironic." She nearly laughed at the humor.

"And of course he could take your money." Chelsea leaned forward as if intent on hearing the facts.

"He told me no, but I'm sure he can renegotiate with the bank if he wants. I could be broke again." Somehow that didn't bother her as much as the fact Broc despised her now and would never trust her.

Chelsea was gazing at the sunset painting. "I think this is one of your best." Then she leaned closer. "Is that Broc on his horse?"

Bliss could not stop the lone tear from slipping from her eye but she vowed it would be the last one she'd shed for Broc Wallace. "Yes, it's from a sketch I made before I met him."

~ * ~

Flynt felt as if his life had been turned upside down twice now, once with this strange lady, Fern, coming into his home and now with his sister sleeping with his best friend. What the hell happened to his well-ordered life? His plans. And an even more pressing question was what was he going to do about changing things?

Raking his hands through his hair, he felt the urge to throw something. Instead, he paced the parlor before finding himself in the library. Yet the sight here didn't calm his nerves as he hoped.

"Fern." He breathed her name as if he didn't want her to hear him.

Yet she did, and she rose, turning toward him, brushing dust from her hands and skirts. "Sir?" Her eyes shimmering as she looked at him. "Chelsea unlocked the door for me."

The dress she wore must have been given to her by one of his sisters. It was made of fine fabric and had barely been worn, but the bust was too tight and she was nearly popping from the bodice. While the style was fresh and new, the color did not suit her at all, made her appear sallow. If he bought dresses for her, they would be gorgeous shades of blue and green, perhaps a few shades of purple thrown into the mix.

Catching his wayward thoughts and needing to put an immediate halt to further thinking in this manner, "What are doing here?" He knew his voice and tone were too stern and commanding, but somehow he couldn't help himself. She didn't deserve his wrath, only Broc deserved to be on the firing end of a pistol. If duels had not been outlawed...

She curtsied and the act looked ridiculous on her. Fern was anything but subservient and the action seemed unnatural. She had this air about her that spoke of aristocracy. Perhaps she was a good actress. He made a mental note to look into the troops in the area.

"Working. Sir. Chelsea, milady, told me I should dust the library and the rest of the house." She smiled at him. "I don't want to be a slacker."

The softening of her expression sent a jolt of pure physical pleasure through him even though her use of the word *sir* sounded cynical. He repeated his father's teachings; one does not have sexual relations with the hired help. In another life this was forbidden. Now it took all his control as well as the knowledge she was afraid of him to keep from seducing her.

Yet it seemed he couldn't help himself. Simply put, he was inexplicably and strangely drawn to her. Reminding himself their brief encounter the other evening did not go very well. She was either frightened to death of him or men in general. He needed to find out the truth.

He nodded at her, "Carry on." That was inane. Did he have noodles for brains? Stepping toward his desk and a small barrier between them, he sat down. Resting his forearms on the top, he stared at her, unable to keep his gaze away from her bodice and what appeared to be beautifully formed breasts, beautifully rounded globes that would fit in his hands quite nicely.

"Are you sure?" Her voice was hesitant as she seemed to step backward, perhaps closer to the door and a quick escape.

For a moment he wondered if she was about to bolt from the room. "Very sure. Don't mind me. I've got some thinking to do and quite enjoy watching you." The moment the words were out of his mouth and he witnessed the expression on her face he understood the new problem he created.

"I'd rather you didn't, sir," she said. Yet she turned back to her work, giving him her back to stare at.

Once again, Flynt noted the way she said sir. This lady had never been servile in her life or she'd been granted liberties no servant should have. By the way she was dusting, though, she did know her way around a hard day's work. Now she was on her knees sweeping all the dust bunnies into her cloth.

"Who are you, Fern? Fern, I don't like that name. I believe I'll call you Hope. Would you like that name better?"

She turned to him, her knees on her dress, pulling the fabric even lower on her breasts. At first she didn't seem to be aware of it then she followed the direction of his gaze to her cleavage and almost apparent nipples, which were all beginning to show quite nicely.

"Oh!" She struggled, trying to wrench the fabric of her gown from beneath her knees while pulling the bodice higher. To no avail, her struggle brought her little to no success. Perhaps causing the bodice to dip even lower.

"Do you like the name Hope? Come, sit down." He nodded toward the sofa near his desk, wishing he dared join her there. No, she'd probably flee the room and right now he needed the diversion she gave him to rid himself of thoughts of Broc and his sister.

"Yes, sir, I like whatever name you want to give me." Finally untangling herself, she found the sofa and sat down, her fingers wound so tightly together, her knuckles turned white.

He poured a glass of brandy for both of them and walking to her handed her the amber liquid. He noticed the color of her eyes matched that of her drink. "You remember anything else about yourself? Something that might help me find your family."

"Don't have any family." Her voice and tone adamant.

"You remember something?"

Returning to his desk, he continued watching her, trying to understand the workings of her mind and waiting to see what truth or falsehood would emanate from her moist and compelling lips.

"No." She looked at the drink but didn't seem to want to try it.

"Drink, the brandy will relax you, Hope." And why would he want her relaxed? Perhaps so he and his probing questions wouldn't frighten her or perhaps she would forget she didn't remember anything and answer truthfully. "Who hurt you, Hope?" He sat down next to her.

Gingerly she sipped then coughed, holding the back of her hand to her lips. "I don't know what you mean, sir."

"Call me Flynt." His fingers thrummed on the arm of the sofa, his leg pressing against hers.

"Flynt." She complied and nearly choked on his name or was it the brandy she just drank?

"Someone, a man, I presume since you're afraid of me, hurt you. Is that why you're running away? Is that why you're pretending you don't know who you are?"

"Don't know what you're talking about, sir," she said and when she met his gaze, "Flynt, sir. I really should get back to work."

"Am I your employer, Hope?"

"Yes, sir," she said.

"Then you will get back to work when I say so and not a moment before." Against his will or perhaps not, his gaze riveted on her rounded breasts, wishing he dared touch her and perhaps more. He would have to sway her to his charming personality first, make her want him as much as he did her.

Looking at her expression again, he needed to laugh but felt the amusement at her expense would not suit his purposes. What was his purpose? Nothing gentlemanly, he admitted, simply because he craved her.

"Never mind, it doesn't matter what you do or don't tell me. We both know someone hurt you. If you speak his name, I'll see he pays."

Shrugging her slim delicate shoulders, "Don't remember. I'd surely tell you if I knew."

Exasperated with her obstinacy, he sighed, his thoughts going back to his sister and best friend and what the bloody hell he should do about them. He couldn't very well give them permission to wed. Broc never asked him for her hand in marriage.

He looked at Hope as if she could shed some light on his problem. "Bliss slept with my best friend. What should I do?" Lord, he must be batty asking for advice from a servant, one who couldn't remember who she was.

"Then you might look at this wording a bit differently. Your best friend slept with your sister. Does that matter to you? Do they love each other?"

The questions as well as her statement were to the point and gave him something more to think about. He never factored love into the equation, because the fellow in question was Broc Wallace and the man had decreed too many times to count that love didn't exist and he wasn't about to marry until he was thirty-five.

"Of course he doesn't love her." Then "how the hell should I know?"

"You don't have to swear." She suddenly became a prim spinster. "A person can make a point in other ways of speaking."

"In this case I do have to swear because it makes me feel better. Answer my question."

"I'm not really sure if I know what that is but, if they are in love, they should marry and have lots of children."

Chapter Eight

A few weeks later, Broc sat in the stable loft, holding the little black and white kitty he promised Bliss. He should take the cat to Bliss but he was afraid to see her, another week maybe and he might be able to look at her without needing her, wanting her desperately. *Fool, you know if you see her, you'll toss her skirts and all intentions, bad or good, would be swept away in the passion of the moment.* Betraying Flynt was not his intention, but he missed Bliss terribly.

He needed to talk to someone who didn't have some type of vested interest in the outcome of his decision. Bloody eyes, but Bliss lied to him about something so important he didn't think he could ever forgive her. Single handedly, she created a bridge between Flynt and himself. Just the condemning look in Flynt's eyes when he realized the naked woman in the loft with him was his sister sent waves of guilt coursing through him, the deception hitting him hard in the gut. The question continued to remain, how did Flynt know his sister was in the loft with him?

Yet, what about Bliss and her feelings...

Before he could see Bliss he had to come to terms with those feelings too.

No, he realized before that moment Flynt must have recognized the horse, Bliss' little brown and white mare in the stable. The swift breath of air he inhaled caught in his throat. Coughing, he sipped the leftover champagne he poured himself before seeing to the kitten.

"You alright?"

He swiveled, liquid sloshing from the glass in his haste to see who was in the loft with him. The voice sounded so much like Bliss' but different. When he looked up, Lacie stood in front of him, her eyes condemning yet seeming to understand his pain. Perhaps the latter was his imagination and wishful thinking.

The littlest MacTavish was a breath of fresh air in his now stagnant life. "Have a seat. Choose a kitten if you like. Anyone but this one," he held it up for better viewing, much to the dislike of the cat who was now mewling frantically and waving his paws in the air. "They can leave their mother anytime now."

"Is it Bliss' kitty?" she asked, picking up a different kitten then taking the time to look each one over. "You didn't do well by her. I guess I'm ashamed right now to call you friend."

He couldn't believe what he was hearing. "No, I suppose I didn't do well and I'll forever regret how we ended. Don't know what to do. Feel as if I'm damned if I do and damned if I don't."

"Really?" She held up a coal black kitten. "I'd like this one but don't think Flynt will allow it. Since all this happened between you and Bliss, he's not really the same. I used to be able to do pretty much anything I like. Now he watches over me, his hawkish gaze constantly riveted on all of us."

"Does he even know you're here?" Broc asked.

"No, he thinks I'm with friends. Truth be told, I don't have any girlfriends. They all seem so silly and frivolous, their minds in the clouds. They gossip about little boys and dresses and what trinkets they want to buy."

"You don't like to talk about those things?"

"No, not little boys. I'd talk about Leslie, but it would get me into trouble."

"I see, so you think you're in love with Leslie. He's much older than you."

"I'll grow up and he's not that much older."

Well, Lacie might also have her mind in the clouds, but in too many ways she was wise beyond her age. "Is Flynt really that domineering? I didn't peg him as that kind of bloke. He's always been the one to suggest something outrageous and the rest of us would follow." Broc needed insight into the moods of his friend as seen by his sister, at least one very vocal and very unintimidating one.

"Where we are concerned and our future husbands, he's an ogre, worse than an ogre." She added for emphasis.

"Worse than an ogre?" He tried to understand but wasn't able to wrap his mind around what she was saying. Flynt was just a man trying to protect his sisters, nothing more or less. Their virtue and future husbands were important. And he was the man Flynt was attempting to protect Bliss from because he'd taken something priceless from her. It was true though. Without a thought, he'd taken her innocence. What man would want her now?

His gut cramped. He couldn't bear the image of another man making love to her.

"Can I try the champagne?" Lacie asked, striding quickly to the bottle and pouring a glass before he decided how to answer.

"Guess so, if you like," he said, watching her down what she poured herself in one gulp.

"Flynt doesn't let us drink. Says we can't until we're eighteen. It's really very good. Why would he keep something like this from us?" she asked him while she poured more before sitting on the quilt, which was still there. "Is this where it all happened?"

Strange, he could not bring himself to change the setting in the loft. *All happened.* "What do you know?" His heart suddenly raced. What did or did not happen here should not become public knowledge.

"Hmm...where to start exactly." She placed a very feminine fingertip to her chin before casting her gaze to the ceiling, the simple gesture reminding him of Bliss. "I learned by listening when no one suspected I was around. I want you to know that Flynt would have never said the things he did if he knew I was within hearing distance."

"Lacie," he spoke sternly, "back to the topic." Then he repeated, hoping she would sidestep and avoid the question at hand. "What is it you've learned about us?"

"Flynt found you and Bliss up here, and she was naked as were you. Well, almost naked. Flynt assumed you had been. Did you make love to my sister? Did she like it?" Lacie asked, grinning almost from ear to ear. "Did you know I want Leslie to make love to me?"

The sip of champagne in Broc's mouth exploded into the air in a mist of fine liquid droplets. "No, you don't."

"Of course I do and you better not tell either my brother or Leslie. I'll never forgive you if you do." She sipped more champagne then pouted prettily, her lashes fluttering flirtatiously. "This is really relaxing."

She truly held the art of flirting in the palm of her hand, and she still had two years to perfect it. Someone should give Leslie an idea of what waited for him in the not so distant future, or perhaps they shouldn't. He would love to see the stoic duke blindsided by this little and very provocative imp.

"And you shouldn't have any more of this. It's not good for your health." Broc reached for the glass to take it away from her, but she turned away from him.

"No, you don't. I'm going to enjoy this one and one more after that." Her words slurred slightly and Broc groaned.

He'd have hell to pay again. "Your brother will call me out if he finds you up here with me. It's bad enough he found Bliss here."

"Naked."

"You don't have to remind me."

Good lord, but this little lady might well be the death of me. As long as no one is found naked, this can most likely be explained away with the kittens. So I'll pray you don't drink too much.

"Broc," she paused thoughtfully, "you won't tell him about Leslie, promise me, please."

Broc had more than one problem with keeping this secret but she was so young and eighteen was so far away for her, anything could happen. Then grudgingly, "I promise."

"Or Leslie about what I just said. It's just a fantasy I have, nothing more. In any case, he's not interested in me at all. Ignores me when I'm around so much so I want to scream at him that I'm not a child."

He wanted to laugh at that statement but held the amusement inside. In a grown man's eyes, she was still a child. "In a few years he might be interested." Broc for some reason, instead of sending Lacie on her way, wanted her company and needed for her to know he would be true to his word. "How long until you're eighteen?"

"Why is eighteen some magic number for all you bad boys?" She leaned against the crate, closing her eyes.

Lacie was very nearly as beautiful as her sister, and Broc supposed in a few years she would be a very attractive woman. Perhaps she'd be the woman Leslie would find hard to resist. "How old are you?"

"Sixteen," she sipped more champagne, "Sixteen and more than a half. I'll be seventeen in January. Seems too long to wait."

"Leslie is twenty-three, way too old for you until you get a few more years under your belt. He probably looks at you as if you're still a little girl not a woman." Once the words were out, Broc realized they weren't the sentiment Lacie must have been looking for.

"That's not the way he looked at me the other night at the card game when he caught up to me in the stable. I thought he wanted to devour me and he kissed me too."

Needing to know more and wanting that knowledge were two entirely different things. Even if he learned something Flynt should know, he didn't believe Flynt would allow him into the house to tell him. This was none of his business anyway, and if Lacie wasn't under the influence of too much champagne, she would have kept her thought-provoking sentiments to herself.

"I need to get you home, Lacie." He smiled as he watched her grimace. "I'm not going to let you go alone and I'm not going to take no for an answer. It's going to be dark out soon and you're drunk."

"No, it's still light out and the sun is still shining. I can ride by myself even though Bliss always said you never let her ride at dark."

"You knew Bliss and I were..."

She waved her hand in the air, a silly grin on her face, "Didn't know it was you, just some devilishly handsome man who she was enamored with. I always suspected it was you though. Everything she didn't say pointed in your direction."

"It was that obvious." He wondered why other people didn't catch on to the game they'd been playing.

"You should go see Bliss." Lacie arranged her riding habit around her legs. "Really, I think she'd like to see you, might have something important to tell you, something you should know."

"I rather doubt that. Rode by the cottage a few days ago and she wasn't there. Looked as if she packed up and left. You wouldn't know where she went?" Broc asked, hoping Lacie would blurt the answer before she couldn't think better of telling him.

"She had to leave, you know. Flynt didn't own the cottage any longer. Told her he sold it and she had to vacate the premises. There's still a bit of champagne in the bottom of the bottle. Mind if I have it?"

"Suit yourself, Lord knows I'm not about to try and stop you. That's Flynt's problem. Did the new owner tell Flynt he wanted Bliss out?"

"That's what Flynt said." Lacie finished the last of her champagne before setting the glass on the crate, a smug expression highlighting her delicate features.

"The bastard. I own that cottage and I never told your brother to have it vacated. Why do you think he'd say such a thing?" Broc knew the answer. He just needed to hear the words from Lacie.

"Flynt wanted Bliss to move home so she'd have to meet the suitors he brought her way." Lacie laughed softly. "But she found a way to get around that horrid situation. She always does. I believe she outsmarts Flynt all the time."

"Lacie." Broc picked up her hands, his gut tightening when he thought of other men courting Bliss, kissing her, touching her. The devil but he didn't intend to let that happen. "Where did Bliss go? I'm pretty sure by what you just said she didn't go home."

"No, she didn't."

"Are you going to make me drag the answer out of you?" His breath seemed to catch in his throat as he waited.

"Maybe. Bliss didn't want anyone to know where she went but Flynt figured it out," Lacie said. "I suppose..."

"Lacie, where did she go." Broc understood it was the alcohol talking. Lacie wasn't perverse by nature. "I have to know." Good God, but his heart nearly double-timed.

"If I tell you, are you going to treat her right?" she asked, tilting her head prettily. "Can't tell you if you don't promise me."

"I promise. I have to see her, find out if she's alright and has everything she needs."

"Then you're going to leave her again." Lacie's voice was

condemning. "Then you can go to the devil."

"Bliss, we can't be together. She lied to me and I don't think I can forgive her, but I still want to help her if she needs it. I care about Bliss. Tell me where she is." He craved her, didn't believe he could live the rest of his life without her, but he couldn't commit, never that.

"I don't believe you care. Seems to be just words to me. You're just afraid to bind yourself to anyone, and this gives you an excuse. You would have left her eventually even if she became your mistress. It's just the way the bad boys are. At least you didn't take her money, not like Flynt. Guess you still could."

Lacie's comments were far too astute for a sixteen year old and might be right, but he didn't think he would have ever left Bliss. If only... "I'll find her whether or not you help me."

"Then what? Make her love you again before you break her heart all over? After that, find some excuse to run out on her? I know life's not fair, but that would be horrible."

Another few questions and comments that were far too astute for this child woman, "I would never break her heart." He paused then, "Not intentionally."

"After that night and you left her without consoling her or even telling her you might be able to forgive her, she cried for nearly a week. Her eyes were red and swollen, but she managed to stay strong. Bliss finished that painting she was going to give you and took it to the gallery. She didn't want anything to do with it. You broke her heart, hurt her more than you could ever understand. Men are like that. They don't understand anything."

"Bliss told me it was mine." One more lie. He felt another loss and it seemed with each step leading him farther away from Bliss, he felt the despair of losing her more deeply.

"You don't deserve the painting. You don't deserve Bliss," she said matter of factly. "Why would she give a precious gift to someone who hurt her so much she had to leave her home? Someone who caused her so much pain she cried for a week?"

"You're right, of course. When you tell me where she is, I'll go to her. Try to make amends, perhaps set all the wrongs to rights."

"She doesn't want to see you and hear all of your excuses. You're just not listening to what I'm trying to tell you. Men..." she accented the word with a long drawn out sigh.

"Is that Bliss talking or Lacie?" he asked, his frustration and anger reaching an extreme level, something he wasn't used to feeling.

"Both," Lacie said, her expression grim. "You can't go see her. It will just hurt her more. I won't tell you..."

"She went to your grandmother's home." And at the sudden change of expression on Lacie's face, he knew the truth. "I'm right, aren't I? Now all you have to do is tell me how to get there." He suddenly felt the need for action. Someone had to rectify all that had transpired between them and gone so very wrong.

"Don't you dare tell her you got that information from me, but it's not as bad if I told you about..." Quickly, she covered her mouth with her hands. "I didn't say anything."

"What aren't you telling me, Lacie?" His voice demanded the truth, but Lacie had turned white and he understood this was probably all he was going to get from her. "What secret is Bliss keeping from me now. It will all go better if I learn the truth sooner than later."

"Nothing. If she lets you see her, you'll discover the truth, but Bliss doesn't want to see you. That's another reason why she left."

He was beside himself thinking of so many, too many different scenarios his mind spun. "Time to see you home. Do you think you can make it down the ladder by yourself?"

He nearly laughed at her stunned expression. Things needed to be taken care of, one of which was to go to the gallery and pay an exorbitant sum for the painting that was meant for him. But that wasn't the first thing he wanted to do. He needed to stop by the cottage again and see if Lacie spoke the truth. Over the weeks he avoided the road to the cottage afraid of what he would do if he did see her. Except for a few days ago when he couldn't help himself. That's when he rode by and the tiny home looked abandoned. He needed to discover the truth, all of it before he could proceed.

"I'm not a child even though I'm only sixteen. What makes you think I can't climb down a measly little ladder? Been climbing ladders for years now and trees as well," she blurted, seemingly indignant with his comment.

He nodded toward her drink, "Champagne can hit you hard if you're not used to it, and you certainly are not used to the effects of alcohol. Shall we go?" He held out his hand to her.

Lacie nodded, suddenly looking a bit unsure of herself. He went first, thinking if she slipped he could catch her. Lacie made her way without mishap as well as the ride to her home.

"I will see you whenever you show up and I'll look forward to our next encounter." He smiled at Lacie, realizing just how much he enjoyed her company. "I will be away though for some time."

"How long?" She dismounted, leading her horse into the stable. "Should I tell Bliss anything? That you're gone somewhere and that you want to see her."

"He's not going to see Bliss." Flynt stepped from the stables. "You wouldn't dare heap shame on her more than you already have. If you go anywhere near my sister, I'll kill you. Stay away from Lacie too."

Flynt's words were a slap in the face. Shame her, what the bloody hell was Flynt talking about? If anything Flynt's words as well as Lacie's hidden innuendos gave him more reason to seek Bliss out. "You don't have to worry. For the next four to six months, I'll be in London on business.

He had hoped to take Bliss with him, show her London, take her to Vauxhall Garden and the opera, show her around the town. That wasn't going to happen, at least not in this lifetime.

"I'll see Bliss when I return. There is nothing you can do to stop me. We have a few things to settle, things that are important." This argument seemed deeper and more consuming than the last one. He'd told Bliss he needed time to think about what happened. Well, he'd thought but he still didn't know the solution.

"I can move her somewhere you'll never find her," Flynt said his voice soft but deadly.

Broc turned, unwilling to continue the conversation, which could explode into something far different with a few more heated words. Wherever Flynt hid Bliss, if he wanted, he would find her. He had the resources and he determined he would use them, resources Flynt new nothing about.

Turning his horse toward the small cottage, Bliss' cottage, he left the MacTavish home and his friend turned enemy behind him. Galloping down the narrow road, he let the wind caress his face and the fading sun warm his skin. He loved autumn. It had always been his favorite time of the year with all the vibrant colors as well as the slow subtle change of the weather.

September had come and gone since that horrible day when he left Bliss. October first was tomorrow. Memories of the hot August days with her filled his head, claimed his heart and occupied his soul. Vividly, he recalled those irretrievable moments in the loft. He'd almost asked her to become his mistress and to stay with him for the rest of their lives.

He was a bloody fool.

His heart belonged to Bliss and he abandoned her because of a friendship that would have continued if he'd done the honorable thing, made her his wife. One didn't have to love in order to marry. Except for love, Bliss was everything to him.

Autumn leaves colored the trees and with the brisk wind the fallen leaves cluttered the ground. She would like to paint this, and he wondered if the landscape was as compelling where she now lived.

This trip was absolutely necessary, and his ship was booked for the afternoon tide. He'd spent too much time with Lacie and now he would have to wait until early morning to ride into Glasgow.

Tying his horse at the hitching post in front of his cottage, he unlocked the door and stepped inside. The silence and the emptiness filled him with anguish. The laugher was gone, vanished with his cruel words as well as his extended absence. The canvasses and easels were nonexistent as well as the scent of oil paints. He'd never really noticed it before.

Everything except what he'd given her was gone. In the bedroom all the garments he bought for her were laid out on the bed he purchased for both of them. Some were still in the packages. The torment and hopelessness nearly sent him to his knees.

What was it Lacie didn't want to tell him? He felt as if he should know, be more intuitive.

Pushing the packages and garments aside, he laid down his hands behind his head, staring at the ceiling. More memories assailed him, memories of Bliss between his arms.

My sweet Bliss...

What have I done? Lost you for now but when I return I'm going to prove to you that you belong with me and not as a mistress but as a wife.

His deep sigh rumbled from his lungs into the darkening room. He had to leave. Tomorrow would be a busy day, and he meant to make the most of it. Yet somehow he couldn't bring himself to depart the cottage. The moon rose and settled in the sky sending a small measure of light to the earth below. Before closing his eyes, he cared for his horse then returned to the empty bed.

This melancholy would do him no favors. As the sun began to brighten the sky, Broc left the cottage, heading for Glasgow and the errands that needed to be done before the afternoon when his ship would sail.

In his apartment he washed then changed his clothes, packing a few items to take with him. Then he sat down at his desk.

First, he addressed the envelope to Lacie.

Lacie, please feel free to read what is inside if you don't trust me. Give it to your sister upon your approval. I know you will and I trust you in this matter. I've no one else and I've not enough time to deliver it to Bliss myself particularly because you wouldn't tell me where your grandmother lives. I trust you.

Dear Bliss,

I've been a bloody fool where you are concerned. I miss you more than I can ever describe in words. You are my heart and my soul. There isn't a second of any day that goes by that I don't think of you.

Lacie tells me you won't forgive me but I pray that isn't true and with time your heart will mend. When I return from London, I plan to court you properly, like a gentleman should court the lady he hopes to make his wife.

I care about you more than life. Don't know if that's love but I pray it will be enough for you at least until I figure things out. I told you I had to think and I guess that's all I've been doing, thinking.

When I finish this I'm going to send it to Lacie with the hope she'll make sure you receive it. Yet even I understand that doesn't mean you'll read the letter and not throw it in the fire. Like I said, I have to go to London or I'd see you tomorrow. Someone in town must know where your grandmother is living and I'm sure someone would be happy to tell me.

Before I leave, I'm going to buy my painting. I'm glad you put it in the gallery for sale just hoping no one has purchased it yet. I'm going to make sure the money for the sunset goes immediately into your account so I know you'll have enough funds to live on until I return.

Please take care of yourself. I pray that I will see you in four to six months.

Yours always,
Broc

He folded and placed the letter in the envelope before sealing it and heading out the door. At the bottom floor he hailed a messenger and giving him explicit directions on who to give this to and who not to, he headed for the docks.

On board the ship he watched the people, the dockworkers and sea captains as they went about their business. The stop at the gallery was fruitful. The painting would be delivered to his apartment and hung in the main sitting room. The money from the sale would be sent to her account.

He was just about to go below to his room when he noticed a tiny figure on the boardwalk. It was Bliss. What the bloody hell was she doing at the docks?

~ * ~

To Bliss it seemed she'd been two steps behind Broc all day. She didn't understand why she'd followed him, knowing he was running from her, that he'd never forgive her but it seemed she couldn't help herself. When he boarded the ship, she knew her worst fears were true. He was leaving Glasgow.

Where was he headed and why? How long would he be gone? She was assailed with questions that were no longer her business.

She rested her hands on her belly, knowing it would not be long before everyone knew she carried a child, Broc's child to those who

179

actually knew her. When that happened, she wasn't going into town. She would have to find another way to transport her work and pick up supplies. Perhaps Nial, her grandmother's second husband would help. It seemed he was happy to do whatever Grams proposed.

Flynt still didn't know she was pregnant. Closing her eyes, she could imagine his fury, but would it be at Broc or her? She'd like to believe this wasn't her fault, but she couldn't do that. The responsibility sat on both their shoulders. After all she could have told him no and maybe everything would have turned out differently.

Bliss watched until the ship was a tiny speck on the horizon then she turned, making her way to a cab. The light mist that had been falling was slowly changing to rain.

"Well, I see he left you too. Doesn't have any loyalty does he now? What did you do to deserve his departure and from Glasgow at that? Thought you were more than his convenient. Guess you're no longer his wife in watercolors."

"Edina," Bliss whispered her name. She prayed she'd never see this woman again and was shocked to meet her on the waterfront. She wasn't quite sure what a wife in watercolors or a convenient was, but she guessed a mistress.

The woman postured, one hand on her hip, her voluptuous breasts thrusting forward then slanting Bliss a malicious glare, "He used to take me with him whenever he traveled to London. Had so much fun. Seems he left you home. Guess your tiny kettle drums just didn't suit him."

Bliss felt heat rise to her face, shocked by Edina's vulgarity and audacity. She wanted to get as far away from her as possible, yet Edina kept pace. She wouldn't put it past this woman to get in the cab with her. A long breath of air emanated from Bliss. Then, "What do you want?"

"Not much you can give me now that your man left you. Was going to see if you could talk him into letting me have that little cottage out in the country he purchased. Thought it was for you but I checked it out and it seems pretty empty."

"Broc doesn't even like you. Wants you to find a new protector. Why would he let you live there?"

"What would you know? You're as much of a little dollymop as I am." She matched her step for step. Even reaching out at one point as if to grab her by the arm to confront her further.

Bliss didn't have any words. Escaping this lady before she attacked her again was paramount in her mind. The starting rain would become another problem if she didn't get under cover.

"You're right. He left me and he's not coming back. Perhaps he'll take you back. You can always try when he returns from wherever it is he's gone." Bliss started down a side street, deciding she would just have to push her out of the vehicle if she tried to get in behind her.

"Well, then you can't put in a good word for me. I'll have to find some other way." She pulled out her rain napper, holding it over her head.

Bliss didn't care, she just needed to have the woman leave her alone. "No, no good words from me to him." Mulling over Edina's earlier words, she inhaled a sharp breath of air. Flynt must have sold it to Broc and he was going to give it to her. Bliss couldn't help herself. She started laughing. Doubled over she was no longer surprised by the things Edina had to say.

"How dare you laugh at me?" she said. One hand on her hip, she was tapping her foot. "You were nothing more to him than a three-penny-upright, cheap and up against a wall.

Bliss puzzled over the things Edina said. Her words were nothing she'd heard before. Then shrugging them off, "I'm sorry, you wouldn't understand the irony about the cottage. I'm leaving. Don't much like getting wet. You obviously can do anything you want. My suggestion is that you find another man."

With that said, Bliss picked up her skirts and hailing a cab, she quickly gave directions then climbed inside and motioned for the vehicle to go. She didn't understand what came over her but for the first time since the day in the loft where her world turned topsy-turvy, she felt at peace.

The carriage pulled up in front of Broc's Glasgow apartment. Bliss reached inside her reticule for the key he'd given her. Confident she'd be alone tonight with her memories, she entered the premises.

Lighting the candles and the lantern, the room was suddenly brighter and painful wistfulness filled her soul. On the balcony and sheltered by the overhang she let the wind blow against her face as well as the few drops of rain carried inward by the stiff breeze.

There would be no sunset tonight, no nostalgia to either warm her heart or face the fact he was truly out of her life. Needing to see if he had anything to eat in the cupboards, she walked into the sitting room from the balcony, refusing to close the door. She wanted to listen to the storm.

In the kitchen, she rummaged and found some cheese and bread that wasn't moldy and a few berry tarts, some of her favorites. The market wasn't far but truly she didn't want to go there tonight. With more searching she found a bottle of wine and opened it.

With the cheese and bread cut and on a plate, she poured the wine. The sunset painting was on the wall in front of her. Feelings and memories pillaged her insides. She fought the tears, keeping them at bay while she studied her work. This was truly one of her best and it now belonged to the man she loved just as she'd intended. She walked to the painting, reaching out, she thought to touch the tiny figure that was Broc. Abruptly changing her mind, she turned away from the heavy reminder of what she lost.

No, she told the tears to vanish, to leave and not return but to no avail. Sobs suddenly racked her body, wishing for something that couldn't be, could never be. Perhaps coming here had been a mistake.

Her hunger disappeared. Backing up she sat down on the settee once again and focused on the painting, stared at it until she thought she would go quite mad. She rose, wandering around the small room until she found herself in the bedroom.

Exhaustion weighed on her, but she couldn't sleep. It seemed her eyes would not shut nor would her mind. All the wonderful moments she spent with Broc flashed through her head.

The sunlight heralding a new day slanted through the window. She'd found his pillow and curled herself around its softness. Nothing like him, she mused but it held his scent, reminding her of his arms around her and the steady beat of his heart when her head rested against his chest.

She stifled the new sob welling up ready to break lose, quickly sitting up. Bliss rose then and straightened her clothing. When she peered outside, the rain fell in torrents. Second thoughts about traveling home swept through her, but she didn't mean to spend any more time in his apartments. The memories were too bittersweet and painful. Reliving them could not be good for her or the babe growing in her womb.

It didn't take long to hire a carriage for the trip to her grandmother's home. Rain pounded the roof, and the miles seemed to take forever as the vehicle slogged through the downpour. Looking through the window, the road turned muddy and swollen with ruts.

Perhaps she should have stayed in town but...

The carriage lurched to a stop, throwing her from one seat to the one in front of her. The driver peered inside. "You alright?"

"I'm not hurt, if that's what you mean?" She rearranged her clothing.

He pushed his hat from his face, water dripping from the brim. "You're going to have to walk the rest of the way."

"You can't go any further?" Thoughts of walking the two miles to get home left her exhausted.

"Wheels stuck, won't be able to get it out until this rain stops and I find an army of men to help dig it out. Until then I'm just as stuck here as the carriage is. You're welcome to sit out the storm inside the carriage, but then I'd have to sit outside. Just as soon you walked."

"I can walk the rest of the way," she told him, not liking the situation or the man's attitude. "I'll be just dandy. You don't need to go with me," she added when he started to follow.

"You sure?" He pushed his hat back as a deluge of water traveled down his back. "Might not be to safe. You might need a man to protect you."

"No one's going to be out in this storm. No one in his or her right mind, in any case. It's only a couple of miles. Should be home long before the hour is up." She started forward, hoping the man would stay put but refusing to look back and check on him.

At times the mud seemed to suck her shoes into the earth. As the minutes passed the walking grew harder and more exhausting. There were moments she didn't think she could move another inch let alone the distance to her home. Determination kept her picking one foot up after another.

Finally, her grandmother's home came into view, and it seemed the grassy land just off the lane was easier to walk. She made her way around the home and to the kitchen door.

Stepping inside, she kicked off her muddy shoes before shaking out her skirts. She needed to rest but wanted a hot bath first and a glass of something stronger than wine.

"What happened to you?"

"Grams, you're home. Thought you would be with the girls. Did Flynt get frustrated with you and kick you out?" Bliss wanted to laugh at Grams expression but stifled it when she saw her grandmother's countenance soften at Flynt's name.

"I'm sure he'd like to but he doesn't dare out of respect for me. He knows I won't take any of his guff. Besides, he also welcomes the help, understanding a man like him is ill equipped to be a young woman's guardian. He overcompensated in every way and unless the man appears less than a man, he won't let Chelsea be courted by him." She paused drawing in a breath of air. "Why haven't you visited us at your brother's home? It's not good for you to stay cooped up here."

"I'd like a hot bath and something to eat first then I'll be happy to chat with you and tell you everything you want to know and probably things you don't want to know. Just walked a couple of miles, and I'm chilled through to the bone."

"I'll take you up on that. We've got a lot to talk over including your young man. Take that bath. The last thing you need is to take sick."

"I'd really rather not speak about the person who used to be my young man. Do you have a pair of warm boots I can wear across the yard to your cottage instead of these?" She looked pointedly at the floor and her muddy boots. "They're wetter than I am if that's possible."

"I'll get something for you to wear and I'll order you a bath." Grams disappeared for a few minutes. She returned holding out a pair of boots with a warm fur lining and a dry cloak.

"Thanks," Bliss sneezed then sneezed again. She groaned softly, thoughts of getting sick an annoying thought sweeping through her head.

"You're welcome, go on home and change out of those wet clothes. There will be hot water in a few minutes. I'll be over in a half hour with a steaming dinner and a chilled bottle of wine and a hot pot of tea if that's what you'd prefer. Go on now," she shooed her out the door but not before wrapping a warm dry cloak around her shoulders.

Bliss trudged out the door, sneezing a few more times before she made it to the door of her grandmother's cottage. Inside her bedroom she stripped from the wet clothing before wrapping herself in a warm robe.

Waiting for the bath, she sipped brandy and watched her grandmother's servants haul the water. She closed her eyes, enjoying the warmth of the liquid as it slid down her throat while desperately trying to keep thoughts of Broc Wallace out of her head.

She soaked in the tub and when she heard the door open and close, she dried off and after putting a warm nightgown and robe on, she met her grandmother with a hug.

"I saw him yesterday." Bliss didn't understand why she blurted that out, something that wasn't important any longer.

"Who did you see?" Her grandmother was dishing up a bowl of steaming hot stew for her.

"Don't be obtuse, Grams, Broc of course." She pulled off a chunk of bread then dipped it in the bowl. "I wouldn't suddenly announce that I saw anyone else."

"And what did he say to you. An apology I hope. He should come to you groveling on his knees and carrying a ring as well." Grams busied herself, pouring wine for both of them before sitting on another chair.

"Saw him on board a ship leaving for somewhere. Of course he didn't have any obligation to tell me he was going away or where his destination was." Bliss curled up on the sofa where she was sitting, an afghan wrapped around her, still shivering from the cold encompassing her that didn't seem to want to go away.

"No, he doesn't, you're right but the man's a bloody fool to let a woman like you get away from him just because he offended your big brother who happens to be his best friend. You're a catch worthy of the best of men, and don't you ever forget those words." Grams downed the glass in a gulp.

"Grams, he couldn't have loved me, you know. If he cared at all he would have at least explained things to me. Instead he refused to talk to me." She didn't want to think about Broc and all the ways she cared about him, but it seemed she could do little else.

"Pshaw," Grams waved a hand in the air. "Men don't know anything. They don't know they're in love when the evidence is staring them in the face and your Broc is no different."

"So you say." Bliss spread the blanket across her lap, studying all the little creases as if they would tell some story she wanted to hear. "He bought the sunset."

"How do you know that? Do I want to know?" Grams asked.

"Maybe, maybe not. It was late last night when I finished with the bank and delivering new paintings to the gallery. Didn't want to drive back. It would be dark before I made it home so I stayed in his apartment."

"Really and how did you get in? Didn't know you could pick locks." Grams laughed. "Although if you want to learn, I'd be happy to teach you. Could teach you a few other things too."

"Obviously, I don't know how. He gave me a key to his apartment. When I saw him sailing on that ship, I decided to make use of that key. When he gave it to me, he told me it was for emergencies. Last night was an emergency. I don't believe he would have been angry if he knew." The nostalgia hit her hard. When she'd been there with him, she'd never thought their short relationship would end quite the way it did.

"Just curious, and you can tell an old lady it's none of her business if that's what you want. Is your money from the paintings still in your name or did he find some way to rob you like your brother did?"

"It's still in my name or one might say our name, Bliss Wallace. Ironic, isn't it?" she laughed then, resting her hands on her tummy. "He still doesn't know and..."

"You have to tell him. Don't you think he has the right to learn about his child?" Grams asked, clearly concerned over this situation.

"Of course he does and when or how do you propose I tell him the wonderful news that he's going to be a daddy?" Shades of anger coated her tone as well as her sentiments. There were too many what ifs in this scenario the two of them were writing and as of this day, none were answered. Now he was indefinitely unattainable.

"Maybe when he returns you can set up a time to meet." Grams seemed to be too logical and rational for Bliss. Her grandmother was living in a fantasyland. Broc would most likely refuse to meet her.

"I've sent him messages; all have been ignored. What makes you think he'll suddenly change his mind and agree to something?" Depression assailed her too many times to count when she thought of her child not having a father even though she knew the baby would be loved dearly by everyone in her family. It wasn't quite the same.

"I have no idea how you'll accomplish anything where he is concerned. You do know him better than me. Changing the subject though, does Flynt know about the child you're carrying?"

Bliss felt blood drain from her face. "No and telling my big brother is going to be even harder than giving Broc the news. He's your grandson. Do you have any idea what he'll do to Broc?"

"Does tar and feathers give you any idea or perhaps a meeting at dawn?" It seemed Grams kept herself from letting a chuckle lose. "The man deserves something menacing to make him think about what he really wants."

"You can't mean that," Bliss said in shock, objecting to her grandmother's assumptions. "This child wasn't entirely his fault. It wasn't like I told him no."

"Of course it's his fault. You were innocent and you had no experience with male sexual games. I'm sure you had no idea how to prevent a pregnancy either. Does Broc have any other children?" Grams asked, the tone in her voice more demanding and condemning than Bliss had ever heard.

"Not that I know of," Bliss said, searching her mind for any mention of children.

"Has he been celibate? Is he as innocent as you?" Grams demanded harshly as if she tried to make a point.

"I don't think so. He could hardly be a bad boy if that were the case, and I know he's had at least one mistress."

"So you know the truth." Grams settled back in her chair, her hands folded neatly as if nothing more needed to be said.

"What truth?" she asked unknowingly, claiming even more innocence.

"Don't lie to me," Grams said.

Bliss couldn't help herself. She let out a long dramatic sigh, "He knows how to prevent children and he chose not to do so with me. I suppose that's what you're looking for."

"And that is the entire truth. He took no precautions and this child is his fault as well as his idea. He wanted you pregnant and that's a fact. Either that or he is a bigger fool than I believed him to be when he let you go."

"You truly believe that don't you, Grams?" she asked, thinking of the other designated bad boys. None of them had children either, and they all had mistresses including her brother.

"I do and that's what makes me believe when he finds out about your condition he will be back and he will marry you," Grams said with conviction. "He will want that baby to have his name."

"That's the problem though, isn't it? I want him to want me for me, not for the baby. I won't marry him if I find out that's how he feels." She spoke with even more conviction than her grandmother, understanding her stubborn nature was not one of her better traits.

"He has the money and the means to compel you to give him the child if you decide to keep the child away from him. If you want to keep this baby, you might have to marry him." She leaned over, placing Bliss' hand in her. "You have time to think about everything. What you must remember is that all the laws are in the man's favor."

"I can leave. Run away where he can't find me." Her hands settled on her belly, fear now becoming a very real part of her pregnancy. "Where do you suppose he went?" she asked, intending to change the subject to something that wasn't quite so personal as to what might happen when he discovered her pregnancy.

"Don't have the slightest idea. I see you're working on more paintings."

"I am. I'll need help getting these into town. Do you think Nial will be willing to go with me when they are ready?" she asked.

"Of course, dear, he would do anything for you, even lie to Broc if he comes around looking for you."

"I can't go into town again, not until after the birth." She counted the months, trying to figure out when the babe would be born. "I think the end of March or the beginning of April. Do you think he'll be back by then?"

"A spring baby, how nice. You'll be able to take the child for walks in the sunshine. It's always nice when they're fussy to get them outside for fresh air," grams recounted, seeming to remember other times.

"When do you think we should tell Flynt?" Bliss wasn't looking forward to that conversation but understood she would have to have it.

"Tell me what?" Flynt strode into the room, reaching out for one of the ginger cookies sitting on the tray. "Glad the rain stopped. Passed a carriage stuck in the mud on the way over here. Was that yours? Now, what were you going to tell me?"

"Nothing," Bliss said quickly but noticed the stern look on her grandmother's face. "Nothing that can't wait."

"The way the two of you were talking, heads together, didn't look like nothing to me." Flynt laughed.

"Well... "

"Did you let Chelsea and Cam take a walk yesterday while the sun was still shining?" Grams asked, a frown on her face. "He's really hovering over those two. Guess he understands Cam better than I do, but Chelsea really does deserve to have a little freedom and you need to trust Cam." She pointed an accusing finger at Flynt.

"Know him too well," Flynt muttered. "And myself. Chelsea's a beautiful woman and she deserves better than..."

"One of your friends?" Grams pointed out accusingly. "Men I assume you trust with your life. Why can't you trust him with your sister?"

"Because he is a man and has needs."

Grams looked at Bliss, "Perhaps this isn't the best time to tell your brother after all. He has this strange way of thinking, and he's the most stubborn man I've ever met including your father, who, until now, held that title."

Bliss decided against Gram's sudden and strange change of opinion. "Perhaps I should get this over with while Broc is out of the country. You wouldn't know where he's gone off to and for how long?"

"London, business, he's sailing the ship James Macmurra purchased a couple of months ago to London, and he also said he would meet with another man." Flynt poured himself a drink.

Bliss let him finish the brandy before she spoke, "I'm pregnant."
The last of the brandy spewed from his mouth. "I'll kill him."

~ * ~

Flynt paced the library, swearing and running his hands through his hair, oblivious that Hope watched him from the doorway. Stopping at the liquor cabinet he poured a drink, downing the contents in one gulp.

"What has you in such a rage?" Hope asked stepping into the room, smiling. "Perhaps I can help."

Her smile always found a way into his heart despite his attempts to resist. She was always sunshine no matter what the day brought, and he often marveled how she could be so agreeable when she didn't even know who she was or where she came from, What bothered him the most was that she ran from something or someone and he couldn't help her.

"Unless you can take me back several months there is nothing to be done. For now I must deal with the present and make sure everything turns out as it should." Flynt turned to her, his gaze riveted on this elusive woman with the vibrant red hair who seemed to have captured his heart.

"I cannot do that," she said, her voice a soft whisper in the semi-darkness of the library. "But I believe I can ease some of your tension."

"And how would you go about doing such a thing?" he asked, skeptical of what she told him and curious as well.

"While I don't remember certain things, there are other things that seem intuitive. Things that seem to be an integral part of my nature or perhaps my past life."

"So," he paused, eager to find out this part of her nature she knew instinctively. "What do you want me to do?"

He watched as she pulled an afghan and pillows from the furniture laying them on the floor. "Take your shirt off," and she pointed to the afghan, "and lie down."

"You're going to seduce me. I'll have to take my pants off too. That will definitely ease the tension, but I don't believe you had any intention of bedding me." He laughed then saw the beautiful expression on her face change to a slight scowl.

After a moment, she laughed, the sweet sound filling him with a small measure of joy at this moment when only darkness seemed to surround him.

"I don't. Are you going to do as I bid?" Once again she pointed to the bedding then looked to him. "I promise you what I have in mind will make you feel better."

"Suppose I'd like to find out what it is you're thinking about doing to my poor man's body." He did lie down on his back, his hands behind his head, grinning at her. "Now what? I'm all yours." Truth be told he'd been all hers for weeks now.

She drew her bottom lip between her teeth, appearing exasperated with him. "Turn over and stop teasing me."

He groaned, feeling the rise of his sex go along with his wishful thinking. "Whatever you have planned would be more comfortable in a bed," he said as he rolled over.

"You're going to feel better soon." She straddled him, her hands massaging his shoulder muscles and his neck.

"Promise?" He felt better already but wasn't too sure how long it would last. Knowing exactly how close to him she was and how easily he could turn and make love to her only meant this relaxation thing was his imagination playing with him.

Her hands and fingers worked magically against his muscles. "Hold tight and don't move, I'm going to walk on you now."

"Do hope you're going to take your shoes off," he mumbled, his thoughts incoherent at best.

"Done."

Then he felt the slight pressure of her weight as she massaged him with her feet. He didn't dare move, didn't dare do anything save breathe as little as possible. Closing his eyes he let the sensations soothe him, relax all of him. Good Lord, but he didn't want her to stop.

When she finally stepped from his back, he wanted to know more about her, how she learned everything she knew. He reached out, wrapping his hand around her ankle.

She froze. He felt it in his fingertips. Slowly, he unwound his hand, wishing he'd remembered her very real fear of men. Gradually, she was letting down her guard but what he'd just done didn't help his cause.

"I'm sorry, Hope." He rose to stand beside her, seeing her eyes glazed over as they had been that first night he barged into her room. "I'm not going to hurt you, Hope. Look at me and see that I'm not whoever it is you fear."

She seemed to hear his words, her eyes focusing on his. Moments later, "I'm not afraid of you, Flynt." She pulled her lips together. "It's just..."

"Just what?" He brushed wayward strands of hair from her face, hoping this gesture wouldn't send her back into a world of her own making.

"I remember something but it's all kind of fuzzy."

"Sit down, and tell me what you can recall." He held her arm, guiding her to the sofa then pulled the pillows and afghan from the floor.

"It's so strange. I remember my mother and sitting in a beautiful garden with flowers all around. We would sit on a blanket but there were stone benches and bird baths."

"A father?"

"If I had one, I don't remember him now."

Flynt chuckled, not meaning any disrespect. "You have a father somewhere."

"I just don't remember anything else. Except mother telling me that someday soon I would leave this place. She would find a way. When I left, I'd have to be very cautious and secretive or they would find me and bring me home. She didn't want me to grow up in that place."

Flynt's gut tightened, every horrible scenario swept through his head. "Were you held captive?"

"I don't know. I don't think so but we never went anywhere. Our rooms were nice and the food was wonderful. There were a lot of other women too. No one left the building."

"Did you ever leave?"

"No, the first I remember of being outside our rooms and the gardens was when I opened my eyes after the carriage accident and the world was cold and the ground was dirty, muddy. I'd never seen mud before, didn't know what to call it until recently."

So, Hope was running from someone. They already guessed that fact and she'd lived somewhere warm with little to no rain. That wasn't much to go on, but he understood discovering who Hope really was, was paramount to keeping her safe and possibly alive.

"How did you learn to give massages and walk on someone's back?" He touched her gently, wishing she would let him kiss her.

For several seconds she closed her eyes, as if searching her mind for the answer. Then she lifted her shoulders in a delicate shrug. "I think it was part of my training. I've so little in my head, but I do remember walking on the backs of other men and another woman holding my hand when I was a little girl and telling me what to do and what would be expected of me."

"Expected of you?"

"Flynt, I think I was a slave of some sort and my mother as well."

Chapter Nine

When Broc was summed to the heir apparent's residence and hauled off the ship bound for Glasgow, anger simmered in his gut. He'd been patient through all the meetings and contracts. The deal making seemed to go on endlessly. During this visit he'd made a small fortune, but he was eager to get home and see Bliss. Now this diversion, an almost kidnapping, was stopping him from his plans of apologizing to Bliss as well as asking her forgiveness, and at the request of someone named Montgomerie. This was no request; it was a summons he wasn't given the opportunity to refuse.

Thoughts of the letters he wrote to Bliss gave him hope that she had already forgiven him and when he finally saw her, she would be waiting for him with open arms. If she received the letters, that is. He had every confidence in his only supporter, Lacie, to do his bidding. Other factors could always intrude, and if she didn't receive the letters, she might have moved on to someone else. In his absence and the manner in which they parted, he was sure she would want to get on with her life.

Now he rode up a tree-lined road to an estate about three miles from London. Five of Montgomerie's men surrounded him, as if he would turn around and go back to the docks if given the chance, and he would. No one told him why he'd been summoned. but it was made abundantly clear he didn't have a choice.

James Macmurra met him at the front porch, motioning for him to go on into the house. Inside the country estate the furnishing were elaborate and tasteful. When he heard a slight noise, a petite woman was walking toward him her hands outstretched in greeting.

"Mr. Wallace?" Her voice was soft and sweet. "I'm Ella Montgomerie. Welcome to our home. Please make yourself comfortable, and let me know if you need anything."

"I am, and thank you," he said, inbred politeness taking over. This woman had nothing to do with the summons, rocking back on his heels still impatient to find out the purpose of this delay and thinking it better be bloody important.

"Follow me, please." She turned, seeming to head into the heart of the home.

Broc trailed behind her to what must be the library. Two men and a woman were chatting until he walked inside. The men rose and strode toward him.

"Drake and Hamilton and Addie." Ella pointed out everyone in introduction. "Please make yourself at ease. I'm sure the meeting will finish in record time, and Drake will have you on the next fastest ship back to Glasgow." Then she left the room.

"Broc Wallace, yes," Montgomerie said, "I'm sure you're wondering why you were summoned so unexpectedly, but this is a matter of grave importance. Would you like a drink and perhaps something to eat? Then we can get on with the information you need to know in order to proceed."

Out of politeness, Broc accepted the food and drink and the seat offered. "I am impatient to return to Scotland. So the sooner we talk the better. I do appreciate the offer of another ship."

"That was James' doing. Under the circumstances, it's the least we can do. He said you've treated him well and that you're probably eager to return to your fiancée."

Broc coughed at Drake's words, clearing his throat in the process. So, James assumed Bliss was his fiancée. It was probably better than assuming she was a great horizontal or his wife in watercolors. A high-class prostitute was the farthest from the truth about Bliss as was her being his mistress.

"You must mean Bliss." Broc sipped the expensive brandy, letting the warmth slide down his throat. So true, he did want Bliss to be his fiancée then his wife, but he held no illusions any of that would come to pass.

"Yes, Bliss, James couldn't recall her name but said you spoke in glowing terms about her." Drake said, seeming to study him as if he sized up an enemy.

"You really should start this story or would you like me to do the honors," Addie asked, getting to the point. "Men can be so obtuse, dancing around the subject when they can just say the words. I'm too impatient to wait and I'm sure Broc feels the same. May I call you Broc?" She turned to the other man, "Don't you think, Hamilton? Men can dance around the subject, never getting to what's really important."

"Of course, Addie, why don't you tell the story? You cut to the most important parts and can get it done before I can even blink," Drake said, grinning and relaxing back in his chair. "You will do a remarkable job I'm sure, and I won't have to concentrate on getting all the facts straight."

"No, you'll just butt in and correct me at every opportunity then feign innocence. Perhaps you can tell the story after all." She waved her hand in the air, frown lines marring her beautiful face. "It's what you want. You were just placating me and mind you, you did a very good job as usual."

"No, be my guest." Drake grinned, motioning with a hand for her to go on with the plan.

She slanted him a look then shrugged slightly. "Don't want to anymore. You've taken all the fun away."

Drake cleared his throat before sitting up straight as if he now meant to get to the business at hand. "Now that everything is settled. There is a very special woman who was abducted about nineteen years ago, and it was believed a sultan in Turkey was the man who stole her away. As the story goes, he was enamored of her beautiful red hair. She has been in his possession since that day."

"What does that have to do with me? I'm not equipped for a rescue mission and from what I've heard around town, you are far more capable of doing that, rescuing the lady in question."

"That's so true, but this isn't about a rescue. This mission is about keeping her daughter safe from the sultan's son who seems to have the same affinity for red hair as his father. At least that is what we've been led to believe. After further reconnaissance, I'm not so sure that is true anymore. He is in Glasgow and has yet to show himself."

"Still am not drawing the connection," Broc said, baffled by the conversation, impatiently drumming his fingers on the armrest.

"It seems your city of Glasgow was her destination. Her mother managed to get her out of the harem and away before we could get to her. Still not sure how that was possible though. In any case, the mother chose to stay. The last we heard, Ayleen Wallace is in residence at the MacTavish estate. We're counting on you to inform your friend and make sure she is protected."

"Bloody hell, how do you know all this about me? Ayleen Wallace, what the devil?" Sweat broke out on his forehead, feeling as if his privacy had been invaded. This was not at all what he expected when he was ushered to the Montgomerie residence. Hell, what had he thought? Rumors about this man were numerous and just how many of them were true?

Drake leaned forward, and it seemed the devil himself stared at him. "It's my job to know who I can trust when there is an upcoming mission. And to learn everything possible about the people involved."

"Why is the woman's last name the same as my own?" His heart throbbed and his nerves shattered as he began to assume things he had no business assuming.

"Because Ayleen is your sister. Your mother was abducted. Correct?"

Broc slowly nodded his head, disliking the tenor of the conversation. "We never knew what happened to her."

"At your father's request and to no avail, I have spent the last few years looking for her then trying to get her out of the sultan's grasp after I found her. Your mother was able to sneak Ayleen from the harem, and she was supposed to send her to London. And as you well know your, father passed away just after he made the request."

"She sent her to Scotland instead," Broc murmured. "Hope is with Flynt. He damn well better treat her right." His hands fisted then he suddenly realized Flynt must have had similar feelings about him when he discovered the two of them in that loft months ago. He suddenly understood all too well.

"So, as you must appreciate, you're invested in this enterprise whether or not you want to be," Drake continued his gaze seeming to pierce into his thoughts.

Addie waved her hand in the air. "Drake, this is not well done of you and you know it. Broc must be in shock and you continue to treat him as if he is the enemy, not the sultan's son, who is the actual foe here."

"You must have decided you can trust us," Broc said, still disconcerted by this man and his probing stare. He felt as if he was back in grade school and his teacher was reprimanding him for being late.

"I like the bad boys very much. Think at one time I could have fit in quite nicely with your little group. My wife would never allow it now though. She likes for me to be a bad boy just with her."

"No, I don't suppose she would," he said, sitting back and trying to put this man in a different light. Then mulling over the man's tale of his sister and mother, he came to some conclusions. He didn't even remember his family. His father spent a better part of ten years in a deep depression, and his mother had been gone since he was a toddler.

"I will send men with you, well trained men." Drake held up his hands, "I know MacTavish has his own men as do you, but they aren't as qualified or as skilled as mine. I do hope no harm has come to Ayleen in the interim. It's taken all my resources and way too much time to locate her and bring her home."

"So, all you want is to keep her safe. What about reuniting with me. I'm her only family."

"Safe and happy. If she's found a new home, a place where she is comfortable and content, then we'd like her to stay. It's entirely up to her. You should keep in mind we've no idea what her mother told her about you and your father. She would have no way of knowing he died."

Drake rose, extending his hand. "Safe travels. My men along with Addie and Hamilton will sail with you. Hamilton and Addie will be in charge of the mission and you're to follow their directions."

"Do I have a choice?" Broc mumbled as he was leaving the room, Addie and Hamilton behind him. He would let them dictate to him, but he made no guarantees he would obey their orders.

"It won't be all bad. You might even find out something about yourself," Addie told him once they were on board the ship.

"Tides good, all the shipment is in the hold as well as all passengers, should we leave right now even though we're not scheduled until tomorrow?" the captain asked Hamilton.

"Sooner the better as far as I'm concerned, and I doubt if anyone else has any reason to stay docked," Hamilton said.

Sailing into Glasgow, Broc stood at the railing, his nerves stripped raw. He needed to go to Bliss, see her, explain how he felt as well as his stupidity when he chose her brother's friendship over his feelings for her. He understood himself and his behavior so much better now. It seemed Addie had been a good listener and her advice sound.

"We'll go to the MacTavish estate first," Hamilton said, striding up beside him. "You can take care of your business later after we secure Ayleen's safety and find out if the sultan's son has discovered her whereabouts.

"Like hell we will." Broc wasn't going to waste any more time in getting to Bliss. "But don't let me stop you."

"Can't let you put Bliss' life in danger. If she is thought to be part of this, she could be abducted and used as a bargaining tool. We have to bring her home. Am I wrong in assuming she took up residence at her grandmother's?"

"You tell me. It seems you know everything, things I didn't know about me and my family." He strode down the gangplank, needing to put distance between him and them. And he didn't believe for a moment Bliss would be in danger if he went to see her. "I'll bring her back to the estate. But how long do you expect us to stay hidden away?"

"Be careful," Addie said, gently placing a hand on his arm and stopping him. "This could prove to be dangerous for all involved."

"I won't take any chances with my life or hers." He looked over his shoulder as he spoke to Addie and Hamilton, who stood with his hands clasped behind his back. It seemed neither of them planned on doing anything to stop him. Striding down the gangplank, he mulled over his destination as well as what he would say to Bliss.

Broc walked down the street, looking to hail a ride. The blow on his head sent him careening to his knees but didn't render him unconscious. He groaned, turning to focus on his attacker, his hands in the air.

"Edina," he whispered before the world went dark.

When he opened his eyes, everything looked fuzzy, his head

spinning and throbbing as well. He closed them again, trying to remember what happened but found his thoughts were incoherent.

A few minutes later he opened them once more trying to make sense of all this. His arms were stretched above his head and when he pulled on them, he discovered they were secured. Needing to take action there was nothing he could do.

"Bloody hell!" He tugged on the bindings, twisting and fighting the bonds securing him. Where the devil were the two people who were supposed to keep him safe? Where were Drake's men? Addie and Hamilton must have stood by and let Edina kidnap him. Addie was probably laughing her head off right now and asking Hamilton if she should rescue him or if Hamilton wanted to do the work.

"It's about time you woke up. It's been nearly all day and I've been so impatient."

"Edina." He'd recognize that sultry purr any day. God knows he'd heard it more times than he wanted to recount.

"You're finally awake. I was wondering... Hmm... Well it doesn't matter any longer."

"What are you doing? You know you won't get away with this abduction." Broc tugged at his bindings again in hopes his first tries weren't real. Perhaps he loosened them.

"I already have," she said, running her nail down his naked chest then back up.

"This won't go well for you when you're caught," he said, cringing at the sensations her touch created. Once he would have taken advantage and seduced her, and now she was trying to seduce him but it was to no avail. There was nothing about her touch that aroused him.

"By the time I let you go, I'll carry your child and you won't let any harm come to me then. You'll even ask me to be your wife." Her fingers rested at his waistband, traced his flesh along the top of the band. "I'll have all the control, so I won't let you withdraw from inside me. We're going to do this until your seed takes root inside me."

He felt only loathing at her caress. "That won't happen. I won't put my seed inside you, ever." He detested her, wanted nothing more than to be free of her. She could not stimulate him because he felt nothing for her.

The touch that once pleased him gave him revulsions now.

She unfastened his doeskins, stroking his shaft with no results. "Perhaps you just crave my mouth."

"I don't crave anything about you, Edina. You make me sick. Give it up and let me go. You can't force me. I'll forget you attacked me and tied me to your bed." He was very nearly willing to do just that, forget what she did if she let him go this instant.

"Actually, it's your bed," she purred, still trying to arouse him. "We made love here so many times I could never keep track. All I need are a few more bliss filled minutes with you inside me."

"That was a long time ago, and it's never going to happen again." Once more he struggled against the ropes tying him to the bed.

"I promise you it will." Her words a soft whisper near his ear. She was sitting beside him, slowly unfastening the bodice of her dress. When she stood, she slipped the gown from her body. She was wearing nothing at all, her breasts huge white globes, her nipples a dark pink. Her waist was slender and her hips wide, still he didn't harden with need for her.

Broc didn't feel anything. All he wanted was to see Bliss and apologize for all the wrongs he had committed against her. "You can't seduce me, Edina. I feel nothing for you save loathing. What we once had is in the past. You can't revive something that is a long time dead."

"Perhaps you are wrong." She straddled him, breasts swaying, her wet core caressing his shaft. "This always made you hungry for me."

Still he remained detached from her efforts without even a conscious thought. "I don't want you," he gritted out between clenched teeth, fury emanating from him. Helplessness was not something he was used to.

It seemed she finally understood what he was trying to tell her. A curse then several more left her lips. "Bloody eyes." She left him then, pouring herself a drink, downing it before pouring another one. "I'm not giving up. I want your baby inside me."

"You should do just that, give up. There will be people looking for me, and when they find me tied up and you keeping me from my desired course of action, it will not go well for you. There is a mission that is more important than either of us that needs my attention." Thoughts of his newly found sister swirled in his head as well as the need to meet her and protect her.

"Liar. No one will look for you, not even your bad boys. They don't know you're here. Have you sent any messages that you've returned? I know you haven't. I've been keeping track."

"There are others who will be concerned about my location and by now they've figured out where you took me. It's really way too obvious and predictable. For God's sake, you took me to my home."

"But very few people know about it."

"My solicitor knows and these people I'm with know everything about my life, about me, who I've been with and probably what I'm thinking as well. I'm sure they know about you."

"How could they unless you told them?" To Broc she sounded indignant and annoyed.

"They're spies, Edina, and if you're not going to untie me, at least have the decency to fasten my pants. They'll be breaking in here soon, and I'm not really wanting to be seen with my privates hanging out." He lost all patience with this woman, and he'd known Addie long enough to understand she'd find this all very amusing, Hamilton as well. They would undoubtedly look for every opportunity to remind him.

"Spies? Why would you be with spies?" She sat down on the bed again, eyeing him critically. "I can't untie you. Maybe I should just leave. When they find you as you say they will undo the bindings, I won't be here and will suffer no repercussions."

"Not this time, Edina. If you don't untie me, I'll hunt you down and have you prosecuted. At the least you'll spend several years in jail." He hoped that bit of news would convince her to do his bidding.

He didn't want to spend any more time on thoughts of this woman. His sister as well as Bliss were far more important. And he prayed Addie and Hamilton wouldn't leave him here. He didn't want this.

It wasn't the first time since learning about her he wondered about his mother's life in a Turkish harem and how she could have possibly survived. He had a sister, Ayleen. How interesting and it seemed Flynt was more interested in her than he should be. The saving factor was that Hope, as they called her, was a servant. The bad boys had all made a pact that servants could not be seduced. It simply wouldn't be tolerated.

His gut tightened at his thoughts of Flynt and his sister, a woman he didn't even know, making love. Would Flynt make Hope his mistress if he got the chance? Had he already done just that? He'd been in London for months now. Anything could have happened in his absence. Hell, she could be with child right now.

Edina cleared her throat before sitting down beside him, "Well, you don't have to act that way." She huffed prettily, batting her lashes at him as if that would convince him to change his mind.

"And what way is that? Like a man tied to his bed after he's been abducted by his ex mistress?"

"You sound angry."

He was trying not to shake his head in disbelief. "I'm more than angry, and perhaps you should dress too. Or do you care if about twelve men barge in here and see you naked?"

"Maybe they would treat me better than you," she said in protest but she started dressing, finding her underclothes and donning them.

"Now, fasten my pants since we've both conceded the fact the sight and feel of you against me does nothing to stimulate me." He was trying to hold his temper in check when he wanted nothing more than to wring her neck and kick her to the gutter. "I treated you well when you were my mistress and after. You've nothing to complain about."

"If I untie you now, what will you do?" Once more she ran her fingernail down his chest, but this time with a defeated and very wistful sigh seeming to accept the fact she lost this game.

He coughed before clearing his throat. "This is a promise. I will have you give me the key to this townhouse, for the life of me I don't understand how you procured it then I will escort you outside. If I ever see you again, I'll have you arrested.

"I guess that sounds almost fair. Could you give me more money?" She moistened her lips as if that gesture would convince him.

"You had more than enough as well as the time to find yourself another man. What happened to that money?" He wasn't about to continue this ongoing fiasco with her.

"I spent it on necessities." She fumbled with the fabric of her skirts, attempting a sheepish look.

"That was lot of necessities. Now my pants..."

Finally, she did fasten them. "Are you happy?"

"More than you could ever guess. The bindings now or you'll come to regret your life." He wasn't sure how he would do that when he never wanted to see her again. Perhaps Addie and Hamilton could help him with that.

"Very well," she spoke softly and moving to the head of the bed, she tugged and pulled on the rope seeming to make no headway.

"What is taking you so long?" His arms began to cramp. His groan echoed around the bedroom.

"I didn't tie these and now I can't undo them. I'm trying, really I am."

"It seems we're going to have company soon," he said, hearing the noises from downstairs. "This might well be out of my hands when I'm discovered tied to a bed and you the attacker. I'm sure my friends saw you from their vantage place. You made no attempt to hide what you did."

"You promised."

"You waited too long," he said as the door burst open.

"Thought we'd never find you," Hamilton said with a snicker in his voice when he saw the woman and his predicament. "Are you enjoying yourself?" Then he turned to Addie, "You want to try this sometime?"

"As long as you're the one tied to the bed," she told him, grinning hands on her hips. "It does look like fun, but for some reason Broc doesn't think so. I assume this woman is not your fiancée."

Broc knew if he allowed it these two could go on forever baiting each other and laughing over all the various possibilities. Then he interrupted, "How long has it been? Seems I was knocked out cold."

"The sun has gone down on the day. Took us a while to sleuth out all the possibilities. We were lucky enough to see Flynt who shed some information on your plight with your ex-mistress," Addie said.

"We also talked to your solicitor, Conway? Or Conrad..." Hamilton waved his hand in the air, "Can't seem to remember. What was his name darling?"

"Not sure." Addie shrugged tiny shoulders with a shared grin between husband and wife.

"Thank god for our untimely arrival, but thank the gods above we found you before your arms rotted off. Looks like she can't get the ropes untied," Hamilton said, his snicker turning to full laughter. Then he turned to Addie and once again brought up the subject, "This has delightful possibilities. Would you like to tie me to our bed sometime?" he asked again as if he meant to waste as much time as possible.

"Absolutely, as long as you never return the favor. Seems a bit claustrophobic to me."

"I'm glad you see the possibilities. We could toast with champagne, strategically placed. I can already taste—"

"Hamilton, stop it. We're not alone now." A shade of pink painted her cheeks.

"Would you two stop playing around with sexual innuendos and just untie me before I've cramps in my arms so bad I can't move?" He was watching as Edina seemed to be slowly backing from the room. He didn't want to say anything, just wanted her out of his life.

"As long as you promise to come with us to the MacTavish estate before you go off on whatever tangent you had planned earlier. It will be dark so you can't possibly—"

"No, I won't promise anything of the sort."

"Tis a pity. Under the circumstances we need to stay in town. The roads at night aren't safe for anyone. Even Montgomerie's most trusted spies," Addie said, preening for Hamilton.

"Then I suppose you'll have to remain tied here," Hamilton said with a bit of a chuckle. "We must procure that promise before we cut the ropes."

"We really could just leave him here for the night and we wouldn't have to watch him," Addie said.

"Really, my dear, do you think that's fair?" Hamilton asked chuckling. "He's only a mere man."

"It's blackmail that's what it is and if I have to promise, I will," Broc said, realizing he had to find out where the grandmother lived before he could find Bliss and the MacTavish estate was as good a place as any to start. If Lacie or any of the other sisters were at home as he guessed they would be, then he'd have a head start.

Addie punched Hamilton in the chest before stepping back, hand on her hips and indignantly saying. "You let her get away when I was trying to untie those horrible bindings."

"And you would have said something if you disagreed with me," Hamilton challenged her. "Besides, Drakes men will never let her go until we give the word."

"That I would. Let's get this thing done so we can eat and get some rest. Tomorrow might be a very busy day."

"There," Hamilton let the ropes drop to the bed. "Feel better?"

Broc sat up, rubbing his arms and swearing softly. "Much better, now the two of you can stay here if you like, but I'm going to my apartment. Don't want to be here any longer than I have to be. Going to see my solicitor again about selling the place. It seems he neglected his job of months ago."

"We can't all stay here?" Addie asked, "Seems like the most logical place since we're already in the townhouse."

"I'm not and I made no promises about tonight's lodging." Broc picked up his coat, heading for the door. "I'll meet you here in the morning."

"How do we know you won't do just as you please?" Addie asked. "You don't."

~ * ~

Bliss sat on a blanket, another one over her lap, sketching the scene in front of her. She smiled when the baby kicked, afterward closing her eyes and wondering if this one little child waiting to be born was a boy or a girl.

She was due in another month, perhaps a bit more. It was nearing the last days of March now and she supposed this would be a spring baby born the end of April. Broc obviously didn't care about her, the infatuation was fast and it seemed to have burned out quickly.

Tiny frogs croaked as if they were the hugest bullfrogs in the pond while squirrels skittered up and down the trees. A bunny hopped by stopping to give her a look. She laughed, her spirits higher than they'd been

206

for months. With the bright warm day it seemed the animals wanted to play.

This sunny and warm weather sent her outdoors for warmth and feel of heat on her face. She'd been cooped up inside since the end of October, the rain not wanting to stop falling. Sitting in the shade of a huge weeping willow, she enjoyed the soft breeze caressing her. While the sun was shining, the wind made it seem colder.

The sketch was almost finished and she intended this one as a watercolor. In her portfolio there were at least four sketches she could turn into paintings. Nial had been in town several times over the last six months, visiting the gallery and checking on her bank account. He didn't seem to mind and actually said he enjoyed the excursion, because on the way home he got to stop by the MacTavish estate and talk to Catherine.

Nial missed Catherine and he was sorely tempted to haul her grandmother over his shoulder and bring her home. Either that or he should bring the girls here and she could chaperone them out of her home instead of Flynt's. To Nial it seemed more practical that way.

He told her he didn't imagine Flynt would care overmuch. The man seemed enamored of the young lady who showed up with no memory and no money. In fact, Flynt might even enjoy having the house to himself and Hope. Who knows what would happen then?

The baby kicked again, this time seeming harder than the last. She pressed on either some elbows or knees trying to make herself more comfortable as she adjusted the baby's position inside her womb. It would surely be nice if all of April flew by without her knowing it. Her nights were uncomfortable as were her days. It seemed the child didn't want her to sleep or even rest, for that matter. She was exhausted constantly, even when she rose in the morning. Men should have to bear children so they would appreciate the process.

She sat up straighter, stretching her back and shoulder muscles, hoping to get some relief from the constant strain of carrying the extra weight. This last month fatigue had been a constant companion and she'd been having some cramping. She was told that was normal.

Nial should show up soon, lecturing her on staying out of the cold. But the sunshine had been so refreshing she couldn't bring herself to leave and go indoors. The weather might turn stormy by tomorrow and she needed to harvest the benefits of good weather as long as the daylight lasted.

True to form, she heard Nial's footsteps. The lecture would come next then he would most likely sit down beside her and watch her draw for a few minutes. She would concede and follow him to her little home and with a hug would send him to the main house.

"Bliss?"

She stiffened, her heart racing while her breath caught in her throat. She closed her eyes before running her tongue along lips that had become suddenly dry. This couldn't be true, could it? Had he come to torment her with more of his harsh words about his friendship to her brother that was worth more to him than he felt about her? Posthaste, she would send him on his way before he could cause any more pain.

"Broc, go away." She slowly looked up to see him studying her, seeming to watch her every move. His feet braced apart, he'd never appeared more handsome and debonair than he did now. "What do you want?" her voice quavered slightly, wishing this confrontation was not about to take place.

He sat down beside her, taking one of her hands in his, "Just to talk. I want to know how you are and hear about the last few months. Have you sold your paintings? Do you have enough money? Is there anything I can get for you?"

"Can't talk now. Haven't you already said enough?" She tugged her hand away and it seemed he begrudgingly let it go. A shiver of dread swept through her as she braced for his scathing words. "I want you to leave." Now before he sees that I'm pregnant.

"Not until I've said what I came here to say. May I look at your sketches?" he asked, seeming to seek a different approach.

"No." She swiftly closed the pad as well as her mind to anything he might try to tell her. Her body shaking with emotions, it was all she could do to stop herself from running into his arms and playing the fool. "Why are you here?"

"To ask for your forgiveness." His voice was quiet yet held a note of wistfulness she'd never before heard from him.

"You should beg, no grovel if you want me to forgive, otherwise this is all a pretense. I don't want to listen to excuses and half truths." Her voice trembled more than the rest of her.

"Did you get my letters? Stupid question. It's obvious you did not. And you're right, I should grovel, just not sure how to go about doing that." He reached out to her then withdrew his hand.

"There were no letters." Yet her heart sped faster at the thought he might have tried to talk to her in the last six months. He wouldn't lie about something that was so important.

"I sent one every week and one before I left. What happened to them? I suppose Flynt might have stopped them from coming here, but I posted the letters to Lacie with instructions not to let Flynt know about them."

"Lacie?" She paid her a visit once a week since Broc left but she wasn't always home. "I do think she brought them and they must have been intercepted. If Lacie promised, she's true to her words. Besides, she likes you and probably forgave you as soon as you smiled at her."

"That's what I was counting on. So, what happened to the letters? Do you have any ideas?"

This time when he picked up her hand she didn't take it away. The same familiar sensations swept through her, and she was reminded of a time that was so long ago but it was also a time she'd never forget. No, the moments when her world crashed in around her would always be vivid in her head. For a short time he meant the world to her.

"Nial," she told him. "You're not his favorite person. He might have kept them from me in the guise of protection." Broc was rubbing gentle, tantalizing circles on the underside of her wrist. The last thing she wanted was to fall under his subtle seduction again, but if truth be told that was exactly what was happening right now and she was allowing it.

"Should we go find out the truth?" He stood, keeping his hand in hers to help her up she supposed.

Swallowing her fear, she stared at him for a second. Well, he would know soon enough about her condition, and she'd known the secret would not be hidden from him forever. The breath of air she inhaled was long and deep. "Yes, I for one would like some clarity. Nial had no right to keep anything from me no matter his good intentions."

With his help, she stood then, his gaze raked over, his eyes widening in what appeared to be surprise. "Why didn't you tell me?" His voice filled with indignation, almost anger, as he stared at her swollen belly.

"I planned on telling you that last night we were together, but you wouldn't let me. After that you wouldn't talk to me," she told him, watching him grit his teeth his jaw twitching. "I sent several messages but you never came, never responded. What was I supposed to do? And the last time I saw you, you were on board a ship sailing away from Glasgow to God knows where. I certainly didn't."

He was holding both her hands, his grip tightening as he gazed at her now a wee bit of awe touching his features. Then he smiled at her. "I wish I had known. When are you due?"

She lifted her shoulders slightly before relaxing, bringing her lips together then, "The end of April, perhaps May."

"You're huge though," he blurted without thought.

"Thank you for telling me something I didn't already know." Her voice curt, she turned from him, the fleeting moment where she almost gave her heart to this man again vanished into the fading sunshine of the day. He had to earn her, she decided, and she would not give anything to him today.

"I'm sorry." He immediately turned contrite. "That was not nice of me, but are you sure you still have another month?"

"Do you want to argue with the midwife?" she asked, trying to gather her sketches but in her present state of mind as well as her condition, she was failing miserably.

"Let me help." He bent over, his arm brushing against hers, sending undeniable shivers up her spine.

"I can do it myself," she said, too curt but made the point she intended. "I'm only pregnant, not sick or incapacitated." She shouldn't feel this way about him, shouldn't react to a simple touch this way.

"Whatever you want." He wisely stepped back, giving her the room she was asking him for, his hands clasped behind his back as he watched her fumble with everything then try to stand.

She managed to put herself in the most awkward position, and she'd never be able to stand and pick up the sketchpad as well as her pencils.

Sitting down and exasperated, tears flowed, turning into sobs.

Once more he sat down beside her. "You don't have to prove anything to me. I'll help with out expecting anything in return." Gently, he brushed tears from her eyes.

Despite the fact she did need to prove something to him but begrudgingly admitted at least to herself and now to him it wasn't going to be this time. "Will you please help me?"

"Yes, I would take on all your burdens if I could." He smiled and with so much ease, he picked up her belongings then helped her stand. He paused as if waiting for a thank you.

"You caused this you know," she told him, yet she accepted his arm.

Her words seemed to give him a reason to smile. He was glad about that but it didn't seem he thought it prudent to tell her, at least not right now. "Do you think it's a boy or a girl?" he whispered next to her ear, his tongue softly touching the lobe, so gentle she wasn't sure at first.

"You need to stop that. I'm not going to fall into your bed tonight despite what you're attempting."

"I'd rather carry you than watch you stumble." He laughed then and the sound was of man satisfied and well pleased with himself.

"I'm too huge." She watched him grimace when she tossed his words back to him.

"You're perfect to me and I do believe you're going to have a very big baby." His steps took on a carefree lilt, most likely a boy.

"You would say that." Just the attempt at standing as well as the verbal sparring with Broc made her tired beyond what she should feel.

"Are you sure you're not due sooner than the end of April?" he asked again. His voice etched with concern.

"The conception would have taken place in July if that's the case," she said, wondering what he thought about that. He would know that wasn't possible. When he took her virginity, he'd been aware of the fact and it wasn't July.

After a swift intake of breath, "We both know that didn't happen. We weren't... we didn't..."

It seemed he was at a loss for words and the thought gave her reason to smile. For the first time, she rendered this man nearly speechless. For the first time in a very long while, she was pleased with herself. A woman well satisfied.

"You are aware that you were my first and my only lover, not that you're my lover any more. Or have you forgotten that?" She leaned against him provocatively, purposely tempting him, but she wasn't sure if it was working or if she even wanted the ploy to work. Of course she didn't. She'd just told him he wouldn't have a place in her bed anytime soon.

"There is nothing about our relationship that I've forgotten," he gritted out, seemingly frustrated or angry.

She couldn't be certain of the emotions driving him, "Neither have I, forgotten anything. I've thought of little else for so many months I've lost count and as my belly has grown and I was sure I'd be a parent with no spouse, understanding people would ostracize me. Still nothing has changed except your arrival here. I will fight you with every breath in my body."

"Fight me?" It seemed he had no idea what she spoke of.

"I won't let you take my baby away from me. You didn't even care enough to...to."

"I've been out of the country on business and why would I take your baby away, our baby?" His question shot home.

She didn't want to put any ideas in his head that weren't already there. And yet, he would pursue this until she answered him, "Because you're a man and you can."

"Again, why would I do that? You're speaking in ways I don't understand and are perhaps beyond my manly sensibilities."

Inhaling a long deep breath filled with frustration along with despair, "We aren't married. If you want him or her, I'm sure the law would give him to you. Over my dead body," she murmured, once more tears threatened.

"First and foremost we are going to be married."

She let go of his arm, trying to distance herself from him, but he caught her, wiling her to look at him. "No..."

"Bliss..."

Stumbling into him, she fell into his arms. "I'm not marrying you just because we've a child together. That's not what marriage is about."

"I won't have a bastard."

"And I won't pledge my life to someone who wants me only because I carry his child. I won't. I just won't." She tried to run from him but stumbled again and would have fallen had he not caught her, saving her from herself.

"Would you marry me if I wanted you because I don't think I can live without you?" he asked, pulling her close, her swollen belly resting against him. "Because I've discovered I need you in my life more than I need to breathe."

"Liar, you say that now because the words will serve your purpose, sway me to your way of thinking. They won't. I remember vividly what you said to me after Flynt caught me naked with you."

"My sweet Bliss, mo mhilse, you are so stubborn and obstinate and adorable. I'm not lying. Should we see if Nial has the letters?"

Bloody hell, but she wanted him to kiss her, touch her, make love to her, but she didn't want to fall for his lies or any ploys he might conceive to make her change her mind. She felt as if she was a puddle of mush. "Yes."

"Good then, I'll prove myself in your eyes as soon as you read them." He was laughing and she didn't understand why. "I'd like to swing you around in my arms and hold you close, you adorable woman. I want to make love to right now and touch your swollen belly. Would I feel my son kick? But I know you need to see the proof of my words before you'll commit to me."

She breathed softly, wishing with all her heart she could believe him, "Commit to a bad boy? Who ever heard of such a thing?"

"I'm not such a bad boy." He stopped, brushing his lips against hers. "But you can be a very naughty lady when you want."

She wanted more, needed his tongue deep inside her mouth, but more than anything she needed to believe in him and trust in him again. "You don't think I know all your manly maneuvers?"

"I would hope I've a few tricks left you don't know. I really hope Nial is the one keeping my letters from you, because I would love a bit of redemption in your eyes and his as well."

"You really want redemption then? Is this part of your groveling or can I expect more after we make up? If we do make up." Her feelings were so meshed together she didn't know what she thought. They so easily fell into an easy camaraderie it seemed they never had an argument and he never left her, never implied to her he would take her brother's friendship over her love.

"Come, before we make any more decisions let's find out the truth." Lightly, he touched a finger to her lips.

"Did you really write me a letter?" She would be happy with one and ecstatic with more.

"Letters every day. I did, but right now we're basing everything on Nial keeping the letters from you and if he didn't, I don't know how I can convince you of anything."

In silence and with her nerves stretched to a breaking point, they walked the rest of the way to the house. Stepping through the kitchen they were met with an ominous silence.

"Nial," she called out. "Nial, are you there?" For some reason she needed Nial's support, longed for Broc to be an important part of her life. And Nial, he could have left for the MacTavish estate, something he did on a regular basis now days.

"Bliss..." Nial rounded the corner. He stopped it seemed when he saw Broc, his voice gruff and demanding. "What are you doing here where you're not welcome?"

"Don't you think Bliss has a right to see the letters I wrote her?" Broc asked as if he knew they'd been delivered and it was Nial who kept them from Bliss.

He paled, "A scoundrel like you is beyond redemption," he growled, his voice low and deep while his hands were fisted at his sides. "The letters might have broken her heart all over again. After what you did and said, you've no privileges in this house."

"All you say is true, but I want to make things right for Bliss and the only way to do that is if you hand over the letters I've been sending for the last six months or more. I need for Bliss to appreciate how I feel and how much I care for her goes beyond the baby she's carrying. Did you read them? You would understand if you did."

"No," Nial said, grumbling. "Didn't want to intrude on her privacy or yours for that matter."

"But you chose to withhold them. Don't you think that's doing the same thing?" Broc spoke, his words sharp and to the point. "They were meant for Bliss and she should have been given the letters, her choice to read or not."

"I'll get them for Bliss. Despite my feelings for you, I suppose you're right. Bliss needs to see for herself if you're the scoundrel I believe you are or if you have at least one redeeming attribute among all of your flaws."

In the parlor, Nial opened a desk drawer and held the letters out to Bliss. "Here they are. Read them and make your decision."

Broc sat down, stretching his legs out, hands folded in his lap with an expression of content. "Finally," he murmured.

She was afraid to open the envelopes, terrified they weren't what she needed to see. She held the messages close to her heart, waiting for the right moment, wishing she had privacy. At this moment her feelings would be evident to Broc. Inhaling, in hopes of a brief moment of courage, she opened the first letter from six months ago. Slowly staring down at it, she read, her heart pounding.

When she finally finished with every word in all the letters, she set them on her lap, unstoppable tears running from her eyes.

"Bliss?" He was on his feet, striding toward before pulling her into his arms. "What's wrong?"

Suddenly, she screamed, bent over in pain. "Oh, my God, not now." She clung to him, her fingers digging into his arms. "No...no..."

"Are you alright?" He swept her into his arms, seemingly terrified.

The pain subsided just as quickly and unexpectedly as the initial contraction. Unbeknownst to anyone, she'd been having small ones for days now. It was too soon for the child to be born, at least a month too soon.

I'm fine." She sighed a soft moan, relieved that perhaps that was the only one for some time. It had been two days since the first pain, but it was much less severe.

"A moment ago you didn't look fine," he said, concern imprinted in his voice and his face. "You should sit down, rest. I'll get you a glass of water." He started for the pitcher of water then turned. "Have you been taking care of yourself?"

"I haven't done anything that would hurt the baby, if that's what you're asking," she told him, peeved at his attitude and the thought she would risk the child she carried in any way.

He returned with the water, handing it to her and seeming to wait for her to down all of it. She sipped before placing it on an end table.

He got down on one knee, taking her hands in his. "Will you marry me now?" He smiled at her but it wasn't with his usual air of confidence.

"I suppose so." She knew her reply wasn't enthusiastic, but at this time it was all she could do, all energy having drained from her body.

His grin changed to one of satisfaction, "I'll have Nial fetch the preacher from the church down the road."

"Is there some hurry I don't know about?"

~ * ~

Addie and Hamilton stepped into the MacTavish parlor a few seconds ahead of Broc, thinking he would stay for the briefing, but he pushed past them to go to the kitchen.

The young woman they traveled to Scotland to protect greeted them. She was tall, a bit too thin but her ginger colored hair caught light from the sun, seeming to set it a blaze. Addie couldn't help but understand how hair like that in a land where most everyone had coal black hair would infatuate a young man.

Addie held her hand out, "I'm Addie and this is Hamilton. I suppose you know the man who stormed into the kitchen without stopping to talk."

"I'm Hope." She accepted Addie's hand, smiling and curtsying. "Please make yourselves comfortable and I'll get Flynt. He's in the library. Yes," she looked his way, "I know Broc but he hasn't been around for quite a while."

"Broc really doesn't matter, I'm sure he has his plans and we can't stop him," Addie said, smiling as she looked in the direction Broc disappeared.

"Tell Flynt we were sent by Drake Montgomerie. I'm sure he will recognize the name and make sure you inform him this is urgent business which concerns the entire family," Hamilton stepped into the conversation seemingly impatient with Addie.

"Really, Hamilton, did you have to make this sound so serious. You'll scare the poor man." Then she waved her hand in the air, "That was really not well done of you."

"Can you think of a better way?" Hamilton shot back. "Besides this is a serious matter, and nothing I said was anything but the truth. Are you going to find out what Broc is up to?"

"My dear husband, we know what Broc is up to, he's off to see Bliss and I'm sure that until some later date we won't hear from him."

"He promised," Hamilton said dryly.

"He fulfilled his promise and left. We no longer have leverage over him." Addie stared at her nails, seemingly bored with the situation.

"What promise?"

Another man strode into the room, "You must be Flynt." Hamilton stepped forward, hand outstretched in greeting. "We've important news and hoped Broc would stay since he has a vested interest in what we're about to tell you. I'm Hamilton and this is Addie."

Flynt nodded toward the door and Hope seemed to understand, turning to leave. "I'll find you when we're finished here."

"This involves Hope too," Addie quickly spoke up before the young woman could vanish into the house.

"Hope?" Flynt asked, "You have news of her, of who she is?"

"We do and of course it's important for her to hear and see if she remembers anything. Perhaps this information about her mother and father will be helpful." Hamilton sat down, crossing his legs and seeming to wait for everyone to settle in.

"May I get everyone something to drink?" Hope asked, assuming her role as a servant.

Addie bristled, "Why don't you sit down and either I'll serve or Flynt can do it."

Flynt tossed her a puzzled look then, "By all means, sit all of you. I will be happy to serve, brandy or tea? Not really sure where or how to do the tea if that's what you prefer," he mumbled, seemingly a bit put off by the quickly changing circumstances.

"Brandy is fine," Addie said, "For all of us. Never knew Hamilton to drink tea unless it was under duress."

"Addie is certainly right about all of what she says. Never want to disagree with her if I want her in my bed at night." Hamilton laughed when he noticed the look on his wife's face.

Addie sat down, smoothing her skirts and patting a place beside her for Hope before accepting the glass from Flynt and enjoying the fact this man was serving a lady as well as his servant.

"I'm not sure..." Hope hesitated before accepting the brandy.

Addie leaned into her, smiling, "It will burn going down, but you'll get used to it. Might even come to like it. Take small sips at first."

Flynt stood, watching over the small group of people that were about to change his life forever. Addie prayed he had not taken Hope's virginity yet. He really needed to know who she was and that she needed to be treated with respect, not, she assumed that he didn't treat women that way but this was different. If he'd taken her innocence, he might feel duty bound to wed her and that wasn't a perfect scenario for a lady.

"Would you like me to begin the story?" Addie asked Hamilton, "Or do you think you can do a better job?"

"You should start. We both know I'll finish and of course, dear, I could never do a better job than you. Carry on," Hamilton said, sitting back, his grin stretching from ear to ear.

"I'm going to start at the very beginning," Addie sipped then set the glass down before clearing her throat a couple of times. She looked in Hope's direction then toward Flynt.

She glared at Flynt, "You were too young to remember any of this and Hope was only a baby when the dastardly deed was carried out."

"A dastardly deed?" Flynt nearly chocked on his drink. "Don't you think that's a bit over dramatic?"

"Oh, no the deed was indeed dastardly." She tuned to look at Hope, "How old are you, my dear?"

For a woman as tall as she was, her shoulders were slim and delicate and when she shrugged it became more obvious. "I'm not sure, but I believe I'm eighteen or nineteen."

"Well, I do know. You are eighteen and will be nineteen on

February twenty-fifth."

Hope's eyes widened. "Really?" She appeared awe struck. "How do you know all that?"

"Over nineteen years ago your mother," Addie paused, obviously to create more drama, "Sara Wallace, was riding in a carriage, on her way home when she was waylaid and abducted."

Addie expected more of a reaction from Flynt. When there was none she went on to say. "Sara Wallace," and turning to Flynt she said, "You do know one Wallace, a Broc Wallace."

Flynt's fingers tightened on his glass and Addie watched as he downed the contents before pouring another. "What does all this mean?" He seemed to suddenly have a good idea.

"We're far from getting to the meaning, at least where you are concerned," Hamilton interjected before looking to his wife for approval or not. Then he lifted his shoulders almost apologetically. "Should I take the next part of the journey?"

"Be my guest," Addie said, gesturing with her hand toward her husband. "My throat is parched, and I've the feeling Flynt is terribly obtuse. This is going to take a very long time. We're going to have to spell out every little nuance. So, it would most likely be prudent if we took our time."

Speaking slowly as if it was for Flynt's sake, "Sara Wallace is Broc's mother as well as Hope's or Ayleen, her birth name. They are brother and sister much the same as you and Bliss are brother and sister."

Addie smiled, watching the myriad of expressions that swept across Flynt's face. Hope might be catching some of this, but Broc had been gone for six months and Addie didn't know how well Hope knew either one of them.

"You said Sara Wallace was abducted. What happened to her?" Flynt asked. "We only heard speculation."

"Sara's not my mother's name," Hope said.

"Do you remember something?" Addie asked, eagerly sitting forward, hopeful the young woman could fill in a few of the blank spaces in the story.

Hope pursed her lips, shaking her head too, "I just know Sara is not her name. That's all. I've never called her by that."

"Sara is her Christian name. I'm sure her captors gave her a different one." Hamilton held his glass to Flynt, silently asking for a second brandy.

"The name you know her by doesn't matter, Hope. What makes a difference here is that your mother is Sara and she wanted desperately to see you escape what was her fate," Hamilton said.

"She knew the sultan's son, the man who captured her and kept her prisoner against her will, wanted you. Sara found a way to get you away, out of the harem and to Scotland. What your mother didn't bargain on was the accident. You were supposed to end up at Deepwood, your family home," Addie said softly, believing with time all the information could be mulled over and accepted.

"I don't remember any of that. I've things that come to me, things I know how to do but specifics I can't remember." Hope rubbed her temples, frown lines marring her delicate features.

Hamilton finished the story, including all the details and specifics they did know. "In any case, you are in danger. We've good sources and we know he's looking for you and will stop at nothing to retrieve his lost concubine."

"Concubine!" Flynt had been silent for some time but now his anger seemed to overcome the silence.

Chapter Ten

"The hurry lies in the fact that I don't want our child born a bastard and it's my belief the baby wants to see the world and his new parents sooner than later." He grinned, smoothing the hair from her face and realizing the last contraction took more energy from her than she wanted to admit. Quickly he brushed his lips across hers in a gentle kiss, one meant to reassure.

"I think we should send for grandmother too, and Hope." Her voice sounded strained as if she understood what he was not so subtly but successfully trying to tell her.

"Wait here for one minute. I'll be right back." He put his hands out. "Don't go away." Broc didn't hesitate. He strode from the room, calling out for Nial who quickly appeared as if he'd been expecting him.

"Get the minister from the church down the road. There is going to be a wedding and send someone to get Catherine." Broc felt as if his heart was going to pound out of his chest. It seemed he couldn't move fast enough.

"Why?" Nial asked gruffly, "Not so sure what all the hurry is about. The midwife and the minister all at the same time, what's got you in such a huff?"

"Bliss is going to have the baby today or tomorrow I'm sure of it. Do you want the child to be born a bastard?" His question was to the point and he watched as the older man turned white. He felt as if his world turned upside down and he'd been thrust into something he was ill prepared for. All he knew though was that he was glad he made it back before the baby was born and he was going to marry Bliss.

"The baby now?" he asked, his voice a gravelly whisper. "The child's not due for another month at least. "Don't you think you're rushing things? You could take your time and have a nice wedding."

"That's why we need Catherine or the midwife, but I'm assuming Catherine's been performing that role since she knew she was pregnant."

He was nodding his head, bobbing up and down. "I'll get the minister and send the stable boy for Catherine. She's not the midwife but I'm sure she'll know what to do."

"Good, tell the boy he must hurry. It's a matter of life and death."

Nial turned from white to grey. "Death?"

"Women have been known to die in childbirth, and I know nothing about the process. I'm sure while her body does all the hard parts, we'd both like someone knowledgeable here to help Bliss if something goes wrong. Now go." He stared hard at Nial. "Have you ever delivered a child?"

Broc prayed Nial understood the gravity of the situation and would pass it on to the stable boy as well as the preacher. He turned, striding to Bliss then helping her to the cottage.

"I need to get you relaxed. How are the contractions?"

He was beside himself, so many questions swirling in his head. His mind seemed a bit incoherent.

Once he settled her on a comfortable chair, "How are you doing?" He needed to know every detail, but he didn't want her to think he was hovering even though he was. "Can I get you anything?"

"I'm fine. You don't have to treat me as if I'll break. I'm pregnant, not on my deathbed." She sounded indignant and he wanted to laugh, but the gravity of this situation hit home with a sudden force. It was a moment of weakness. Bloody hell, he'd been away, unable to protect her and help her through any difficulties. She wasn't alone now and he was going to make damn sure she knew he was here for her.

"I understand you can walk, but we both know this little boy is not going to wait until the end of April to make his appearance. You need to rest right now and make sure you have the strength you're going to need to get through this."

"You don't know it's a boy. This child could just as easily be a girl. Would you care?" Yet she sounded as if she convinced herself he was right.

"Don't know why, but I'm pretty sure I'm right. Now, what can I

222

get for you? Something to eat? You are going to need your strength." He felt tongue-tied and it seemed he kept repeating himself. "I don't care if our baby is a boy or a girl, just healthy." And he realized he cared as much or more for Bliss' health.

"What could I possibly need?" she asked, putting her feet on a table before inhaling a deep breath.

"I could have done that for you," he told her, bringing her a quilt and covering her. He was acting like a fool but he couldn't help himself.

"What has come over you? Where is Broc and can I have him back, please?" she mumbled, yet it seemed she snuggled into the cover with a yawn. Then, closing her eyes, "I am tired. Seems like I've been on the verge of exhaustion for the longest time."

"That's a good idea, close your eyes. You can take a short nap before the minister arrives."

She sat up, ignoring his words. "What is going on here?"

"I sent Nial for the minister and he in turn has sent the stable boy for your grandmother. We will be wed in about an hour, and we will also have someone competent to deliver this child when the time arrives."

"Who would that be?" she asked, stretching her back and grimacing as if every part of her was in pain.

"Catherine, your grandmother, the midwife, isn't she?" he asked, baffled for the first time then realized Nial just told him the same thing. Good Lord, he was losing his mind.

She was smiling and shaking her head. "Catherine is not my midwife. I've been seeing..." she broke off as another contraction ripped through her.

To Broc, the pain seemed to last the longest time. He set his hand on her belly as if that would help and felt the muscles clench as if preparing for the birth. Awe swept through him. The contraction stopped then, and he watched as she closed her eyes and struggled to push herself upward.

Needing to help, yet he didn't know what to do. She was already sitting, with something to drink. "Should you lie down?"

"No, I think I'd like to walk a bit. Just around the room. Could you help me stand?"

In a second he was beside her, helping her, wishing he knew what the hell he was doing. "Is this good for you, walking? Don't you really think you should be in bed, resting?" he asked, too unsure of himself to even pretend to think straight.

She shrugged then, "How would I know? I've never done this before, and I wasn't very old myself when my sisters were born. Just to change the conversation, why don't you tell me what you did in London?"

"Found my sister," he mumbled, thinking on that subject and the fact Hope was with Flynt and under his roof. "Not really in the mood to talk about myself. I was told about her and where she was."

"Sister...?" She stopped walking. "Didn't know you had one."

"Neither did I." He proceeded to tell Bliss all about the lost sister, Hope, and the mother he barely knew. His feelings were in such a jumble over that, but he didn't have time to think about anything or anyone except Bliss.

"How do you feel about this development?" She turned to him, seemingly concerned. "Hope is living with Flynt."

"About the baby, excited, terrified, hopeful and I think I could keep listing things. Don't have any idea what to do with one."

"About your sister," she clarified, "come, let's sit. I think I need a shoulder to lean on. I'm tired and terrified too. I'm afraid of what's about to happen to me."

"It's a bit ironic don't you think that Flynt is attracted to my sister unbeknownst to him. Can't say as I feel overly protective though. He's probably learning the truth right now."

"You should and you shouldn't. Flynt won't hurt her just like you never intended to hurt me," Bliss whispered, settling into his arms. "You only hurt me when you left and never told me why you cared more about Flynt's friendship than our relationship."

"But I did and I think Catherine will make sure Flynt either woos her correctly and as a gentleman or weds her right now. I know he's interested in her. I've seen the way he watches her."

With a bit of hesitancy, "Are you really marrying me for me and not the child?"

"Yes." He couldn't think of a rational explanation for it. He did want the child in every conceivable way but if the mother wasn't Bliss, he wouldn't have sought out a preacher. He would have provided for the baby but marrying the mother would have been out of the question.

"Is that all, just yes?" she asked tentatively. "I'd hoped to hear something more. But then..."

"But then what?" he asked, wondering what more she could want to know. "I want you and I want to spend the rest of my life going to bed and waking up in the morning with you in my arms."

"I want that too, but I've known it for a long..." Another contractions gripped her as she moaned in pain.

"They're getting closer together." His fingers drummed the chair as nervous energy coursed through him, wishing Nial would make an appearance with the preacher this instant.

"It's the first child. There is lots of time, so I've been told. Sometimes they take all day to finally be born."

"And sometimes I'm sure it doesn't take that long."

"We're here, I brought the minister along with his wife. Can we come in?" Nial called from the doorway.

"Please, thank goodness." he said, relieved at least the wedding would take place before the birth.

"Are all parties willing?" the minister asked, looking to Bliss then back to him. "Won't do this any other way on such a spur of the moment."

Nial must have said something to him about the urgency and their unsteady relationship. Nial didn't like him or trust him. "We are," Broc spoke up before Bliss could answer.

"I am too," she spoke softly. "I want to marry Broc if he still wants me and please, before the baby is born."

Broc was sure she was hiding another contraction, her face was strained and lines were etched across her forehead. "Then we need to start the ceremony right now."

The minister stood in front of the fireplace, Broc beside him, his hands clasped behind his back, and he suddenly realized he had no ring to give her. He would have to get one soon. For now they would have to make do with nothing.

Nial cleared his throat then seeming to read his mind, "One minute, I think Catherine would like Bliss to have this." He vanished out the front door and a few minutes later he returned. "This is the engagement ring from your grandfather to your grandmother, Bliss. Your mother's ring will go to your brother."

Tears formed in Bliss' eyes. "If it's alright with Broc."

"I didn't have a ring for you. This all happened in such a hurry. The ring will be perfect."

"And you had such a long time to purchase one but then you decided to marry me when? When you saw I carried your child?" Her words were accusatory but made their point.

They'd already been over this and as far as Broc was concerned, once was enough. He told her how he felt. That should be enough. "When I was on my way back from London but you couldn't know that. You have to trust in me and my word. Can you do that, Bliss, trust me?"

She looked down, hiding her eyes from him as well as her expression. He knew then this was not going to be easy, but there were more pressing problems confronting him. He didn't think he was wrong, but Bliss' contractions were very close together. This wedding was taking longer than he expected, and it wasn't going to be another twelve hours before his son arrived.

"Then should we start?" The minister's wife asked, seemingly as impatient as he was. "There is no time like the present."

"Not until Hope and I get settled. Dear, you can't marry without your grandmother at the wedding." Catherine walked inside, arms open wide. "And your dress... Oh my," Her gaze settled on Bliss. "We best get started."

It seemed Catherine saw the tensions lines radiating in Bliss' face also and knew more than she was saying.

"You and Nial can sit, turn the chairs around. Grandmother, will you give me away?" Bliss asked.

"I'd be honored. Oh dear there is no bouquet. This is not the wedding I would have dreamed for you. Remember when you were little and we used to..." She stopped staring at Broc and his hard expression.

"Grandmother, we really should begin. We can reminisce later." With Broc's help, she stood.

"No," Hope spoke up. "You've all waited too long. The baby is coming any second now."

Broc's heart seemed to lodge in his throat along with more frustration he'd ever felt before. "We're getting married now." He tried to stand firm in the face of increasing opposition.

"And this baby is going to be born before you can finish with the vows," Hope insisted. "You need to think of Bliss first, not yourself. No one will consider your baby a bastard if you wed after they are born. Indeed, no one in this room would dare say otherwise."

Broc felt as if that was what he was doing, but the world seemed to be caving in all around him and he could do nothing to stop it. He looked to the minister, "Give us the shortest version possible," then to Catherine, "Please..."

Bliss inhaled swiftly again, another contraction taking control of her body. But she held onto Catherine, slowly taking the steps toward him.

"You really should..." Hope began but was cut off by Nial.

"Hush..." Nial whispered, stopping Hope from whatever it was she planned on saying. "This has to take place now before the child is born. The baby won't be born in the next five minutes."

"I suppose things are different here than where I come from, but one thing is the same. When babies are ready to make their way into the world, they do. But you're right, not in the next five minutes."

"Who gives this woman...?" the minister asked, appearing confused yet taking control of the ceremony in light of all that was happening.

"I do and with love." Catherine spoke, handing her to Broc who took Bliss' hands in his.

The minister's words as well as the short ceremony seemed a hazy fog in Broc's mind. This was the culmination of one life and the beginning of another, one he was looking forward to and thrilled to discover all of Bliss and the opportunities they could share together.

"I do," Bliss said her voice barely audible.

"You may kiss the bride," the minister said.

"Finally." He breathed against her lips, brushing his softly against hers, thinking to deepen the kiss just a bit.

"Broc!"

"What is it?" He stepped back, concerned as Bliss doubled over, seeming to lose control over her body.

"My water broke." She stood in a pool of liquid. "I..."

"Did anyone go for the midwife?" Catherine asked, a strange expression on her face, yet seemingly oblivious to the fact Hope had been performing that duty. Broc wondered what they weren't saying and why.

"I can deliver the babies." Hope stepped forward. "It's one of those things I don't remember why I know. I just do. I've been visiting Bliss and I suppose one could say I've been her midwife for the past six months."

"Thank god. Babies?" Broc breathed as he held her up more terrified now than he had been five minutes ago but at least they were wed. The signing of the papers could wait until the birth. "We should get you to a chair."

"No, she should walk as long as she feels able, then get the tarp I'm sure Catherine has purchased and cover the bed with it. Broc, you can help then I trust you will keep to yourself out here in the parlor. Sip some brandy play some cards or whatever it is men do when their women are doing all the work for them and their future heirs."

Broc heard recrimination in Hope's voice and wasn't sure what to make of it. In truth, he had no idea how to think about his sister at all and the knowledge his mother lived in a harem and his sister had been brought up in the way of the women there.

"Bliss is giving birth now?" Flynt strode into the room, his body rigid. "I thought..." he began.

"It's all true and Bliss is my wife now so I want you to remember that." Broc watched the man he called friend for so many years sit down, the strain of all this seeming to get the better of him, he rubbed his hand across his jaw.

"Where's Hope," Flynt asked.

"Right here. Bliss, we're ready for you now." Hope turned to Broc. "Will you help get her into the bedroom and ready."

Flynt rose to do what Hope bade as if Bliss was still his responsibility. Broc shook his head at him then turned toward his wife. He liked the way that word sounded in his thoughts, and he was sure he'd love the way wife sounded when he spoke it and he was about to have a child. Did Hope say babies? Plural?

"Bliss is mine now, Flynt. Don't you ever forget it." Broc said.

"I suppose she is. Can't seem to help the brotherly instincts though. I've been her guardian for so long."

"Just remember Hope is my sister." Broc said the words slowly as if he meant to emphasize every word.

Inside the room, Hope closed the door. All business now, she began, "You need to help her out of her clothes and into her nightdress. I understand you haven't been married long, but it seems you must have been intimate." Hope smiled at him and he was struck by her beauty, wondering if their mother looked anything like Hope.

A few minutes later Bliss was dressed and on the bed, appearing terrified, her face blanched of all color. "I'll stay by you," he told her as he sat down on the side of the bed.

"No, you won't," Hope said. "Men are to wait outside so they won't faint when babies are born, causing more trouble. We've enough to do caring for the mother and the newborn without having to worry about the father's health. Personally, I would leave you sprawled on the floor, but I'm sure Catherine wouldn't like that."

There it was again, babies.

Bliss cried out then, the scream piercing Broc's heart. He would do anything he could to alleviate the pain or take it into himself. He tried to stand firm. "I'm staying."

"No." Hope was shaking her head while she grabbed his arm leading him to the exit. "If you don't leave now, I'll call Flynt."

Those words were enough incentive for Broc. He didn't want Flynt seeing Bliss this way. "I'll go but if I hear anything or think Bliss needs me, you're to call me. I promise you I won't stay out here, and if I'm in the room, I won't faint."

"If she needs you, I'll call you. Men have a way though, of getting in the way." Once again she smiled that angelic smile that would sway any man to her purpose. And again his mind traveled to his mother.

Bliss screamed again and when he started toward her, Catherine stepped in his path. "Hope says no, so I'm going to honor her command as well as her knowledge in these events."

"Has she been her midwife all along?"

Catherine nodded, "Yes, and her knowledge is beyond anyone I've known. Bliss is in good hands. Everything will be fine. Go out with the men and have a drink or two. I don't think it will be long before your child is born."

Broc slowly backed from the room, his gaze riveted on Bliss, yet he acknowledged the fact this was beyond anything he understood.

"Don't let anything happen to her," Broc said, his voice harsh as he spoke to Hope. "You're my sister of only a few days and if anything happens to the..." to the woman he loved.

His heart stopped for a moment and when it started beating again, it seemed hers beat along with his. He needed to stay here and lend his support, but he wasn't sure about asserting himself.

"Nothing will happen to your wife," Hope said, "I promise. So far her pregnancy has been normal except for the early arrival which could mean a couple of things."

"What?" Broc jumped on the statement.

Hope waved her hand in the air then turned to Bliss as another scream wrenched the silence of the room. "Nothing right now is as important as Bliss. Now go. We've business to take care of here and rest assured I'll call you as soon as the babies are born."

Slowly, Broc backed out of the room and watched as Catherine closed the door in his face. He'd never felt more alone than he did now. The slap on his back woke him from the strange feelings.

"Let's get a drink. I've a feeling we're going to be waiting awhile," Flynt said, his voice laced with humor. "You're going to be a father. Didn't see that one coming a year ago. Did you?"

"Neither did I." Broc looked to the closed door wishing he had the courage to break in and watch the birth of his child. "And you're going to be an uncle."

"We're getting old," Flynt said, laughing. "Marriage, kids, what else is around the corner?"

"She changed me and I never saw it coming. Thought I'd stay a bachelor until I was thirty-five." Broc paced the room, stopping long enough to except the glass of whiskey Flynt poured for them. Yet somehow from the very beginning he'd hoped for this and he acknowledged he never took precautions. That in and of itself was strange.

"Women folk have a way of doing that," Nial spoke up, grinning. "Changing everything. Never thought I'd get married a second time then I met Catherine. She stole my heart the first day I saw her. My life hasn't been the same ever since."

"Guess you won't be coming to our weekly card games any longer." Flynt laughed, "You'll have better things to do."

"Like what?" Broc asked, still pacing and reeling inside, his gut cramping with every scream of pain coming from behind the closed door.

"Darned if I know." Flynt shrugged, making himself comfortable in a large chair before sipping his drink. "Most of it's women's work I suppose. Don't even know what that is though. Suppose you should hire a nanny to help take care of the child."

"Then why'd you bring it up if you don't know what you're talking about?" Broc finally sat down, his forearms resting on his thighs, his head in his hands.

"Walking the baby in the middle of the night. Perhaps changing a diaper or two," Nial said seeming to laugh at the two men who considered themselves wise in the ways of women but knew nothing about babies.

"Why would anyone have to do that?" Broc asked.

"To put the baby to sleep. They've got their own hours to do things, and it's got nothing to do with what's natural and right." Nial tried to explain. "Then you do need to learn to change the diapers. It isn't all women's work. A good man helps with their creation then the duties afterwards."

A piercing scream then another, the sounds nearly sent Broc to his knees. "I'm going in there."

Flynt stood by the door, blocking him from entering the room. "You can't, not until they're ready for you. Hope said she'd call you when he's born."

"Bloody hell." He turned away, striding through the house and out the door, inhaling ragged breaths of air. He walked in the cold spring air, to the creek behind the house before doubling back to find himself on the patio.

He'd never been here before today and it had been months since he'd talked to Bliss. Now suddenly he was married and expecting a child. He sat down on a patio chair, his head resting in his hands. On the ship from London he never bargained for a baby, just the wedding. Thought they'd have months together before there would be three of them in his household.

So far, he'd not done this well. Bliss deserved better and he'd have to find some way to make it up to her.

Marriage to Bliss had been on his mind for quite some time but a baby… *You're a damn fool, Broc Wallace, a damn fool. What did you expect when you made love to her so many times and never protected her?*

He couldn't help himself, but he was shaking his head, aware now that getting her with child must have been his intention. Why though? To bind her to him? He'd been afraid of her leaving him. She'd had so many secrets, he was sure what they had between them wouldn't last, and he knew the first time he kissed her, he couldn't live without her.

Why on earth had he been so cruel that day in the loft? He didn't understand his actions and least of all what he said then, but what he knew now was that he loved her, loved Bliss with all his heart. He would spend his life making it up to her.

My sweet Bliss...mo mhilse

Now that he knew how he felt, he had to tell her. She would want to know that he loved her. Good god did she love him? Bliss never spoke of love or even asked him if he loved her. Were women like that?

Didn't they care about love?

Edina always told him she loved him, but he'd known she loved his money and his other mistress had always spoken of love. He never believed them. The truth of it was before he met Bliss, he didn't really believe love could exist.

Until now...

"You've got to come," Flynt stood by him. "I think the baby is here. Hope asked for me to find you."

Broc wiped his sweaty hands on his pants then swallowing the lump in his throat stepped through the door just as another scream ripped the air. He rushed through the door, Catherine trying to hold him back. What happened? He'd thought the baby had been born and that was why he was called.

"What...?" His question echoed in the room that seemed to be filled with chaos. The women reacted swiftly to something but he had no idea what that was.

He stopped, seeming to freeze in midstride, studying the scene. What he saw stole his breath. Bliss was still in labor. A child was... "Hope!"

Quickly Hope turned then handing a baby to Catherine, "It's twins, just as I expected. You get two babies to take care of. You should be pleased. You've been twice blessed."

"Two babies..." He didn't know what to do with one.

The blood, it seemed as if it was everywhere, coating the floor and Bliss wasn't screaming any longer. She was silent. Something was wrong. His breath stopped for a moment.

"Go to her," Hope's voice was urgent.

Broc heard the concern and a touch of fear in her voice. Shivers stole through him. "And do what?" Yet he knew in his heart she needed him now more than ever. He strode to her, sitting down beside her, he smoothed the damp hair from her face.

"Comfort her, give her your support and talk to her," Hope spoke softly even while she worked.

"You can do this, Bliss," he told her, looking at Hope then Catherine seeking their approval. "You're strong. A moment more and you will have your child, children in your arms. I'll help."

Her eyes were glazed yet his words seemed to give her strength as he watched her. "Broc." She whispered his name and it made him smile. "Stay with me. Don't go away. I couldn't bear it if you left me again."

"Of course, never ever leave you again." He looked to Hope. "If your midwife lets me." Yet nothing could drag him from her. Not when she asked for him and needed him.

"Tell her to push. Sit behind her and hold her in your arms. I can see the head. Just a few more pushes and she'll be finished and she can rest."

Broc bent close to her ear whispering, "You can do it, Bliss, push and I'll try to help. On the count of three, one, two, three, push."

"One more," Hope said. "Count again, she's so tired that's the only thing that will help."

Broc knew real fear. He didn't want any more children. He'd remain celibate for the rest of his life because she shouldn't have to go through anything like this. But he nodded at Hope then he counted again. "Now push with all your strength."

Bliss did then slumped into his arms. Her body was damp and her face pale, but two crying babies were now making their presence and demands known. Catherine accepted the second child after placing the first and oldest, a boy, in Bliss' arms.

She cradled him and Broc heaved a huge sigh, relieved Bliss seemed stronger now. "I told you we were going to have a boy," he whispered.

"Give him a nipple and he'll know what to do," Hope said, a blush creeping over her face at her words.

Broc grinned as the baby latched on just as Hope said he would do. A wave of paternal pride swept through him.

"Here you go, Papa," Catherine handed Broc the second child, another boy.

Then to Bliss, "When that one finishes, you can nurse the youngster."

"What should we name them?" Broc had a few names in mind but understood he should run this past his wife.

"Let's think about it. Right now, all I want is to sleep, and I've a feeling these boys don't want the same thing," Bliss said, smiling down at the child in her arms.

"Here you go," Hope wound a piece of green string around the oldest boy's wrist before tying a blue one around the youngest. "Until you can tell them apart this will tell you who's who."

"We've only one crib." Bliss turned to Broc as if he could make this right. "You have to find another one."

"Tonight?"

~ * ~

Bliss woke, her heart pounding to the cry of her babies, both of them. The night had been hectic, a wedding as well as the birth of her twins consumed most of it. Broc slept next to her. It seemed as if an eternity had passed since they passed a night together. Now the night was spent feeding the infants and changing the babies' diapers.

Well, this was the beginning of their future and they had no plans as of yet as well as no names for the boys. Broc told her he had some in mind though. She hoped they weren't really common names. She wanted ones that would set her boys apart.

"Time to get up," she whispered close to his ear. "The boys are awake and needing attention."

"Again? We need a nanny," he mumbled while he sat up, raking his hands through his already disheveled hair. "Never expected my wedding night to be like this."

Bliss laughed, bending over to kiss him quickly on the lips. "Just what did you expect?"

"Carnal pleasure with my wife." But he pushed the covers away, striding to the crib where the boys were wailing. "I'm giving you the youngest first this time. Don't want him to think he always has to wait for big brother," he said as he placed the boy in her arms.

"Knowing this is what happens when you make love to me, the best bet is to keep you celibate." She accepted the boy into her arms. When he was finished, she traded with Broc.

"At least they sleep and eat at the same time. When do you think they'll sleep through the night?" he asked, cradling the youngest while rocking on his feet.

"Not for a while yet. They aren't even a day old and you're expecting them to act like children." She laughed at him, not knowing the answer to his questions either. "Think we should speak with Hope. I've a feeling she knows more about things like this than anyone ever expected."

"When you grow up in a harem you get an entirely different view on life I suppose." Broc said, placing the boy in the crib and walking to Bliss. "Think Mr. Blue is asleep again."

"Here, so is Mr. Green. We really do need to come up with two adorable..."

"Manly..." he added, correcting her in the process.

"Names for them. I would never name them anything that is not manly." She punched him in the arm, laughing as he tackled her, pinning her to the bed. He kissed her then, closing his lips around hers, brushing them with his tongue and groaning when she opened for him.

When he pulled away, "I've missed you, my sweet Bliss, *ma mhilse,* more than I could ever say. Don't ever leave me like that again."

"Broc Wallace, of all the incorrigible things to say to me that one is the worst. You know I would never leave you as you also know the reason we were apart for so long was because you left me. Your mistress even had the audacity to tell me you always took her with you."

"Now, that was a lie."

"I figured as much."

"I will take you every where I go. I did wish I could have taken you to London. When I saw you as the ship was leaving, I almost made the blasted thing turn around but didn't know what kind of reception I would receive." His lips found hers once more.

She felt the heat and for a second a searing need for him deep inside her. "I do think I might want to have another child but we have time. We don't have to decide something like that today. We just have to be careful, you know."

"You would do this again?" he asked, rolling from her and bringing her so he could cradle her next to his body. "There was a fraction of time during your labor I thought I would lose you."

"I was so tired but you gave me strength. No more children at least not in the next year or possibly two. How many toddlers do you want running around the house at the same time? What if we had a second set of twins?" She could well imagine just how hectic life could be. It was what her mother and father had done though. Four children in five years' time, but for some reason there were six between her and her brother.

A puzzle she doubted she would ever be able to solve.

"None, can't they just pass by that age and become older boys perhaps thirteen. I've a pretty good idea what to do with a boy at that age." Lightly, he stroked her arm, trailing a finger up then down.

She shivered in response, thinking too much time had passed between them without lovemaking. "Don't think that's possible, besides

I'm not sure about your knowing what to do with them. I don't want you to corrupt them."

Throwing his head back, he laughed. "I would never corrupt my boys, just teach them things they need to know."

"That could be the problem. Your idea of what they need to know and mine is most likely very different." She tried to stifle a yawn, hoping he wouldn't see and leave her alone. She liked his arms around her. It had been so long.

"While they are sleeping, I'm going to the kitchen to get something for both of us to eat. You need to sleep also." Leaving the bed, he tucked the covers around her. "I'll be back and when you wake up, we can talk about moving home."

Strange, but she felt at home here in this little cottage, and she knew it would always hold a special place in her heart. She yawned again, snuggling into the covers, dreaming of the future, their future.

The clattering of dishes put her in a dreamy half awake and half asleep then the scent of coffee woke Bliss. Sunshine filled the room and it seemed the day would be another sunny one. She sat up, brushing hair from her eyes and watching Broc cradle both boys.

"How long did I sleep?" She held out her arms, silently asking for one of the babies to feed.

"About five hours," He gave her the oldest child.

"Look at that, you've diapered him and they went five hours without food. I would have never thought..." she broke off at the expression on his face. "I'm grateful for the sleep as well as everything else you've done."

"I'd like to move home later today if you think you're up to it. Nial and Catherine have gone ahead and they are opening up the house. I haven't been there since I left for London. I suppose things are going to be a bit musty."

"Home... Do you have a nursery ready?" She smoothed the top of the boy's head, amazed at the tiny miracle she was holding.

"Catherine is taking care of the room for the children." They switched babies.

"We should shop for clothes." She cuddled with the other child now. "And names, we need to name them. I don't want to call them Mr. Green string and Mr. Blue string forever."

"I've a few picked out. What do you think of Houston?" he asked, laughing. "That will take care of one if you like it."

"I like Payton but do you want to name them both with the same beginning letter?" she asked, thinking that would be adorable and very twin-like.

"So, easy for them to confuse people. Do you think they'll be incorrigible?" He was grinning as he rocked the child almost as if he hoped they would be just that. "I like Garett and Grant."

"I don't know if I can decide. Should we ask for a third opinion?"

"And who would that be? Your brother? Never. I won't give him any say in our children's names after the way he treated both of us." He sat down, still holding the child who was now growing sleepy eyed.

"In any case, we don't need to decide at this moment."

"We should sleep on it," Broc said.

"Well that will be quite easy since it seems that's all I want to do is sleep and eat just like our boys. But first I'm going to eat and take a bath." She swept her hair back, tying it in a knot to keep it from her eyes.

"I'll get you hot water. Then you'll probably have to feed the braw lads again. Perhaps after our midday meal we can make the move. I'm eager to get home."

"And see what Grandmother has done with the nursery," she said, smiling at the beautiful yet sudden change in her life. For the first time in a great while she was optimistic about the future.

"That too."

"As you said, but I feel at home here." She gazed around the bedroom, wondering what the rest of her life would look like. They still knew so little about each other. They pleased each other in bed and they had good conversation. She really enjoyed his company. What else was necessary?

He sat down beside her, taking her hand in his. "In time you'll appreciate the Wallace estate, Deepwood. Now, I'll get you that hot water. We can talk later." He left her alone with her thoughts as well as the boys, most having to do with their future and the direction it would take.

This was not going to be easy, she knew. Standing, she walked to the crib, stroking the cheek of both boys. The future was promising. She was in love with an amazing man one who stole her heart the first time she saw him, but she didn't think she would ever tell him that.

Telling him how much she loved him would make her too vulnerable.

Day one of her new and rapidly changing life and she understood it was up to her to make sure her life stayed on track needing nothing more than to keep Broc happy. She didn't want him to revert to his bad boy status. If he grew tired of her, he could easily take another mistress. She didn't think she could live with that. She certainly wasn't the type to share her man. That possibility was one of the reasons Flynt didn't want him to court her. Of course Broc didn't court her. He seduced her.

"You should be in bed." Broc stood just inside the door, framed by the sunlight filtering through the window and into the babies' crib.

"Why? I feel fine, just a little tired but so much better than when we woke up this morning."

"You just gave birth. You need to be in bed." He made his way to the bed then turned down the covers, seeming to wait for her.

"I'm fully clothed, in case you haven't noticed, and I'm ready to leave the cottage. While you were gone, Catherine helped me pack the necessities. We can leave anytime you like." She wanted to laugh at his changing expressions.

"I've changed my mind. In light of your condition, we should stay at least a month maybe longer." Critically, he eyed the bed then her.

"If we aren't leaving, I'd like to maybe go outdoors for a short walk." She knew she was pushing him but she needed to move her feet and breathe some fresh air.

"That's not wise," he said, standing in front of the door as if he meant to prevent her from leaving. "Moving too much could cause complications."

"Where did you get that crazy statement? It certainly didn't come from Hope."

"It just makes sense," he told her indignantly, his hands on her shoulders as if he meant to push her to the bed.

"You can either accompany me or not but either way..." She brushed past him and into the parlor. Looking over her shoulder, she smiled inwardly when she saw he was following.

"You should be in bed," he mumbled, tagging along. Then with a very masculine huff that gave Bliss more reason to smile he wrapped an arm around her pulling her close.

"Catherine will watch the boys. I talked to her earlier," Bliss waved to her grandmother as they walked through the kitchen. "Only ten minutes."

"They'll be fine dear, nothing an experienced grandmother can't handle I'm sure. If I need you sooner, I'll send Nial to fetch you."

~ * ~

Bliss walked into the bedchamber where Broc was stretched out on the bed, his hands behind his head.

"Hope told me..." Bliss looked at the floor, moistening her lips and finding flames simmering within that seemed to heat her from the inside out. "Anyway, Grandmother is taking care of the boys and the wet nurse will be there all night unless there is some kind of emergency the two of them can't take care of."

He patted the bed beside him. "She told me also that you could make love anytime we wanted to now. Come here."

Her heart raced, anticipation a heady thing, yet her feet didn't seem to want to move. The children were born three months ago and while they shared a bed, he barely touched her. It had been nearly a year since that horrible day in the loft. "I..." she began but couldn't think of anything to say. Nerves inundated her.

"It seemed easier before, didn't it? You don't need to be frightened." He rose from the bed, sensing her hesitancy.

"You always seduced me." Her voice shook with apprehension or need, she wasn't sure which. Maybe what she was feeling was passion. Perhaps she just wanted him so much she couldn't talk.

"And I will again if that's what you want." He brushed hair away from her neck, his lips lightly caressing and his breath whisper soft against her flesh. "If you want me."

"I want you, it's just that I'm unsure after all this time. I feel as if I, we've never done this before. We have two children and I suddenly feel as if I'm still a virgin."

She turned to face him, gently reaching upward to touch his face. Gazing into his eyes, she was reminded of the steel blue simmer of desire that was always in his eyes. He caressed her with the gentlest of touches, almost as if he thought she was fragile. She wasn't delicate in any way, but he would always see her in that light.

His lips brushed softly against hers, a feather light caress that tickled more than seduced. She giggled and he looked up askance at the sound. "You mock me?"

"This seems like the first time. Perhaps we should play a game." His groan at her comment made her smile.

"No games, I don't have the patience. I need you, Bliss, in every possible way and I need you now."

"Yes, you should be up for sainthood. You've waited so long but you remember why, don't you?" She giggled but his lips covered hers, silencing any further banter.

"Should we make another baby?" he asked as his nimble fingers found the fastenings on her dress. Within seconds the fabric slipped from her shoulders.

"No." At his words, she panicked slightly "Not yet. Can we still make love?" She pushed away from him. He held her away, gazing at her milk-swollen breast, lightly touching one, mesmerized by the drop forming at the tip.

"Of course, until the twins I never sired any children," he murmured softly, as he finished undressing her.

"I'm glad of that." She let her head fall back giving him better access, but she found the fastenings on his doeskins, pushing them down his legs.

He kicked them off before he carried her to the bed. She touched him, cradled his arousal in her hand. He groaned deep in the back of his throat. "Not yet. Let me pleasure you first."

The tiny sounds of longing and desire settling in the back of her throat left him smiling. "Please, Broc." Her hips rose to the rhythm he set.

"You want me inside you?"

"Yes, now," she gasped as ripples of pleasure swept through her.

She felt him as he thrust inside, bringing her more pleasure, touching the very essence of her love for him.

Then he withdrew and his seed spilled on her. He cried out as his body shuddered in sexual release. Then he rolled off, yet pulling her close. "Bliss, I've never told you this, but I love you."

Her hand roamed, finding his shaft again, touching him until he was aroused once more. *I love you so much.*

"Naughty." He teased her and kissed her again.

"It takes a naughty girl to love a bad boy." She assured him with a soft smile.

He laughed and it turned out that they made love again. The boys were safe and secure with their grandmother and wet nurse. As it turned out they had all night.

"I love you too, Broc," she whispered as his fingers once again danced over her body. "My sweet Broc," she murmured.

"My sweet Bliss, I love you more than life."

Coming March 2020
by
Christine Young

Crazy for Cam
Bad Boys Book One

Chapter One

1824 Glasgow Scotland

Lord Colin Angus Monroe MacEwen Viscount of Rosehill, better known as Cam to his friends, stood on the balcony of his townhouse in Glasgow, Scotland, thinking over the last cowardly nine months of his life. He had made promises to a lovely lass, Chelsea MacTavish. Promises he was unable or perhaps terrified to keep might be a better word to describe his behavior.

The promise was to court her. Instead he stayed away, ran from her to be exact. Chelsea was not for him. He was a womanizer and a cad and never expected to be anything else. Bad boys didn't change. Until he met Chels he had no intention of marrying until he was at least thirty-five and only because he wanted an heir. As his male friends claimed, he and his friends were the bad boys of Glasgow. Everyone knew they'd never reform.

Broc changed, he reminded himself. If one bad boy could do it, so could he. Blessed hell, but he wanted and yearned to have Chels in his arms, loving her for the rest of his life.

These last nine months had not been among his finer moments.

When Cam closed his eyes, when he tried to sleep, all he could see were Chelsea's lips and he didn't have to try very hard to recall the feel of them against his, their tongues dancing a beautiful duet. That night almost a year ago now had been a major mistake, one he was having a difficult time recovering from. When he saw her, in her quaint little hiding place staring at him, her eyes huge which he read as passion, he couldn't resist her.

It was not well done of him, but he had to have her.

The bad boys were gambling and when he noticed her, she bolted from the room, dashing through the hallway to hide behind a door. The challenge she issued was explicit in the shimmer of her eyes. If he had any sense about him, he would have left her there, knowing she wasn't for him. Chelsea was a lady, and she deserved a gentleman who would treat her right. He could not leave though because he found himself inexorably drawn to her beguiling smile and passion-drenched eyes. A taste of her, he told himself would be enough.

It wasn't enough. That one taste created an appetite he couldn't fill.

At the time, he believed that day had been the beginning of the rest of his life. She allowed him inside and he kissed her, not a chaste kiss, not one he might give a woman he was courting. No, this kiss was meant to seduce, raw and hungry, deliciously sensual. He found he wanted her in the most elemental and primal ways, and he craved to be her first lover.

Nothing else would do for him.

The wonderful thing was, he paused in thought to sip the brandy he poured for himself. Well, she seemed to want him as much as he did her. She didn't resist or tell him no even though he suggested she do that very thing several times. The feel of her breast beneath his hand, the hardened nipple veiled by the fabric of her gown, haunted him day and night, awake and asleep. He should not have touched her so brazenly but he'd been unable to resist her sweet siren's call.

The very next day he met her again and made more promises to her, agreements he now understood he could never fulfill, not unless he reformed. Her brother Flynt was right. He wasn't good enough for her. Hell, he never got rid of his mistress although that woman moved on when he stopped seeing her almost to the day he first kissed Chelsea. He'd been celibate for nine long months. Laughing at the irony, he downed the glass of brandy before throwing the crystal glass against the wall and watching it shatter into a million tiny pieces.

The violence didn't make him feel better.

The idea of properly courting a woman, not just any woman but Chelsea MacTavish, was not something he could wrap his mind around. When he was with her, all he could think about was stripping her naked and tasting every inch of her beautiful body. Bloody eyes, but he didn't even know what she looked like naked but he could fantasize. His imagination kept him in a state of constant arousal.

"What did that glass do to you?" Flynt MacTavish, Chelsea's older brother and proclaimed guardian of the MacTavish sisters clapped him on the shoulder. "Shouldn't you be getting back to the game so I can win more money from you."

The need to rid himself of the primal energy and sexual thoughts surrounding Chelsea pulsed through him. A ride and a cold swim in the river would do just fine. After all, it was almost dawn. Maybe he could reach his house near the ocean by the evening. Suitable company even for the other bad boys, he was not.

"You wouldn't like it if I told you," he said, smiling as he once more relived the few kisses he shared with Flynt's sister. "If you knew, you might string me up by my balls."

He roared with laughter. "That bad? Try me and it better not have anything to do with one of my sisters."

Cam was shaking his head, pacing the room now. "No. Like I told you. You wouldn't like my thoughts. Might even skewer me through." Cam laughed at the thought, knowing it was the truth.

"You want another glass of brandy?" Donal, another bad boy stood by his side. "Don't know what's wrong, but it's got to have something to with a woman."

"Like to drown in it." Cam knew a ride, a cold swim, nothing would stop the constant ache except possessing Chelsea, perhaps not even then would he find relief.

"That can be arranged," Leslie said, smirking as if he knew what was going through his head. "Let's get back to the game or call it quits so I can still find some bliss in my mistress' arms tonight."

"I'm not good company. Do whatever you like." Cam sat down on a chair, one leg slung over the arm, the other stretched out in front of him. The nearly full bottle of brandy sat on the table beside him. If he had it his way, he'd finish it tonight before crashing for a few hours.

"If it's not your mistress, who has you needing to see double and wake up with a pounding head?" Flynt asked, still laughing too hard for Cam's taste. "Must be a pretty special woman then. She denying you heavenly comforts or are you going to go the way of Broc and settle down, babies and all?"

Cam frowned at him, feeling the effects of too much alcohol and realizing the truth of Flynt's words. "Hardly going down that road." He didn't dare say more. If Flynt discovered his feelings for one of his little sisters, he'd keep Chelsea locked in her room until she turned thirty. Even her grams who seemed to take over the finding of suitable husbands for the MacTavish women wouldn't be able to persuade Flynt to hand over the key.

"Not until you're thirty," Leslie reminded them.

"Thirty-five, and she'll be out of the picture by then," Cam muttered, wishing he hadn't said the words but beginning to lose control of his thoughts and speech. Sullenly, he poured more brandy and hoped that in his drunken state he wouldn't reveal the woman of his dreams.

"Think it's time to leave this man to wallow in his misery. If you want the woman, do something about getting her. Shouldn't be too hard for a man of your specific talents," Flynt said, chuckling. "After all, what parent or guardian wouldn't welcome you into their fold? You've inherited money as well as a steady income and you come with a title. You're moderately good looking. Face it, you're a catch worthy of any young woman."

Any but a MacTavish lady. He was glad he had enough control not to say the words aloud. Or did he? The scowl on Flynt's face told him something else or was it a scowl. He downed the glass before closing his eyes and willing his friends from his townhouse. Truth be told he needed to wallow in his misery and wake up to a pounding head as well, just to remind him that he had to change his ways if he was going to court the woman of his dreams.

"You should see your mistress. A good douse of carnal sex might relieve the ache between your legs." Donal pulled his coat from the stand. "I'll see all of you next week at my place." Then he left.

"Good night," Leslie said, following in Donal's footsteps.

"Suppose I'll take my leave also. You're not in any condition to be good company. My suggestion," he paused, "find the chit and make love to her until you get her out of your system," Flynt said as he too exited his home.

When the door closed behind Flynt MacTavish, Cam let out a loud roar of laughter. Find the chit and make love to her until you get her out of your system, he recalled the words. And wouldn't you just be the happiest guardian in the world when I threw your words in your face? Unknowingly, Flynt just gave him permission to ravish his sister.

Chelsea deserved more than that kind of behavior from a suitor. Yet that was exactly why he didn't court her. He knew he would do just that, make love to her until...

...but he didn't believe for a second he would ever get her out of his system.

The ticking of the clock was now the only sound he heard until the birds began to chirp nonstop. Sunlight filled the room and the pounding in his head was incessant. Squinting his eyes, he breathed in deeply, willing the alcohol-induced pain to vanish. Still his head throbbed and his gut churned. A quick massage to the back of his neck as well as his temples did nothing to alleviate the horrendous problem.

Too many mornings he woke in this condition in a fervent yet unsuccessful attempt to rid Chelsea MacTavish from his thoughts. If he could go back to that night so many months ago, he would have never chased her into that empty room, never would have kissed her or felt her heart beat beneath his hand. Just the thought of the way her soft womanly curves felt against the hard planes of his body had him aroused and aching.

Standing, he ran his fingers through his hair. His servant left a pot of hot coffee for him, anticipating his needs and when he wandered through his home, he found a still steaming bath had been left for him. Stripping and with the cup of coffee in hand, he settled into the water, pretending he was ready to start his day.

Once more his imagination got the best of him though. He needed to do something about his condition. No other woman would do and he knew it. So he would have to change the course of his actions but to what?

He had no idea how to court a lady properly. All he knew was how to bed them and give them pleasure. This was a predicament if bedding and pleasure weren't prerequisites for courting. He would have to make it a point to ask someone who might know. Problem was, he didn't really know or trust anyone like that.

Bloody hell, but he wasn't going to allow some other man to win over Chelsea's heart. He finished his coffee as well as his bath before heading off to the university. Some of his proper and stuffy colleagues might have some advice for him.

In the hallway and near his office, "Cam, you teaching today?"

"No, just have some paperwork then I'm heading home. Got business to attend to." The first matter on hand was to ride out to the MacTavish estate and discover if Chelsea was home and in the process get permission from Flynt to court her. Rumor was since Broc Wallace purged the waters, Flynt was a bit easier to deal with.

"Cam," another colleague approached him. "What are you doing here today? You're not scheduled to lecture."

"Looking for advice and you're just the man I'd like to hear from." Cam opened the door to his office, waiting for his colleague to join him.

"Advice from me?" Leod asked, pointing to his now puffed up chest. "Seems unusual. You've always appeared confidant. Never asked me anything before."

"Have a seat." Cam gestured to a chair while he removed his coat, thinking about what he should say or ask. He knew this man was courting someone, his gut clenching when he thought the woman might be Chelsea, but he also understood the man might have something more to offer than he could see on the surface.

The man cleared his throat, running a finger around his collar as if it was too tight. "What do you want?"

"Need to learn how you court a woman properly," Cam said, watching Leod's face turn a brilliant shade of red. He poured two glasses of whiskey before holding one out to the man who ignored him. In one gulp he downed his, more curious now than he'd ever been.

"You're asking me that?" He coughed in a feeble attempt to clear his throat. "Don't know why you need help with something like that. Heard you were a Casanova, one of the self-proclaimed bad boys in town. You shouldn't need help in that department."

For a moment Cam was taken aback. He'd never thought of himself as a Casanova. He enjoyed women, true, but he never took advantage of a situation, at least not until he met Chelsea MacTavish.

"Don't need to know why. My reasons are my own. Understand you're courting a young lady. Just have to know what's proper and what is not." Cam wasn't at all sure this conversation was going anywhere, and as the seconds passed, he was surer than ever this colleague would never be able to shed light on his question.

"Like what?" The man squirmed, fidgeting with his neck cloth. "What you're really asking me isn't apparent. I've heard stories about your prowess where it comes to women. I'm not like that. I don't bed every woman I call on, wouldn't want to in any case."

Cam waved his hand in the air. "Whiskey?" he queried again then immediately had a second thought on that matter.

"Don't drink."

"Mind if I do?" Cam understood how drinking might make this man uncomfortable. He would be shocked to learn Chelsea liked her brandy and wine. That was all he knew about her except the fact he craved her and she was sweet. Well, he also knew first hand how she melted in his arms and the way her blue eyes shone with raw passion when he kissed her and how her beautiful blond hair shimmered in the sunlight.

"It's your office."

"I'll take that as a confirmation that you don't care." Cam poured a second glass of whiskey then sat on the edge of his desk, watching the man. Not liking the idea that people, his colleagues, talked about him behind his back, he asked? "What do you know about my, er, prowess with women?"

The man wiped his sweaty forehead, "Just talk. You've had more than one mistress, I've heard. Women swoon when you walk by, no, perhaps that was an exaggeration. Not really sure in any case."

"True." He tossed back the whiskey and grinned. "That's one of the reasons I'm asking for advice. While I'm an expert where it comes to mistresses and giving a woman her pleasure, I've no idea what a man can and can't do with a proper lady when they are courting. Do you give your women pleasure?"

"What?" he sputtered.

"Never mind, let's get back to courting."

"For instance..."

"Have you kissed this woman you've been seeing?" Cam asked,

pretty sure what the answer would entail if he went into detail.

"Once," he confessed, the shade of his face had not changed since the first questions. His visage was still a brilliant crimson.

"And was this kiss chaste? A peck on the cheek or did you take her mouth into yours and taste her. Did you stick your tongue between her lips and deep inside her mouth?" Why the devil was he provoking this man when all he wanted was some answers to important questions?

He stood quickly rocking the chair he'd been sitting on. "Sir."

"I take it there were no tongues involved." He rose, striding to the window. Looking over campus, he watched the people waking around and wondering just how many of those students would react to his question the same as his colleague. Perhaps he was a bad boy. He realized then he didn't like Leod at all.

"No, no, of course not. A gentleman wouldn't do such a thing. A peck on the cheek is all that is proper, if you must know. Nothing more, no tongues involved." He was breathing hard clearly agitated by his questions.

Cam couldn't help himself. He sighed heavily, understanding all too well he would never be able to keep his hands to himself let alone his tongue where Chelsea was concerned. "Haven't you ever wondered what it would feel like to taste the woman you want to marry before the nuptials? What do you think?"

The man was shaking his head back and forth while he righted his chair and sat down. "No, no I haven't. Don't know what you mean by tasting. Doesn't seem at all proper to me."

For a moment Cam thought the man might swoon. "You should really try it sometime. I can find you a lady of the night who is clean, a woman who could teach you how to make love to a woman so she has her pleasure not just you. You don't want to be selfish do you?"

"I don't know what you mean," he said, droplets of sweat running down his face and into his shirt, his armpits soaked through.

"Would you like a woman to teach you?" Cam persisted, wishing all men would discover the secrets before they wed. Women deserved better than fumbling fingers and grunts that led nowhere.

He could still remember the woman his father brought him to at the tender age of fourteen. The lady was a widow. Her husband left his fortune to his son from another woman, failing to provide for his wife. At the time the lady needed funds just to live. He also remembered just how beautiful she was. If he ever had a son, he would make sure he treated his son to that very valuable education.

"I can't imagine doing such a thing."

Cam turned his attention back to his colleague, discovering a bit of disdain for this pious self-satisfied man. "Have you held her hand? Traced tiny intoxicating circles on her wrists and heard the first tiny sounds of desire a woman makes when she likes what you are doing?" Cam was beside himself. This was turning out to be detrimental to his case.

The man was sputtering now, "I've held her hand but not the other. Why would I want to do that?"

"You should try it, and you could suck her fingers into your mouth. I guarantee you'll enjoy the tiny sounds of pleasure your actions will cause. You do want to pleasure your woman."

"Professor MacEwen, I daresay the things you are proposing are outrageous very improper. Doing those things would ruin my reputation. Why, people would talk about me the way they do you."

Cam grinned again, wondering for a moment how people talked about him before realizing he didn't really care. "Of course they are improper. That's why I needed to know how to approach this woman properly. You see..." He was about to tell this stuffy and oh too prim man that he'd done all he'd said with the very woman his colleague might be courting. No, he hadn't sucked her fingers into his mouth but he would. Not for a moment did Cam believe Chelsea would ever give her heart to a man who only kissed her chastely on the cheek. At least that's what he presumed had been done.

"I don't see anything at all," he objected. "The young lady I'm seeing would never allow me to do such things and neither would her brother, Mr. MacTavish. I would most likely go to hell if I only tried."

Cam let out a huge sigh, realizing suddenly he might have been giving the man ideas. The last thing he wanted was for this man to taste any part of Chelsea. "Yes, yes, I suppose you're right. It was a crazy notion of mine, and you haven't touched her breast either, felt her nipple tighten beneath your hand. That is all good and proper. I'll try to remember your advice."

Cam couldn't stop the outrageous statements. Truth be told he had no interest in making his colleague uncomfortable, but jealousy swept through him the moment the man told him he'd kissed her and held her hand. He was pretty sure this person would never follow through with his suggestions, thank god.

Months had passed since he touched Chelsea, and his body ached night and day just to see her let alone run his hands along her waist to her breasts kiss her deeply. Bloody hell, but he was going insane just thinking, talking about sex with Chelsea's face prominent in his head.

Imagining himself sitting next to Chelsea while doing nothing more than holding her hand made him sweat. Where she was concerned, control like that didn't exist for him and he realized he was doomed before he even began to try the proper way to court her.

The man stood, starting for the door. "This is all none of your business and very inappropriate." He left, slamming the door behind him.

Cam plopped down on the chair behind his desk, closing his eyes, head back and wondering what the devil he was going to do about courting Chelsea. The man was right, of course. Flynt, Chelsea's brother, wouldn't let him anywhere near her. Flynt knew all too well his reputation around women. They'd honed that very reputation together.

But what would her grams, Catherine, do? Probably feed him ginger cookies. He groaned. In any case, she was the official guardian now having assumed the position after Flynt made so many mistakes with Bliss, the oldest sister. Of course Catherine would never approve of him either. If she knew the things he and Chelsea had already done, she would ban him from the home.

All you need do is behave yourself when the older woman is close and if you're lucky enough to find privacy, well then, you don't have to behave. He smiled, realizing right then his next stop would be the MacTavish townhouse. He'd prolonged this moment far too long. Chelsea was in town for the next few days. He remembered that he heard that tidbit from Flynt just last night.

Playing by the rules had never been a strong suit of his. Now, if his end game were to be achieved, he would have to do just that at least around the chaperones.

Play by the rules... A new concept for him, one he meant to cultivate where it was advantageous.

A different colleague poked his head into his office, laughing. "Heard you've been asking questions about proper courting."

"You heard right..." Cam was no longer in the mood, his answer sounding gruff.

"Got a drink for me? I can tell you many a tale if that's what you'd like," he told him.

"I think I've heard enough about proper and prim. Not something that appeals to me."

The man let his head fall back, roaring with laughter. "She's really got you by the balls, doesn't she."

Cam thought about that for a second. "True." His eyebrows rose a notch, studying his friend. "I want her and the only way I can have her is to seduce her or court her."

"I know which I'd prefer," the man said. "But do you want her for more than a week or two or is this for a lifetime?"

Cam felt his nerves begin to snap while his fingers tightened around his glass. "Don't know yet." He hadn't thought that far ahead. What did he want? Now, he needed her this very moment.

"You should make up your mind before it's too late for either scenario. If you seduce her and toss her away, you'll ruin her life as well as her prospects for a decent marriage. If you seduce her and mean to keep her as your wife, your life will change in too many ways to count."

"I'm not a cad," he growled, yet at the same time marriage had never been in his thoughts. His plan was to marry when he turned thirty-five and not a moment before. He wanted an heir too. He was only twenty-four, eons stretched in front of him before he would need to make a commitment.

"If you go through with your plans, you will be just that, a cad, unless of course, this lady is mistress material. Hardly believe that though. You'd already have her set up in your old mistress' home if that were true."

Cam drummed his fingers on his desk, thinking and wondering if his set in stone plans could change. Chelsea would never wait for him eleven years. She would be wed and bedded before he could blink.

He thought nine months had been a long time to stay away from her. Hell, nine years was a lifetime. What to do?

"Think about what I said." His colleague left.

Silence, cold and hard, echoed in Cam's ears. Everything he planned and saved for would vanish in a blink if he let go of his dreams. Yet he craved Chelsea, his body did anyway. Wasn't there more to a relationship than just sex or lust? He didn't have an answer for that. Sex, for him, had always been the driving force where women were concerned.

Bad boys, he mused thoughtfully. They all had been christened as such, by themselves of course. Now the community did the same.

Bad boy, what's she gonna do when I come for her?

Cam was determined to do just that. He was coming for her and he craved her in every way a man craved a woman. She would have to tell him no if they ever found privacy or he would teach her everything he knew about lovemaking.

So far she'd never told him no. Chelsea was older now though. And he'd also ignored her for a significant amount of time.

Anything could happen.

~ * ~

"There's a young man waiting for you downstairs," Catherine told her granddaughter as she stepped inside Chelsea's bedroom, a large grin on her face. "He seems a bit impatient to see you. While he was polite enough, there was an edge to his voice."

"And he wants to sit in the parlor and talk?" Chelsea asked, incredulous. "I've had enough of that for a lifetime. I don't even want any of these men Flynt has found to court me for a friend, let alone a partner for life." No, she craved more and the only man who could fill that had lost interest in her despite his promises.

"You should at least give this man a chance," Grams said.

"Why?"

"Most who have courted you don't know how to ride a horse, and I for one am heartily glad I don't have to chaperone you and your suitors in a carriage. Sitting in the parlor and engaging in polite conversation is just fine with me." Catherine laughed, still smiling fondly at her granddaughter. "I would have your word you won't let this beau touch you below the waist though or do anything but kiss. Kisses are just fine."

How was this man different from the others? For a few seconds she stared out the window, wishing no one was downstairs and she could go for an unchaperoned ride all by herself. She knew just where she would go if given the chance. No, she wouldn't. It would only make her recall Cam and his kisses, the way he played her body. Not chaste, dry kisses her suitors had given her on the cheek, but deep soul shattering, heat raising delicious kisses only Cam could give her. She wanted to taste him again and feel his tongue against hers.

Then, with a heavy sigh and a reluctance to exist in the next few hours, "Why would I have to give my word now? Most of the men who visit me don't touch my hand let alone somewhere below my waist. I'm really not up to this, Grams. Tell him to go away."

"Stop moping around. You've got the rest of your life in front of you. If you want him to go away, you'll have to tell the man yourself. I don't want to hear what you have to say if he leaves without your seeing him," Catherine said with another chuckle while she smoothed her skirts and donned an exasperating look.

"You're far too secretive for my taste. Just spit it out. Tell me who this man is and I'll make the decision. I'll tell him to go away if that's what I want." Chelsea was plucking at her skirt, nervous energy seeming to sweep through her. The air around her seemed charged.

"Tell who to go away," Daryl and Lacey, two of her sisters joined them, plopping down on the bed together. "Tell us. Who exactly do you want to go away?"

"Whoever it is in the parlor," Chelsea began with a huff and a very negative attitude. "I don't know who it is, and I really don't care anymore. I'm never going to marry anyone anyway. Grams seems to think I'd like to see this man. Don't know why." Considering suitors just to make Flynt and Grams happy had her exhausted and wishing she could run away to some island and never have to talk to or see another man.

"Would you like us to see who it is for you?" Lacey asked, cocking her head to the side as if she was studying her. Then she grinned, her signature Lacey smile that told Chelsea her sister had something devilish in mind. "I know I'd want to know who was waiting for me in the parlor, especially if Grams thinks you might want to see him."

"Who would you like to see, Chelsea?" Daryl asked, prompting her curiosity as Daryl well knew there was only one man she would consider, and he was on her bad side now. Cam broke promises to her. "You can narrow down the possibilities if you look at the situation that way."

The only man she'd like to see right now was Cam just so she could tell him what she thought of the abandonment as well as the broken promise. She wanted to rail at him and hit him until she felt better inside. Anger at his rejection of her simmered deep inside, had for the last nine months, growing more as each day passed. At her sides her fists clenched and unclenched, frustrated that there was nothing she could do about this situation. Obviously, she couldn't just show up at his townhouse. If she were a man, she could call him out.

Irritated, she crossed her arms in front of her then clenching her teeth, she gritted out just for spite, "I don't want to see anyone. They can all go...they can go..."

"Jump in a lake. Perhaps that would be a good remedy for what is probably ailing your man," Grams offered, with a wink as if she knew something no one else knew. "I'll tell him you're under the weather and he can come by tomorrow. That should suffice for today, but you'll need another excuse tomorrow."

"Why would you get rid of him today just to invite him back tomorrow?" Chelsea asked, now furious with her grandmother. "It's obvious to most people that your words make no sense. If I didn't know better, I'd wager you're playing matchmaker and that has to stop."

"No." Lacey blocked the way, holding her hands out to stop her grams from leaving the room. "Let me see who it is then you can decide. Is that alright? We shouldn't make this permanent, at least not yet. It might be Cam."

"I don't want to see him either."

"Of course you do," Lacey said. "Quit acting like a fool and denying yourself something you desperately want."

Chelsea wasn't sure how to react to her well-meaning sisters and the groping suitors who came to see if she would be a suitable wife for them. This had to be another one just like the others. The man downstairs wasn't Cam. She wasn't anyone's suitable wife. "I suppose you can go see. Nothing you discover will make me want to go somewhere with whoever it is or sit in the parlor and talk nonsense about the weather or who is performing at the theater. And I won't pretend for anyone that I don't like brandy and wine."

"Good, then it's settled. You'll have much needed information to make up your mind with." She turned to Daryl, grinning as if she couldn't wait to see who sat in their parlor. "You coming with me?"

"Keep me away? Not on your life. I bet it's Cam," Daryl said, just as the pair exited the room. "And what do you suppose she'll do if it is him?"

"Maybe he's finally come to his senses. We'll be back in a few minutes with the valued information. Don't go anywhere," Lacey said when she turned to look at her over her shoulder.

"Where would I go?" Chelsea sighed softly with a little emphasizing lift of her shoulders. Almost nine months ago she'd seen a future with Cam now... There was nothing now and if it was Cam in the parlor, what the bloody eyes did he want? To play with her emotions before he left her again? She wasn't going to allow that to happen. He'd have to get down on his knees and grovel on the floor before she'd consent to anything he might have planned.

"You could sneak down the servant's staircase. If you got to your horse before anyone knew what you were doing, well...you could be miles away before the man knew you'd left the house just to get away from him," Lacey said, returning to the room to further irritate her.

"If it's Cam waiting for you down there when he found out, I bet he'd go after you and just like on that night you'd let him catch you," Daryl said, pointing a knowing finger at her. "You'd do it again, let him catch you, kiss you, fondle parts of you, intimate parts."

"I did not do that." Chelsea protested to no avail, understanding just how astute her sisters were. "Would not," she protested but her voice was weak and she knew the lie.

"You told us you did and you also told us he kissed you. Is that why you don't like any of the other suitors? They can't kiss like Cam?" Lacey asked, now tapping her toe impatiently and seeming a bit reluctant to accomplish her mission.

Bliss walked into the room. "What's Cam doing downstairs? He finally come to his senses? Did he decide he wanted to court you properly?"

"You ruined our fun," Lacey said, hands on her hips, a pout on her pretty face. "We were teasing Chelsea about her anonymous suitor, and now she knows Cam is waiting to see her."

"I don't understand." Bliss sat down next to Catherine. "What are you talking about?"

"Chelsea's debating whether or not she wants to go downstairs and talk to him. Of course until this moment, she didn't know it was Cam waiting for her," Daryl said. "Now that she knows she should be racing down the steps eager to tell him what she thinks."

"Really, Chelsea." Grams leaned over and placed her hand on hers. "You absolutely should see what he wants. You might be pleased. I'm certain I don't want to watch you mope around the house for another second let alone another nine months. Go see the man and stop wallowing in self-pity. This might well be the dawn of a new life for you."

"How can I just forgive that man after what he did?" Chelsea felt betrayed and abused by him. He made assurances to her he didn't keep. "I can't trust him now, never will."

Grams chuckled softly, "He's a man. You will have to learn that where their women as well as their hearts are concerned, they don't seem to know what they want. I'm sure he meant what he said at the time as I'm also sure he will move heaven and earth for you to grant your forgiveness."

"They want sex," Bliss said softly, smiling as if she understood the opposite sex better than most. "Nothing else matters to them until other things jump in and blind side them. Deny him what he wants the most and see what happens."

"Look how that worked out for you." Chelsea couldn't help the sarcasm. "You barely had your babies before Broc wed you."

"That's just it. I didn't deny him anything, and it took forever to work out, forever for him to come to the recollection he loved me and wanted me in his life," Bliss said. "Perhaps if I'd told him no..."

"Flynt still wouldn't have let him court you," Lacey said and that was the crux of Bliss' problem. "You forged the way for the rest of us, even though nothing is perfect yet."

"That wasn't how it all started though. Even before...well I allowed Broc to do things I shouldn't have," Bliss said.

"And he won't let Cam court me anymore than he would have let Broc court you. Perhaps I should visit him at his townhouse and get pregnant."

"No!" They all chorused.

Then Catherine cleared her throat, "Lest you forget, I'm in charge of those chaperone duties now, not Flynt. Getting yourself with child is not the solution. It might be a means to an end but never the solution."

"Flynt doesn't understand the fact you are now our guardian. He's still searching out men who he deems worthy husband material and presenting them to me."

"Where are the twins?" Grams asked in a not very subtle attempt to change the subject.

"Broc needed to see Flynt for some reason I didn't quiet understand. He has the babies, and I'm sure he will bring the twins to me as soon as either one starts crying or needs a diaper change. Right now he just wants to show off his heirs. So, I'm going to enjoy a few minutes with my sisters."

"You're sure it's Cam you saw?" Chelsea asked, her heart in her throat while she tried to figure out what she would say to the hideous man. If she should chastise him for leaving her alone for so long without a word as to why, or if she should count her blessing and try to find some time alone with him.

"Yes," Bliss said, "I'm sure I know who he is and that I saw Cam. If you want him, you have to decide how to proceed. Walking down those stairs to the parlor could be the first step toward a new tomorrow. Staying here, well, it certainly won't put you one step further in your quest to wed him."

"What does that mean? How to proceed?" She breathed in long and deep, her emotions in a jumble of incoherent thoughts that made no sense. "Walking down a set of stairs won't change the fact he broke his promise and my heart. Won't change the fact he abandoned me for whatever reason."

"Can I assume you've allowed him liberties you've granted to no one else?" Bliss asked, prying into Chelsea's private life. "Of course you don't have to answer anyone but yourself."

Chelsea gazed at Catherine then back to Bliss, unwilling to say the truth with Grams present even while she understood her sisters knew most of what happened between herself and Cam. She licked her lips before sucking the bottom one between her teeth.

"I did let him kiss me, a couple of times and I—they made me..." she paused, staring at Bliss as if waiting for an answer.

"As if you can't think," Grams answered for her. "As if you don't have any bones in your body. Dear, we've all been there. And some of us, including, me have given liberties to their men they shouldn't have. You have nothing to be ashamed of or feel guilty about. If you didn't care for Cam MacEwen, you wouldn't have let him kiss you or touch you either."

"When you're in love it's terribly hard to deny them anything. Especially when they caress you in certain ways," Bliss said with a starry eyed look. Then shrugging, "I still can't deny Broc when he looks at me."

"I never thought you lacked courage," Daryl said directly to Chelsea. "You've always been the boldest and the most fearless; a bricky lass is what everyone calls you. Don't change now. Act before it's too late and you have regrets."

"You all really think I should go see what he wants?" Chelsea felt her knees begin to wobble. "Not sure I can actually walk down those steps. I'll most likely fall flat on my face."

"He'll be there to pick you up," Daryl laughed and that will give him another chance to kiss you."

"Put on that beautiful blue day dress you purchased the last time we went shopping. We can all help you and lace the corset tight so you have the tiniest waist. He won't be able to resist you," Grams spoke fondly to her. "Bliss can help you with your hair and Lacey, you go down and keep Cam company until Chelsea looks more than presentable."

"I'd like that. I used to talk to Broc, too, but I never knew it was you, Bliss, who he fell in love with. He was always so elusive and secretive. At least this time I know the woman of his choice and I can give him the proper incentive to treat you right." With that set, the youngest of the MacTavish clan vanished from the room so quickly it seemed she wasn't even there.

"What if he doesn't wait for me? We've all been talking for quite some time. He might have left already." Chelsea felt a wave of insecurity pass through her as her sisters and grandmother dressed and coifed her. Cam was a busy man although she didn't know what he did to make money. It had always seemed he was on the go doing this or that.

"Some powder on your cheeks, a bit of tint to the eyelids and lips; after that we'll blacken your lashes, and you'll be even more gorgeous than you are already."

"It's time," Bliss said, holding out her arms before twirling her around. "I'll walk down the steps with you. Steady you if you think you're going to fall. You can do this. Cam is a lucky man if he can catch you. Mark my words, don't make courtship too easy for him. It's best if they have to work a little bit."

"You don't have to hold me," Chelsea whispered, discovering the corset was cinched in so far she could barely take a breath. "Really, I want to think I'm a grown woman even though at the moment I'm realizing I'm not acting that way."

"I'm sure Broc is ready to hand over the twins. He's lasted longer than I expected." Bliss patted Chelsea on the hand. "As soon as you say the word, we can confront this man you want."

Chelsea nodded. "Ready as I'll ever be."

In the parlor, Chelsea's feet seemed to freeze to the floor. Not only did Cam sit in the room, but the sultan as well as someone who'd been here once before. When she first saw, Cam she had the horrific urge to run into his arms then anger began to build inside. He abandoned her and as Bliss told her, he should have to work for her affections.

Yet, if he crooked his little finger, she'd undoubtedly give in to him and whatever it was he was asking for.

She fanned her hot face with her hand, yet she couldn't seem to cool herself or the uncontrollable fury rising to the surface. Her gaze remained on Cam, but it was Arie who seemed to understand her predicament.

Arie suddenly stood beside her, his hand on her shoulder as he bent close, "Are you all right? I will sweep you away from all this. Just say the word, my petite. We will run away together, you and I."

"No." She was shaking her head and trying to swallow, knees trembling. "That's Cam." She tried not to look at him again. "What does he want with me now?"

"I know who he is. If you recall you've told me a lot about what transpired between the two of you," he whispered close to her ear, laughing. "May I escort you into the room where you can confront the beast? Be sure to make him beg before you forgive him."

Her shaking head turned to nodding while she remained thoughtless and without any notion of what was happening or how she would make him beg. Arie seemed to have this meeting under control. He brought her to a chair to sit in while he poured everyone a glass of wine and graciously handed the drinks out.

When she looked at Cam, he appeared so arrogant and cocky her fury grew. She would throttle him if they were left alone. The silence echoed in the room as her discomfort grew.

"Well, it seems Chelsea has several suitors to choose from. This is such a fine day." Catherine entered the parlor with her hands clasped in front of her. "The conversation does seem a bit boring, nonexistent to be exact. Perhaps," and she turned to Chelsea with a look of encouragement on her face, "you would like to take a stroll in the gardens with one of these men."

Cam stood as if she would pick him, but the way her sensibilities were tumbling all over themselves she dared not. Turning to Arie, she began, her heart pounding out of synch, "I think perhaps..."

He was quick to reject her preliminary choice, seeming to understand after seeing Cam she needed more time, "You should take this other man." Then looking at the third man in the room, "What is your name?"

"Leod," Chelsea said but she didn't want to go for a walk with him in the gardens or anywhere else. "He's been here before. I thought I made it perfectly clear to him. I did..."

Arie cut her off, seeming to have some other agenda in mind. "I would like to speak with Lord MacEwen privately. The viscount needs to understand a few things. So, I'll come find you as soon as I've had a word with him."

"I don't know why you'd want a word with me. I've nothing to say to you." Cam rose, extending a hand to Chelsea and ignoring Arie. "I've come to see the lady and don't want to speak with anyone else."

"Go on," Arie said with a smile and a push of his hands in the air. "Have faith in me and in what I plan to do here, petite. Go with Leod. One of us will be with you shortly."

"I do have faith but..." She didn't trust Cam one tiny bit, but she was coming to trust Arie even given his role here and what they all expected of him. He had come to reclaim Hope, who had run away from his father's harem. The story was long and involved but despite his father's intentions, Arie wasn't attracted to Hope and Flynt was. Now Arie was just having fun, enjoying the Scottish atmosphere and the women in Glasgow as well. Chelsea didn't think Arie ever had plans for Hope.

"Wait in the gazebo. Whoever survives this encounter will find you." Arie laughed a full rich belly laugh.

"Come, Chelsea," Leod said, holding out his arm. "I want to clear the air. We've much to talk about."

Chelsea didn't accept his arm but she did follow him. "Don't talk to me as if I'm your lap dog. As far as I'm concerned, we've nothing in common, and therefore there is nothing further for us to speak of to each other. I'm only accompanying you because Arie asked."

Leod looked back to the room then to Chelsea. "Of course I don't think of you as my lap dog, you're a woman. I'd prefer it if you accepted my arm." His voice cracked when he said preferred.

"Don't need any man's arm to walk," she muttered softly. "Been doing it alone since before I was one."

"What?" he demanded, touching her chin and making her look at him.

"Nothing." She jerked away from his hold then inhaled, praying Arie would not be much longer and that he would also find a way to send Cam home. Despite feeling eager yet apprehensive to see Cam earlier, she no longer felt that way. Her anger was just too close to the surface and unpredictable as well.

Chelsea had no idea what Arie had been thinking sending her to the garden with Leod. He knew she didn't want anything to do with this man and had express instructions along with her grams to turn him away if he ever came to the house again.

So, why had her wishes been so blatantly ignored?

Arie obviously didn't know how to follow instructions or keep a promise and neither did Grams. "Men," she muttered, hoping Leod didn't hear her. They do exactly what they want, when they want.

Outside the scent of Roses filled the air as did the site of all the lovely summer flowers beginning to bloom. The blue sky and sunshine should have brightened her day but it didn't. Chelsea tried desperately to keep her mind focused on herself and what she needed to say to both men. When Leod placed her hand in his, she cringed, jerking away, but he held it tight.

"Let me go," she grit out. "I don't want you to touch me."

"Never." His voice was gruff, determined and different from the way he usually spoke to her.

She told herself this was only for a few minutes more but when they walked into the gazebo and he placed an arm around her pulling her to him, she panicked. Her hands on his chest she tried to push him away, but he was too strong. His lips slanted over hers while he forced his tongue inside her mouth.

Chelsea didn't know where the strength came from, but she shoved him hard, screaming, "No!"

Turning, she ran into Cam's arms, her body quivering. He held her close, her head on his chest while his hands ran the length of her trembling back. "I suggest you leave, Leod, and never return here." Cam growled low in his throat. "Chelsea is mine."

"You were the one who told me I should do that." Leod tried to shift some of this problem on to Cam.

"Only to a willing woman. If you recall, I offered to find one for you. Chelsea seems far from agreeable."

"I didn't know we were courting the same woman," Leod said, seeming to be taken aback by Cam's appearance and the way he held Chelsea in his arms.

"We're not." Cam spoke calmly. "I'm the only man courting Chelsea. Best you don't come around here again," Cam reminded him.

This time Chelsea pushed away from Cam, staring into his eyes. "You told him to do that? Stick his tongue in my mouth?" She inhaled, coughing when she couldn't get enough air.

"Yes and no." Yet he didn't release her but turned her and helped her to find a place to sit inside the gazebo.

"Yes and no, what the bloody eyes is that supposed to mean?" She couldn't believe Cam would tell another man, anyone to do that to her. "You are a cad of the worst sort."

"If you'll have me, I'm your cad."

"If..."

Sitting down beside her, he placed her hand in his, slowly tracing tiny circles on the underside of her wrist. "It's a long story. Are you willing to listen?"

"Does it begin nine months ago?" She wanted a complete explanation. "You're a cad," she told him again, turning her head away, unwilling to fall victim to his compelling eyes as well as the wide charming grin that stole her heart every time she saw it.

"Yes and no about the time period, not my being a cad. Where you're concerned, I guess I deserve the title." When she looked at him again, he placed a fingertip on her lips, stopping her comment. "Let's start with me and what happened this morning in my office."

She meant to remain cautious. Cam could rip her heart out and tear it into tiny shreds if she let him. Arie had told her as much, caution, and don't give him everything he asks for, her sister's advice.

"I'm listening." She moistened her lips, almost as if she anticipated a kiss.

"This morning I asked Leod for some advice, and I ended up giving him some of my own which, when I realized what I was telling him, he might apply to you since in the process I discovered he was courting you. At that point I wasn't sure what to do, so I offered a willing woman to him, one who could teach him how to treat a lady."

"You asked Leod for advice. I've a hard time believing that." The confession nearly made her laugh and quite literally stole her anger for the moment. She would have to remain stronger.

He traced the line of her neck, sending goose bumps down her arms. "It's the God's honest truth, but I do find I won't be able to use any of his advice. His way of courting just won't work for me. I wanted to do this properly, and I'm still going to try but..."

"Why is that?" she interrupted needing to run her finger along the smile forming on his lips. She realized instantly he would suck her finger into his mouth and she would allow him to do anything. If this was her version of not giving into this man, it wasn't going to work.

"Your just too beautiful and hard to resist," Cam murmured, his mouth so close to her ear she felt his breath as he spoke. She thought he might touch the tip with his tongue.

"Cam...why really," Her voice shook as her body seemed to be melting.

"Because I'm going to kiss you like I did so long ago, not a chaste kiss but one where I'll hear those tiny sounds in the back of your throat.

The ones that make all of me smile."

"Arrogant." She did touch him then, traced his lips with her finger, wishing she dared give into everything he asked for. Perhaps that ploy would result in all her dreams coming true.

"Self-confidant." He pulled her finger into his mouth, sucking, biting gently. "I truly don't like the word arrogant."

"You didn't do that before. Suck my finger into your mouth. What's a girl supposed to do when she's angry and wants you to beg forgiveness?" She closed her eyes, trying to inhale a deep breath of air and finding the task impossible. "Dear lord, my corset is too tight. I think I'm going to faint."

He laughed, a deep belly laugh. "If you like, I can fix that." His mouth descended on hers before she could answer. Her lips encased in his, his hands on both sides of her head holding her still, he slipped his tongue deep inside, played and dueled with her.

She recalled all the vivid sensations as he bit and laved her mouth with teeth and tongue. Over and over again, he kissed her and kissed her until her body cried out for him, for something more. She did want him to touch her breasts, cup them in his hands like he did before, run his thumb across her clothed nipple, perhaps even take the tip into his mouth as he did her fingers.

When they parted for a moment and he gazed into her eyes, "I really can't breathe. Cam, I do think I might faint."

"I promised Arie I wouldn't do anything to compromise you," he whispered, even as his nimble fingers unfastened the buttons on the back of her dress. Before she understood what he was doing, he untied her corset then laced it back, much looser. "You should turn now. Not too sure if I can fasten the buttons without seeing the tiny things. Let it be known, though this is the last thing I want to do at the moment."

"Thank you." She inhaled long and deep. "My sisters..."

"They did this to you?" He couldn't understand anything about women's clothing, least of all corsets.

"They wanted me to look my best for you and well... a tiny waist..." She was amazed by the myriad of expressions crossing his face.

"Good god, woman, you're so tiny without the corset I can wrap my hands around your waist. Why would you want to be smaller?"

She shrugged her shoulders, unable to think of an answer to his question but needing a diversion. "I'm still angry with you, Cam. Doesn't matter that you kissed me and l liked it and want more. You have a lot of months to make up for, and I don't intend to be an easy conquest."

"I'm just glad you still like my kisses." His smile captured her heart again.

"I wanted to hit you and hit you until all the anger vanished, but I let you kiss me instead."

"Ach lass, is the anger gone now?"

"Not yet." She touched his lips again, needing more of him. "You should kiss me again and maybe I'll forgive you."

He roared with laughter. "So, if I kiss you again, you won't be quite so angry and you won't take your fury out on my humble man's body. Hmm...should I just keep kissing you until there is no more fury to vanquish? Kissing. That's my choice."

"Or until Grams finds us. Don't do anything that will have her banishing you from the house. I don't think I could live through another desertion. Grams told me kissing was fine. Just kissing. Nothing below the waist."

"And what would that be, my sweet one? What could I possibly want below your waist?" He laughed and she somehow thought he knew more than he was allowing her to know.

"I'm hardly sweet and you know that," Chelsea protested, hitting him on the shoulder with her fisted hand.

"Not at all. Now, what would get me banished from the house?"

~ * ~

Arie handed Leod a glass of whiskey that he wished was laced with arsenic. "Drink this." The sniveling little man tried to take liberties the lady didn't want to give. Chelsea valiantly fought her own battle. He'd been a few steps behind Cam when he watched her shove Leod away.

"Don't drink." Leod told him. "Don't like the stuff."

"Very well. Let it be known from this day forward you're not welcome to court the lady MacTavish. You need to set your sights on someone else, someone more appropriate for your expectations." Arie cared more than he wanted to admit that Chelsea touched his heart. If she wasn't so adverse to becoming his fourth wife, he would spirit her away and make sweet love to her, make her forget Cam.

"Why should I pay any attention to what you, a foreigner has to say?" Leod sneered seeming to have no idea the power the sultan possessed. "I've no intention of finding a different woman."

"Slavery is something my people enjoy. They've found it easy to abduct women and men to work for them, serve them in anyway they please, physical labor as well as sexual slaves. There is little the various governments can do to stop them once a person disappears behind harem walls." Arie spoke slowly and pointedly, watching the play of expressions on Leod's face.

"You wouldn't dare. I'm a free man. You have no right to enslave me." His voice wavered on the last words.

"Only as long as I want you to remain free. Do something I don't like..." The sultan spoke nonchalantly, staring at Leod, looking for any sign of weakness of which there were many.

While he was surprised his subtle threat didn't seem to register with this man, he was pleased too. His unwillingness to believe would make the task so much easier if it ever came to his enslavement.

Arie could think of no greater pleasure than watching this man labor throughout the day for the rest of his life. Or, he paused in thought, he could sell him to another man as a paramour. The thought got better with each passing second, and he almost hoped Leod would defy him, and in doing so test the truth of his words.

Leod didn't have the courage for defiance. Arie was sure Leod would crumble to his will.

"What's that supposed to mean?" Leod asked. "I am free. I won't work for any man unless it's of my choosing."

"You should look around you and see everything as it really is. My people don't live by the same societal rules as you do. I've money, power, friends and the means to abduct you to my country. If I do so, you'll never leave, never see Scotland again and you will be under another man's thumb for the rest of your life." Arie knew just the man to sell Leod to.

Leod grumbled for a moment then chose not to speak.

"I was sent here for another purpose, but found it didn't appeal to me. You, on the other hand..." He let the sentence hang, wondering what spin Leod would put on this.

Leod downed his whiskey, sputtering and coughing as it seemed he felt the affects of the alcohol. Then after setting the glass down hard, "Are you threatening me?"

"Of course not." Arie loved the way this was beginning to play out. "Me? I would never threaten something so dastardly or a loyal Scotsman. This is just a version of what could happen in the future if you don't play by my rules."

Leod held his glass out silently, asking for more whiskey. "I should be able to do anything I want."

Arie smiled while he filled Leod's glass. Thoughts of getting this man so drunk he couldn't think and putting him on ship bound for some place far away flitted through his head. He couldn't though, but what he could do was serve him a lesson he wouldn't soon forget.

"You can do anything but court Miss MacTavish." Arie persisted as a plan slowly took shape in his head. "Where you are concerned, I've only one consideration, and that is for you to leave this lady alone."

"I want her." He said, his eyes closing. "Don't want to give her up. One way or the other she will be my wife."

Once more Arie filled Leod's glass.

"Sadly, for you my friend there is no choice in this matter" Arie said before he nodded at one of his retainers. From the earlier conversation, the man in Arie's employ must have guessed his intent and left to return a few glasses of whiskey later.

"Where is she?" Leod stood, unable to keep his balance sat down. "Need to say goodbye."

"Let my men help you to your carriage, or did you ride a horse?"

Leod held up his glass, "Like this stuff better than I ever though possible."

Arie obliged as he smiled and watched his men escort him from the house. His man stopped, waiting for further directions.

"Take him into town, strip him of all his clothes save his small clothes and leave him in the town square. No, perhaps you should leave him naked. If that doesn't bring the point home, nothing will."

"Or we can resort to stronger measures."

"Only if he doesn't learn the lesson we are teaching him." Arie sat back, grinning and thoroughly enjoying the scenario he set in motion.

Foolish for Piper

The pickpocket...

Piper has spent her life surviving the streets of St. Giles Parish in London, a den of iniquity and crime. Masquerading as a boy she escapes the whorehouses the young girls are sent to as they come of age. The day she encounters Brett MacLachlan begins the same as every other one. When she picks his pocket, she has no idea her life is going to change irreversibly.

...and the mark

Handsome aristocrat Brett MacLachlan has come to London for his amusement only to find his world turned upside down by a thief and her dog. From the moment he spots her, Brett knows there is something intrinsically wrong. In his arms, Piper discovers passion and joy. Yet secrets of her past haunt her, and a scar will tell the true tale as well as her identity.

Taylor's Destiny

She traveled to another time and place to changing destiny...

Enjoying a day of sailing, Taylor Maxwell never expected after a suffering a concussion she would wake up in another century. A resilient independent woman in the twenty-first century, the blond beauty is ill prepared for life in the 1800s. Her first sight of the naval captain who rescues her makes her heart stop, giving her hope for her future.

His life is transformed by a woman who appears from nowhere...

Born to a life of ease, Reid Stewart defies the dictates of those born to aristocracy and chooses a life of adventure in the navy and as a spy for the crown. When he discovers a nearly naked woman on the bow of small sailing ship, his heart warms. His love for Taylor and his need to protect her from a man who pursues her might cost him his life as well as hers.

Caitlin's Duke

She played a fiddle in an Irish pub....

Caitlin O'Shea Is the most beautiful woman Roc Leighton has ever seen. With her blue violet eyes and long black hair she captivates him. In turn he mesmerizes Caitlin. Caught in the power of his gaze as he watches her, she is wise enough to know he desires her but will never give his heart to her. Caitlin has vowed to never be any man's mistress.

And fell in love with an English Lord...

Roc knows the first time he watches her play the fiddle and dance around the pub, she will be his next mistress. Despite her protest, he will find a way to convince her that her place is with him. While Caitlin's determination to keep her vows, fate takes a cruel turn and she is forced to seek refuge with Roc.

Catching Meara
Book One in the McKenna Clan Series

Meara Thorton was a feisty, world-class computer hacker—cornered by the FBI and shockingly given the chance to be their newly acquired technical analyst. Brilliant and intuitive, yet aching with the loss of everyone she has cared about, her restless heart led her to discover a love she fought and a world she didn't know could possibly exist.

Sweet Sexy Sadie
Book Two in the McKenna Clan Series

From the first time Sadie's eyes met those of Brody McKenna in the hot Sierra Madre Mountains, theirs was a potent attraction—not gentle, slow, and easy, but hot, hard, and all-consuming. The daughter of a dysfunctional family, Sadie had dreams no man could wrench from her with hot sex and an all-consuming passion. She'd challenge this alpha male with all the strength she possessed. But her red hair, fiery temperament, and indomitable spirit obsessed Brody...and he knew he had to find a way to show her he was more than he appeared and convince her to make a life with him.

Sweet Misbehavin'
Book Three in the McKenna Clan Series

Cast adrift after fleeing the home of Jokul, the ice demon, Atantsi, a firestarter, grew to womanhood as she moved through time to keep the demon from finding her. Though stubborn and courageous, she was ill prepared to use powers she had not been taught. Her first sight of the intoxicating Carr McKenna left her breathless, and her second encounter gave her hope for a future she never thought she had.

A playboy, a second son and a shifter, a man who thought his life would be carefree, Carr McKenna was shocked to discover the woman he'd paid as an escort is a firestarter who is running for her life. He is the leader of all the McKennas around the world and that he has multiple powers. His passion for Margo and the need to defend her might cost him his life as well as hers.

Sweet Talkin' Sugar
Book Four in the McKenna Clan Series

Lyonesse McKenna, was dreaming or was she? From the instant Lyn saw Deacon McClain across a black jack table in a crowed Las Vegas casino the unmistakable attraction sent Lyn's senses flying into overdrive. Her family of shapeshifters believed in soul mates. She'd always been skeptical yet she couldn't help but question the way her heart sped when he looked at her.

When Deacon appeared in Las Vegas he knew his first job was to save Lyn from a Sea Demon, but the next order of business was to convince her he would someday mean more to her than she'd ever expected. But her stubborn nature and unbendable spirit consumed Deacon...and he had to chase away all the demons real and imagined in order to win her heart.

Sweet Surrender
Book Five in the McKenna Clan Series

Ripped from her family at the top of Infinity Cliff, Kimi McKenna finds herself thrust somewhere into the future. Dark elements threaten to destroy the earth unless Kimi can work together with the white witch to stop the destruction. Confused by her mate's role in the conspiracy, she refuses to acknowledge the connection. But amidst raging fire and attacks on the people she is coming to hold dear, she allows Maska O'keefe into her heart.

Maska O'keefe has loved the beautiful shapeshifter for years. Unable to save her life years ago, he vows to watch over her as he is given a second chance to convince her that even though he is a witch and not a shifter, they are indeed soul mates. Kimi's divided loyalties between her family and the cause she is now a part of will determine their relationship. Only the part she plays as the messiah can bring this to a conclusion in the final battle.

Dakota's Bride
The first book in the Lakota/Pinkerton Series

When Emma St. John received her brother's letter imploring her to escape her stepfather's vengeful scheme and to trust Dakota Barringer with her life, she was willing to chance it. But the handsome, brooding riverboat owner Emma found in Natchez a danger of another kind. For Emma soon found herself surrendering to an unrelenting desire.

Raised by the Sioux when his parents were killed, Dakota had been betrayed once before by a white woman. He wasn't about to trust another, especially one claiming that her stepfather, a powerful U.S. senator, had framed her as a murderess. But he couldn't let Emma's intoxicating effect on him. Now Dakota would risk his very life to protect the innocent beauty who had seduced him with her tender love.

My Angel
The second book in the Lakota/Pinkerton Series

A BEAUTY IN BUCKSKINS
When her father decided to send her to a finishing school back East, Angela Chamberlain refused to be confined to stuffy drawing rooms. Instead, the daring spitfire who could shoot like a man and ride like the wind longed for a life of adventure and romance—and she knew exactly who could give it to her. Devil Blackmoor was a hired gun with a dangerous reputation. But Angela was willing to go to the ends of the earth to capture the handsome devil's heart.

A DEVIL IN DISGUISE
He'd come to America looking for excitement, but Devil Blackmoor got more than he bargained for when he encountered a beautiful rebel who

answered his kisses with a wild innocence that touched his very soul. Yet standing between them were more obstacles than either ever dreamed. For Devil had strapped on a gun for the wrong man. And that made Angela his enemy. Now he'll have to choose between his duty and the woman he loves more than life.

The Locket
The third book in the Lakota/Pinkerton Series

The year is 1894. Seeking revenge for crimes against his family, Misha Petrovich follows a path that leads straight to Ariel Cameron's boarding house in Mist Harbor, Oregon. A family heirloom in Ariel's possession leads Misha to believe she is guilty. The locket has been handed down to the oldest girl in the Petrovich family for generations. Ariel is innocent of wrong doing, but her father is not. Misha is torn by his feelings for Ariel and his need for restitution against her father. Knowing that the relationship between them is fragile, Misha does everything in his power to protect Ariel's father. His efforts are to no avail when her father is shot. Ariel comes to realize Misha's steadfast courage and determination to protect her and her father despite what has happened to his family. Ariel's love and devotion heals Misha's heart.

The Talisman
The fourth book in the Lakota/Pinkerton Series

Running from a marriage that lasted one night, Dr. Moriah McKeown discovers the land she has settled on is coveted by determined and lawless men. Yet the proud young woman who once vowed never to abandon her home has second thoughts when her adopted children are threatened. Her only recourse is to enlist the aid of a dark, dangerous gun for hire.
Haunted by the past and a betrayal he will never forgive, Ian Civanovich uses his fast gun and his reckless courage to forget the faithlessness of a woman in his past. He will trust no female—nor will he rest until the threat hovering over Moriah McKeown is put to rest.

Forever His
The fifth book in the Lakota/Pinkerton Series

Struggling to come to terms with the part she played in Jacob St. John's death, Etta Barringer resigns from Pinkerton Agency and seeks peace and solace in a Rocky Mountain Cabin.
Jacob has vowed to discover the reason Etta has betrayed him, sold him out to his enemy and left him for dead.
Isolated in their cabin, they discover their love for each other and learn to trust. But the trust is shattered when Jacob learns she is married to his sworn enemy; the man who left him in the desert to die.

Allura's Secret
Twelve Dancing Princesses Book One

Allura McClellan is horrified by her father's decision to take out an ad in the Times awarding her to the man strong enough and smart enough to win her hand and uncover her secrets. She's an intelligent young woman who takes great delight in the freedom allotted to her by her father. She's well aware that marriage would effectively curtail the adventures she's shared with her sisters and cousins.
Hunter Gray is nothing like the other men who've arrived to vie for Allura's hand in marriage and everything that goes along with it. However, he is the first to refuse to concede defeat and pursue her despite her attempts to disguise her true appearance. It's her temperament that is of more concern to him than her looks. Hunter has worked all his life with the hope of someday owning his own land. Now that it looks like there's a very real possibility that everything he's ever wanted is within reach nothing is going to deter him – including Miss Allura's disagreeable disposition.

Amorica's Wager
Twelve Dancing Princesses Book Two

Amorica Hepburn was sent to London to find a husband. Finding a man was the last item on her agenda. With her two cousins, Amorica wagers she can dissuade her suitor before the others. Despite her efforts she discovers a chemistry that cannot be denied. Suddenly she is the arrogant man's wife, pledged to a marriage neither desire. But swept off to his ancestral home above the Dover cliffs and into his strong embrace, Amorica is soon possessed by a raging passion for the husband she had vowed to despise… Damian Andrews couldn't afford to trust the emerald-eyed spitfire who happened upon his secret. Amorica's hatred of all men of his kind only inflames the war that rages between them. Still, he can not control the intense desire his stubborn bride inspires, or make her surrender to his will until he has conquered the headstrong beauty on the battlefield of love…

Ravyn's Marriage of Inconvenience
Twelve Dancing Princesses Book Three

A REGAL BEAUTY
When the duchess decides to wed her to a wastrel and a fop, Ravyn Grahm takes matters into her own hands and declares her engagement to another man. Instead of fessing up and telling her great aunt what she has done, she goes through with the pretense. Aric Lakeland is the bastard son of an earl and has a dangerous reputation. But Ravyn is willing to do most anything to keep the duchess from discovering the lie.

A DEVIL-MAY-CARE SMUGGLER
He'd bought land in America, looking to put down roots and end his life of adventure, but Aric Lakeland got more than he bargained for when he encountered a beautiful heiress who made a promise she didn't want to keep. But the promise could not be undone and standing between them were more obstacles than either ever dreamed. Aric had made plans to spend the rest of his life in America and that was at odds with Ravyn's plan of living in England and running her father's estate. Now, he'll have to choose between his dreams and the woman he loves more than life.

Christel's Sunrise
Twelve Dancing Princesses Book Four

He Made Her An Offer...

Life has thrown Christel McClellan some experiences that could have devastated a less determined woman. Beautiful, self-assured and fiercely independent, she is trying to forget the loss of her stillborn child. But is the child alive?

She Couldn't Deny...

Life is carefree for Ryder MacLaren who loves to see what is on the other side of the sunrise. Laird of Clan MacLaren, he is wealthy, handsome and happily unencumbered...until stunning Christel McClellan enters his life. When he hears her story, he believes the child she thought dead has been sold to a wealthy buyer.

Storm's Passion
Twelve Dancing Princesses Book Five

SHE MADE A PROPOSAL...

Life strikes Storm Graham a shattering blow when she learns her father has bartered her to a man she detests. Storm is beautiful, self–assured and fiercely independent, and refuses to be a pawn in her father's schemes, yet she can find no way out of this bargain made in hell. Going on the offensive she asks the wealthiest man on the eastern coast of England to marry her, never believing she might fall in love.

HE TRIED TO REFUSE...

For Hadden Johnston life has provided everything he ever wanted, including a sanctuary for homeless children. He is wealthy, handsome and happily unencumbered...until stunning Storm Graham marches into his life and proposes a marriage of convenience. Yet this type of marriage to a woman who inflames his senses is far from acceptable. If he's going to be tied down, he will move heaven and earth to have this woman warming his bed.

Gotta Have Fayth
Twelve Dancing Princesses Book Six

A regal beauty with raven hair and piercing blue eyes, Fayth Graham is unwilling to parade herself in front of the wealthy Lords of England during the season. Seeking a means to dissuade any man wishing to wed her, she seeks a way to ruin herself for marriage. When she unexpectedly meets a man with sparkling gray eyes and an infectious grin, she decides this is the man who will keep her from agreeing to obey.

He returned from six months at sea, looking for a few nights of pleasure with a willing lass, but Jarret Kinsley got more than he bargained for when he met a beautiful debutant who responded to his kisses with a wild innocence that touched his heart. Yet the obstacles looming between them might rip them apart. Both had vowed never to marry, so when consequences of their dalliances got in the way, Jarret would have to choose between the life he's always desired and the woman he loves more than life.

Ella's Pleasure
Twelve Dancing Princesses Book Seven

A WHISPER OF PLEASURE

Ella Hepburn was an auburn haired debutant from the harsh Scottish coastline—a wild innocent to be seduced and tamed. A spirited beauty, she captivated Drake Montgomerie's jaded heart—while succumbing to the smoldering desire she felt for her unyielding suitor.

A WHISPER OF DANGER

In Drake Montgomerie's glittering world of money and privilege, young Ella discovered passion and desire could overcome everything she'd been taught to resist—entangling Drake, the heir apparent, in a lethal coil of aristocratic family intrigue. But grave peril would only nurse the sparks of a love that knew no limits and a magnificent ecstasy that would not be denied.

Eveleen's Seduction
Twelve Dancing Princesses Book Eight

A WHISPER OF SEDUCTION

A brutal attack on Eveleen Hepburn's cherished island off the Scottish coastline leaves her shattered and bewildered. Learning a man she once trusted can kill as easily as he can breathe even though the deed saves her life, creates questions that need answers. An innocent beauty, she enchants Logan Maxwell's cynical heart—giving in to the raging passion she feels for her mysterious suitor.

A WHISPER OF INTRIGUE

In Logan's Maxwell's world of espionage and privilege, young Eveleen discovers truths about herself she never expected, and a need for passion and love can overcome all her fears if she learns to accept certain truths. She finds herself entangled in a lethal battle for land that was once owned by French nobility, taken from them during the revolution and sold to Maxwell. But grave peril would unleash the flames of love that simmers, creating a magical union that cannot be refuted.

Tavia's Deception
Twelve Dancing Princesses Book Nine

WHISPERS OF DECEPTION

When her father decides to send her to London for her season, Tavia Hepburn resolves to see the world instead. The raven haired beauty decides to disguise herself as a lad and find employment on a ship bound for Barcelona as a cabin boy. But she never bargains on finding passion and love to a red haired sea captain who rescues her from certain death.

WHISPERS OF MURDER

For James Macmurra, the world is black and white until he meets a young debutante, who turns his world upside down. He's unable to deny Tavia's intoxicating effect on him. In a match tense with obstacles, unwillingness to divulge secrets, and unforeseen peril, irresistible desire and passion grows into undeniable love. James would risk his life to shelter and protect the innocent debutante who seduces him with her sweet love.

Larena's Fascination
Twelve Dancing Princesses Book Ten

WHISPERS OF FASCINATION

Fiery, free spirited Larena Graham never wanted to marry a duke. She is thrilled to be in love with the fourth son of an aristocrat, Gavin Broon. But when it seems Gavin ignores her, she set her sights on politics and bettering human life. Unsuspecting intrigue and a plot against her, she continues her dangerous plans despite Gavin's wishes.

WHISPERS OF TRUST

Gavin has every intention of properly courting the beautiful Larena until he must leave the city in order to put his affairs in order. Returning to

London, he finds the woman he means to make his own is embroiled in political protests that could lead to a prison ship. Larena must learn to trust the handsome Scotsman whose most pressing mission is to protect her and keep her from harm.

Tira's Eeucation
Twelve Dancing Princesses Book Eleven

WHISPERS OF EDUCATION

Learning how to build ships is Tira Hepburn's only dream until she meets Jamie Lundin and her world is turned upside down. With her raven black hair and vivid green eyes, she tempts Jamie and pushes him to defy his vows. She never bargains on finding an irrevocable love and a passion to a man who cannot fulfill her dreams despite his burning desire for her.

WHISPERS OF A BARGAIN

Arrogant and self-assured Jamie is brought up short when Tira captures his heart. All his carefully made plans are put to the test when he decides to teach her the art of ship building if she will spend a week with him alone on his ship. He is unable to deny Tira's intoxicating effect on him. When Tira leaves him behind unwilling to live with him without the benefit of marriage, he races after her. Jamie will risk everything to shelter and protect the innocent debutante who seduces him with her sweet love.

Tira's Eeucation
Twelve Dancing Princesses Book Twelve
Whispers of Love

Aidan McLellan has loved since she first set eyes on him as a young girl. Spontaneous, wild and eager to grow up, Aidan haunts his waking thoughts day and night, insinuating herself into his life. With her fiery red hair and sparkling sapphire eyes, she seizes Blade's heart even while he tries to resist the innocent child until she becomes a woman.

Whispers of Courage

Blade has waited what seems a lifetime to claim the woman who captures his heart as a little girl. Claiming his inheritance before his younger brother takes what is rightfully his, Blade must convince Aidan of his sincerity after years of avoidance and wed her before his father dies so he can return home, securing his rightful place. Everything is put to the test when his life as well as Aidan's is threatened by the man who once called him brother.

Twelve Days to Love

When Archer Steele shows up at Calanthe Durand's failing plantation with an alligator over his shoulder, Cali thinks she's never seen a more handsome man. During the war she had to defend herself and her servants from both union and confederate soldiers. Independent and self-sufficient, she vows to never marry.

But Archer Steele has different ideas. The first time Archer sees Cali in town, he feels an instant attraction. He decides he will do everything and anything to convince the beautiful Miss Durand he is worthy of her love. During the weeks leading up to Christmas, he gives her twelve gifts in hopes she will fall in love with him. Yet they are faced with challenges they must overcome before Cali can commit to a marriage.

Door to Heaven

Jessica Lawrence is the stepdaughter of a woman born in the twentieth century transported back in time to the year 1868. An acclaimed suffragette, she raises Jessica to believe in the equality of women. Jess Law believes everything she was taught, and when the time is right she becomes a private investigator. Courageous and impetuous, Jess finds danger in her quest to save all women from white slavery. Her passionate mission results in a wedding to Roc Newman, a man she knows can steal her heart...

Roc can't trust the sapphire-eyed spitfire who invades his home in search of secret papers and knocks him flat with her karate moves. Jessica's refusal to obey his wishes serves to inflame the war between them. Still, he cannot control the intense desire his reluctant bride inspires, or make her surrender her independence, until he has conquered the headstrong beauty on the battlefield of love...

Rebel Heart

HER REBEL SPIRIT DEFIED HIS OUTSIDERS SOUL...She was velvet and silk, eyes the color of a summer storm and amber hair. Victoria DeMontville, because of a promise and a codicil to her father's will, was forced to marry one man to protect her from another. She hated Cameron Savage with a fierce passion. But to hold on to her genetic research and find a cure for the deadly Signe virus, she must pretend to love the enemy at her door, come with weapons of fire to melt her icy heart...

HIS OUTSIDERS TOUCH IGNITED RAGING PASSIONS...He wore a mask, disguised as the Phantom, a true legend come to life. Even as war and debate over new genetic research engulfed them all, he would find his greatest adversary in the beauty who'd branded him an outsider and barbarian, the woman he was born to possess, his soul mate.

Safari Moon

Solo St. John, a wildlife photographer, is preparing for a trip to Alaska. Suddenly, Solo finds women of all sorts invading his privacy, his home and his office, all cooing nonsense words and blatantly throwing themselves at him. Solo doesn't know why, and he has no idea how to rid himself of the persistent women. He finally decides to beg a favor of his best buddy Nyssa Harrington.

In love with Solo for the past ten years and knowing he doesn't return her feelings Nyssa doesn't want to talk to Solo. She knows if she accepts his phone call, she will not be able to resist the temptation to hope again.

Straight to Heaven

Running from demons, Alexandra McMurdie stumbles into Forbidden Ground where up is down and elements of nature are contested. Though a strong independent woman in the twenty-first century' she is unprepared for life in the 1800s. Her first site of the formidable James Lawrence makes her heart skip a beat, giving her cause to reconsider her desperate need to find a way home.

Born with a silver spoon, James' life was torn apart during the War Between the States. Moving west he vows to put the life he once knew in the past. When he discovers a half-frozen woman near Gold Hill, his heart begins to thaw. His love for Alexandra and his need to keep her from a man who has pursued her through time might cost him his life as well as hers.

Stories from the Heart

The Lending Library-a fantasy by Christie L. Kraemer

Faeries try to fit into the human world when the forest where they make their home is destroyed by a mysterious enemy.

Chasing Rainbows-a contemporary romance by Genene Valleau

An eccentric aunt, an inventive uncle, a mother who wears poodle skirts, and a brother who wears pearls provide a hilarious backdrop for the courtship of a young woman who yearns for a "normal" family.

The Gift-an historical romance by Christine Young

A man and a woman on opposite sides of the Civil War get a second chance at love after one final battle returns soldiers to their war-torn homes to rebuild their lives.

A Touch of the Blarney
by
Christine Young, C. L. Kraemer, Genene Valleau

Tumble through time…

…to Ireland in 1817, when tensions are high between Protestants and Catholics and faey people guide the fate of villagers. A lovely Catholic lass stumbles upon the weakly ritual fisticuffing between Irish lads. She falls into the lap of a handsome young Protestant. Family ties, grudges, and two conniving faeries threaten their budding love. But the faeries outsmart themselves when they hijack a time machine that has mysteriously appeared in their forest and are whisked to…

…Eugene, Oregon in the 20th century, amid a property feud between the local faeries and night elves. The conniving faeries from Olde Ireland try to stir up more mischief. However, a warrior gnome convinces the magic folk to control their own destiny, and forces the intruding faeries to take refuge in the time machine again, spinning their way toward…

…A modern day castle in western Oregon. An eccentric inventor is determined to reclaim his wayward time machine and save his beloved wife from her latest misadventure. If only they can travel safely past the black hole…

a May Day Anthology
by
Christine Young, C. L. Kraemer, Rosemary Indra, Genene Valleau

Highland Miracle — Christine Young

HURTLED THROUGH TIME, Sean Michael Sterling, landed in the midst of a May Day celebration he didn't understand, assuming the role of Laird Sterling.
ILLIGITAMATE CHILD OF NOBILITY, Reagan Douglas searches for a way out of her half brother's house.

Defying the Odds — C.L. Kraemer

The night elves on the hill aren't happy without their magic. They concoct a plan to punish those who were involved in the act that rendered them almost human. Meanwhile, Uther, the rogue night elf, has returned to woo the Librarian to be his eternal mate.

Love in Bloom — Rosemary Indra

When childhood friends reunite it takes two fairies and a matchmaking daughter to help them admit their true love for each other.

No More Poodle Skirts — Genie Gabriel

After drifting for years in the innocent age of the 1950s, a woman struggles to join today's world by finding a career and a new love, with some help from her zany family.

Once Upon a Christmas Moon
by
Christine Young, C. L. Kraemer, Genene Valleau

TWELVE DAYS TO LOVE

When Archer Steele shows up at Calanthe Durand's failing plantation with an alligator over his shoulder, Cali thinks she's never seen a more handsome man. During the war she had to defend herself and her servants from both union and confederate soldiers. Independent and self-sufficient, she vows to never marry. But Archer Steele has different ideas. The first time Archer sees Cali in town, he feels an instant attraction. He decides he will do everything and anything to convince the beautiful Miss Durand he is worthy of her love. During the weeks leading up to Christmas, he gives her twelve gifts in hopes she will fall in love with him.

BOOTS AND BLADES

An ancient evil from the old country has arrived in the high desert of Oregon. Gnome children are vanishing then re-appearing, showing various stages of traumatization. Tiamoon, warrior gnome, will put her skills to use alongside Killian, a handsome warrior, also in need of a cause.

CHRISTMAS PAWSIBILITIES

With their world destroyed and their space ship malfunctioning, the dogizens of Planet Canid have little choice but to crash land on Earth. They face tortuous experiments at the hands of the Geeks in Green...or they can trust an eccentric inventor and his zany family to deliver the Canine Queen's puppies and help them celebrate new lives.